LARGE
PRINT
EDITION

RANDOM
HOUSE

# ACTS
# of LOVE

## JUDITH MICHAEL

Published by Random House Large Print
in association with Crown Publishers, Inc.
New York   1997

*Library of Congress Cataloging-in-Publication Data*
Michael, Judith.
Acts of love / Judith Michael.
p.   cm.
ISBN 0-679-77418-1
1. Large type books.   I. Title.
[PS3563.I254A65   1997]
813'.54—dc20        96-41589
CIP

Random House Web Address:
http://www.randomhouse.com/
*Printed in the United States of America*
FIRST LARGE PRINT EDITION

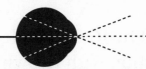

This Large Print Book carries the
Seal of Approval of N.A.V.H.

I dipt into the future, far as human eye could see,
Saw the Vision of the world, and all the wonder
that would be.

*Locksley Hall*
Alfred, Lord Tennyson

# ACKNOWLEDGMENTS

Many people helped with the research for this story.
Special gratitude is due:

Harry M. Miller, Sue Greaves,
Ann Churchill-Brown, Leon Fink, Pam Jennings and
the Sydney Theater Company—
Sydney, Australia

Maya Friedler—Chicago, Illinois

Sam Fifer, attorney—Chicago, Illinois

David Shapiro, M.D., and Judy Solomon, R.N.—
Evanston, Illinois

Also, for extraordinary insights into the lives
of directors and actors:

Uta Hagen
for her book *A Challenge for the Actor*

Alan Schneider, Robert Falls and Zelda Fichthandler in
*The Director's Voice:*
interviews by Arthur Bartow

Peter Brook
for *The Open Door*

William Gibson,
for *The Seesaw Log*

# NEW YORK

# CHAPTER 1

Jessica and Luke had met only a few times before she disappeared. They had met casually and briefly, and they had not liked each other.

"*Why* don't you like her?" his grandmother had demanded. "Good Lord, Luke, you're a director; she's an actress—one of the most brilliant in the world, which you know perfectly well—she'll take my place if I ever retire, and I'm sure you know that, too—and she's gloriously beautiful *and* a friend of mine even though she's young enough to be my granddaughter, *and you don't like her.* You don't even know her. What did you two talk about last night?"

"The play," he said. "How wonderfully the two of you work together on stage. The usual things at an opening night party."

"*The usual things.* Luke, you have the whole world to talk about! You share the theater and she's warm and clever and interested in everything—"

"She's interested in herself." He heard the impatience in his voice and tried to soften it. "Opening nights don't lend themselves to leisurely conversations; you know that. It was her night, and yours, and it was a triumph, and everyone wanted to talk to the two of you. She wasn't interested in me and I wasn't impressed with her. Except on stage, of course; do you know how many times I've called her agent because I wanted her for one of my plays? She's always been busy, or she's been in London; she spends a lot of time there."

"She likes it there and London audiences love her. Oh, Luke, I had hoped . . ." She laid her hand along his face and after a moment said, very gently, "Do you think you might not have been at your best last night?"

"You mean because of Claudia. That had nothing to do with it." His impatience was back and his words came out clipped and hard, in spite of himself. Masking his anger, he took her hand between his, and kissed her cheek. "We'd both be happier if you'd let me handle my social life in my own way."

"Well, you might be," his grandmother said crisply, "but I see no reason why that would add to my happiness at all."

They had laughed together, as, almost always, they did after having been at cross-purposes, and had gone on to other things. In the following years, Constance tried a few more times to bring Luke and Jessica together, but their crowded schedules intervened and they were not interested enough to give her any help. And then, many years later, Constance died, and Luke went to Italy to close up her villa and, in a strange and unexpected way, came face-to-face with Jessica.

He sat in Constance's airy library, in the velvet wing-backed chair where she had died in her sleep, and ran his fingers over all the things she had touched in the last hours of her life: a round, damask-covered table; a decanter and glass that had been filled with wine; a silver-framed montage of pictures of himself as a boy of seven, when he had first come to live with her, as a student in high school and in college, as a director with the poster for his first play and at the awards ceremony where he had won his first Tony for direction of *Ah, Wilderness!;* and, closest to Constance's hand, an Italian box, elaborately carved, inlaid with gold and amber and polished to a soft black luster. Inside were letters, hundreds of them, crammed together, the oldest-looking at the front. Luke ran his finger along the top of them, making a sound like a stick dragged along a picket fence. It seemed that the same handwriting was on all of them. He took one out and opened it.

Dear, dearest Constance, I want to thank you again (and again and again and again if I only knew different ways to do it!) for your wonderful, warm, generous encouragement last night. When you said I did a fine job playing Peggy, I knew I really was an actress and I'd be one for the rest of my life because Constance Bernhardt said so. The play is all you, of course, and probably no one else even noticed me, but it means the world to me just to be on stage with you. My mother said 16 was too young for summer stock, but I had to try and oh, I'm so glad I did! Thank you, thank you again! With my eternal love, Jessica.

Jessica, Luke thought. A young Jessica Fontaine at the very beginning of her career, bubbling with excitement. He glanced at the date at the top of the letter. Twenty-four years ago. So she would be forty now. And she's been writing all these years, which means my grandmother was writing, too. A long friendship. But Constance told me that, more times than I could count.

He pulled out another letter at random and unfolded it.

Dearest Constance, you won't believe this but Peter Calder got the male lead, which means I've got to do two love scenes with him. Wasn't it just last year that you and I swore we'd never get within ten feet of him? Well, here I am and now I'll be fighting off his gelatinous hands for the run of the play.

Luke burst out laughing. *Gelatinous.* The perfect word for Peter Calder. It was the reason Luke and almost every other director had stopped giving him parts years ago. But Jessica had had two love scenes with him—when? He read the date: seventeen years ago. She'd gone from a bit part in a play with his grandmother to a role opposite Calder—who in those days was one of the top actors on Broadway and in films—in only seven years. He had forgotten how swiftly her success had come. That was the year, he remembered, that he had gotten his first job on Broadway. He had been twenty-eight, and for six years, since graduating from college, he'd been directing plays for small, struggling theater companies in lofts, church basements and old movie houses. They drew tiny audiences that often did not fill their forty or fifty seats, but occasionally critics came and soon people in the theater were talking about him. "Lucas Cameron's masterful direction . . . ," began one review in *The New York Times,* and two months later he was offered a job as assistant director of a Broadway play. That was what he remembered about that year.

Oh, and Claudia, Luke thought. That was the year we were married.

Idly, he took a third letter from the box, about halfway in. A newspaper clipping fell from it and he unfolded it. It was from the *International Herald Tribune,* picked up from an Associated Press story in the *Vancouver Tribune.*

### *Fatal Derailment in Canada*

More than fifty passengers were killed and three hundred injured Monday evening, about 10:30 P.M., when *The Canada Flyer* derailed in Fraser River Canyon, eighty miles northeast of Vancouver. Using searchlights and rescue dogs, teams from nearby towns searched through the night in the wreckage and along the rocky banks of the Fraser River in temperatures that fell well below freezing. Among those rescued near dawn on Tuesday morning was Jessica Fontaine, world-renowned stage and film star, who had been in

Vancouver for the past four months starring in a production of *The Heiress*. She is listed in critical condition. The train, bound for Toronto, had left Vancouver at 8 P.M. Cause of the accident, the worst in the history of Canadian rail travel, is not known.

Luke remembered the story. There had been rumors that Jessica Fontaine was on her deathbed, that she would be unable to act for a year, two years, three years, that she had escaped serious injury, that she would be back in town in a week, two weeks, a month. No one could reach her to learn the truth. Her friends, her agent, her colleagues, television and newspaper reporters, all called the hospital in Toronto, where she had been taken, but all of them heard the same message: Miss Fontaine could not have visitors, and she would not accept telephone calls. Her friends kept calling; her agent went to the hospital; but, week after week, no one was allowed to talk to her or see her. And finally, one day six months after the accident, they were told that she was gone, without leaving a forwarding address or telephone number or any clues as to where she could be reached.

Then there was silence. Jessica Fontaine had been the most sought after stage star in America and London; she had starred in at least two films that Luke knew of; and suddenly, after only eighteen years, she was gone. A meteor, Luke thought. Arcing luminously through the sky, then vanishing into darkness.

He replaced the letters and the newspaper clipping and ran his fingers over the box that held them. Constance had chosen one of her most beautiful possessions to hold Jessica's letters, and had kept it beside her favorite chair in the library. How she must have loved her, Luke thought. How they must have loved each other. What must it be like, to have a friend like that? I have no idea.

The telephone rang and he picked it up. "Signora Bernhardt's residence."

"Luke," demanded Claudia, "why didn't you tell me you were going to Italy? I had to ask Martin where you were . . . you know I hate asking butlers where people are."

He held the telephone away from his ear and gazed through the French doors at the softly sculptured hills and valleys of Umbria that surrounded his grandmother's villa. "Claudia, this trip has nothing to do with you."

"It does and you know it. We had a date for dinner last night."

"I'm sorry. I forgot. You're right; I should have called. Constance died, Claudia, and I left as soon as I heard. I wasn't thinking of anything else."

"Oh. I'm sorry." There was a pause and he could almost hear her reorganizing her thoughts. "That's sad, Luke. You were so close to her. She never liked me, you know, she made that perfectly clear. . . . Oh, I shouldn't have said that. I'm sorry, Luke, but this hasn't been a great week and then when you didn't show up and I had to call

Martin to find out where you were . . . but I shouldn't have said that about Constance. I mean, what difference does it make now, whether she liked me or not? But I was so upset when you weren't here. I do rely on you, Luke, a little understanding, a little support. I don't think that's too much to ask."

Luke shifted in his chair, as if about to run. He was four thousand miles from Claudia and he sat in his grandmother's bright library warmed by the afternoon sun, but still he felt stifled. Which was exactly the way he had felt after two months of being married to Claudia, though it had taken him five years to ask her for a divorce. Now, eleven years after their divorce was final, he recognized almost every word of their dialogue: it was like a bad script, he thought, that no playwright could improve. But, still, he could not sweep her aside. "I'll be back in a week. We'll have dinner then."

"What night? When will you be back?"

"I haven't decided. Wednesday or Thursday. I'll call you."

"I might be busy, you know."

"We'll find a time when you're free."

"Call me before you leave Italy."

"I'll call when I get to New York. Claudia, I have to go; I have a lot of work to do."

"What? What are you doing? You must have had the funeral by now."

"I'm closing up her house. And mourning." He slammed down the phone, angry at Claudia, angry at himself for getting angry at her. He knew better; why did he let her get to him?

It's this house, he thought. The lady of this house, the only lady I've ever loved, is dead, and so is her house. Everywhere I go, in every room, there she is . . . and yet she's nowhere. I can't fathom her absence; she was mother and mentor and closest friend to me all my life. How can she be gone?

He was shaken by the loss of her. His memories of her were so vivid that he could still hear her strong voice—deep, almost husky, and so compelling that audiences had sat motionless through every play so as not to miss a word—praising him when he was growing up and hungry for encouragement; calling to him to share the beauty of a sunset or a painting or to notice the oddities of someone's speech or gait; challenging him to defend his opinions, making him a better thinker and a far better stage director. Her opinions were more important to him than those of any teacher or basketball coach or friend. Remembering her, he could hear her laughter the last time he had visited her here, he could feel her hand on his arm as they walked through her gardens, and feel her breath on his cheek as she kissed him good-bye and said, "I am so very proud of you and I do love you, my dear Luke." That was the last time he had seen her; almost the last time they had talked. She died less than a week later.

He was crying. No one in New York would believe it, he thought, not of Lucas Cameron, whose emotions, they said, were locked away, except in the theater, where he truly came to life. Through his tears, the olive and cypress trees that shaded his grandmother's flower gardens wavered as if fading away—the way she had—and he jerked himself upright, willing the tears away. Too much to do, he thought; tears are an indulgence.

He walked back to the main salon, but still the memories came, this time of his grandmother, eight years ago, when the doctors told her her heart was getting weaker and she would die if she continued to act. "Then I'll die on stage," she had declared to Luke. "I'm only seventy-seven; no one leaves the stage that early. I always expected to die on stage; it's where I belong. It's my home. Where else would I want to die? Only a fool would leave home to die in a strange place."

"What about the other actors?" Luke asked. "If you die in the middle of their big scene, they'll never forgive you."

After a long moment, she laughed, a short, bitter laugh, and a few months later she gave in. But she would not stay in New York. She bought a white marble villa nestled in solitary majesty at the top of a long hill, with the landscape of Umbria spread grandly below, furnished it with an exquisite collection gathered in a lifetime of travel, and re-created herself as if she were creating a character on stage. She held telephone conversations with American friends every afternoon; she allowed visitors only after they made appointments far in advance; only Luke was welcome at any time. She and her housekeeper held elaborate discussions every morning about the food for the day and how best to prepare it. She walked in sunlight or showers through the acres of her gardens, conferring with her gardeners in her barely adequate Italian, with many gestures and much laughter; she paused frequently for rests on the smooth rims of dozens of fountains she had brought in from all over Italy, each one fashioned with a column in the center of a still pool that reflected the mythological creatures poised in marble and granite above, and once rested, she threaded her way through the maze of tightly pruned hedges that were one of the reasons she had bought the villa—to confound her guests, she said.

Unable to sleep more than two or three hours at a time, she read late into every night, devouring the books she had put aside in a lifetime of acting. Often, in the silence of her library, she read aloud the plays that playwrights and directors sent her from all over the world, the next day, or the next week, dictating her critiques for her secretary to type and mail.

And she corresponded with Jessica Fontaine, Luke thought, and never told me about it. I wonder why.

In the large salon, he went back to taking inventory and organizing Constance's possessions. Some he was taking for himself; some would be sent to storage in New York; much would be given away according to Constance's will. *My salon furniture to my housekeeper, plus everything in the kitchen, which she has made hers through abundant and excellent use; my dressing table and mirror and all my clothes to my housekeeper's daughter, who has eyed them longingly but never was so rude as to inquire if she might have them; my paintings and sculptures to you, Luke, and all my jewels, in the hope that someday you will find a woman to whom you wish to give them; my collection of plays to Jessica Fontaine—*

The plays were on a table near the piano. Luke had watched the collection of rare first editions grow through the years as Constance found them in theater and opera libraries and in bookstores throughout the world. They were worth many thousands of dollars, Luke knew, but they were treasures mainly because most of them had notes in the handwriting of their first directors and of authors—George Bernard Shaw, Henrik Ibsen, Corneille, Racine, Chekhov—who often were the directors themselves. Priceless, Luke thought; Constance must have told Jessica she was leaving them to her. But there was no address in her will. *How the devil does she expect me to find Jessica Fontaine?*

He packed the plays in a large carton that he set alongside the others he was shipping to his apartment in New York. He layered them with tissue paper, double- and triple-wrapping the most fragile ones, then sealed the box and marked it "JF" on the outside, so that he could ship it to Jessica later, when he had her address.

At noon, he ate a cold frittata and an arugula salad left by the housekeeper, who insisted on coming once a day to take care of him. He sat on the broad terrace that ran the length of the villa, looking out over hills and vineyards, a sinuous silver river and distant villas barely visible in their groves of trees. His grandmother had sat here for hundreds of hours, reading, writing, contemplating. "Sitting here, my whole being gathers in the wonders of this lush, serene landscape," she had written to Luke in the last week of her life, "and I feel I am its caretaker. But of course we all are, aren't we?—all of us who have been given a world filled with such richness and beauty and abundance. We are its caretakers—and each other's caretakers, too—and there should be nothing but gratitude in our hearts. I'm grateful for you, dear Luke."

He had called to say he would be back in a month, just before beginning to cast his new play. But four nights later, in the deep-cushioned chair in her library where she read late into the night, with a book in her hand and the box of Jessica's letters beside her, Constance died.

Luke wandered restlessly through the villa and came again to the library and stood beside the chair where she had died. The sun had moved lower and its long rays picked out a Greek statue of a young boy in the gardens just beyond the terrace. He was lithe and wary, but fierce with determination, and Constance had said he reminded her of Luke at seven years old, when his parents died. "I stood beside you at the funeral," she had told him, "and we barely knew each other, but you kept leaning toward me, a degree at a time, until your skinny body was against mine, and when I put my arm around your shoulders you were trembling so hard it seemed you would never stop. I saw you look at the casket with terror—your mother, my daughter, gone so soon, so terribly young—and then you looked at me with the most awful desperation, because you thought there was no one to take care of you. And when I saw that desperation and terror—and by then your body was pushing so hard against mine that I thought you'd knock us both over—well, I loved you from that moment. You were child and grandchild to me. I cannot imagine a life without you."

From then on, he was always with her. He grew up in her dressing rooms and backstage in every theater where she appeared, studying with tutors and learning as much or more from the wild variety of actors and crew members who moved in and out of his grandmother's orbit. They treated him like a mascot and taught him everything they knew, about every part of the theater, on stage and backstage. By the time he was in his teens, tall and lanky, his hawklike face and unswerving gaze making him look older than his years, he knew more about the theater than any school could have taught him. Still, when Constance insisted, he went to college, but, like a yo-yo, he sprang back to her at every vacation. But, as Constance pointed out, she wasn't the only attraction: he also came back to be in the theater. Because by then it was clear to both of them that he would never be able to stay away from it for long.

Luke sat in Constance's chair and put his head back. I ought to get to work, he thought, but he stayed still, feeling her presence. The box of letters from Jessica Fontaine was within reach; he had replaced it in the exact spot where his grandmother had kept it. He opened it and once again ran his finger along their top edges. *I wonder what happened to her. She can't be acting anymore; I haven't heard her name in years. To disappear like that, at the height of the most brilliant career since Constance's . . . how could she do it? Why would she do it?*

A little more than halfway through the box, the stationery changed: it had been pale blue, now it was ivory. Luke took out the first letter on the ivory stationery. It was only a paragraph, and the handwriting was that of someone else.

Dear Constance, I haven't written because I was in a terrible accident. You may have heard about it or read about it, but I know that often you don't bother with the news. Anyway, you remember I wrote you that I was going to take a train trip across Canada and I was so excited because it would give me a chance to unwind and get away from everything. But it was terrible . . . oh, God, I almost can't say it. The train fell into a canyon. Fraser River Canyon. I have nightmares about it every night, and every day, too. I've been sleeping a lot. In fact, for four weeks I was pretty much out of it. I'm sorry if you were worried when I didn't write, but I was in and out of surgery I don't know how many times and I couldn't do anything until now. I still don't want to talk on the phone, so I'm dictating this letter to a lovely young nurse who's been holding my hand all these weeks, stroking my brow and telling me I'm going to be fine. She spins such a convincing tale I've told her she's as good an actress as Constance Bernhardt ever was, but today I feel a few timid stirrings of life, so perhaps there's some truth in what she's been saying. Oh, that's enough, I'm too tired. I'm sorry, Constance, dear Constance, I do miss you so . . . But that's not a complaint, and it's not a hint; I don't want you to come here, it would be too much for you and you've got to think about your own health. I just want you to know that I'm thinking about you and I'll write again, I promise. All my love, Jessica.

A courageous woman, Luke thought. Thinking of Constance while going through her own hell. A different Jessica from the one he thought he had known.

He replaced the letter and stood up to go back to the salon. But this time he took the box with him. Maybe, when I have time, I'll read a few more, he thought.

Slowly, through that long day, as he sorted and packed, the salon emptied. Its white marble floors shone cold and hard in the last light of the lingering June evening; the walls, stripped of their paintings, appeared to recede and vanish, so that the room seemed no place to live, but only a space to pass through. Done in here, Luke thought, anxious to be finished and gone. His footsteps echoed; his shadow beneath the lighted wall sconces was long and thin, sharply bent where the wall met the floor, as if it were racing ahead of him. *Constance's bedroom and her desk in the library, and that will be it. Two days at the most, and I can leave. And never come back.*

He had parked his rented car in front of the villa and he drove to the village where he was meeting the realtor. At the trattoria, he sat at a table near the doorway just as the door swung open and the realtor came in to sit opposite him. He waved the waiter away. "We will pour our own wine." He raised his glass. "Signore, you have thought about this? You are certain you truly wish to sell?" The realtor was an unhappy man. It was good to have Americans own property in the area; it drove prices up and gave jobs to housekeepers, caretakers, gardeners . . . If he had known this was the reason Signore Cameron had invited him to dinner at the best trattoria in the village he would not have come; he would have delayed; he would have begun a campaign against selling. But now here he was and time was short. He spoke slowly, leaving hopeful pauses in which Luke could change his mind. "You have considered keeping it for yourself? For yourself and your family? This is truly a good place to bring children for the vacations."

"I have no children. And yes, I'm sure—"

"But for yourself, signore! It is truly good for the restoration of the self after hard work. And I must confide in you, signore: the market is abominably slow right now. Perhaps you would wish to keep the villa furnished and ready for you to use while you are trying to sell it. We cannot know how long it will take to get a truly excellent price—"

"A reasonable price. You'll call me with every offer. I'm not coming back."

The realtor sighed deeply. "As you wish, signore." It was impossible, he thought: the man had no children and he was a director of stage plays; there was nothing in his life to make him human. He was impressive, of course: tall and broad-shouldered, not truly handsome, his face too sharp, with heavy brows and black eyes that bored into one, and black hair shot with gray, hair so thick it was to be envied by those like the realtor who each morning had to artfully arrange the few strands left on a shiny field. An imposing man, Signore Cameron, but rigid in his ideas.

"Now tell me more about the town," Luke said

as platters of *ossobuco* were set before them. He tore another piece of bread from the loaf in the center of the table and poured more of the Brunello. "Tell me about the people."

Wherever he went, he always asked about the people. Claudia hated it. Once she called him a voyeur; she thought it was his fascination with other people that had led him to find her wanting. But that was not it at all. Luke collected people. At home, he made notes on their quirks and eccentricities, their troubles and longings and passions, their private stories and public conduct, their unique vocabulary and speech patterns, the different ways they laughed, the look in their eyes when something wonderful or fearsome happened. They became a wellspring of knowledge that he used to help his actors and actresses develop their characters. And he used it too in a private world where he tried to write his own plays, struggling in his spare time to learn the craft of writing: how to tell a story, write dialogue, build characters, create tension. He had finished two scripts but they lay in his desk; so far, he had shown them to no one.

When he returned to the villa after dinner, he sat in the library, making notes on the realtor's tales of the village, seeing it as he knew his grandmother had. Then he went to the salon and retrieved the box of letters he had left there. The more powerfully he was able to evoke his grandmother's spirit, the more palpable Jessica Fontaine seemed to him: a real woman whose life was entwined with Constance's, a woman whom he now realized he knew almost nothing about, but whose story was here, left to him, he thought, by Constance. Because of course she had done this on purpose. Instead of destroying the letters, she had left them for him to find, so sure of his curiosity and his hunger for people's stories that she knew he would not be able to resist looking into them and then delving deeper, to learn as much about his grandmother, perhaps, as about Jessica. And as he sat in the empty villa, remembering Constance, it seemed that Jessica was there, too; that he could not separate them, nor would they want him to.

Much too mystical, Luke thought, shaking his head. Jessica was more practical than that. Wasn't she?

Dear Constance,

began the second letter in the inlaid box.

I'm so glad you liked the roses . . . I wasn't sure you even like roses, but I thought they were beautiful and I couldn't let your birthday go by without sending you something of beauty. But every day is beautiful, isn't it? I wake up and help my mother around the house, and it's very ordinary, but then I think about getting to the theater and being on stage, watching you and learning from you and everything is beautiful again. Oh, I am so happy!

Thank you for being you. Happy, happy birthday, with all my love, Jessica.

The next morning, it was that joyous letter and
the realtor's tales of the townspeople that Luke
thought about, fending off the tomblike feeling of
the villa. He went to his grandmother's bedroom.
He had put it off, knowing it would be the hardest
part—her bedroom and the library where she had
spent most of the last year of her life—and he went
through both rooms without stopping to rest or
eat. He shut his mind to images of Constance using
the delicate blown-glass perfume flasks and the
gold hand mirror and comb on her dressing table,
or lacing the sleek Italian shoes she had so loved,
or reclining each night against the lace-edged pillows on her bed, half-sitting because it helped her
to breathe, reading until she felt drowsy, then
reaching out to turn off the gilded lamp and sleep.
He got through the day without tears, handling
everything his grandmother had handled; method-
ically labeling and organizing everything so that he
could leave a day earlier than he had planned.
On the last morning, he walked through the
rooms one last time with the shipping agent, tag-
ging furniture and boxes, going over directions.
"And this, signore?" the agent asked, picking up
the inlaid box.
"I'm taking that with me."
"It is heavy to carry. I can ship it with the paintings and boxes of—"

"No, I'll take it." He knew it was foolish, this reluctance to let the box go, but he would take no chance that it might be lost. That afternoon, he packed the few clothes he had brought in his roll-on luggage and wedged the box among them.

He closed the door and turned to leave Constance's villa for the last time. Briefly, he glanced back at the shuttered windows and the gardens empty of gardeners, empty of Constance, and a wave of melancholy swept over him. But then he thought about Jessica's letters. Hundreds of them: intriguing and already important enough to keep close by, for reasons he could not even analyze. To please Constance. To satisfy my curiosity. To understand a woman who now seems almost a mystery. And for whatever other reasons I may find when I read them: reasons that Constance, even at the end of her life, thought of when she left them for me to find . . . and to read.

# CHAPTER 2

The air-conditioning had turned the air frigid and Luke pulled on his jacket as he came into his office from the muggy streets. He had been back only a month, but the memory of green hills and the cool marble walls of his grandmother's villa had melted in New York's stifling heat and been swept away by his overcrowded schedule. No time for memories, he thought, glancing at his grandmother's photograph on his desk. And as if she were beside him, he heard her say, "But Luke, dear Luke, when did you ever let yourself indulge in memories? You're always starting over . . . a new play, a new lady, a new life. Am I truly the only person you hold on to?"

"Yes," Luke murmured in the silence of his office. "The only one."

He walked past his desk to stand beside the low couch that stretched the length of one wall and looked down at the script of *The Magician*. He had been working on it late into the night before and had left the pages scattered over the coffee table, as colorful as a garden with lines and arrows, checks and asterisks made with different color marking pens, one for each character, each scene, each shift in emotion or sudden change in relationships. By now, three months after the playwright had sent it to him, he knew every word by heart and the characters were as familiar as if he had known them for years; they peopled his thoughts and even his dreams. It was the same each time he took on a new play. He plunged into a world that he would spend the next weeks and months shaping to his own vision, a world challenging enough to fill his life and sufficiently enthralling to convince him that these were intimacies enough for him. He needed no others.

He swept the pages together, striking the edges

on the table to square them, then slipped the manuscript into his briefcase and went back outside,
into the wall of heat that was New York in mid-
July. When the light changed at 59th Street and
Madison Avenue, the pedestrians surged across,
complaining about the heat, the humidity, and the
government, as if they all were related, and Luke
imagined a scene on stage with just such a mass of
perspiring, grumbling humanity tossing out just
these comments. Probably not, he thought as a
taxi stopped for him. Too many people; too expensive for anything but a musical.

"Hot," said the taxi driver, meeting Luke's eyes
in the rearview mirror. "Same hot in Pakistan, too.
My wife, she says so why are we here? Why not
some place different from Pakistan? I tell her, here
is different. Here is job, here is money." He waited
for a reply. "Right?" he asked.

"Right," Luke said, and repeated it to himself.
Here is job, here is money. That's why we're all
here, instead of a cool hilltop villa in Italy.

*But every day is beautiful, isn't it?*

The thought seemed to come from nowhere.
Luke frowned, trying to remember where he had
heard it. No, not heard: it was something he had
read. And then, as the taxi inched its way downtown, he remembered. *I wake up and help my
mother around the house, and it's very ordinary, but
then I think about getting to the theater and being
on stage, watching you and learning from you and
everything is beautiful again.*

Jessica. He'd meant to read her letters on the flight from Italy, or when he got home, but he had not even opened the box. The instant he took his seat on the plane his focus shifted from Italy to New York and he forgot the letters and Jessica and even the grief of his echoing footsteps in the empty villa. It was as if, on his way home, he was already there, absorbed in the new play, dealing with Claudia, taking Tricia Delacorte to dinner a few hours after he landed, setting up a meeting with Monte Gerhart, the producer of *The Magician,* Tommy Webb, the casting director, and Fritz Palfrey, the stage manager, and, after them, all the others who would be working backstage and at the front of the house to bring the play to opening night in late September, a little over two months from now.

At Madison Park, the taxi pulled up at a reddish-brown turn-of-the-century office building, one of the city's early skyscrapers, its sandstone lintels and doorways carved into curves and leaves and mythical figures. Luke pulled on his jacket again as he rode the chilled elevator to Monte Gerhart's office, thinking that it was one of Monte's many oddities that he had chosen that particular building, then decorated his enormous office with glass-and-steel furniture, a geometrically patterned carpet and huge modern paintings that made the windowless room a muffled cocoon of dark colors slashed by beams of light that shot from recessed ceiling fixtures like spotlights on a stage.

One of the spotlights formed a halo around Gerhart at his desk. He was a huge man with a full gray beard that hid his neck, square wire-rimmed glasses and long gray hair curling over his ears and onto his shoulders. His shirtsleeves were rolled above the elbows, revealing a heavy gold watch and two gold link bracelets; his loosened tie was bright with butterflies; and he sat at an oval desk drawing buxom nude women on an artist's sketch pad. "Luke! Have a seat. Have something to eat." He remained in his chair, but gestured with a powerful hand. "Coffee and iced tea in the corner; sweet rolls, muffins; whatever looks good."

Luke poured coffee over ice cubes. "Can I bring you something?"

"I'm on a diet. My wife says."

Luke's eyebrows rose.

"Right; it's bullshit. I'll have a few sweet rolls or whatever's there; I've got coffee here. Well, now, sit down. I reread the play last night. Great play, but like I told you, I've got problems with Lena. She's too old. Nobody gives a damn about eighty-plus women; they don't want to think about getting old; reminds them they'll die one of these days."

Son of a bitch, Luke thought. You've had this play a month and never mentioned this. But all he said was, "How old would you make her?"

"Not sure. Fifty, maybe. Forty's probably too young."

"And the three great-grandchildren?"

"Well, obviously not. Grandchildren, maybe. If

she's fifty and she got married young . . . twenty? . . . twenty-one? . . . something like that. It's not a big deal, you know; Kent can rewrite it in a week or so; most of it would stay the same. Lena and her grandson . . . well, it would have to be her son. But the important thing is how she changes him, right? That's okay whether he's her son or grandson, right? And the love story can stay the same; it's great the way it is. Kent can handle it. He'll be here in a few minutes; once we get him going on it, we're ready to roll. Should be smooth, right? It's not like you and I are strangers; we did another play together, one of your first, right?"

"It was the first." Luke kept his voice casual and amused. "Almost thirteen years ago to the day and you're exactly the same, Monte. Still trying to up-stage the playwright."

Gerhart drew two large circles for breasts and began shading in the nipples. "Everybody needs help, you know, even playwrights. Hey, we talked about this, Luke. A month ago? Something like that."

Luke sat back, stretching his legs. He looked relaxed, but those who knew him well would recognize the tension in his body and his eyes. "Give it up, Monte. We never talked about Lena's age; you just dreamed it up. The whole story revolves around her and her grandson, and we aren't going to make her one year younger. Or older, for that matter."

Gerhart took off his square-rimmed glasses and

contemplated Luke through pale eyes that looked small and newly laundered without lenses shielding them. "Nobody likes old women."

"Who told you that?"

"I didn't have to be told. *I* don't like old women."

"I'm sorry to hear it. Most audiences do, you know. How else would you explain Jessica Tandy and Ethel Barrymore and Constance Bernhardt?"

"Constance— Your grandmother. That's why you're so hot for this play!"

"Lena does remind me of Constance. But that wouldn't be enough. This is a terrific play, Monte, and you know it. It's hard to believe that Kent wrote it—that he knows so much at his age—but somehow he got it all right: it's a solid story with wonderful lines and the characters are absolutely true to—" He stopped as the buzzer on Gerhart's desk sounded.

"Well, the great playwright's here," Gerhart said. "We'll see what he has to say."

"He won't like it," Luke said flatly.

There was a rush of air, as if a tornado had spun into the office. Kent Horne was young, tall and thin and flamboyantly good-looking, with a shock of black hair, dark blue eyes magnified by wire-rimmed glasses and a long neck that made his head seem like a kind of beacon, swiveling to take in the world. He wore faded blue jeans, a belt with a silver-and-turquoise buckle and a white open-necked shirt, and he was talking before he was more than two steps inside the door. "I've got a great idea for act two, not a change really, but a terrific way to make Daniel look stronger a little earlier, we don't have to wait quite so long to see what he's really like inside. I'd thought of it earlier, actually, but—"

"Good morning," Monte said, standing behind his desk.

Kent looked at his outstretched hand. "Pretty formal, Monte. I mean, we're practically related, right? When you do a play . . ." He looked at Luke. "Hi."

"Monte thinks structure is a good thing," Luke said, amused, and Kent shrugged and went to the desk to shake Monte's hand.

"Good morning," he said, emphasizing the words. "Glad to see you looking so well. Glad to see everybody looking so well. God, it's nice to be cool. I walked from my apartment and I could feel myself melting, starting with my feet and sinking into a puddle, like the Wicked Witch of the West—"

"We're talking about rewriting Lena so she's fifty," Monte said, sitting down. "Better for audience identifica—"

"Fifty? *Fifty years old* instead of eighty-two? You're not serious."

"If we're talking about it, we're serious."

"You can't be. You're out of your mind. Luke?" Kent turned to him. "You're serious about this?"

"I wouldn't tolerate it."

"Then why the hell are we talking about it?"

"Because I want to," Gerhart growled. He drew wide hips, curving them into mountainous thighs, then threw down his pen. "Listen, damn it, I've produced fifteen plays and twelve of them made money. Twelve! Four are still making money. That's a hell of a record, and you know it, and I had something to say about every one of those plays. Just because I spent my time making money instead of going to college doesn't mean I don't know what's wrong with the theater. You people talk to each other too much; you forget ordinary folks. And ordinary folks like young; *they don't like old.*"

"Bullshit." Kent had been prowling the room; now he stood in the center of it, legs apart. *"The Magician* is about Lena—Christ, Monte, you *know* this—who's the real magician, the way she makes things happen between people, and it's partly because of her age. I mean, you don't have all that wisdom when you're young."

"You're young."

"I'm different, I'm a genius. What the hell, this play is about real people and *it's about a woman who isn't young!*"

"Fifty isn't young."

"You just said it was; you said that's why you want to change her age."

"Not *young* young. But not old. Old is out, damn it. There's no way I'm going to produce a play about an old hag who people will think is a witch, not a magician."

There was a silence. Son of a bitch, Luke thought again, seething. No one was going to tell him how to direct *The Magician;* he'd lived with the script for three months and by now it was his far more than it was anyone else's. But still he had to go through this charade to get where he had thought he was when he first walked in twenty minutes ago. They're midgets when it comes to directing, he thought, and then, with a glance at Gerhart's huge frame, he broke into a chuckle. *Midgets.*

"What's so funny?" Kent demanded.

"Not a lot." He stood up. "I didn't come here to listen to you two hack away at each other. We're going to talk about getting this play produced or we'll drop the whole project and I'll put together a new team."

"Lena's age stays the way I wrote it," Kent said flatly. "It doesn't change by one year. Not by one goddamn day!"

Luke nodded. "We understand that."

"Look, it's a no-brainer," Gerhart said. "Do a draft, Kent, give us something to talk about. Couple days, that's all. Well, take a week. Can't talk without something in front of us, right?"

"No. Damn it, Monte, how many times do I have to say it? No. No. No."

Luke leaned forward, his hands on Gerhart's

desk. "Monte, read the play again, straight through. I don't intend to have this discussion again, so this is what I want you to think about." Pulling a pad of paper to him, he scrawled three lines, tore off the sheet and put it in front of Gerhart. "First, you know who fills most theaters these days: older people who can afford the price of a ticket. You think they won't understand Lena, and admire and identify with her? Second, when there are young people in the audience, whom are they going to lean toward? We know they'll identify with the lovers, but what about Lena, who'll remind them of their grandmother . . . or make them wish they had a grandmother like her? Third, when Lena's grandson falls in love, it's very much like the love affair Lena had when she was young; she feels more protective of it precisely because she's in her eighties—sixty years removed from that passion. A woman of fifty could look forward to another love affair; Lena can't. I have notes on all those points, but before I show them to you I want you to read the play again, beginning to end, not stopping for single lines or even scenes. Get a feel for the whole thing." He waited. "I assume you'll have time to do that," he said evenly.

Gerhart was drawing again, concentrating on bulging calves fading to slender ankles. After a moment he looked up and grinned. "Well, you're a tough hombre, Luke. I don't mind that; it's why you're the best director around. I thought of those things—you're right about the old people in the audience; you might be right about everything else, I don't know, but I did think about all that and it's a hell of a good play just the way it is. I knew that last night. No question I'd like her younger—I think with some rewriting we could make it work—and you know I always try to get my way and I will again—fair warning, Luke, I always try to get my way—but for now, with Lena, you've got a good case, so, okay, we leave her alone."

Kent was staring at him. *"So okay?* We've been playing a game? Monte, I have better things to do with my time than play your little games."

"I'm paying for your play, *Mr.* Horne, and if I want to play a game now and then, I'll play it and so will you. This wasn't a game, though, this was serious. I wanted her younger. I fight for what I believe. You don't understand that? Look at you, standing there like Clint Eastwood ready to shoot me through my whatsit. I tried and I lost. Sometimes you'll try and you'll lose. That's how it goes."

"I don't lose."

"The hell you don't. You'd better think again about that."

"Let it go," Luke said. "It's going to be a rough two months of togetherness if you two can't learn to get along. That's your assignment. Both of you." He opened the office door. "Monte, ten o'clock tomorrow? We'll start again. Tommy will be here, too."

"Tommy?" Kent asked.

"Webb," Monte said. "Casting director. Ten o'clock, Luke."

"I'll be here, too," Kent said aggressively.

"Of course you will," Luke said, "it's your play. But I shouldn't have to tell you that this isn't a one-man show: not yours, not mine, not Monte's. The theater—at least my theater—is no place for tyranny. You've never had a play produced, but whether you had or not, here you do it our way. Some lines—what the hell, sometimes whole scenes—always need rewriting; the minute rehearsals begin you can hear when lines that look terrific on paper just don't work when they're spoken. I'll never deliberately compromise your integrity as a writer, but I'm telling you now, you'll be rewriting as we go along."

"I don't rewrite. It's perfect the way it is."

"I've never seen a perfect play. Neither have you. *The Magician* is a wonderful play, but I can't promise I won't ask for changes, and if that doesn't satisfy you, you'd better pull out now."

There was a silence. "You know I wouldn't do that."

"I'm glad to hear it. Tomorrow at ten?"

Kent nodded. Monte was drawing shoes on his nude woman. Luke left. He had a lot of planning to do, or it was going to be a hell of a long two months.

"It doesn't seem long enough to put on a major play," said Marian Lodge as they sat in Luke's office an hour later. She was tall and thin with hair slicked back and gold loops swaying from her ears, and she wore a linen suit and a silk rep tie. She sat erect in an armchair, a malachite roller-ball pen poised over the pad of yellow lined paper on her lap and a tiny tape recorder hissing faintly on the arm of Luke's chair. "Readers of *The New Yorker* profiles demand verisimilitude, you know, so I'll want all the details. How do you get everything done in two months? Don't actors need more time to learn their lines and psych out their characters, and then rehearse? And what about all the rest of it—costumes, stage sets, lighting, props . . . I'm fascinated by the theater, you know; I could talk about it forever."

"I don't have quite that much time," Luke said with a smile that was caught by the photographer who prowled about the room, his camera's automatic shutter making a rapid staccato as he photographed Luke, the few prominent, abstract sculptures, the leather-and-suede furnishings and the signed photographs that covered the walls. Luke held his smile and masked his impatience. He had only agreed to the interview because Tina Brown had asked him to do it as part of a double issue on the arts, and already he was regretting it. "Let's see how much we can do in an hour. As for the two months, preparation for a production can go on too long: not only does it reach a plateau, it can slide backward and lose whatever freshness—"

"So how do you decide how long to rehearse?"

epends on the complexity of a play, and the
of characters. But I'd think something
wrong if a play took much more than six
rehearsal."

ded. "Now, I know you and Claudia are
but do you have children?"

, Luke shrugged. He knew all about
f interviewer. She would skim the sur-
g now and then into the real details of
t never enough to interfere with the
lation she was really after. "No," he

would you like children . . . or are your plays
your children?"

"Plays are like children: they need nurturing
and shaping, they need a creative atmosphere in
order to reach their fullest potential, they—"

"Yes, but what about you, Mr. Cameron? Surely
you've thought about your own children . . .
you're—I have this in my notes somewhere—how
old you are—"

"Forty-five. Of course I've thought about children; my grandmother liked the idea of having
great-grandchildren. She talked about it until the
day she died. I was seven when I went to live with
her—my parents had died quite suddenly, within
two months of each other—and Constance took
me in. I grew up backstage, with tutors and various casts and crews to teach me everything that tutors didn't know. I remember once, when I was ten,
we were in San Francisco touring *How Green Was*

*My Valley* and everybody was talking about Haight Ashbury. It sounded like pure romance and excitement—sexual excitement, though I think, at ten, I could barely have defined or recognized it—so one day when my tutor was sick I took off by myself. I had a little money and I bought a map and a candy bar and some kind of soft drink, and I actually got to within a few blocks of where I thought I was going when one of the cast members, Terry Evans, plucked me off the sidewalk. Constance had enlisted everyone—cast, crew, even the cleaning staff—and sent them to scour San Francisco to find me. But Terry didn't take me right back. He called Constance to tell her he'd found me and then he took me on a tour of the Haight, a real one, including dinner at some little place that's long since disappeared. He gave a running commentary that even a ten-year-old could understand, so I saw that there really was romance and excitement there, and a kind of innocence that's rare today. But Terry also made me see the young people who were lost in drugs and fantasies and were vulnerable to exploitation. In fact, that was what he made sure I learned that day: how brutally some people prey on the innocent. There was sexual exploitation and financial exploitation—shopkeepers and landlords who robbed those kids blind—and con artists who used them to make a buck by running bus tours through the Haight, filming it for television, writing cockeyed newspaper stories about it, using real names and photographs. Of all the examples of man's inhumanity to man, the Haight, under Terry's tutelage, was probably the most devastating. And it's still in me, in the way I direct, in the way I feel about the undercurrents of relationships, the power struggles between people. I guess I was pretty shaken up, because by the time I got back to the theater that night I remember being relieved to know that there were new rules about my not going off alone, and from then on Constance made time to be my fellow explorer. She and I explored three dozen cities before I went away for high school and then college. We were a great team."

"A charming story." Marian Lodge smiled brightly. "But speaking of exploring, I do want to explore your ideas about your marriage and marriage in general, your friends and of course children."

"Miss Lodge." She looked at him expectantly, her pen poised. "I thought you'd be able to grasp the reason I told that story. I thought I was making it clear that I have no intention of talking about my marriage or my friends or my feelings about children. I'll be glad to talk to you about my grandmother and the plays I've directed and those I plan to direct and what I'm trying to achieve in my directing. Giving you the benefit of the doubt, I assume that's what you came to hear."

"Well. Do you always tell interviewers what kind of an interview they can do?"

"Always."

"So you direct the interview the same way you do a play. Did you direct your marriage that way? Oh, dear me, I'm sorry," she said quickly as Luke stood up. "That slipped out. I apologize. May I rephrase it? Do you direct any of the events of your life in the same way?"

He smiled. "No."

"*Would* you sit down again? I *am* sorry. It's just that I'm known"—she smiled again, a confidential smile—"for getting all those intimate details no one else can get. Those are what make a person come alive on the printed page: I'm sure you know that."

"A good writer makes people come alive through language and imagery, not titillation."

She flushed. "Well, yes, of course. But I'm thinking of our readers, you know; they expect to read about your personal life; they want to *know* you."

"They'll know me through my work. I'd think that's what *The New Yorker* readers would be most interested in." He remained standing, leaning casually against the wall behind his desk. "From the time I was seven to my thirteenth birthday, when Constance decided I needed a real high school, and after that on summer vacations, I lived backstage, watching, listening, asking questions, pestering the crews to let me work on stage sets, lighting design, props, everything that goes into a production. When I was fifteen I knew I'd be a director and I was already criticizing the way plays were being staged. I was an unbearably arrogant teenager, absolutely sure I'd already learned everything I needed to know. Constance listened to me with great patience and more than a little humor and then told me that I had a few things left to learn and I was going off to college, whether that was part of my lifetime plan or not."

Having launched himself, he talked easily about his early years in the theater and then all phases of theater life, using anecdotes, famous names, a sprinkling of technical backstage terms, an inside look at scandals of the past and his own style of directing, especially in the plays and films that had made his name one of the most famous on Broadway. Then he added the statistics magazine editors love: how many plays he had directed, where they had opened and later toured, the number of tickets sold, how many people were involved in the production of a play and how many people in the theater made a good living at it (very few).

By the time he stopped, almost two hours had gone by, the photographer had long since left, and Marian Lodge had changed her tape twice and filled her notepad. Not bad, Luke thought when she left. He had no desire to see his picture or his quotes in yet another magazine, but if profiles such as this one led to larger audiences, longer runs of his plays, more great scripts sent to him from known or unknown playwrights, then the two hours had been well spent. In fact, he would do anything within reason to help his plays and the theater in general.

*I wake up and help my mother around the house . . . but then I think about getting to the theater and being on stage . . . and everything is beautiful again.*

Jessica again. Odd how her words, from only those few letters that he had read, kept weaving through his thoughts. But the words fit his life, slipping smoothly into whatever he was doing. Well, we're both so deeply a part of the theater, he thought. Or at least she was. Good God, how she must miss it. The way my grandmother felt when she moved to Italy. Jessica must have written about that. I'll find out, one of these days, when I have a chance to get back to her letters.

He ate a sandwich at his desk and worked through the afternoon. He liked his office: the serene quiet that was accentuated by faint sounds of traffic from the street eleven stories below, the cool black, gray and blue furnishings his decorator had chosen, one book-lined wall and two walls covered with photographs of the stars with whom he had worked, and of presidents, senators, prime ministers, kings and queens, all standing beside him, smiling into the camera, or shaking his hand, or bestowing a medal or award, or presenting him with a gift after he had visited a country to oversee the staging of a play. He knew it was faintly childish to exhibit the photographs—splashing his importance all over his walls—but he told himself he did it to impress visitors, and so each season there were new ones to add to the collection. He worked contentedly through the afternoon, mostly undisturbed, letting his secretary screen his calls, until, as he was about to leave, Claudia called.

"Dinner tomorrow night?" she asked brightly. "I haven't seen you for ages."

"You'll see me tonight, at the benefit."

"With five hundred other people in the St. Regis ballroom. Luke, don't be coy. You know I meant just the two of us."

He glanced at his calendar. "I'm going to Joe and Ilene's cocktail party tomorrow night, and then to Monte Gerhart's. We could have a drink before that, if you'd like."

"Luke, I need to talk to you; there are some things I can't handle. . . . Why are you doing this to me?"

"All right, tomorrow night, but not dinner; we'll have drinks at Pompeii. Eleven o'clock. I'll meet you there."

"You could pick me up."

"Claudia, it's half a block from your building. Meet me there and I'll walk home with you afterward. Make a list of what you want to ask me; you're always forgetting something."

"*Make a list?* I don't plan my dates as if they're board meetings; life should be spontaneous. Anyway, I won't forget; it's mostly about money."

And Claudia never forgets anything involving money, Luke thought as he hung up; she still talks about the time she had to pay for dinner at the Terrace because I'd left my wallet backstage. That was before we were married and she was on her best behavior, so she paid with a smile and a little joke about absentminded directors, but she never forgot it.

His limousine was waiting downstairs and as he sat back in its cool interior, his driver turned to scrutinize him. Arlen O'Day had been Constance Bernhardt's driver for thirty years and had watched Luke grow up before going to work for him when Constance went to Italy, and with all his Irish intensity he took over as Constance's stand-in, watching over Luke, worrying about him, offering advice. He studied Luke's face for a moment before starting the car and pulling out into traffic. "Bad day, Mr. Cameron? Or just the heat? It's a killer, the heat; God must be punishing somebody, but I don't know why the rest of us have to get it, too."

Luke smiled. "I don't think it's punishment for anyone. And I didn't have a bad day; it was a pretty good one, at least the afternoon." He fell silent, thinking about his day. Indoors, all of it, arguing with Monte Gerhart, giving Kent Horne a lesson about the theater, probably the first of many, fending off a persistent interviewer, dealing with his ex-wife, who insisted on calling it a date when Luke agreed to take her out for a drink, having his most normal conversations with a taxi driver from Pakistan and a limousine driver from Dublin. Suddenly he felt stifled, wanting to run.

Run where? He didn't know. Somewhere. To find
something. But he had no idea what he wanted or
where to look for it.

Forty-five years old, he thought. Healthy, finan-
cially secure, internationally known, admired,
maybe envied. Unmarried. Unattached.

"Shall I wait, Mr. Cameron?" Arlen asked as he
turned onto Fifth Avenue.

"Yes. I'll be about half an hour." I'm attached to
Arlen, he thought ruefully: the only person who
always waits for me. Good God, that sounds
maudlin. It's the heat, as everyone says. Or the beginning of a new play; for me that's always the
hardest time, when nothing yet has a shape, when
I have a manuscript but no actors, no characters
coming to life, nothing to mold. I'm always tense
at the beginning of a project; it doesn't mean a
thing.

But the truth was, there was something else that
he wanted, something he hadn't achieved, and
even though he could not define it, he often felt a
longing that crept up on him, as just now, taking
him by surprise. It always faded, but it always
came back.

Across the street from the Metropolitan Museum, Arlen pulled up at a limestone building fes-
tooned with stone gargoyles and rearing dragons
and wrought-iron balconies that stretched the
width of the building at each floor. A doorman
reached for the limousine door as Luke opened it.
"Well, sir, Mr. Cameron, it's a hot one, and hotter

tomorrow, the radio says." Luke wondered how many times that day he had said those words to other residents of the building, how many times he had ducked inside for a breath of cool air and a swig of something iced, how many times he had mopped his face and changed his white gloves to keep them pristine. We all have stifling days, he thought, but his own restlessness, a kind of urgency, still gripped him, and he wished, as the second doorman took him to his penthouse in the self-service elevator that the residents insisted be run by a doorman, that he could stay home that night and try to figure out what was wrong with him.

But there were almost no nights that he could stay home, and so he greeted his butler, who told him that it was exceedingly hot outside but that the apartment was blessedly cool, swiftly took a shower, shaved and changed into his tuxedo and returned to the street. Arlen pulled up just as he emerged and, without being told, drove to the glass-and-steel tower on Madison Avenue where Tricia Delacorte was coming toward him across the lobby. She kissed Luke lightly as her doorman closed the car door behind her. "My, you do look handsome; your hair is different."

"Still wet from the shower." He looked at her with pleasure, admiring her cultivated beauty and the expensive perfection of her ball gown that exposed a good part of her creamy skin between puffed sleeves in a rainbow of colors. She had been born Teresa Pshevorski on the west side of Chicago, but at seventeen, newly arrived in Los Angeles, she got her first job as a maid, as Tricia Delacorte, a name from a novel long since forgotten. She had planned to marry a famous actor or director she met while serving hors d'oeuvres at parties, but the years went by and it never happened, and one day, bored and angry, she wrote an article for a neighborhood newspaper describing the scandals of fictitious characters as if they were major names in Hollywood: the high and mighty who ate and drank but ignored the maid. Her writing was lively and racy and attracted the attention of the editor of the *Los Angeles Times,* who called her in.

By then she had had two face-lifts and could talk like an insider, using the storehouse of gossip and movie lore she had overheard in years of parties. She talked her way to a column in the *Los Angeles Times,* which was soon picked up by a national syndicate, and then she was offered a column in *The Sophisticate,* a glossy weekly magazine for those who thought they were sophisticated even if others did not. Soon she no longer needed fictitious names because she was invited everywhere and her telephone rang constantly with tips on impending marriages, divorces, births, the end or beginning of affairs, a son or daughter on drugs, a fortune lost or made, an engagement broken, a criminal indictment in the works. The most enticing appeared in her column with names in boldface. Occasionally she ran a blind item: "Who ducked out of Spago the other night rather than answer questions about the agreement in the works between his wife, his mistress and his two teenage children?" She was the sole arbiter of whether such questions ever were answered, or were left to dangle in the steamy air.

By the time Luke met her, she divided her week between apartments in Los Angeles and New York, collecting tidbits about actors, actresses, directors and producers who now were scattered as widely as Aspen, the plains of Montana, and Sharon, Connecticut. She had never used an item about Luke.

"Well, they did it again," she said to him in the limousine, sliding along the leather seat until her thigh was against his. "You'd think they'd have some sense of responsibility."

"Should I know what you're talking about?" he asked.

"I did tell you. Joe and Ilene Fassbrough were quarreling at LAX when they came back from Europe; they fought all the way through customs. Well, last night they had a major blowup at Freddy Parkington's dinner—stopped the entrée from being served for a good ten minutes—and then Joe actually told me I should ignore the whole thing, that he had the flu and was feverish and said a lot of things he didn't mean. But these people have a responsibility, you know: the rest of the world looks up to them and sickness is no reason to absolutely lose your standards of behavior. If he really was sick. He looked fine to me. But of course men always look wonderful in tuxedos."

"Did you say he was sick in today's column?"

"Of course not; I said that he and Ilene stopped the entrée from being served. It's a much livelier item, Luke, you know that; it would be a wonderful scene in a play. I wanted to say something about people who let down their social class by behaving badly, but that really doesn't belong in the column. Maybe in *The Sophisticate* next month."

Luke sat back, his arm along the seat behind her shoulders. "What social class is this?"

"Ours. Oh, Luke, don't be tiresome. You know what I mean."

"You mean that Joe and Ilene Fassbrough, who are two of the most asinine people I know, and dull besides, are role models for an upper class."

"They spend a lot of money, people recognize them and like to be seen with them, and they're invited everywhere. It's more than upper class, Luke, it's like royalty, if we had royalty. Well, we don't, but Americans really would love it if we did—why else do you think every magazine with Charles and Di on the cover sells out in five minutes? Instead we have people like Joe and Ilene, who are movie stars and who do all those royal things like sponsoring benefits and getting their pictures in the paper and buying a lot of art. Readers love to read about them. And if you think they're asinine and dull, why are you going to their house tomorrow night?"

"A good question. They've invited a playwright from the former Yugoslavia; I've heard of him and I want to meet him."

"Invite him for dinner at your house."

"It's easier to meet him at the Fassbroughs' and see if we have anything to talk about."

"Why do you think they're asinine and dull?"

"Because they prattle about money, and measure people by money, and because they're exhibitionists, which I find infantile."

"But they're famous."

"And you write about famous people, so you certainly should write about them. But as if they're royalty? You don't really believe that."

"I believe they're as important as royalty, and that's what counts."

He shrugged. He knew that Tricia's enormous success was due in large part to just that sort of serious naiveté, her pure belief that the people she documented—most of whom were shallow and unimportant—were as newsworthy as royalty, their doings every bit as interesting to her readers as the machinations of presidents, generals and crooks.

And he knew that that was exactly what he asked of his audiences: that they suspend their disbelief and let themselves be swept into the worlds he created. All his work as a director was toward that end: to bring to life the work of the play-wright so that audiences responded to it with a pure belief in its reality and importance. For that reason he understood Tricia and even sympa-thized with her. She had the kind of belief that children have in fairy tales and adults have in fan-tasies that make their lives tolerable by keeping everything on the surface, avoiding depth and complexity. Together with her blond beauty and endless store of anecdotes, that had kept him amused and interested for almost four months.

He liked her fame, too. He always chose to be with beautiful, well-known women and he was used to attracting photographers, and the night at the St. Regis was no different. For Luke, the whole evening—the auction to raise money for a cause he had not bothered to notice, the dinner and danc-ing, the fragments of conversation snatched from the air as groups gathered, broke apart and re-formed—seemed to float on the attention that sur-rounded him and Tricia. It was a way of getting through the evening without feeling boredom or impatience.

*Without feeling anything.* The words flashed and were gone, but they left him feeling as he had in his limousine earlier that long day: stifled, waiting for something and trying to figure out what it was.

He danced with Tricia, made conversation, bid on and won three items in the silent auction, and engaged in a fierce battle in the live auction for a sculpture he had determined to own. He won there, too, and the crowd broke into applause. In the limousine, he gave Tricia the necklace he had bought in the silent auction, and she cuddled against him. "Are you getting serious about me, Luke?"

"As serious as you are about me," he said easily.

She frowned. After a moment, she said, "I think someday I might like to marry you. I'm just not sure. I think you'd be hard to live with."

"You're probably right." The limousine stopped in front of her building; Luke sent Arlen home and he and Tricia went upstairs.

"What does that mean?" she asked. "That I'm probably right. What does that mean?"

"That I would most likely be very hard to live with." He walked with easy familiarity through her living room, a large, coldly modern square space filled with clusters of wood-framed glass tables, white couches and armchairs, marble floors with Stark geometric rugs and a scattering of minimalist paintings on the white walls. Luke disliked it all, finding it neither beautiful nor comfortable, but a major designer had done it for a sum of money that even Tricia found excessive and so she defended it vigorously and wore bright colors that made her stand out like a brilliant flower in a black-and-white photograph. Luke went to the bar and made Tricia a drink and she sipped it while he made one for himself. Then he sat beside her on the couch and took her in his arms. "It's not something we need to talk about now."

She held herself slightly away from him. "Do you want to get married again?"

"Probably not."

"Luke, you keep using those words. Probably. Most likely. Aren't you sure?"

"Probably not," he said, smiling, and kissed her, pulling her into his arms and feeling her move pliantly against him. Her tongue tasted of the martini he had made her; her skin became flushed beneath his hands, as supple as warm, polished taffy. She led Luke to the bedroom and when they lay on the silk coverlet of her bed she fit herself beneath him with rippling movements that came from her own experience and her familiarity with him. So skilled was she that she blurred into anonymity. In sex, as in the times they were apart, Luke never spoke her name; in fact, he barely thought about her. He did not think that was a bad thing or a good one; it was as if their moves had been scripted—they could have been any two people in bed after an evening on the town—but he was aware of Tricia's skill at making him feel that whatever he wanted she would do: she would bend and sway and stretch and open to him however he wished because at this moment nothing in the world was important to her but pleasing him. And that was enough to make him dismiss their conversation, and if Tricia remembered it or let it intrude on the next few hours, she never said a word to Luke. As far as he was concerned, marriage was as far from her thoughts as his.

But when he walked home just before dawn, striding through the oddly quiet streets, his restlessness returned. When he let himself into his silent apartment, he went to his study and sat at his desk and thought of reading for half an hour before going to sleep: a few scenes from *The Magician* or a new novel. He did neither of those things. Instead, he reached for Constance's box of letters, and pulled one out at random.

Dearest Constance, I can't believe we're in another play together! Do you know it's exactly two years since we met? And I feel just the same as I did then: I wake up and the world is bright and exciting, sort of holding its breath, waiting for evening, when I'll be with you. I've been working *so* hard—I've hardly seen anybody at all because I'm trying to do everything you told me to do. I'm taking classes in ballet and modern dance and speech. When you wrote, "You must learn about your own body, every movement you make, and about your voice, how it sounds to others, how you can control and vary it, how the shape of your mouth changes when you speak with anger or joy, or with an accent . . . if you learn all this, when you are on stage, you will be in command of it," I shivered when I read that; the idea of *being in command* . . . Anyway, I'm also in a yoga class—I guess it *is* discipline of mind and body, the way you said it was, but mostly it's a lot of fun—and I'm reading lots of biographies and autobiographies, which you also said I should do, to understand all kinds of people in all kinds of situations. With all that, I'm much better than I was two years ago; I can feel it and it makes up for being alone so much. I hope *you* think I'm better. If I am, it's all because of you.

She'd be eighteen, Luke thought. Constance would have been—he calculated rapidly—sixty-three. Two years had gone by without a letter—at least, there were none in the box—but in that time Jessica had done everything Constance had suggested. He was touched by the image of a lonely young woman steadfastly following the advice of someone she worshiped but did not see or hear from for two years. And she must indeed have improved, because here she was, appearing once again with Constance. He wondered if Constance helped her get the part.

He returned the letter to its place in the box and took another at random, much farther toward the back.

I know, I know, Constance, of course you're right, but I'm so angry I can't think straight. It isn't enough to say that I'm alive and life has so much to offer—I know it does, but *it isn't enough!* I want what I had . . . oh, God, I want it back and it eats away at me that I can't have it. I'm sorry, dearest Constance, I shouldn't pour all this out on you, but I know you understand, because you're living on your mountain in Italy and that isn't enough for you, either, is it?

This must have been after the train accident, Luke thought. *It eats away at me that I can't have it.* She meant the theater, of course, but why couldn't she have it? What had happened to her?

Holding the letter, he gazed through his tall, leaded windows as the sky brightened, thinking that Jessica Fontaine was turning out to be far more interesting than he had ever thought she was, more interesting, in fact, than anyone he knew right now. A remarkable, mysterious woman. Something drew him to her: perhaps the tragedy of her life and her disappearance, perhaps her greatness before that, perhaps her friendship with Constance. He did not know the reason; he only knew that the box of letters was like a magnet that tugged at him wherever he was. I need a quiet evening, he thought, to start at the beginning and read them in the order she wrote them. He looked at his calendar for that night. Cocktails at Joe and Ilene's. Dinner at Monte's. A late supper with Claudia. He flipped through the pages for the rest of that week, and the next. God damn it, he needed a night at home. Well, tomorrow night. He wrote a note to make his apologies to Joe and Ilene and to Monte, then slipped Jessica's letter back in the box. He had a few hours to sleep before he was due at Monte's office. And that evening he would come back to Jessica, and find out what happened to her: why she vanished from the stage, where she was now, whether she knew about Constance. What she knew about him.

And he realized, as he went to his bedroom, that he was already thinking he might want to see her again. Not for any special reason, he thought; just out of curiosity. And then, at last, he went to sleep.

## CHAPTER 3

Dearest Constance, it seems so weird to be back in high school, spending my time with all these people who have no idea what I was feeling all summer, how much I learned, how different I am. A boy I met last year, Wesley Minturn, very tall and thin and stooped (like a stork peering down to see what the rest of us are up to) asked me to go to a movie. He said he had his father's car and he even told me what kind—a six-cylinder Alfa-Romeo convertible, red, with black leather seats—I guess he thought I'd find that irresistible but actually I thought it was pretty sad that he couldn't trust himself to be the main attraction of the evening. He made me feel old . . . well, older than him anyway, because I do trust myself, maybe for the first time in my life. I think I won't date at all for the rest of high school; I'm just too different from everybody here, I've seen too much of the world, I'm *world-weary* (I'm pretty sure I know what that means) and even though I'm an actress I won't act like all the other seventeen-year-olds in my class. I'm sure I'll be lonely, but that's the price one pays for being an artist. If we don't suffer, how can we ever become great? I hope you're fine and please write to me. All my love, Jessica.

Luke smiled. *World-weary.* Hardly. She was young, charming, full of energy and hope, and dramatic as only a seventeen-year-old could be: acting a role even when writing a letter. Constance probably had seen herself, at seventeen, in that letter. No wonder they'd become friends.

He slipped Jessica's letter back in its place and sat back, his gaze moving around the library. It was large and square with a deep green cove ceiling, mahogany shelves lining three walls and a mahogany-carved fireplace within a green marble surround. A red, green and brown Bessarabian covered the floor and the long couches were the same red, startling and dramatic against dark green velvet drapes. "Like a stage set," his grandmother had said with satisfaction, and she had sat like a queen in the center of one of the couches, looking up to the ceiling with its wrought-iron chandelier and down to the vast coffee table covered with stacks of books, most of them bristling with bookmarks. I miss her, Luke thought; those weekly telephone calls, our visits, just knowing she was there, part of my life.

The telephone rang and he reached for it. "Luke," said Tricia, somewhere between annoyance and alarm, "I'm at Joe and Ilene's; why aren't you here?"

"I decided to stay home and read."

"*Stay home?* You never stay home! And this playwright you wanted to meet—"

"I called him; we made a date for lunch next week."

"Something's wrong. Was it last night? Because I talked about getting married? I wasn't serious, you know; and anyway, I said I didn't want to, so—"

"It has nothing to do with you. I enjoy being home and I don't do it often enough."

There was a pause. "Are you going to Monte's dinner?"

"No."

"Luke, he's your producer!"

"He's having sixty people for dinner; he won't miss me. I'm sorry I'm not with you, but you'll find plenty of scandals for tomorrow's column and that's the real reason you're there, isn't it?"

"Well, and to be with you."

"I'll call you tomorrow. We'll do something on

Friday if you're free. Right now I'm going back to my reading."

When he hung up, he refilled his glass from the bottle of Scotch that Martin had left for him earlier that evening and added ice cubes from the insulated ice bucket. "You'll be having dinner at home?" Martin had asked. "About eight," Luke replied. "Something light."

He reached for another letter, and the telephone rang again. "What the hell," he said, and thought of letting Martin get it, but instead picked it up.

"Luke!" Claudia exclaimed. "Why are you home? You said you'd be at Joe and Ilene's, and then Monte's, *and then we had a date!*"

Oh, Christ, he thought, remembering, and felt annoyed and resentful as he saw his private evening slip away. But at the same time he saw the humor in it: two women trying to drag him out of his home when all he wanted was to be alone with a third woman's letters.

"It's because you don't want to see me, isn't it? You never stay home; you're just looking for an excuse—"

"It has nothing to do with you." It was amazing how people made themselves crucial to every event, he thought, seeing themselves as the cause of what other people do. He drained his glass and mentally shrugged. "I'll have a quick supper with you. Italia at nine. I'll see you there."

He told Martin he would not, after all, be dining at home and asked him to call the restaurant to reserve a table. He poured himself another drink and took out the next letter. He had an hour.

Oh, what a magnificent gift! Dearest Constance, how wonderful you are, the necklace is absolutely the most gorgeous gift I've ever had. The cameo looks so rare and precious, and I love the silver chain, and I'm going to wear it forever, starting tomorrow afternoon with graduation and then the prom. Well, yes, I actually am going to the prom. I remember I told you I wouldn't date for the rest of high school and you said I'd feel as if I was in a play and got sick and my understudy went on and *nobody missed me.* You were absolutely right, so after a while I started going to parties and things and I even had a good time. Well, some of the time I did; do you have any idea how *young* high school boys are? They only have three or four things to talk about and then they start using their hands. You wouldn't believe it: one minute they're talking about the school football team or something else I couldn't care less about, and then all of a sudden their hands are all over the place, poking, rubbing, pawing . . . unbelievably crude! And sloppy! They have absolutely no finesse . . . they're like puppies, all panting and nuzzling. The problem is, once in a while lately I've started responding—well, my body has, anyway, and I think, oh, well, why not?—which

I find totally embarrassing because there's nothing *romantic* happening, and then it all seems so dumb, and I tell whoever it is to take me home. But what happened about the prom was that a really handsome guy who just moved here, very smooth—lots of finesse!—asked me to go, and I thought, what a change, so I'm going with him. . . . He just called and asked me what I'm wearing so he could choose an orchid to match! I told him black. It has lace *barely* covering my front, *very* sophisticated—and can't you imagine how the cameo will look against black silk? More later, all of it in *great* detail.

Crude and sloppy, Luke thought. Puppies. He remembered himself in high school, all arms and legs, awkward and uncoordinated the minute a girl approached; his voice unreliable, his penis willfully springing to attention, obeying no master but itself. She doesn't know a damn thing about it, he grumbled. But then he chuckled, remembering that the letter had been written some twenty-three years earlier. Past history, he thought; she's learned a lot since then, and so have I. He opened the next letter and ran a casual eye over it, not interested in descriptions of a high school prom, but suddenly a sentence stopped him.

I'm so ashamed of the letters I've been sending you, so incredibly childish.

Something happened, he thought; she's changed. And it looks like it's been a long time since the last letter. He went back to the beginning.

Dearest Constance, your letter was forwarded to me here, at Yale, where I'm finishing up my first year. I'm sorry I haven't written, I think of you all the time but I just couldn't write. I'm so ashamed of the letters I've been sending you, so incredibly childish. I can't believe I ever was that person, so *young* and uncaring, never wondering if you had time in your life for a twittering teenager who kept throwing herself at you, demanding that you love her. I did want you to love me, for lots of reasons, but partly because I thought my parents didn't. Well, now they're dead and all I know for sure is that I never really knew them and that makes me so despairing that I think I'll explode with it because there's *nothing I can do about it.* I'm not sure I ever really looked at them, you know; it seems to me I was always looking somewhere else when they were in the room. So I never saw who they really were. They told me they loved me and wanted to protect me, but that meant keeping me in our little town, safely married, doing something with my drawing and painting—like interior design, or something—but I'd told them over and over that that was just a hobby. They never understood that New York means the theater and *you* and *life* to me, and all I wanted was to be there, and we quarreled about that and *now* I think of things I should have said, or things I should have said differently, or not said at all. I know they loved me and they weren't bad people . . . oh, it's crazy and scary to think that I'll never see them again or tell them all these things I've figured out how to say. They were driving to a movie and they stopped for a red light and a car rammed them from behind and pushed them into the path of a truck. I had nightmares about that for months, even after I came to Yale, and then I got sick and ended up in the infirmary. A psychiatrist, Dr. Leppard, came to see me, a wonderful man who reminds me of my father, and we talked for months, three times a week, and after a while I was able to sleep again. But I didn't care about anything; I felt like some kind of mechanical doll that makes all the right moves and passes tests in class and talks to people—everybody was so nice, but it was like they were talking to me from far away—I felt all empty inside—not alive. Then one day Dr. Leppard asked why wasn't I in the theater program? That was funny, because of course it was the reason I came to Yale and I hadn't even thought about it. So I went over to the theater and they were casting a play and I got a part right away. It was small, but it got me back on stage. But then the most awful thing happened. When I came to the first rehearsal and looked at all the empty seats in front of me and the rest of the cast all around me and the director sitting on the edge of the stage with the script in his hand, I started to cry. Because right then, for the first time, I really believed that my parents were dead and I'd never be with them again and it was as if I'd thumbed my nose at them the minute I walked out on stage. I mean, I'd chosen this other world that they didn't approve of and it was like a betrayal. Of course they'd never know it, but still . . . oh, I don't know, it was the most confused time in my life. Everybody came to help and I finally stopped crying, and afterwards I felt like I'd become somebody else. I wasn't my parents' daughter and I never would be, ever again. And I was alone. I didn't have anybody behind me, waiting for me to come home, keeping my bedroom ready and leaving the front door unlocked and the living room lamp lit. But after a while I remembered that I have you to write to, and your letters to read—I read them hundreds of times, did I ever tell you that?—and I knew that I really do have a family and a home and that's the theater. It's the one place I know I belong. I'm going to work as hard as I can, and I'll be the best of all—except for you, of course; but maybe someday I'll be as good as you— because that's what I want more than anything in the world. I don't want a family or children

or any of those ordinary things that get so
messy and hurt so much. I just want to act.
Once I thought the theater was all I wanted;
now I know it's all I can have. I miss my
parents. I miss knowing they're at home, talking about what we'll do when I visit. I miss
having them miss me. I hope you're fine and
that you'll write to me again even if I've spent
all this time talking about myself. Are you fine?
What are you starring in now? All my love,
Jessica.

"Luke, what in the world is the matter with
you?" Claudia exclaimed. "We're *waiting* for you!"

Luke looked up and met the patient gaze of the
sommelier, looking as timeless as the murals of
Pompeii and Herculaneum on the walls and the
antique draperies at the windows. "Sorry." He ran
his eye down the wine list he had been staring at,
unseeing. "We'll have the Conterno Poderi Barolo
if you still have the '90. And ask our waiter to
bring us an order of calamari to start."

"What *were* you thinking about? Or should I
say, *who?*"

"An eighteen-year-old girl whose parents were
killed in an automobile accident."

She stared at him. "Who is it? I didn't know you
knew any eighteen-year-olds. Oh, is it the new play
you've just started working on? You haven't told
me anything about it."

"No." The sommelier brought the wine and

Luke sat back and looked at Claudia. She was wearing a dark blue dinner suit, beaded at the deep cuffs and collar and cut with such dramatic angles that it was almost a costume. She wore it with style, attracting glances. But they were brief, because her beauty was the kind that left people feeling puzzled, wondering why they were not drawn to such perfection. Her face was a perfect oval framed by straight black hair that swung smoothly when she turned her head; her black eyes were spaced perfectly, her cheekbones made gentle shadows in her smooth, lightly powdered skin. Her mouth . . . well, that was one of the problems, Luke thought. Her mouth would have been perfect but for the tiny tug of dissatisfaction at each corner, like a perpetual complaint that the world was not living up to Claudia Cameron's expectations. And then there was something wrong with her perfection itself: she always looked a little as if she were lacquered, her features unmarked by warmth. Even when she smiled, her eyes were watchful and a little suspicious.

Once, Luke had been overwhelmed by her beauty, when he was young and beginning to be noticed. He knew she would help him to be noticed, and she did: they were such a striking couple that their photographs appeared in magazines more often than couples with greater fame and more impressive credentials. And Claudia helped him in other ways. She was an amiable hostess who followed Luke's directions perfectly in hiring caterers, florists and valets; she tolerated unexpected guests with a bright smile; and she could talk lightly and amusingly at parties of ten or a hundred for an entire evening without saying one word of significance or making one remark that anyone could construe as controversial.

"What are you thinking about?" she asked, having held her pose for several minutes so that he could gaze at her without interruption.

Luke nodded to the sommelier to pour the wine. "What a good hostess you are."

"Oh, was. I don't entertain anymore. There doesn't seem to be any point. Is the eighteen-year-old real, or is she in a play?"

"She's real."

"Who is she?"

"An actress."

"At eighteen?"

"She's in the theater program at Yale."

"And fired up with ambition? That's what you find so attractive about her?"

"Do I find her attractive?"

"Enough to make you forget I'm sitting here."

"I didn't forget; I was distracted. What was it you wanted to talk to me about?"

Claudia beckoned to the waiter. *"Ravioli alla quattro funghi,"* she said, "and the *tre colore* salad to start. Keep the dressing on the side. What are you having, Luke? Maybe the same thing? You always did like mushrooms."

An old trick, Luke thought, remembering all

the ways Claudia had tried to bind them into one when it was clear their marriage had failed to do that. "Lobster risotto," he said to the waiter, "and the same salad as the lady." He turned to Claudia. "Is it money again?"

"Oh, Luke, how crude you are."

"You're right. I'm sorry. But you did say you had to talk to me."

"Well, I am." He made a gesture of impatience that she recognized and she said hastily, "It's just that I need to talk. You know that, Luke. All these years and I haven't found one person who understands me the way you do. You know there's more to me than people think. I *was* a good hostess, wasn't I? People always talked about our parties; some of them would have killed to get invitations. I loved being your hostess; I remember every party we ever gave. Remember the time that prince, the short one, what's-his-name . . ."

Luke drank his wine and welcomed the arrival of his salad and then their dinners. It became increasingly clear that Claudia had nothing particular to talk to him about or, if she did, was putting it off to another night, to make sure there would indeed be another night.

". . . and of course it was such fun, all those people telling you how wonderful you were, and I was part of it. Nobody notices me now; do you know how awful that is? No, how could you? It's the worst thing in the world; it's like I've disappeared."

"You have at least five hundred friends; you're busy every night."

"Well, thank God; that's what keeps me alive. But, you know, Luke, those are acquaintances; they're not really friends who truly care about me. I mean, they think I'm somebody because I was married to you and I still see you, I mean, we still date once in a while, but when you come right down to it, you know, there is absolutely nobody waiting for me when I get home at night. Just that empty apartment."

*I didn't have people behind me, waiting for me to come home, keeping my bedroom ready and leaving the front door unlocked and the living room lamp lit.*

Luke felt a flicker of pity, which surprised him and left him momentarily silent. He seldom felt pity: he believed most people were the cause of their own troubles and had it in their power to clear them up if they so chose. Claudia especially— beautiful, spoiled, self-centered—had undercut their marriage from the beginning by refusing to share with him in building it. She had clung to him for everything: the fame he brought her, their travel, their friends, their social life, the way she organized her days, demanding of him that he tell her what to do with herself and how to do it. "You have a good sense of design," he had said, and she had gone to design school until it bored her. "I'll be an actress," she had declared, staring down Luke's look of disbelief, and she had gone to acting classes until even she had admitted that she had no talent and no real interest. Over and over, she had forced him to direct their marriage as he directed plays, but when something upset her she called him a tyrant. She preened at the attention they got when they went out, then sulked at home because people wanted to talk to Luke, not to her.

"What do you want?" he had demanded when they had been married almost five years.

"I want you to help me!" she flung at him.

"I've helped you for five years," he said quietly.

"Not enough!"

But by then he did not care whether it was enough or not. Whatever she wanted, it was more than he could give her and he was exhausted by her incessant demands. He said he wanted a divorce, and she went through with it, rigid with anger and the fear of being alone. She left New York and for a year Luke did not see her. But then she began calling him, first from Europe, to tell him she was coming home, then irregularly, begging to see him. And, almost always, Luke made the time to see her.

"You shouldn't have married her," Constance had told him. "You know perfectly well that you can't tolerate dependent people and you knew from the time you met Claudia that she would lean on you for everything. But you can't just cut her out of your life; you still have some responsibility for her."

"Luke, you're drifting again!" Claudia exclaimed. "I wish, just once, you'd concentrate on me. We'd still be married if you'd been willing to do that." Luke smiled and she looked at him defiantly. "I don't see what you find amusing in that."

"I'm amused by the contortions people go through to explain the past. It's not just you, it's everyone, including me. Such convolutions to find ways to soothe our vanity."

"You're saying I'm lying?"

"I'm saying you've written your own script and it satisfies you, so it needn't have even a remote resemblance to mine." His pity had faded; he was exactly where he was every time he was with Claudia: impatient to be gone. And now he could be; they had finished their coffee and had no reason to linger. "Come on, I'll walk you home."

"Already? Are you nervous? You always get nervous when I talk about our marriage."

"I never recognize our marriage when you talk about it. And I'm not nervous; I want to get home. I have work to do; we begin casting next week."

"Can I watch the rehearsals?"

"I leave that up to the cast. You know that." He signaled for the check.

"I was at the Phelans' last week," Claudia said, very casually, and then Luke knew what this dinner was about, and he knew that she had held off talking about it until it was clear that, otherwise, the evening would be over.

He sat back, ignoring the check the waiter put beside him. "How much did you lose?"

"You could give me the benefit of the doubt. I might have won." He looked at her steadily and she flushed deeply. "A little over five thousand."

"You promised me you wouldn't go there again."

"I was lonely."

"More likely bored."

"That's part of being lonely. So when they called and said they missed me and they had some really interesting people and a new roulette wheel with a terrific new croupier—and I felt lucky—and God knows *I've* missed *them*—well, anyway, I said yes. And they gave me the front bedroom, you know, the blue-and-silver one, and I had such a good time. They're wonderful people, Luke; they make me feel wanted."

"They want your money."

"They want me! They could get tons of people with money, but they always call me first. Why can't you believe that people really like me?"

"I know that people like you. I also know the Phelans." He skimmed the dinner check, then laid it inside its leather folder with his credit card. "How much over five thousand?"

There was a pause. "Actually, it was closer to ten."

"How much closer?"

"A little over nine. Just a little. Nine, three. But I have it, Luke, you don't have to worry about me."

"You don't have it. The Phelans know you don't have it, but they know you can get it. Why else would they let you play all weekend just on your signature?"

"How do you know—"

"I told you: I know them. You didn't spend a penny at their house, did you? They never asked you to. And what little token of affection did they give you when you left? Earrings? An Hermès scarf? A bracelet?" Claudia was silent. "What was it?"

"Lapel pin," she whispered.

"Ninety-three hundred dollars for a lapel pin," he said contemptuously.

"It was a gift! Because they love me! And if I want to believe that, who the hell are you to tell me I'm wrong?"

"Your banker," he said.

Her shoulders slumped. She stared into space, running a finger around the rim of her wineglass. "I have until day after tomorrow."

The waiter took the leather folder and vanished, and Luke pulled out his checkbook. An expensive dinner, he thought, and no sign of anything changing soon. *Why the hell can't she find another husband?* But he knew the answer to that: she clung to the fantasy that they would get together again. Like a child, she believed that saying or thinking something often enough would make it a reality. And in one way she was right: he kept covering her gambling debts.

He wrote the check and held it out until, with a whispered "Thank you," she took it and slipped it into her purse. Then he signed the charge slip for dinner and finally shoved back his chair and stood up. "I'll walk you home," he said, and turned to lead the way out of the restaurant, letting Claudia trail behind.

"Thank you," she said again when they reached her building. "I do appreciate it, Luke, your help, your being close to me . . . it means everything to me. I won't go back there, you know, the Phelans', if you don't want me to."

"I didn't want you to go the last time. You knew that."

"But I hadn't gone for such a long time. . . . And you know, they *are* my friends."

"Next time you want to go, call me first."

"Like AA." She smiled brightly. "I can't think of anyone I'd rather have for a buddy." She put her hand on his arm. "Won't you come up for a drink? I bought your favorite cognac."

*He even told me what kind of car . . . I guess he thought I'd find that irresistible but I thought it was pretty sad that he couldn't trust himself to be the main attraction of the evening.*

"No," Luke said. "Good night." And he walked away, leaving Claudia with her doorman, who patiently held the door, averting his eyes but not missing a word.

Dearest Constance, how can I ever thank you enough for your wonderful letter. I'm so sorry about your daughter dying . . . I guess that sounds silly because I know it happened thirty-six years ago, but the way you described it, I was crying, it was so sad and I couldn't bear to think of how you suffered, even though you said having your daughter's little boy helped a lot. And it helped me, knowing what you'd gone through, and of course the most important part was when you said "I didn't tell her often enough how much I loved her and what a good person and good mother I thought she was; I took it for granted that somehow she knew all that. But nothing in re- lationships can be taken for granted, repaired or restored when all the opportunities have slipped through our fingers." I showed that to Dr. Leppard and he said you're a very wise woman, and you are, and how lucky your grandson was to grow up with you. Lucas Cameron, what a nice name; he must be a won- derful man. And he wants to be a director! That's so exciting for you! I'm sorry he was in Europe when I met you in summer stock, and now he's finishing graduate school, but I know I'll meet him someday because he's going to be famous, I just know it, because you brought him up and maybe someday he'll direct both of us in a play; wouldn't that be wonderful? Please tell me how you're going to play Miss Moffat. I've loved *The Corn Is Green* all my life and I've thought about how I'd play her and I'm sure that deep inside she's very insecure and fighting to discover who she is and what she can be. Is that how you see her? Thank you again, thank you so much, for your letter and most of all for your friendship. I do love you. Jessica.

Luke reread the last few sentences. He remembered talking to Constance about *The Corn Is Green*. She had come to his graduation when he received his Ph.D. and they had talked about the play, soon to begin rehearsals. Constance had said that a friend thought that Miss Moffat was insecure and what did Luke think about that? "You've got a smart friend," Luke had said. And it was Jessica, he thought, refolding the letter. About nineteen years old, for the first time broaching her ideas to Constance as an equal: one actress to another. Good for her.

He fit the letter into its place in the box. As sure of herself at nineteen as I was, he reflected. And she thought I'd be famous someday. He smiled to himself. *What amazing insight.*

He finished his drink and looked at his watch. A little after midnight; time for a few more letters. He pulled out a handful, all from Yale, describing her courses, her part-time jobs and her acting. By her third year she was regularly starring in the Yale Repertory Theater, one of the most prestigious in the country, and halfway through her senior year her letters reflected this: they grew more assured with every part she played, never casual but often casually confident. She was no longer a wide-eyed ingenue, but a professional who approached each play as a set of problems to be solved, a challenge to be confronted, a joyous time of discoveries about herself and the world.

He looked up as his butler appeared in the doorway. "Still awake? Martin, it's almost one o'clock."

"Mr. Cameron, I just discovered a message the housekeeper took this afternoon when I was out. Mr. Kent Horne says he's worried about Monte's pushing to make Lena older—those are his exact words—and he wants to talk to you, whatever time you arrive home."

"Thank you, Martin."

"His voice sounded urgent, the housekeeper said."

"His voice always sounds urgent. If he calls again, tell him we'll talk in the morning. Better yet, turn off the main phone and go to bed."

Martin's face grew stern. "I could never do that. Emergencies occur, tragedies happen. One cannot cut oneself off, ever, from the tumult of the world, however much it may, momentarily, seem desirable."

Amused, Luke shook his head when Martin left. *I'm surrounded by drama. Probably I create the atmosphere and everyone else jumps in.* He glanced at the last paragraph of the letter in his hand. *Including Jessica.*

I know you're thinking of my happiness when you keep asking if I'm dating, but dear, dear Constance, I've told you so many times that I'm not and I don't want to. Maybe someday that will change, but, believe me, I don't feel deprived by not dating and jouncing around in bed the way almost everybody else does. It's just too far from anything I really care about. I suppose if I met someone really special . . . but I haven't, so it's foolish to speculate. I'd rather think about the chance that you'll come to New Haven for graduation in two weeks. That would be so splendid! Please let me know the very second you decide; I've already reserved a room for you, just in case, and the best table in the best restaurant for dinner. Now, THE BIGGEST NEWS OF ALL. (I've been saving it for last, hugging it, you know, like a precious secret that I'm sharing for now just with you.) Two days after graduation I'm going to Chicago to read for John Malkovich at Steppenwolf! The theater manager called and invited me! The play is something I don't know, by Sam Shepherd— they're sending it to me and I should have it in a day or two—but I don't care what it is; you of all people know that this is a dream come true—the chance to work with Malkovich and Gary Sinise and Joan Allen and Glenne Headley . . . oh, Constance, I'm sending prayers to all the theater gods that they ask me to join them. *Please* come to see me graduate; I want to see you, the real you, not the picture of you in my head when I write or read your letters. I can't wait. Much love, Jessica.

Luke read the long paragraph again, sharing Jessica's excitement, the exhilaration that comes with that first opening of a door to the future. He had felt it when he got his first job as assistant to one of the greatest directors on Broadway; he had known then that he was on his way and nothing would stop him. And Jessica, too, he thought. I wonder if Constance went to her graduation.

He wanted to read more, to be with her for a while longer and find out what happened next, but it was late and he had an early meeting. Reluctantly he closed the box and switched off the desk lamp. Tomorrow night, he thought. I'll come back to her then. But at least I know this much. She's on her way.

## CHAPTER 4

Kent called early the next morning. Luke was at breakfast in a shaded corner of his terrace where two wicker armchairs flanked a low brass chest that held the telephone, a stack of newspapers and his breakfast tray. The terrace was deep and long, paved with brick and wrapping around the corner of the building. Roses climbed its low brick wall, crabapple and plum trees grew in deep wooden tubs, dappling the light that fell on cushioned wrought-iron furniture, and gaillardia, cosmos, campanula and dahlias were massed in terra-cotta pots and planters. The air was still; the city brooded, somnolent in the heat, its skyscraper windows reflecting the sun like sheets of foil flinging back the white light. In the distance, the George Washington Bridge hung in the heavy air beneath wisps of clouds barely visible against the pale sky. Without looking up from his newspaper, Luke reached for the telephone when it rang.

"Luke, the thing is, I don't trust Monte." Kent's deep voice came in a barrage of syllables. "I have to see you, I mean we have to talk about this and get it settled before Monte gets set in stone, I mean, before he gets used to the idea of changing things or trying them out on us or whatever the hell he was doing with all that shit about making Lena younger. He can't do that every time he gets a bright idea, you know, he can't—"

"He can do it whenever he wants," Luke said. "We'll all have ideas about the play and we'll talk them out and you'll have to get used to that."

" 'All'? Who's all?"

"Mainly Monte and me and the cast. But you'll find that Fritz has—"

"Fritz?"

"The stage manager. Fritz will have suggestions

and so will the props manager and the set designer and just about everyone else who gets a look at rehearsals. Most of them are pretty casual and don't take up much time, but when cast members have ideas about their lines or the ways their characters are shaping up, we take them seriously."

"Damn it, Luke, plays aren't written by committee! They don't come out of happy little meetings where everybody says, 'Oh, listen, I've got the *best* idea . . .' and they go off spinning some crap from some childhood trauma or something. Plays are written by playwrights working *alone.* You don't understand that, because you aren't one, but—"

"I've done some writing," Luke said coldly, "and I work with writers. I know it's tough. But you chose it."

"Over pumping gas, right. It's what I do, and I'm good at it, but it's my whole life, it's *me,* and if you think I'm going to change *one scene*—what the hell, *one word*—because some half-assed actor thinks he knows better—"

"We'll talk about it at lunch," Luke said. "Right now I have some calls to make. I'll see you at Monte's office."

"You're not hanging up on me!"

"I'm going to hang up because I have work to do before we begin casting your play. I said we'd talk about this at lunch; I assume you heard me say that."

"Yeah, well—"

"You can tell me all your problems then. I'll see you in a little while." He hung up, and began to pace on the terrace, stretching his muscles. *God save us from geniuses who somehow, miraculously, write a brilliant play but still have a lot of growing up to do, so that on top of everything else, we have to educate them.*

The telephone rang and he ignored it, sure that Kent was calling back. But in a moment Martin came to tell him that Monte Gerhart was calling. Luke picked it up, sitting on the edge of his chair. "Luke, it's Monte. I just wanted you to know I've got the perfect Lena; I'm bringing her to the casting session; didn't want to spring her on you, but she's the greatest, Abigail Deming, you know her, wait 'til you hear her, I am *crazy* about her, she absolutely *is* Lena, wait 'til you—"

Luke's frustration, still churning, exploded. "You damn fool, you promised it to her, didn't you?"

"Hey, hold your horses, you didn't hear me say—"

*"Did you promise it to her?"*

"Christ, what's eating you this morning? Well, not exactly. I said I thought she was perfect and I was sure you'd agree. I guess I shouldn't have done that—"

"You know damn well you shouldn't have done that. We talked about this—remember? We agreed—"

"I know, I know, but, damn it, Luke, I took her

to dinner last night and she's got a way with her, you wouldn't think so, a woman that old—"

"You were drinking."

"No, it's not that. You know, she's tough, and she's no beauty, but she's got this way of putting her hand on your arm, just this little touch, and looking straight at you and all of a sudden she's gorgeous and you're melting. I know that sounds crazy, but she really pulls it off and I know she could pull off Lena, too."

"For God's sake. I'll see you at ten." He slammed down the phone and stood at the wall of his terrace, trying to control his anger. Far below, traffic inched through narrow streets on hot asphalt, pedestrians darted between the cars, often walking across two bumpers so close they seemed locked together, and the cacophony of horns rose with angry volume to Luke's celestial terrace, enveloping him in its stridency. Everyone is angry, he thought. He imagined the anxiety of pedestrians, wilting as they hustled to meetings where they were expected to look alert and unwrinkled, and the frustration and rage of drivers beating tattoos on their steering wheels as they moved forward a few infuriating feet at a time, and his anger began to dissolve into humor. *It could be worse: instead of dealing with Monte and Kent, I could be driving a cab.*

Martin stood in the doorway holding out a sheaf of telephone messages. "None of them seemed urgent, so I didn't interrupt you."

Luke flipped through the slips of paper. "Call Miss Delacorte; tell her I'll pick her up a little after seven for a play and dinner afterward. Tell the Neals no; I never go to costume parties. And this one, from Renaldi, about the sale of the villa . . ." He paused. "Tell him to call about midnight New York time; we can talk about the buyer then." He scanned the remaining messages. The last one was from Fritz Palfrey, stage manager for *The Magician.* "Need to talk to Luke; set designer has peculiar ideas, not workable. Call me."

Suddenly Luke wished himself in his library, sharing the silence with Jessica's letters, far from backstage squabbles and clashing egos, the adolescent storms of Kent Horne, the thousands of mediations and decisions that stretched before him. Then he shrugged. What had he told Kent? *You chose it.* This was his job, it was his life, and it was the only one he wanted. Jessica Fontaine, if he found time for her, was a minor diversion at best.

And he forgot Jessica, and almost everything else, as soon as casting began in a theater Monte had gained permission to use for the day. Luke loved this early part of the production where, for the first time, the lines of the play were spoken aloud, at last taking wing from a typescript and beginning to soar. The theater was as silent and empty as a ghost town, with a single spotlight illuminating the center of the stage, leaving the rest of it, furnished for that evening's play, almost invisible. In the spotlight, the actors stood alone or in pairs, reading parts of scenes, and Luke, sitting in the sixth row, felt a deep sense of comfort. Everything he was, everything he did, was, for this moment and the moments to come, building on each other to that one moment when the stage sprang to life on opening night.

"God," Kent breathed, sitting with the others, "God, listen to them!"

Luke barely heard him. Monte Gerhart was on his left, Tommy Webb, the casting director, on his right. In the wings, Fritz Palfrey, a few stagehands, and the technical director sat on stools, watching. In the back of the theater, the house manager slipped in and took a seat on the aisle of the last row.

Luke glanced at the script in his lap, then looked at Abigail Deming, standing in the center of the stage, reading Lena's farewell speech to her grandson Daniel. She was small but held herself well; her gestures were controlled; her face, as pale and wrinkled as old linen, was not as expressive as Luke would have liked, but her voice was strong, with clear modulations. She was a good actress, not in a league with Constance Bernhardt, but better than most and she had fifty years of experience . . . and a reputation for being a terror if she did not approve of the way things were going. Which was why Luke had not called her to read for the part.

But as she read now, he knew she was good. The other actors, and Tommy Webb, sitting beside him, all knew it, too, and when she finished her speech and Daniel spoke the last line of the play, Luke heard Kent let out a long breath. "It's like I've died and gone to heaven."

"What do you think?" Luke asked Tommy Webb.

"Dynamite. Both of them, Abby and what's-his-name. Cort Hastings. *Cort*. Where do they get these names? I'd heard he doesn't get good 'til after a month of rehearsals, but he sounds pretty good right now."

Luke turned to Monte. "She's very good. Tommy and I think both of them will be fine."

"Agreed. Thanks, Luke; I thought you'd be so mad at me you'd dump her. But she is good, isn't she? Tough inside, but when she looks at you . . . well, you know what I mean."

"So now we need the girl," Tommy said. "I've got two of them here; I like them both. One might be too beautiful: distracting, you know? When do you want them, Luke?"

"After lunch. All right with you, Monte? Kent?" When they nodded, he said to Tommy, "What about the three small parts?"

"I've picked 'em, tentatively. Videotapes for you in my office."

"After we do the girl. Between three and four, I'd say. Fritz wants to talk to me about the set design. Do you know anything about that?"

"He doesn't like Marilyn Marks; he thinks she's

too far out. He likes stages that look like your great-grandmother's living room, the one nobody ever goes into. What can I say? He's a great stage manager and he's a pain in the ass."

Luke chuckled. "I'll see him after I look at the videos. I'm going to talk to Abby and Cort, and then go to lunch. Two o'clock back here?"

"Right."

A small group stood at the side of the stage, talking in low voices, and Luke joined them. "Fritz, I'll buy you a drink this afternoon. Meet me at Orso; I should be there by five. Abby, Cort, that was very fine. We think it's going to be a pleasure working with you."

Abigail nodded with satisfaction. "I'm looking forward to it."

Amused, Luke heard the note of grandeur in her voice—royalty condescending to work with him—but he said only, "We all are. It's an exciting play."

Cort nodded vigorously. "I like this guy, Daniel, and I had a grandmother like Lena who I was crazy about."

"Who's the girl?" Abigail asked.

"We'll know after lunch. The three of you—"

"I should be part of that casting, Luke; she has her most important scenes with me."

"The hell she does," Cort said. "I mean, this is a love story, right? Lena's a big part of it, but audiences come to see love stories, and this girl—

Martha, right?—Martha and I've got a couple of truly steamy scenes. So I'm the one who ought to help choose her."

"Tommy and I do the casting," Luke said easily, "though we're always interested in your ideas. Now, I want the first run-through day after tomorrow, ten o'clock; Fritz has the address of the rehearsal space. Bring questions, ideas, suggestions, whatever you think of. The playwright's vision is what we're here for, but I want your input, too, all the way along." He kissed Abby on both cheeks. "You're going to be a magnificent Lena. Cort, you're going to be a fine Daniel. And we're going to have a terrific production."

Cort nodded. "I've got some ideas about Daniel, you know; I really know what he's all about."

"Write them down. We'll go over all of them."

"Oh, let's start now," Abigail said energetically. "Why wait?" She put her arm through Cort's and reached for Luke. "Let's have lunch. We can talk and talk for hours."

"Tommy and I have more readings this afternoon, and I'm having lunch with our playwright. Both of you should get my phone and fax numbers from Fritz and get in touch with me anytime you have a question or an idea, a suggestion, a problem, anything. If I'm not at home, I'll get back to you as soon as I can. From now on, we're a family; we don't stand on ceremony. Okay, I have to go; I'll see you in a couple of days."

He turned to the audience. "Kent?"

Kent came out of his trance and followed Luke through the wings and along a corridor to a steel door that led to an alley and from there to a small, unobtrusive restaurant a block away with an anchor suspended above the door.

They sat in a booth with high partitions for privacy. The booths and the wood floor were dark, and paintings of the sea hung on the dark walls, each in its own circle of light. Kent scanned the menu and ordered what seemed to Luke to be three meals. Looking up, Kent saw his bemused expression. "Growing boy," he said, grinning, and when Luke had ordered, he sat back and sighed. "No problems, Luke. I don't know what we have to talk about. I'm a happy man."

"Put it in writing," Luke said, "so I can remind you of it a month from now."

"Nope, it's going to be rosy all the way, I can tell. They're going to make my play *live.* I mean, you heard them—they need a few little things that I'll clue them in on, you know, emphasis, gestures, things like that—but we're practically ready for opening night. God, they're so good!"

Luke gazed at him. "Why are you so sure they'll sound like that on opening night?"

He reared back as the waiter brought salads and bread. "Of course that's how they'll sound! I mean, after I give them some clues. But I'll tell you, Luke, it was pretty close to perfect."

"I don't think so."

Kent's eyes narrowed. "You're telling me I don't know my own play?"

"Absolutely, from your perspective. But not from the audience's, and not from mine, and I'm the director." He pushed his salad aside and folded his arms on the table. "Do you know what a director does, Kent?"

"For Christ's sake, Luke, everybody knows—"

"Let me tell you how I direct a play. First of all, you wrote that script from somewhere inside you, and a lot of the time you looked at your words and wondered where they came from, how that phrase happened to come out just that—"

"How the hell do you know that?"

"It's possible that I know a lot more than you give me credit for. So there you are, with a script that came from inside you, your subconscious or whatever you want to call it. My job is to find the deepest meanings in it, the richest dimensions of character, angles you may not even be aware of, and reveal them to the audience through the actors. Everything the actors do has meaning, and one of my jobs is to help them find the details that make every part of this play—every bit of dialogue or wave of the hand or lifting a glass, whatever it is—have a special meaning that illuminates the special meaning of the play. That's how we reach the audience. A director in Chicago calls it rock 'n' roll theater because every production should be heightened and explosive and as aware of the audience as a rock 'n' roll band is. I mostly agree with that. Otherwise we might as well be putting on plays for ourselves in small dark rooms."

Kent was staring at him. "I don't know any directors who sound like you."

"Good. Just remember that the goal of all this is to make your story wonderfully alive, and to realize as much of your vision as we can. We'll discuss and argue and get passionate about our ideas—the more passionate the better the production will be—and you'll be in the thick of it. And that's the way it should be, as long as you see yourself as part of a collaboration, not the Lord sending us a tablet that we're supposed to accept with religious devotion."

"I never said I was God."

"I think I recall you talking about perfection."

After a moment Kent laughed. "Well, yeah, but, you know, I mean I went over it like fifty or a hundred times, editing and rewriting, and by the time I sent it to you it was— Well, I mean, I thought it was pretty good."

"It's terrific. Eat your lunch. We have to get back."

They walked into the theater just as Tommy Webb was looking around for them. A young woman stood on stage with Cort Hastings and Abigail Deming. "Okay, Tommy," Luke said, and the three on stage began to read as he and Kent reached the row where Tommy and Monte sat.

They listened to two women read, then called

back the first, and asked her to read Martha's long monologue in the second act. She stood stiffly on the stage and read carefully, as if measuring each word. As she went on, her pace picked up and became smoother and she began to move about the stage, matching her actions to her words. Better, Luke thought. Still not right, but we can work with her. And physically she's right for Martha.

Suddenly he saw Jessica playing Laura in *The Glass Menagerie.* That had been fifteen years ago, but he remembered every detail of her performance: an actress of extraordinary grace and beauty turning herself into a plain, crippled, painfully shy young girl. And she'd transform herself into Martha, he thought. I wish she were here. She'd give Martha more depth than even Kent could imagine.

But Jessica was not here and he focused on the young woman on stage. Her name was Rachel Ilsberg and he knew they could work with her. He looked at Tommy, who nodded, and then at Monte. "Yeah, she's okay," Monte said.

"She's really Martha," Kent added.

"Well, not yet," Tommy murmured. "But she'll be fine. Not too beautiful. Tall, but not too tall for Cort. Good carriage. Nice voice."

Luke looked at his watch. "Tommy, let's look at those videos tomorrow; it's almost five and I have to see Fritz. And would you talk to Rachel? Tell her how impressed we are, that we're—"

"Excited and eager to begin," Tommy finished.

"And a run-through day after tomorrow. I'll have contracts for everybody by then. Ten o'clock for the videos?"

"Can you make it nine?"

*"Nine?* Well, sure. Just don't make a habit of it. Okay with you, Kent?"

"Sure. God, I've finished my run in the park by nine o'clock; that's halfway to noon."

Luke turned to the stage where Rachel stood. "Thank you. We liked it very much. Tommy will talk to you about it." He went to the side aisle and up the five steps that led to the stage, then ducked into the wings and made his way to the stage door. Outside, he blinked in the sunlight. *Daylight. We forget what it looks like.*

Fritz Palfrey was standing beside a table in the window of Orso, waiting. "I'm having wine, something red. You?"

"Fine."

He waved to the waitress. "Luke, listen, I know she's hot right now, but listen, I can't work with her."

"You're talking about Marilyn Marks?"

"Who else? Look, I've got a grandmother just like Lena, she's in her eighties and I know what kind of apartment she likes and this set Marilyn designed, it's not a grandmother's apartment."

"You mean it's not your grandmother's," Luke said gently.

"Grandmothers in their eighties like things normal and . . . sort of dull. Not dramatic. I *know* what Lena is like, Luke, believe me. She's just like my grandmother."

*And that's one of the brilliant aspects of Kent's play; everyone sees Lena as his or her grandmother. But no play is a true mirror of real life; theater compresses and exaggerates real life to create its own universe. And Fritz knows that.*

The waitress brought their wine and Fritz held his up to the light. "Nice color. So what do you think?"

"Have you seen Marilyn's final drawings?"

"How could I? She's only done preliminaries. I want to head her off at the pass."

"Let's not do that. I don't pass judgement until I see drawings and a model."

"Luke, I can't work with that set."

"Let's wait until we see the model." He pushed back his chair. "We'll meet with Marilyn and props and costumes next week—Thursday or Friday around three—let me know what works for everybody. And Fritz." He put his hand on Fritz's shoulder. "I appreciate your ideas. You're the best stage manager in the business and I promise you we'll work together on this."

"Right, well, we'll see what happens. You didn't finish your wine."

"I'm going to a friend's dress rehearsal tonight; I have to stay awake."

He made his way through the late-afternoon crowds to Fifth Avenue, and turned uptown, feeling the slight coolness of shade trees when he came to the cobblestone walk along the low brick wall bordering Central Park. He dodged Rollerbladers and women pushing strollers and tried to find a steady pace between people coming to a halt for passionate debate, lovers walking in step and making way for no one, crowds leafing through used books stacked on folding tables, and children chasing an errant whiffle ball. Finally he crossed to the other side of the street, close to the buildings, where there were no crowds. By the time he reached his building he was perspiring and frustrated—he never had enough time out of doors and when he did it seemed, lately, that it was usually uncomfortable—and he bypassed his library to go straight to his bedroom, where he stripped and stepped into his shower.

It was not until midnight that he finally sat on the leather couch in his library and stretched out his legs. He had taken two telephone calls from Kent, a call from Marilyn Marks and one from Monte, he had taken Tricia to the dress rehearsal of his friend's play and then to dinner with the playwright, director and crew, and then had told Tricia, with some truth, that he still had work to do and in any event was exhausted and so could not go upstairs with her when he took her home. But what he really had wanted was just what he finally had: silence, the seclusion of his library, and a tray provided by Martin with a sandwich in case he was hungry, cognac, coffee and a bowl of pistachios placed conveniently at his right hand.

He sat for a time, enjoying the silence. He watched a newscast on television, then enjoyed the silence again, letting the day unwind in his thoughts like a movie reel, speeding up, slowing down, reversing.

They had a cast for *The Magician,* or they would have one by tomorrow when they filled the minor parts. Marilyn was working on sets; Fritz was agonizing, as he always did; the theater was booked, the rehearsal space rented, the first run-through set for Thursday. Everything was on schedule.

He finished his cognac and reached out to put the glass on the tray, and his glance fell on the box of Jessica's letters. *No time tonight. I'm too tired.* But he continued to gaze at the box. *Well, maybe just one.*

Dearest Constance, I'm sorry I haven't written in so long; I've missed writing to you even though we talk on the telephone now. It really is wonderful to hear your voice (even better to be with you, oh, so long ago now . . . wasn't that a splendid day we had together at my graduation?) but there's something special about letters so I decided to write this time instead of calling. I was sorry to leave Steppenwolf—those were the most wonderful two years of my life and I've never learned so much so fast—but you were right: *Anna Christie* on Broadway is much more important. Did I tell

you what Phil Ballan said when he called? This
was how it went:

Deep, deep voice: "Miss Fontaine, I was in
Chicago last week and caught the latest play at
Steppenwolf." Then he stopped and it took me
a minute to understand that he was waiting for
me to say something. *"Really?"* said I, just a
trifle breathlessly. His voice got deeper. "I must
tell you that I have never been as impressed
with a performance at Steppenwolf as I was
with yours." He stopped again, waiting, and I
said, "Oh, thank you"—so unutterably *dull*—
why couldn't I think of something clever? But I
couldn't quite get myself together because except for you nobody from Broadway has ever
told me I'm really good. "And," he said, dragging it out like Santa with his presents, "we
want you to come to New York and read for
*Anna Christie.* I think you'll be an absolutely
splendid Anna. And I'm never wrong about
my judgement." Another time I might have
laughed, but not this time: he could have whin-
nied like a horse and I would have thought it
was a beautiful sound. And then he said, "Are
you still there? You're coming to New York?"
and "Yes!" burst out of me, and then I apolo-
gized because I thought I'd blown that poor
man's ear off through the telephone.

So now here I am, back in New York—so
enormous and hectic after Chicago and my
"family" at Steppenwolf, but in another way a

lot of fun: like walking into a huge party where I don't know anyone but they all look familiar. I found a tiny apartment in SoHo; it barely has room to turn around but it has a window and for about forty minutes a day it gets sunshine. Of course I'm almost never home for those forty minutes, but it's nice to know it's there anyway. Isn't it amazing how little sunshine we see when we're working on a play? It's like we forget what daylight looks like. I've had two long talks with the director about how to play Anna; he has some ideas I never thought of that might work. The best part is, he cares about what I think and I've thought about nothing else but playing Anna since that phone call so I have some very definite ideas of my own. Do you believe we should do just what the director tells us, or do you think we should insist that we play a part the way we feel inside? We've never talked about that as much as I'd like to. Would you tell me what you think?

There is a problem with being in *Anna*: one of the producers seems to have taken a fancy to me—what an old-fashioned phrase!—and now he haunts the theater, wandering around backstage like a little boy set down in a strange neighborhood, pretending to "run into" me, then saying, "Well, now that we've run into each other, why don't we have dinner?" And he comes across too hearty, too anxious, when what he's obviously trying for is a *bon vivant*—casual, debonair, irresistible. There's nothing really wrong with him, in fact I think he's probably very nice, but I'm in *Anna Christie!* In New York! How can I think about anything else? I'm so nervous I just want to be left alone. He says I'd be better off with a companion to relax with. I suppose he could be right, but he seems so absolutely sure that it makes me suspicious. A lot of people around here are like that, always saying things like "You've *got* to do this" or "I will *not* read that line" or "I have the perfect person for that" or "I will absolutely *not* tolerate this lighting" or . . . oh, you know; you've heard it all. Wouldn't it be novel if someone, just once, said, "Well now, that seems like a prodigiously stupid idea but we're here to experiment and learn, so why don't we give it a try?" Everyone would probably be stunned into a very uncharacteristic silence, but it certainly would lighten the atmosphere.

Luke chuckled. He read the last line again, smiling, and then it occurred to him that it was as if Jessica had been with him all day, her lively young voice cutting through sham and histrionics, sweeping away melodrama, sharing her observations with him when they were alone. He looked up from her letter and gazed across the room at a Picasso print of a dancing woman. He remembered Jessica

Fontaine's voice from the times when he had seen her on stage: a magical voice, musical and rich, with a lilt that was like the faintest trace of a foreign accent. He imagined hearing her now, her freshness and honesty, the rill of laughter that ran beneath her words, the unexpected phrases that sparked her sentences. He liked her companionship; he liked hearing her comments at the end of his day.

His fatigue had vanished. It was late, but he felt fine. Plenty of time for a few more, he thought, and, reaching into the box he pulled out a handful of letters and settled back to read.

## CHAPTER 5

Jessica Fontaine in *Anna Christie* mesmerized an opening night audience at the Helen Hayes Theatre last night as has no one else since Constance Bernhardt played Anna almost forty years ago.

The newspaper clipping had fallen out of the letter and Luke read it first.

It is rare that an actor totally inhabits the *space* of a character: a past history, hints of a future, quirks and eccentricities, mannerisms, a way of moving across the stage as if it is the whole world. Great actors do this without intellectualizing it;

they get "out of their head," if you will, and into that mysterious well of the instinct that draws on some kind of inner magic and on a lifetime of experience. Jessica Fontaine is too young to have a lot of experience—she turned twenty-five a week before *Anna Christie* opened—and she is still untried in many roles, but she has that inner magic and she is wondrous to watch. I predict we'll be watching her a lot, from now on.

Dearest Constance, how wonderful you were to call last night—opening night! I felt you beside me while I waited to go on; I was so scared I was shaking and my legs felt heavy and rubbery but I started saying over and over what you'd said on the phone—that *you're* so nervous you feel sick every time before making your first entrance—and I repeated it without stopping—Constance gets nervous, too; Constance gets nervous, too—until I almost hypnotized myself with it and actually began to feel better. I could really hear you talking to me and feel your hand on my arm and you stayed with me all through the play, even at the curtain calls . . . there were *fourteen,* can you believe it? I have so much to tell you, but I can't write a long letter today because we have to work on the second act to tighten it up, but I promise I'll write as soon as things settle down. I just wanted you to know that I'm grateful for you, always, and I love you. Jessica.

Why didn't I see her in that play? Luke wondered. He thought back. She was twenty-five, so I was thirty—and that was the year Claudia and I spent in San Francisco while I was directing at the Berkeley Rep. We saw Constance out there when she was playing in *The Visit* in Los Angeles, and the three of us took some weekend trips until Claudia got bored and then Constance and I went by ourselves, as far north as the Olympic Peninsula, as far south as Baja. We were away from New York for almost two years; I went to Los Angeles to direct another play and then Claudia and I went to London to see Constance open in *Oedipus,* and then Paris. So Jessica had her triumph without Constance. But Constance called. A loving friend.

Dearest Constance, thank you so much for your telephone call last night and I do apologize; how could I let four months go by without writing to you? Maybe it's because I think of you all the time, and talk to you inside my head, so perhaps I think I've written when in fact I haven't. But now here I am on my way to London—and you! Do you know how I've dreamed of this—to be in another play with you, to *work* with you, to learn from you . . . I am so incredibly excited I can't begin to describe it. I'll just call it paradise. My paradise: playing Vivie Warren to your Kitty Warren. Playing your daughter, even though there's not much daughterly feeling in the

whole play. What a wonderful time we'll have!
Oh, one thing, you'll meet Terence in London.
I wrote to you about him; he's the producer
who kept wandering around backstage. We've
been going out since *Anna* closed and he's really quite nice. His name is Terence Alban (and
woe to the person who calls him Terry!) and
he's from Dublin and London and Cape Town,
but even after all that moving around and
some pretty sophisticated living he's still
unbelievably timid about a lot of things,
including me. I have to urge him on now
and then, even (especially!) in intimate
moments. It's not that he doesn't know what to
do or how to do it, it's just that he can't believe
anyone would truly be attracted to him and he
really believes it's better not to try than to find
out someone doesn't want him. So after a
while *I* kissed *him* and undid his tie (what a curious reversal of roles; it made me feel quite
different about everything), and then I made a
few casual suggestions and eventually we pro-
gressed to his bedroom (we were in his living
room at the time, overlooking all of Central
Park under a full moon . . . so very beautiful,
but I thought if I commented on it Terence
would think he was a failure because my attention was wandering, so I didn't mention it) . . .
well, please forgive this peculiar sentence; it
seems to be wandering all over the place . . . so
we got to his bedroom—

Luke looked up from the letter. He felt uncomfortable: a voyeur pawing through letters meant only for his grandmother's eyes. But he was angry, too. Why couldn't she see through Terence Alban? Luke had known Alban for a long time; they'd met through Monte Gerhart and Alban had put money into two of Luke's productions. He'd been hanging around the theater for years: too much money, too much time, nothing to do but get his kicks by attaching himself to famous people. He wasn't good enough for Jessica; all he had was a fake, cloying insecurity that made women want to stroke him and build him up. Bringing out the mother in all of them, Luke thought contemptuously; you'd think she'd be too smart to be taken in by that.

Time for bed, he thought, and stuffed the letters back in the box. But their crushed mass made him feel guilty, thinking of the care his grandmother had taken with them, folding each one and lining it up perfectly with all the others, so he pulled them out again and smoothed them on his knee. A few fell to the floor and he picked them up and spread them out on the coffee table and, in so doing, once again began to read.

The only thing wrong with the past year, dearest Constance, was that you and I didn't write to each other. But in every other way it was absolutely the most perfect year of my life. First of all, being on stage with you, watching

the miracle of your transformation into Mrs.
Warren, and feeling my own strength increase
because of yours. I think daughters in real life
must feel like that when their mothers are people they truly long to grow into. I wonder how
often that happens. I loved my mother but I
never wanted to be her, while I've wanted to be
you ever since the day we met. When you and
I work together, I have a feeling of great
power . . . well, actually I have it all the time
I'm on stage, but it's even greater when I'm
with you. We've talked about this but now I'm
truly beginning to understand it: the feeling
that we can do anything when we slip into one
character and then another—young girl to
middle-aged woman to old woman, prostitute
to suburban matron, schoolgirl to royalty—
and then, when we take our curtain calls and
hear the applause and see all those smiles and
bright faces in the audience, we know we've
brought them with us, *we've made them believe
in us.* I can't imagine more power than that,
and nothing in the world gives me so much joy,
such a feeling of freedom, as if I'd learned to
fly and now I soar over everything and there's
nowhere I can't go, nothing I can't do.

But you're part of that, and the most perfect
moment of this perfect year was the last curtain call of our final performance when you
took my hand and the two of us stood alone
on stage, and the whole audience was standing,

and their applause wrapped around us in a huge roaring embrace, and when the curtain finally came down and stayed down you said, "You and I, dearest Jessica, are much more together than either of us is alone; we enhance each other. I am very grateful for that." But *I'm* the one who is grateful and I thank you with all my heart for saying that. I will never forget it.

Of course part of what made me happy in London was Larry, as long as it lasted. It was very strange to be in a play opposite someone I was having an affair with, and I was very mournful when it ended—I liked him a lot and we had fun together and I couldn't understand why he kept insisting that we get married. Why couldn't he just have a good time and be happy, the way I was? Oh, dear, what a lot of quarrels we had when we could have been making love and laughing. Such a shame.

When Terence came back from New York I put him off as long as I could, but after a month I ran out of reasons for not going out with him, so we started up again, only I couldn't go to bed with him because I was still, in a way, mourning Larry and missing him, and that drove Terence crazy; he slid back to thinking he wasn't worth anything and after a while I got awfully tired of all the stroking he needed, the bucking-up, the *mothering,* so I broke that off, too.

This all happened a week ago, after you'd
left for Sydney and I was wishing that I could
have stowed away in your luggage. Instead, I'm
going to Hollywood, to make a movie, and the
next time you hear from me I'll be sitting in
some house in Malibu (never been there, but
the studio rented it for me), missing you, missing the stage. I cannot imagine working without the driving energy of an audience. You said
you got used to playing to the camera and to
the other actors. Did you really, or were you
saying that to encourage me to try it? More
soon; I love you; Jessica.

Luke leafed through the next letters.

Dearest Constance, I know you're right and
I should be grateful that *my* reviews were all
good, but you know as well as I do that the
worst thing in the world is to be part of something that everyone hates. You know how much
*I* hated it; you probably got sick of hearing me
tell you. Oh, I am so angry! I've never been
part of a failure before and it doesn't matter
that the reviews said I was good; I feel tainted
by that film.
     **** It's an hour later now. How wonderful
everything is! All it took was one telephone
call to change everything. Edward Courier just
called! *The* Edward Courier, asking me if I'd be
interested in reading for *Who's Afraid of Vir-*

*ginia Woolf* opposite Constance Bernhardt!
Would I be interested! Good heavens, what a
question! So if they like the way I read, we'll be
together again, in New York, in about six
months—oh, I could sing a Hallelujah for that!
In the meantime I've been asked to work with
a repertory company in Los Angeles and that's
wonderful experience, so I'll stay in the Malibu
house, which is very beautiful and I love living
on the ocean.

By the way, Larry showed up the other day
and we had a very romantic reunion. I was surprised at how glad I was to see him, and he
says he won't talk about marriage, so maybe
we'll have as good a time here as we had in
London. Maybe he finally understands what
I've been trying to tell him: that I can't
separate me—who I am and what I am and
what I want to be ten, twenty, thirty years in
the future—from the theater. I want to be the
absolute best, but I want more than that: I
want to do good in the theater. If I have this
gift—this power you and I feel on stage—then
I can help people by bringing plays to life so
that maybe they can understand things they
couldn't understand before. I read the other
day that theater exposes our internal feelings
so we can *see* them instead of having them just
flutter around inside us. If I can help people
understand their feelings, that's better than

anything, isn't it: to do good while you're doing the thing you love best?

Well, that's what I've been trying to explain to Larry. I think he finally understands it, though now and then he pretends we've never talked about it. He's staying with me in the Malibu house, which is strange, because I'm used to living alone, but he wanted to be here and I said we'd see how it worked out. So far it's okay; in fact, a lot of the time it's rather pleasant.

Larry, Luke thought. Who the hell is he? On the bookshelves at the other end of the library he found a thick volume and opened it to the index. They were together in *Mrs. Warren's Profession,* he mused, so he would have been Frank Gardner, Vivie Warren's suitor. He turned to the page listing the play's history. In the New York production fifteen years ago, Mrs. Kitty Warren had been played by Constance Bernhardt, Vivie Warren by Jessica Fontaine and Frank Gardner by Lawrence Swain.

*Oh, for Christ's sake. Larry Swain. He's not good enough for her.*

Larry Swain. Muscular, handsome, with those classic good looks that seemed to belong in books on Greek sculpture more than in the everyday world. A good actor, not exceptional, but good enough for television, which was what he'd been doing for the past ten years or more. And he was known to be smart, with a pretty good wit, though not exceptionally smart, or exceptionally witty. In fact, Luke thought, he wasn't exceptional at anything. And Jessica Fontaine deserved someone who was exceptional in every way. *Why does she keep choosing men who aren't half as good as she is?*

He glanced at the letter beneath the one he had been reading. Too long for tonight, he told himself, and was about to return it to the box when he saw, on the second page, his own name. There was no way he could put off reading about himself. He poured another glass of cognac and once again settled back to read, starting, this time, on the second page.

. . . people at the opening night party were so amusing, all of them looking intense and holding forth with lots of eight-syllable words—the more the better!—to sound profound about what the play really meant. I wish people could just relax and enjoy the world and take from it what is important to them without always having to analyze it. I was glad to meet your grandson at long last—I've been reading about him. I like his looks—not especially handsome; he reminds me of a hawk who soars miles above the earth and isn't especially interested in coming down for a more intimate look. Strong, though, and intelligent, and his eyes are very sexy, or would be, is my guess, if they ever warmed up. He and I didn't

spend much time together; there were too
many people wanting to talk to me about the
play, and everybody was all keyed up, waiting
for the first reviews. Anyway, I got the feeling
that Luke was very . . . oh, prickly, I guess . . .
does he seem that way to you? He didn't seem
warm or at all interested in me; in fact, for a
while I thought he was like the worst of the directors I've known: aloof, observing the rest of
us, being critical—the hawk again! But then I
thought there was more going on inside him:
he seemed angry or frustrated or maybe just
wary. He wasn't open and giving, at least to
me, the way you are, and I guess I expected
him to be more like you in every way. I'm sure
he came to the party just to see you; I couldn't
see any other reason for him to be there.

Maybe his problem is his divorce. I shouldn't
know about it, but the papers were so full of
it—why do people allow their failures to be
smeared all over the newspapers? I'd make sure
only my triumphs were public—and it sounded
so messy, if it was my divorce I'd probably
glower at parties, too. I know the stories came
from Claudia, but still, the two of them should
have been able to work something out to keep
it quiet. Of course, if they could have agreed
on that, maybe they could have stayed married.
I remember thinking that my parents had
made their marriage last by kind of tiptoeing
around places they knew would make them ex-

plode into one of those fights where people say unforgivable things. I guess Luke and Claudia aren't the tiptoeing kind.

Anyway, I'm sorry I didn't like him better because he's your grandson and you love him, but it was clear he didn't like me, either. Actually, what he reminded me of, even more than a hawk, was a lighthouse, all alone out there on his rock, straight and tall and looking out to sea, away from towns and people and society, showing everybody else the right way to go but never joining them. I'd like to work under his direction sometime, but he doesn't seem the least bit interested in working with me, so it all seems pretty doubtful.

Luke gazed unseeingly into the dark fireplace. He remembered that opening night party; he remembered coming home and sitting here, staring into the fireplace as he was now, cursing himself for his coldness, for being rude at his grandmother's triumphant celebration. Martin had set a fire for him that night; when was it? He thought back. Eleven years ago. October. A cold, misty October night a few months after his divorce from Claudia. He'd come home early, disgusted with himself, restless and at loose ends. I wasn't directing anything then, he remembered; I felt I had no connections, with the theater, with anyone, with anything.

*He seemed angry or frustrated or maybe just wary.*

Wary. Well, she'd hit it. It was not only that he had no play in production at the moment, it was that he'd been divorced in the most public way, with Claudia suing him for ten million dollars—which he didn't have—to make up, she said, for what he'd promised her, and all her hangers-on testifying that Luke had promised to take care of her and bring her great wealth, not to mention fame, adulation, the world at her feet.

That same year, he had directed *Vigilance,* a new play that told the story of a small town destroying itself through greed over the ownership of a new oil field, and a marriage that grew in strength as the town disintegrated. The play was the hit of the season, a powerful production that Luke drove relentlessly from the moment the oil well was discovered through the crescendo of greed and violence that tore apart generations of families to the tenderness of the final scene when hope rose from chaos.

By then Luke and Claudia's marriage was over and Luke knew why: it had none of the strength, none of the trust and hope, of the marriage in *Vigilance.* "Oh, my dearest Luke," his grandmother had said, "you've fallen into the trap of confusing your own life with the life you're creating on stage."

"I'm comparing ideas about marriage," he had responded heatedly. "That's all I'm doing."

"Don't scowl at me, dear boy. And relax; you're quite rigid and opinionated these days. If you're going to compare marriages, choose one that has something in common with your own. Do you know anyone who has a marriage like the one in *Vigilance*? Of course you don't, because there couldn't be one: it needed the destruction of the town to find itself, and you won't find many towns destroying themselves as part of everyday life. My dear, you've created a vision of reality, not reality itself, and I shouldn't have to tell you that, because that is the definition of theater. You know perfectly well that however hard you look for a marriage like that one, you won't find it."

"I'm not looking for any marriage."

"Of course you're not; it's too soon. But when you do—"

He shook his head. "Not after this one. I keep going over it and it makes no sense. How could I be so blind? And stupid. I'm a lot smarter buying a car than I was getting married. What the hell happened to me?"

"You wanted to be married. You thought I had a rather empty life and you could do better."

"I never thought that. My marriage had nothing to do with you."

"Of course it did. You wanted a life different from mine. There's nothing wrong with that; it doesn't mean you loved me any less. Somewhere inside you, I think, there's a spark of anger at me for not marrying and giving you a father. I did think about it; I surveyed the contenders and not one of them would have been the father I would have wished for you, much less a husband for me. But you didn't know that, so you were angry and when you grew up you decided to show me how someone could have great success in the theater and also a happy marriage and a full life. A truly fine goal, dear Luke; I applaud it. It's still a good goal. One failure is no reason to toss it away. My dear boy, you're thirty-four years old and you've just become the most exciting and talked-about director in America. Give yourself some time to figure out what you expect of yourself and what you want from other people. Live alone: that's good for you. But also, go out on the town, be a *bon vivant* for a change. You've always been too serious. And after a while, perhaps I'll introduce you to someone, a young woman with whom I've been having a most delightful correspondence. You've met her, but you don't know her, and I think the two of you might be very good together."

"I'll find my own women," Luke said harshly, uncomfortable with his grandmother's insights. He had, in fact, blamed her for not providing him with a father, but he had not thought she knew it. Now he felt himself squirm, like a schoolboy who'd been caught out, and that made him lash out more angrily. "I'll make my own way; I don't need advice or little shoves from the wings."

"Oh, aren't we the tough one? You need advice *and* help; you need to learn a few things about finding someone who will be good for you instead of—"

"Spoken by an expert in marriage."

"In relationships," she said crisply. "I do know a good deal about relationships; more than you, I daresay. And why are you attacking me, Luke? It doesn't change the facts."

"You don't know anything about the facts of my life. I'll handle them my own way. Just leave me alone." And then, ashamed, he said, "Don't bother about me. I know you worry, but I'll be fine."

"Well. Well, then, I'll just hope that you learn to get close to people, and that you learn to play. I'm afraid I didn't teach you how to do those things, not very well, anyway."

Sitting in his library, holding Jessica's letter, Luke remembered every word of that speech and for the first time realized that Constance had been trying to tell him about Jessica. *But I wasn't ready, and after that she didn't try again.*

He had not argued with her about marriage— what good would that have done?—but he did take her advice about going out on the town, and soon he was one of those single men sought by hostesses to fill out their dinner tables, providing symmetry and the titillation of availability.

He also was busier than ever, directing one play after another, taking out one woman after another, working six days a week, playing tennis at seven o'clock in the mornings—the only time he could fit it in—and spending Sundays with a group of theater people who stabled their horses in New Jersey and rode from breakfast to an early supper before going back to the city.

"I said 'learn to play,' " Constance scolded him. Six months earlier, she had been ordered by her doctor to retire from the stage and now she was having a farewell dinner with Luke before leaving for Italy. "Look at you: you're working all the time, even when you're riding. You and your friends make it a contest or a race, as if some stallion is nipping at your heels. Luke, when will you learn to relax? You've got years of work and life ahead of you, but you're not giving yourself time to stoke the furnace."

He chuckled. "If I'm able to do so much, my furnace must be pretty well stoked already."

"No," she said gravely. "You're using up your reserves. I'll drink a toast, my dearest Luke. To many, many visits to Italy—I want you to come whenever you have the chance, even for a few days—to successful plays, and to a life that has room for love and laughter."

He touched his glass to hers. "I love you," he said, and both of them knew she was the only person to whom he said those words.

Luke opened his eyes and realized he had fallen asleep in his chair and had dreamt about Constance. He remembered almost everything she had ever said to him—he knew that could not be true, but his memories were so vivid that it seemed true—and he missed her the most when he thought of all the advice she had given him, often rejected but never forgotten. He stood up to go to bed, found himself still holding Jessica's letter, and realized he had not finished it. Standing beside his chair, he read the last page.

I don't think I've properly thanked you for your advice about Harold. You were very wise; you saw him much more clearly than I did. (I seem to have a blind spot about men; it takes me a long time to figure them out. I have to work on that.) Harold is probably the most charming man I've ever known, but you were right: he has a way of sucking people into his orbit that's quite destructive. I was beginning to feel as if I'd been caught in a web, but it was so charming and intricately beautiful that I didn't realize I was saying the things he wanted me to say and maybe I was even becoming what he wanted me to be. You made me understand that, and I'm very grateful.

I'll see you soon, when I welcome you to my new apartment. It's so wonderful that I can't wait to share it with you. As soon as I move in and get settled, I'm going to give lots of dinner parties, and you're invited to every one: my door is always open—wide, wide open—to you. All my love, Jessica.

It was almost daylight when Luke closed the box and went to bed. I would have liked to know her the way Constance did, he mused drowsily, and then he was asleep.

Four hours later, as he sat at breakfast on his terrace, the telephone rang. "Luke," Kent said, "why hasn't anybody told me when we open, and where?"

"It wasn't deliberate. We open the third week in September at the Vivian Beaumont. You could have asked me that when we're in Tommy's office."

"I couldn't wait. I'm not good at waiting. Where are the rehearsals?"

"At a studio we've rented on Forty-fifth Street. We'll rehearse there until dress rehearsal out of town."

"Where?"

"Philadelphia. A good town for theater. Any other questions?"

"I should have known all this!"

"Yes, you should. Maybe you heard it and forgot it in the excitement of casting."

"I never forget anything. Like, I had another idea about the set this morning when I was jogging—"

A jet pulled a long contrail, pale against the washed-out sky, across Luke's field of vision. He concentrated on it. "Why don't you wait until we meet with Marilyn?" he asked at last, and eventually was able to put down the telephone.

The day was going to be as hot as the day before. Luke wondered briefly and futilely why one of the world's greatest centers of commerce and the arts couldn't have been built in a benign climate, then turned back to his newspaper and his breakfast, in a silence that he found comforting and restful. A visitor from the country would have wondered at his idea of silence, filled as it was with the cacophony of car horns, screeching tires, air brakes and pneumatic hammers that rose from the street. But Luke heard none of them, or heard them only as components of city silence. Had they all stopped, he would have been alarmed at the strange vacuum, convinced that some disaster had occurred.

The sounds of the city wove through his day in a rhythm that rose and fell as he went in and out of office buildings. By late afternoon, when he and Kent returned to his office from the sixth meeting of the day, all the sounds had run together: traffic, conversation, elevator music, the click of office computer keys, the greetings of secretaries and doormen. "God, what a schedule!" Kent groaned, flopping into a chair in Luke's office. "How do you put on a play if you're in meetings all the time?"

"Productions begin with meetings." Luke filled two glasses with ice water and handed one to Kent as he walked around him to reach his desk chair. "We have one more: Marilyn Marks is bringing a model of her set design. Fritz doesn't like her ideas, but he hasn't seen the model, so I asked him to come at five-thirty. That gives Marilyn half an hour without interruptions."

"What doesn't Fritz like?"

"We'll see when he gets here."

"Close to the vest, Luke."

"Everybody gets an equal chance," Luke said evenly as Marilyn Marks came in, carrying her model. She was small and fragile-looking, with a thin face framed by a cap of brown hair, brown eyes close together above a thin blade of a nose, and a thin mouth that tightened even more when she concentrated on her work. "Hi, Luke, here it is," she said, setting the model on the round conference table. Luke introduced her to Kent and the three of them stood at the table.

Marilyn bent over the model, using a pencil to point out different parts of the Styrofoam-and-cardboard stage set. "Lena's living room: everything is a little off center. I see her as a woman at the end of her life who can't figure out why this grandson she's absolutely nuts about doesn't seem to love her. Of course he does in the end, but until then she's got a lot of *tsuros* about it. It's like a dream that she's trapped in. I know that Fritz hates it, but Fritz doesn't like anything that's offbeat."

"Dynamite!" Kent cried exuberantly. Luke was more cautious; he thought the set veered too far from realism, but he wanted to study the model and think about it, so for the moment he said nothing.

The telephone rang. His secretary and assistant

had long since gone home, so he answered it. "Luke," said Tricia, "I've cooked dinner. Please come. Seven-thirty. I've missed you."

I'd like a quiet evening at home, Luke thought, to go over everything. And when I can't think about it anymore, I could take a break and read Jessica's letters. But that doesn't make sense. As my grandmother would say, it's no way for a healthy growing boy to spend his evenings. "Fine," he said. "Is red wine all right?"

"Wonderful. And, Luke, be very casual. It's just the two of us."

"Good."

Kent and Marilyn left his office together, talking about the set. Luke walked home, barely aware of the crowds, thinking mostly of the oppressive heat of New York's streets, somehow feeling trapped by it. In the quiet coolness of his apartment he showered and read his mail, then walked to Tricia's apartment, arriving exactly at seven-thirty.

"I love it that you're always on time," she said, her arms around his neck. "I'm glad to see you. Tell me you're glad to see me."

"I'm glad to see you." And he was. She had nothing to do with *The Magician,* nothing, in fact, to do with the theater, and she was cool and fresh and beautiful. She wore a long slim dress of blue silk, gold ballerina slippers and a white apron trimmed with gold braid, and her hair was perfectly combed, a few strands falling with artful casualness across her forehead. "You look lovely," Luke said. "But not as if you'd been spending much time in the kitchen."

"That was earlier. I believe in entertaining my man, not stirring and chopping while he sits alone in the living room."

"I could help stir and chop."

"Do you do much of that?"

"None. No one has ever asked me to try."

"Well, maybe no one has felt very domestic with you. Come look at my column for tomorrow. Scotch?" she asked over her shoulder as she went to the bar.

"Fine." He found the column on the coffee table and sat down to read it. Her picture was at the top, tiny and grainy but identifiable, her expression somber, as if the news she imparted was too profound for smiles. "Behind Closed Doors" was the name of the column, and Luke skipped from one boldfaced name to the next until he came to a blind item. "What former wife of New York's hottest director leaves tomorrow on a cruise with companion Edwin Peruggia, Hollywood's favorite lawyer, who tried but failed to invest in her former husband's new play?"

"What the hell is this?" he demanded when Tricia turned from the bar with their drinks.

"That's why I wanted you to read it. You never told me you were turning down investors, Luke."

"We're not. Monte would have told me. Where did you get this?"

"Luke, you know I never reveal my sources."

"Someone in Peruggia's office, I suppose. It can't have been Monte's staff. Who was it?"

"My lips are sealed."

"It never happened, Trish. Doesn't that bother you? Where did you get it?"

"My God, you are so stubborn. One of Ed's new lawyers, just out of school. He said he got it from Ed's secretary."

"And you didn't check it."

"I don't have time to check everything. Would it really bother you if it runs? It's free publicity, you know."

"Take it out. It doesn't serve any purpose."

"It titillates, Luke. That's what it's supposed to do."

"It produces nothing. Like stirring a cauldron without making soup or stew or sauce."

"It produces *interest*. Amusement, curiosity, envy, contempt . . . emotions. People feel alive when they have emotions. What else do you produce in the theater, for heaven's sake? You're so high and mighty, but you do exactly what I do. Only I reach more people every day than you do in five years."

"You left out understanding."

"Oh, Luke, good heavens, nobody reads a gossip column for *understanding;* they read it to feel superior to people who are richer and more famous and more beautiful than they are. I'm not trying to write the truth of the ages, you know; I'm just giving people what they want. Now could we change the subject? I'm sure it isn't good for the digestion to have deep philosophical discussions before dinner. You really didn't turn him down? You might have done it because you don't like his morals. Or distinct lack of them. Or you heard he was squiring your ex-wife and you— No, I see from your face that that won't fly. Just tell me if he ever wanted to invest in any of your plays."

"No."

"Well. I'd believe you before one of Ed's little underlings." She led him back to the couch and sat beside him, kissing him lightly. "Tell me about the play. I heard Abby Deming is going to star; that's money in the bank for you, isn't it? I mean, she's such a draw; it's amazing, at her age, and as far as I can tell she's never had her face done. And it's extra good, isn't it, because you've got an unknown playwright. What's his name? Tell me about him."

"Dinner, Miss Delacorte." In the dining alcove, Tricia's maid lit the candles on the small round table and filled the wineglasses, then vanished through the swinging door into the kitchen.

Tricia took Luke's arm to walk across the room. "We can talk over my excellent dinner." Luke held her chair as she sat down. "Now, Luke," she said as he sat opposite her. "What's the name of your newest genius? Tell me all about him."

Luke was looking past her through the wide windows at thousands of other illuminated windows filling his field of vision. They were the same lights he saw from his own dining room, at a slightly different angle, and it occurred to him that his world was a narrow one, without a change of scene or, it appeared, a change of subject, even when he went to dinner.

"Luke!"

"Kent Horne," he said. "Very young, brilliant, occasionally charming, unfortunately also immature and hyperactive." He put his hand over hers. "You will not put an item in your column that Lucas Cameron's new play has been written by an immature young man who is going to be hard to control."

"What makes you think—"

"You were planning it. Forget it, Trish. Not a word about any of this, or I can't talk to you. You know that."

"This is my livelihood we're talking about."

"Your livelihood does not stand or fall on items about Kent, who hasn't made a name yet."

"Will he?"

"Yes."

"Well, then I'll write about him when he does."

The maid cleared their soup plates and served soft-shelled crabs and a wild rice salad. Luke refilled their glasses. The candles slowly burned down. And for the rest of the evening, and into the night, they shared the common ground of New York and its celebrities that had brought them together.

But much later, when Tricia drowsily stretched on her silk sheets as he got up to dress, and asked him to stay the night, he shook his head. "I still have a few hours of work. Thank you for everything; it was just what I needed."

He bent to kiss her, then made his way through the apartment, skirting furniture that hulked like indistinct ghosts in the faint light that filtered in from a city only half asleep, and took the elevator to the street. It was barely cooler than when he had arrived, but he did not look for a taxi; he walked the mile to his building, past sleeping figures in doorways bundled up as if it were winter; past lovers pausing to kiss, or taking an extra skip to make their footsteps match; past a woman in a frayed down coat and wool hat pushing a grocery cart piled high with possessions; past a couple in the midst of a quarrel, spitting accusations, neither hearing the other; past two boys whispering, plotting, darting glances all around; past someone laughing at something her companion had said; past someone weeping at something her companion had said.

Not such a narrow world, Luke thought as his doorman held open the door to his building. If I get out of apartments and theaters and keep walking, I'll see everything.

Martin had left notes on his desk: Tommy Webb had called. So had Monte Gerhart, Kent Horne, Marian Lodge—*who's Marian Lodge? Oh, the writer from* The New Yorker. *I can't even remember what I said to her*—Fritz Palfrey, and Cort Hastings saying he'd been reading *The Magician* and he didn't think he liked Daniel as much as he'd thought at first, so he needed some time with Luke tomorrow, and also the playwright, whose name he couldn't remember.

*Don't these people ever sleep? Or take some time off?* Luke swept the messages into a pile and left them by the telephone. He looked at his watch. *Not so late. Time for one or two letters.* And with that he knew that he had been waiting for this moment, anticipating the letters in the same way that a child anticipated bedtime stories: a reward for a good day, a treat for the time when everything else had been accomplished. He was faintly embarrassed by his eagerness . . . but why not? he thought. Jessica was Constance's friend; obviously I'd want to know more about her. He went to his chair, where he saw that, once again, Martin had left a tray on the round table, this time with a plate of chocolate cookies beside the thermos of coffee and bottle of cognac. He settled himself, poured cognac and coffee, munched a cookie. Then he opened the box and pulled out a cluster of letters.

. . . can't believe there could be a theater without—

The pages were out of order. Luke reorganized them. It was a short letter, the handwriting agitated.

Dearest Constance, I just got your letter. Oh, damn, that I'm stuck in London when I ought to be with you. Have you known about this for a long time? Well, you must have; good heavens, if your heart is so weak that you have to leave the stage, you must have been worrying about it for months . . . years . . . And never a word to me. Every time I said you looked pale or tired—and thinking back I realize I said that a lot, especially when we took our last play to Los Angeles—you always passed it off: too many late nights, a mild cold, a touch of the flu. You said in your letter that you didn't want to worry me, but aren't we closer than that? I thought you would have shared . . . Well, you didn't and I wish you had, but the thing is, what do we do now? I could come to New York overnight to be with you before you leave; would you like that? Or—I have a much better idea—could you stop in London on your way to Italy? My hotel suite has an extra bedroom and we could have a few days together; you could see me in *A Doll's House*— I'd love to know what you think of it—and I've got a new friend I'd like you to meet. But most of the time it would be just the two of us. We could be as busy or as quiet as you want but at least we'd be together before you go into this strange exile you've chosen. Please let me know your schedule; please write or call, anytime. All my love, Jessica.

Dearest Constance, four perfect days in London (and every time you had to stop and rest we had a chance to try another pub!), but that was two months ago and now I'm back in New York and you're in Italy and I feel as if we're on different planets. I never realized how much I counted on you being on a stage somewhere; it made me feel less alone. I didn't even know I felt alone until now. You said you do, too, when we talked yesterday afternoon, and I was up all night thinking about you. This must be about the hardest thing you've ever done, isn't it? I understand all your reasons—that you wanted to be far away from New York, that you feel you're a different person when you're not on stage and so you went all the way and made a new life to go with the new person you are. I understand it, but still it amazes me that you had the courage to do it.

Your aloneness is much more stark than mine—it makes me feel ashamed even to talk about mine, but you asked about it on the phone. The fact is, I've never had a close woman friend other than you, I have no man I care about, I have no family. You were all of those for me. Until now, and so again—as so many times before—what I have left is the theater. And I do have a new excitement there, because suddenly writers are sending me plays, or sending them to my agent, so I feel that, now,

I'm part of the beginning of things. Not quite the creation but close to it.

Still, I wish you were with me. The other day *The New York Times* said, "Now that Constance Bernhardt has retired, Jessica Fontaine is the dominant actress of the American stage." Imposing words . . . but I'd rather share it with you; I'd rather we dominated together. I do so miss you.

But I have your photographs. Thank you for sending them to me; I like being able to picture you in your villa when I write to you. And yes, I will come to visit, as soon as I can. How lovely of you to quote an old letter of mine: "My door is always open, wide, wide open, to you." That means everything to me. Be well, I love you, Jessica.

Luke put his head back and closed his eyes. *I've never had a close woman friend other than you, I have no man I care about, I have no family. You were all of those for me.* Two of a kind, he thought: Jessica and I. Constance filled all those roles for both of us. And now she's gone. I wonder if Jessica has found someone to replace her.

After a minute, he looked through the other letters he had removed from the box but not yet read. They listed plays in which she had starred, and another movie, this one a Merchant-Ivory production that received rave reviews, as did Jessica. And then she wrote that she had moved to a house on 10th Street near Grace Church.

I saw it on a Monday and bought it that afternoon; closed two weeks later, and by Friday had workers renovating it. I'd spent those two weeks making drawings of what I wanted, and I can't wait to move in. I'm hoping for a whole new kind of life here. There are still so many roles I want to play—my calendar is booked for the next three years—but now that I have this house I'll have new views out of my windows, new friends, new walks to take and new rooms to come home to from touring and visiting you. Someday you may even come to visit me here—I have a bedroom just for you. What a lovely prospect!

Luke skimmed the next letters describing the decorating of the new house, and then came to the last letter he held. Folded inside was a clipping from the *Vancouver Tribune* announcing the new theater season, which would culminate with Jessica Fontaine's long-awaited first appearance in Canada. She would star in *The Heiress* for a six-week run beginning on February 1, and already the performances were sold out. Luke opened the letter.

Dearest Constance, I'm so glad you're feeling better and that you had a good visit with

Luke. It's lovely for you that he gets there so often. Will he be there in March? Well, *I* plan to be! I'm going to Vancouver in February, to do *The Heiress,* and then, about mid-March, I'll take a train trip across Canada to unwind. Then, when I get to Toronto, I plan to leap on the first plane for Italy and spend a couple of weeks—if that's not too long for you—lolling on your terrace, breathing your pure Italian country air, hiking those hills and fields around your villa that I so loved last time, and just being with you. Does that sound all right to you? I'm so much looking forward to seeing you. I'll call you from Toronto, but I plan to write long letters from the train, chock full of adjectives and exclamation points; I'm told it's a beautiful trip, especially through the Fraser River Canyon and the Canadian Rockies. I'm really very excited about it. More soon, I love you, Jessica.

# CHAPTER 6

Rehearsals for *The Magician* started on a day that would be proclaimed by television's weather people the hottest day of the decade. New York lay in a torpor: dog walkers clung to the shade, forcing their pets to find new venues, pretzel vendors stood at arm's length from the radiating heat of their stands, and even the children turning on fire hydrants seemed to be moving in slow motion. As the cast for *The Magician* gathered in the studio Monte had rented on 45th Street, they all offered elaborate comments on the heat, and Luke, sitting at a table some distance away, heard in their voices a note of pride, as if they felt that New York's heat was far more intense than that afflicting other cities—just as its cold, its crowds, its crises, were more intense—but because they were people of ingenuity and wiliness they would come through just fine.

"Hell of a place to live," Monte Gerhart muttered as he took the chair beside Luke. "Always something: trial by fire every goddamn day of the year. Other cities, they've got normal weather, they live normal lives, dull but normal. They'd have a hell of a time getting through an hour here, talk about a lifetime. I got Tracy's budget. Seems high in spots. Two hundred fifty thousand for publicity?"

"That doesn't buy much these days. We'll look at it again, though. What other spots?"

"Costumes. Props. We're not putting on *Phantom of the Opera,* you know; it ought to be pretty simple."

"I agree; I thought those were high, too. We'll ask Tracy when she gets here; she must have a reason for those numbers. Anything else?"

"No, that's it. The money's coming in, Luke; it

rolled in as soon as I wrote to a few people that we had Abby Deming, *plus* I had Abby write a P.S. that she's all excited about Rachel and Cort. I mean, those kids've only done a few TV things, I couldn't raise a dime on their names, but if Abby gives thumbs up, a lot of people pull out their checkbooks. But that doesn't mean we don't watch the budget; you never know what's coming."

Luke nodded. He remembered from the earlier time they had worked together that it had taken him a few weeks to get used to Monte's apparent crudeness and bumbling manner that disguised one of the sharpest producers in the business. Clever of him to have Abby add a postscript to his letter; it was probably enough to tip the scales in their favor with any would-be investors worried about her reputation as a terror. And am I worried about that reputation? Luke asked himself as he stood up to greet Abby and the rest of the cast. You bet I am.

The room, on the second floor of an old warehouse, had been remodeled as a dance studio, and one wall was mirrored, with a bar running along it. On the opposite wall, high windows stretched from one end of the room to the other. Klieg lights hung from the ceiling, and Luke had turned on a few to illuminate the area he had marked with tape to represent the stage. Folding chairs and packing boxes were scattered about to be used as furniture; there would be no stage set, furnishings or props until dress rehearsals in Philadelphia, in six weeks.

This was a decision Luke and Monte had made together, to avoid the expense of the stagehands union, which would have moved in if there had been any piece of furniture or props on the makeshift stage. Three window air conditioners labored against the heat, sounding like asthmatic patients walking up a flight of stairs.

"Good morning, I'm glad to see you all," Luke said. "I'm looking forward to the next weeks—we have an extraordinary cast and an extraordinary play and we'll have a good time putting it all together. Most of you haven't worked with me before. I won't give you a laundry list of my peculiarities, but I will say that I don't give orders and 'should' isn't a big word in my vocabulary, though I do know how to use it. Rehearsals are a conversation between us to figure out the emotions and meanings behind everyone's lines and bring out the strengths of the play. Any questions or comments? Okay, then, I'd like to start by going straight through the first act. Kent's given us a few stage directions and you can follow them, but most of the time you should move around any way you want. If you feel like sitting, grab a chair and put it wherever you want. Action springs from words and emotions, and I'm not going to tell you what to do; you'll find out when it happens. And it will happen, and then change over and over again, as your understanding of your lines changes, and as you refine the way you play your parts. If you have questions that absolutely can't wait, we'll stop, but I hope you can save most of them until we've gone through the whole act. Okay, let's get started."

He moved back to the table. "Where the hell is Kent?" Monte demanded in a loud whisper.

"He said he'd be here. You'd think he'd be the first." Luke cleared a space on the table amid paper cups half-filled with coffee, thermoses of coffee and iced tea, bagels and sweet rolls, cans of soft drinks, extra copies of the script, jars crammed with sharpened pencils, and a stack of yellow notepads, and put one of the notepads and three pencils in the clearing in front of him.

"Well, look who's here," Monte said as Kent came in. "We always start on time," he told him.

"Sorry." Kent put a bulky string-tied package on the table and began to work at the knot. "Listen, you've got to see this; it's the most—"

"Later," Luke said, his eyes on the actors.

Kent turned. His body grew still and then curved forward in an arc of pure intensity, as if he were being drawn the length of the room and into the cast . . . as he truly was, thought Luke, glancing at him. He was hearing his lines—all of them, the entire play—delivered for the first time by professionals and Luke knew that they sounded to him even newer than they had at the casting. He turned to Luke, his eyes glistening. "It sounds okay," he whispered. "I mean, it sounds *good.*"

Luke smiled, for the first time beginning to like him. But he did not take his eyes off the actors, and Kent and Monte watched with him as the first act of the play unwound. Luke was tense and watchful, but he was also exhilarated. This was one of the best times: everything beginning, everything unformed, a world waiting to be created. The week before, the cast had gathered around an oval table in Monte's office and twice read the play aloud without any attempt to dramatize it. It was a way for them to hear their lines in context with all the other lines, and to hear the play as a whole. Now, in a bare room, on a makeshift stage beneath glaring lights, speaking above the wheezing air conditioners, they were taking their first steps in building their characters and constructing a story, and so this time there was emotion and laughter as they read their lines and moved about, and they eyed each other like strangers getting acquainted, circling, touching, sitting, standing, finding their own rhythm and their own space that set each of them distinctively apart from the others but always kept them part of a whole.

They all felt the same exhilaration that Luke felt, and the undercurrent of anticipation built as voices grew stronger and the shape and momentum of the story became clear. When the first act ended, there was a brief silence, like that of diners savoring a good meal. Then, slowly, they began to move away from the stage, relaxing, preparing for the next act. Cort sat down at the table where Monte was opening a package of croissants.

"What's this?" he asked, gesturing toward the bulky package Kent had carried in.

"I want Luke to see it," Kent said. He untied the string. "Marilyn designed another set. I told her to go all out; get really dramatic. Here's the model." He pulled off the wrapping paper.

There was a long silence.

"All those dark little rooms," said Abigail. "It looks like a whorehouse."

Kent flushed. "No, it—"

"Marilyn designed this?" Monte demanded. "She wants to build this set?"

"Well, actually, she said it was up to all of you."

"When did she do this?" Luke asked.

"Well, I was at her studio, and she showed me this . . . she'd done it for another play, as a kind of experiment, and never used it—"

"For obvious reasons," said Abigail.

"And I thought . . . all these rooms, you know, all the parts of Lena's psyche, it would be like looking inside her head. I mean, this play is about how we learn to trust ourselves enough to believe that other people will love us for what we really are, not some kind of image they have of us, and I thought these rooms would be a metaphor for all the ways Lena acts and thinks. . . ." His voice trailed away.

"*Metaphor,*" Monte said. "Fritz will have a heart attack."

"Fritz won't see this," Luke said. "Kent, we're

not using it. It may say something special to you, but it won't to audiences, and that's what we have to think about. I've already asked Marilyn to simplify the other design and she—"

"*Simplify?* She didn't tell me that! I mean, I was there all weekend—"

"Which we weren't going to tell anyone," Marilyn said, coming up behind him. "What a gallant gentleman you are, Kent."

Kent reeled back. "I didn't know you were coming this morning."

"I brought sketches for Luke." She turned her back on Kent, unrolling a large sheet of paper. "What do you think?"

Luke and Monte bent over it. "This looks good," Luke said. "Monte?"

"Nice idea, living room, bedroom, screened-in porch. And you've got the windows and doors sort of off center like before, but not so much. I like it. Luke?"

"I do, too. Do you have a model, Marilyn?"

"I've started it. I can have it in a couple of days."

"Bring it in when it's ready. We can't make a final decision until we see it, but I think we're very close. Thanks, Marilyn. This is a good job."

"It's a good play," she said quietly. She looked around the room. "I thought you'd be rehearsing."

"That was the idea," Luke said drily. "We're about to start again; do you want to stay?"

"If nobody minds. I love this part of it, the beginning."

"Have a seat." Monte pulled out the chair beside his.

Luke walked toward the stage. "I'd like to start again and go through all three acts without stopping. We'll break for lunch at one o'clock. If anyone has comments or questions, hold them until afternoon. Okay. From the top."

Kent stood behind Marilyn's chair. "Could we go out later? I mean, lunch or coffee or whatever you want. Please."

She did not turn around. "I'll think about it."

"Kent," Luke said. "We're starting."

"See you later," Kent said, and touched Marilyn's shoulder as he walked to a chair near the stage.

At the end of the first act, Luke waited for comments or complaints, but there were none. "Act two," he said, and picked up his pencil. His list was already several pages long, and he knew how many hours lay ahead, in his office and at home, when he would go over each point to find ways to communicate his ideas to the actors, to incorporate their suggestions, if possible, and to shape each scene so that, one by one, they built to a final scene that audiences would feel was inevitable and right.

"Luke," Abigail said, "I'm going to be on stage at the beginning of the act instead of coming in later."

Kent's head shot up. "But—"

"Go ahead and try it," Luke said. "And then go straight on, Abby; any way you feel comfortable."

They settled into the play, and the rehearsal filled the rest of the day, with a brief break for lunch in which Marilyn and Kent disappeared for fifteen minutes and he came back alone. "It'll get worked out, or maybe it won't," he said cryptically to Luke. At the end of the day Luke sent his actors home with a promise that the next day they would talk about their parts. "We'll go over everything: questions, problems, any kind of discomfort with your lines. It will probably be the only day we devote to that and nothing else. Day after tomorrow we'll be rehearsing again."

A few minutes later the lighting director arrived. "I know it's earlier than I usually get started on a play," he said, "but I just saw Marilyn's model and I'd like to sit in on a few rehearsals. I had some ideas when I saw the model. . . ."

He and Luke went over the sketches in his notebook, until Kent grew bored. "Think I'll take off," he said to Luke and Monte, and they nodded, still talking about lights.

When the lighting director left, Monte pushed back his chair and stretched. "I feel deprived; only one meal today. Gladys would be thrilled. I'll tell her I planned it that way. You ready for a drink?"

"In a minute. Marilyn wants to do costumes, Monte. I told her it was all right with me."

"Fine with me. She's dressed a lot of shows. She's good. Classy, too."

Luke was looking at his schedule. "Sketches of costumes by the end of next week. By then Marilyn should have the new model to Sprowell for set construction. He's slow; I like to give him plenty of time. When are you seeing Aiken?"

"Tomorrow before I come over here. Luke, has he ever managed a theater before?"

"In San Francisco. Why?"

"He's too calm. He makes me nervous."

Luke chuckled. "If you're nervous enough, he'll catch it from you, and then you'll feel better. He's good, Monte. When you get a schedule for ticket sales and theater posters, let me have a copy. And you'll talk to him about theater parties?"

"Right."

"Okay, then, the budget. Did you talk to Tracy?"

"I thought you were going to do that. It doesn't matter; I should have done it. I'll call her when I get home. Five o'clock tomorrow, assuming she can make it?"

"Fine."

"Anything else?"

"No, that's it." Luke walked around the room, gazing at his tape on the floor, the chairs and boxes the cast was using for furniture, the table where he and Monte sat, heaped with everyone's cups, leftover food and Styrofoam containers that would all be cleaned up before they arrived the next morning.

"Luke, let's go."

He nodded and forced himself to walk away. Once rehearsals began, he was always reluctant to leave. They all were like that as the play sprang to life. In another month it would seem as if, for them, there was no city, no climate, no families: only the theater. But Monte was waiting, one hand on the doorknob. "I don't mean to rush you; it's just that I invited somebody to join us for a drink and she's always on time."

Luke looked at him. It had been a long day, heavy on drama. "Why?"

"Why did I invite her? Because you're always looking for new ideas and she's got some terrific ones. Because you'll like her. Because *I* like her."

"I'm not looking for new ideas when I'm just beginning a new play."

"I just met her, Luke; I got enthusiastic. Humor me."

Luke strode ahead and Monte puffed, barely keeping pace, as they walked crosstown on 44th Street. As they neared the Algonquin, Luke at last slowed down. "One short drink," he said. "I'll give you that much."

"It won't be punishment, Luke; you'll like her."

Amid the clusters of fringed velvet couches and armchairs in the Algonquin's inner lobby, an attractive woman waited. "Luke Cameron, Sondra Murphy," Monte said. "You haven't ordered?" he asked Sondra.

"I waited for you."

Monte hailed a waiter and they ordered drinks and then sat for a moment in silence. Sondra, serene and assured, seemed content to wait indefinitely, but Monte began to fidget. "I've got this idea about adapting some of Sondra's books for the stage," he said to Luke. "Children's books, about a bear named Abbey. Of course, we'd have to change the name."

Sondra was contemplating Luke's impassive face. "I don't think it will work," she said to him. "When I met Monte at a dinner party it seemed cruel to clamp down on his enthusiasm—it's so refreshing—but I don't think my books have anything for adults, and certainly not for the theater."

Luke looked at her with interest. She was blond and attractive, with strikingly vivid features; confident, and not captivated by Monte's vision. "Why does Monte think it would work for adults?"

"I don't like to speak for him—"

"Go right ahead," Monte said.

"Abbey has a lot to say about the world through her adventures. She tours Japan, she meets the American president at his inaugural ball, she goes to Paris for a Fourth of July party at the American embassy, all the time commenting on people and politics. Monte thought that could be the core of a play or a musical."

"You're right, it wouldn't work," Luke said, and they smiled together, as if Monte had temporarily disappeared. "But is all that firsthand?" he asked. "You've done all the things your bear has done?"

"All of them. I've been involved in politics for a long time. But I don't write political books; these were fun projects with my daughter."

They talked on, with Monte listening, and when they parted, Luke said that he hoped to see her again. It probably would not happen; they both were too busy and their lives were too far apart, but he was drawn to her, partly because of her attractiveness and the clear way she spoke about herself and the political and social worlds she inhabited, but also because she reminded him of Jessica. They both were women who created their own reality without waiting for others to do it for them. *The kind of woman I could stay with. The kind of woman my grandmother would approve of.*

"You were right," Monte grumbled when they turned to walk up Seventh Avenue. "Waste of time."

Luke laughed. "I had a better time than you did. Just don't have any more ideas about new shows until we've taken care of this one. Keep a diary. I'll read it in a few months."

His step was light as he walked toward home. Sondra Murphy had been a good tonic: someone who had nothing to do with the world of make-believe or gossip, someone whose life was rooted in gritty realism. Maybe that was why Jessica left the stage, he thought. No, of course not. Sondra and Jessica were not really alike. It was just that his thoughts these days, wherever they started, had a way of ending up with Jessica.

*And I need to get back to her letters; it's been a long time.*

But *The Magician* was in its fourth week of rehearsals before Luke had a chance to return to Jessica's letters. Every night, coming home from an evening out, he would sit at the desk in his library, working on his notes for the play and on the script itself. And often there was a midnight call from Claudia. "I miss you, Luke. Tell me how you are. Tell me about the play."

"What have you been doing?"

"Nothing."

"Monte told me he talked to you the other day and said you should call Gladys, that she could find things for you to do."

"She's unbearably dull, Luke, even if she is Monte's wife. And I'm not sure he likes her, either. Do you know what he called her? The volunteer queen of the eastern seaboard, always knocking herself out for some good cause or other. God, can you imagine anyone describing me that way?"

Luke let that pass. "Why not call her? You don't know what to do with yourself and she has jobs that need doing."

"Washing the feet of poor people."

"I think the only one who still does that is the pope. Look, damn it, she and her friends do a lot of good things that wouldn't get done if they weren't around. And it makes them feel good. It might make you feel good, too. Call her, Claudia. Give it a chance."

"Well, I may get to it one of these days. I'm not excited about it, you know, Luke; I really don't think I'm a good works kind of person."

There seemed to be no answer to that, so Luke made none. He looked down at the fanned-out sheets of Marilyn's watercolor paintings; one of the dresses for Lena bothered him and he was trying to figure out what was wrong with it.

"Luke, tell me about the play," Claudia said. "Please, you know I love to hear about it. Is Cort still complaining?"

It was against his better judgement, but it seemed to keep her happy and away from rehearsals, and so he told her more than he ever told an outsider about what went on within their small group. "Not as vociferously. He's discovered how powerful his part is in the third act."

"But you said Kent was rewriting something for him? You made him do it?"

"I asked him to try it, that we could always change back, that nothing was written in stone. And he agreed, but what he really thought was that stone was too common; he thinks of his pages as cast in bronze, hammered to perfection for posterity, so my comments weren't exactly welcome."

Claudia laughed, a long merry laugh that coiled around him, and Luke found himself wanting her close; he could feel his arms around her. He needed someone outside the theater to listen to him, to laugh with him, to share the dramas, small and large, that filled his life. Then he caught himself. Not Claudia. Not ever again.

But he'd been working too hard. He'd seen Tricia only three times in the past month and had been distracted when they were together, and Claudia's voice was warm, her laughter intimate.

*And I'm lonely.*

*No.* He backed away from it; it contradicted his image of himself. *Not lonely. Just a little low. And tired.*

"So then what happened?" Claudia asked.

Luke stared at the drawings, his head resting on his hand, and pictured Claudia, sitting at her telephone, making small circles with her right foot as she always did, wrapping a strand of hair around her finger, slipping it off, wrapping it again, gazing into space.

"Well, Kent actually rewrote parts of the first and second acts, but then Abby would charge in like the cavalry, her chin up—I don't know how a cavalry has its chin up, but if anyone could figure it out, Abby could—saying, 'It does not *work.* Luke, I will not tolerate this . . . it is *wrong, wrong, wrong!*'"

"Oh, perfect." Claudia was laughing again. "I can just hear her. And everybody shuts up as soon as she does that."

"Exactly. Even Cort. But the first act is weak because he's not putting himself into it; he really doesn't like it—"

"Luke, why don't I come over for a while? Just to have a visit, much nicer than a telephone call. You could even offer me a drink. Please, Luke, wouldn't you like that?"

He would. He wanted companionship, and Claudia knew the people and the vocabulary of the theater as Tricia did not; that was one thing— perhaps the only thing—she had learned in their marriage. But not Claudia, he thought again. It never worked. Within an hour of their coming together, she slipped from companion to dependent, looking to him to provide her with activities to fill her hours, ideas to fill her thoughts, a structure for her life. Luke knew that there were people who seemed unable to organize their life in a way that was meaningful and productive, but he did not intend to spend time with them. Even—especially— an ex-wife.

So it would not be Claudia to whom he would turn for companionship.

*Well, who, then? Who's going to come along to fill this gap that seems to be bigger and more noticeable than ever before?*

"Luke? Did you hear me?"

*Probably no one. If it hasn't happened yet, the chances are . . .*

"Luke!"

"No, you can't come over. I'm exhausted, Claudia; I have a few more notes to finish and then I'm going to bed. I'll call you."

"When?"

"When I have time."

"No, that's no good, you have to be more definite. Oh, why do you make me go through this every time? I need you, Luke. You're the only one I can talk to, the only one who understands me. I need to know when I'll see you. If I know we'll have dinner on Tuesday or Monday or whatever, I feel better."

"You have hundreds of friends. I've never known you to be without a string of men ready to take you wherever you want to go or do whatever you—"

"I have acquaintances. Hundreds, thousands. This city is full of acquaintances who don't want to listen; they just want to talk and preen because they're with a beautiful woman. The Phelans are the only people who truly are friends, who really listen to me, and you don't want me to see them."

"They're friends as long as you spend money at their gambling tables. Can't you understand that?"

"They're friends because they care about me!"

"Damn it, we go over the same things, time and again. Can't you look at them and see what they are?"

"If I don't know when I'm going to see you, I'll look at them a lot!"

"Then you're on your own. You know how I

feel." Angry and frustrated, he slammed down the telephone. What made her think he would find her childishness attractive or desirable? Probably the fact that once he had married her and had stayed with her for five years. And still agreed to see her, still paid her gambling debts, still called now and then to see how she was. And as angry as he was now, he knew he would call her in the next few days and take her to dinner and listen to her complaints, and that he would do it as often as she demanded, because, though no one knew this, Constance had told him to.

Not in so many words. But after listening sympathetically on the rare occasions when he brought his frustrations with Claudia to her, she nodded when he told her he was getting a divorce and then said, "So now you plan to shut the door in her face and walk off. Can you do that?"

He had sat in silence, feeling like a boy again, wrapped round by that sense of being pinned down that boys have when they are on the verge of manhood and can no longer hide behind fecklessness. "Probably not. I'll do what I can for her."

Forget it, Luke told himself. He tried to concentrate on Marilyn's drawings, but in a moment he knew he was too tired to analyze whatever it was that was bothering him about them. He went to his armchair. On the round table, Martin had arranged a thermos and a bottle of burgundy beside sandwiches under a bell-shaped cover, slices of chocolate cake, and a silver bowl of glazed apricots. Martin has an exaggerated sense of my appetite, Luke thought, but when he tasted an apricot he realized how hungry he was and remembered that he had not eaten dinner. He had canceled a date with Monte and Gladys to stay home and make notes for Kent on the last scene of the play and had told Martin to leave something for him. Well, here it was, and he was ravenous. He found a newscast on television, poured a glass of wine, and ate two sandwiches while his thoughts roamed from the newscast to the notes he had just finished, then to Claudia, then to his grandmother, and, from her, to Jessica.

It had been a month since he had read one of her letters or even thought about her. A long month, Luke thought. Maybe it isn't the company of one or another woman that I've missed; maybe it's her letters.

He had put a marker in the box where he had left off reading and he pulled out a few of the letters behind it. Folded inside the first was a piece of a column torn from a newspaper, and Luke found himself looking at Tricia's photograph and her name beneath the title "Behind Closed Doors." In the second item, it was Jessica's name, in boldface, that leaped out at him.

Famed Broadway and Hollywood actress **Jessica Fontaine** is hospitalized with devastating injuries suffered in a train derailment in Canada. Insiders say she is an invalid who has lost the power of speech. Her agent has no comment.

Written in the margin, in a shaky handwriting, were the words "This is not true."

I missed that, Luke thought, but then I never read this stuff until I met Tricia. He opened the letter. It was written on the same blue stationery and in the same handwriting as the one he had read when he first found the box, telling Constance about the train wreck. That one had been dictated to a nurse and so, it seemed, was this one.

> Dearest Constance, I don't imagine you'll see this in Italy, but who knows what papers reprint this garbage and maybe you did read it, so I'm sending a copy with my commentary. *It isn't true.* I haven't lost the power of speech and I'm not an invalid and the doctors say I won't be one. I have some broken bones and torn tendons, and so on . . . I guess that's not dramatic enough for a gossip columnist. I can't imagine how someone can make a living putting rumors and outright lies into newspapers where readers will assume that they're true. What an awful way to live.

Luke thought of all the times he had been amused and entertained by Tricia and had not bothered to ask her the source of her items. He felt ashamed and folded the letter and put it away, as if turning his back on Jessica's accusing voice. The next letter was still in the nurse's handwriting.

My dear, dear Constance, I miss you, and it's
only a few days since you left my bedside. It
was magical to see you, and of course totally
unexpected since I had written you, quite
firmly as I recall, that you were not to come,
that you weren't strong enough for such a trip.
But when did you ever obey orders?

Luke imagined the scene in his mind: two
women in a room at twilight, one in a chair, leaning forward, holding the hand of a woman lying
partially propped up, bandaged, her eyes closed,
or perhaps just opening. Everything else fell away.
All the conflicts and pleasures of his day in the
theater, Tricia, Claudia, all of it vanished. He felt
he was in that hospital room with his grandmother
and Jessica, and when he took up the letter again,
it was almost as if Jessica were talking to him, as
well as to Constance.

We talked a fair bit, didn't we? A lot of it I
can't remember. I'm having trouble remembering little day-to-day things . . . they float
through my mind like bits of confetti, here for
a drifting moment, then gone, then, maybe,
back in a day or two with other images swirling
about, overlapping, blurring together . . . good
heavens, I'm babbling. My nurse is writing
this—of course you know that, from the handwriting—and she is so wonderfully kind that

she writes anything I say, even the words
that wander in and out like people trying to
find their way through an unfamiliar
neighborhood. More babbling; forgive me.

Even though I miss you, I'm glad you've
gone back to Italy; you looked so pale that last
afternoon we were together, and one time when
you thought I was asleep I watched you and I
could see that your animation and vigor were
an act—still acting, dearest Constance, and
how good you are at it!—that you were in fact
exhausted and needed to be home.

So there were many things we never talked
about and one of them was the train accident.
It was strange and quite scary that whenever I
tried to talk about it I started shaking. Yesterday, I don't know why, I brought it up and the
nurse brought me newspapers with stories and
photos of the derailment. I can't imagine sur-
viving it. So many didn't, they say . . . more
than fifty. I know I will never fathom the mystery of why I survived and others did not.

There were other mysteries: how quickly the
police and medics came, and hundreds of others I'll never know about; the kindness and
concern and stubbornness of the doctors and
nurses who kept trying, through all my operations, to put back together—or try to—all my
broken bones and dislocations and severed
nerves (well, yes, there was more going on than

just those three fractures I told you about in my other letter). But everyone says I'll be all right—they've said that over and over. With luck, they say, I'll be absolutely all right. I'm trying to believe them. Someday, when I get back to the stage, I'll thank all of them publicly, every doctor, every nurse, every nurse's aide. Until then, I thank them silently every day when I awake and see the sunlight. But for now, I'm very tired, dear Constance, so I'll say good night. I love you and thank you so much for coming here; it meant the world to me, as I kept saying until you told me to stop, that you got the point. But it did . . . the world . . . Jessica.

Luke looked up from the letter, repeating its phrases in his mind. He could almost hear Jessica's voice, an actor's voice. *When I get back to the stage, I'll thank all of them publicly* . . . But she never got back to the stage. She was not forgotten—revivals of her films, and videotapes of many of her performances shown on public television, kept her brilliance alive and were still used in acting classes—but the world of the theater closed around the space she had left and after a period of shock and a sense of loss, they all, like Luke, went on with their lives. Jessica Fontaine was gone.

Why? What had happened to her? Everyone had asked that question six years ago, at the time of the accident. Luke had asked it himself. But now it seemed more important than ever that he find the answer.

He opened the next letter in the cluster he had taken from the box. The stationery had the imprint of a condominium complex in Scottsdale, Arizona. The handwriting once again was Jessica's, though more slanted and slightly stiff, as if each stroke had been drawn with attentive care.

Dearest Constance, I'm sorry, I'm sorry, forgive me . . . you wrote and called, so many times, and I ignored you. I cried when I read your letters, and when they told me you were on the telephone, but I couldn't talk, not to anyone, because I couldn't think of anything worth saying; it all seemed such a waste of time. I did what everyone in the hospital told me to do, I ate and slept, I went to physical therapy twice a day, seven days a week, but I never spoke except when I absolutely had to. All my life I've depended on words, and loved them, but in the hospital they seemed weak, stupid, all empty air.

At first I tried to joke about what had happened in the accident, to make light of it, but the more I did, the darker everything got and finally there was no light at all, no warmth, and no hope, because it wasn't possible to deny what I had become. I don't want to bore you with medical jargon, but you've asked so many times that I'll tell you. I was in shock when I was rescued, with a concussion and three fractures. One is a fracture/dislocation of my hip and so far I've had three operations to repair the hip joint and fit everything together again. The doctors say I'll probably need a hip replacement, because of degeneration of the bones; that's one of the prospects I have ahead of me. The other two fractures are in my femur and upper arm, including a torn rotator cuff, and they don't seem to be healing properly, even after two surgeries. I had cuts on my face and body from flying glass, and I lost a lot of blood. I'm so thin I look like a refugee from a famine, and I know that my face shows all the pain and the painkillers I've been taking. I can't say for sure because I'm afraid to look in a mirror.

I've been having different kinds of therapy; one of them is called passive therapy, where I lie on a table while a therapist lifts and bends and stretches my completely limp arm and leg. This is supposed to keep everything from freezing up while the torn tendons heal. If I did the exercises myself before they heal, "firing up" my muscles, the stitches could tear apart. So day after day I lie there and watch my scrawny arm and leg being manipulated by a strong, beautiful young woman who has her whole life ahead of her, while mine is over. I can't imagine why she bothers. Why does anyone care about this shell or spend time on it? Why do they pretend all this pushing and pulling will make a difference?

Oh, Constance, who am I? I always took such joy and pride in my body—so strong and responsive—and my looks and my energy and my control of my life—I could do anything, I thought—and now I look at the flat shape of my body barely disturbing the sheet on my bed and I don't recognize it. *I don't know whose body it is.* And I don't know where I belong. The world is so drab, with no colors or curves or angles, just a flat smear of *things* . . . meaningless and a waste of time. I'd run away, but I can't run. I'd put myself to sleep forever, but I can't seem to do it. So every night when I go to bed for the two or three hours of sleep that I manage before pain or terrible dreams wake me up, I pray I won't wake up. But I always do. Why does such a wreck of a body keep working?

I'm doing my therapy at a place called the Landor Clinic, the best of its kind in the world, people say, as if I care, and I got here by being pushed in a wheelchair to and from the airplane and then to this townhouse, which I bought sight unseen because it didn't matter where I lived. The main thing is that the master bedroom is on the first floor so I don't have to deal with stairs.

The doctors are talking about two years of therapy, and by then I'm supposed to be recombined, renovated, restored, rebuilt, rehabilitated, and retreaded . . . something like a tire, I suppose, ready to roll again. They're lying, of course, to keep me motivated—that's their big word—at therapy and eating and sleeping and all those important things. But nothing is important. I know that, even if they don't.

I'm sorry for dumping all this on you—I tried not to—but I don't have anyone else and I can't bear the loneliness and darkness without at least talking to you on paper. I look at the pen in my hand and feel it touching you. I need that so much; I hug it to me. I'll try to be more cheerful next time. All my love, Jessica.

Luke looked up, shaken, almost in tears. He had grown so accustomed to her optimism, her exhilaration at being alive, her wry humor and sharp insights—in fact, he had almost come to depend upon them—that he could not believe this was the same woman. Devastated, he thought. Broken. And without friends or family to keep her from hitting bottom. No wonder she vanished from New York. But . . . what happened after the two years? People recover, even from the worst of accidents, and pick up their lives. What kept her away?

Dear Constance, I'm not ready to talk on the telephone, maybe soon, but not now. My nurse was too abrupt, and I've chastised her, but please don't insist. Can't we just have letters for a while, as we did long ago? I'll answer all your questions, though I haven't anything interesting to write about except my rigid routine—I'm as organized as if I punched a time clock every hour on the hour.

My nurse—Prudence Etheridge, a scuba diver from Sydney who is working her way around the world, a year in every city—pushes my wheelchair to the car twice a day and drives me to therapy, then brings me home, stopping off at the supermarket, or the pharmacy for yet another prescription, or a bookstore. She wants to take me to movies, too, but the thought of watching a movie makes me ill. Twice a day she holds me up while I shuffle around the large room that is living room, dining room and kitchen, and when she loosens her grip I panic and grab her, and she says, in her broad Australian accent, "Miss Fontaine, you are infinitely better than you think you are." Of course, she's trained to say that sort of thing.

Lately she's been prodding me to take an evening art class in a community center and last night I let her take me there. I did some sketching and began a watercolor—I did it as a hobby, you know, in another life—and it was the first evening that the hours didn't seem to drag on endlessly. I did a watercolor at home this morning, a child in a garden, and the time flew by again. So I think I'll go back to the class, and keep going as long as it's interesting and fills the hours.

One thing I don't have to worry about is money. I managed to put away a great deal in my years on the stage, all efficiently invested by a fund manager in stocks and bonds and real estate. And there's the money from the Canadian railroad, a huge amount. I wouldn't have sued them in any case, but they made their offer and, over my lawyer's objections (he thought I could get much more), I accepted it.

But aside from money, what's gone is . . . everything. The theater, New York, the long walks I loved, the people I knew, the house I just bought and fixed up so beautifully, the future. My life. I start shaking when I write that; I want to scream. What am I doing here? This isn't me, this isn't where I belong, this isn't how I fill my days and nights. *Where is my life?*

Prudence gave me a needlepoint, framed and ready for hanging. It says, *The only answer to "Why me?" is "Why not me?"*

Do you believe that? I don't want to. A random world, incomprehensible, bitter, cruelly indifferent . . . with no pattern, ever, to the bad things that happen to us, or the good ones, either. Unless . . . Lately I've started wondering, in the long nights when I can't sleep, if my life has been too easy. I never had a bad review (even in that awful film that everyone hated); I never had a time when there was no work because no one wanted me. Maybe, when everything goes so well, something bad happens, to even the score, so to speak. Well, I'm even. They've done their worst, whatever gods are interested in making us pay for happiness, and now I suppose they'll leave me alone. Now, when it doesn't matter anymore.

One of these days I promise I'll pick up the telephone and call you; until then, please don't call anymore. So much is jumbled in my head, anger and fear and confusion and *rage,* that I'm afraid a scream will come out if I open my mouth to talk. But I will try to write more often than I have in the past weeks. I hope you're well. When I was in the hospital, I thought of hiding in your maze, where no one could find me and I'd never leave it. Did you ever feel that way? I think of you, all the time, and I love you. Jessica.

Luke read the letter twice, then a third time, Jessica's despair flooding him with its bitterness. *What's gone is . . . everything.* Why? Because she'd been told it would be two years before she could get back to the stage? There had to be something more. He picked up the next letter. It was different from all those that had gone before, the paper a soft ivory, subtly textured, with an embossed fountain in the upper left-hand corner and, beneath it, three embossed lines: "The Fountain, Lopez Island, Washington State."

Lopez Island. Luke had never heard of it. But if it was Washington State, it was probably in

Puget Sound. He took an atlas from the shelf and looked it up. Puget Sound. A broad waterway bounded by Washington State, Vancouver Island and British Columbia, with dozens of islands scattered across it like confetti. One cluster of islands north of Seattle was named the San Juans. And within that cluster was Lopez Island. A dot on a map, a tiny island three thousand miles from New York. It was as if she had gone as far west as she could—and then dropped off the edge of the continent.

Dearest Constance, I've saved all your letters and taken them out to read and reread in the darkest nights. Thank you for writing without demanding replies; thank you for not scolding me again, thank you for your patience in all these twenty months. Twenty endless months, but then they didn't stretch to two years, as originally predicted, so I should be grateful. And of course I am. I have my health back, my energy, I have no more pain, which seems a miracle after living with it for so long, the scars and bruises and swelling on my face from all the plastic surgery are gone, and I have a new life here, on this most peaceful and beautiful island. You'll say it's a long way from New York, and so it is, but that's part of its charm. I've lost all interest in the theater, you see, so what better place to be than a tiny spot where theater as we know it does not exist?

Luke scowled at the words. They made no sense. Recovered, free of pain, whole again . . . why wasn't she singing with joy, filled with exultation and excitement and hope? She wrote of life, but sounded as depressed as she had in her letters from the hospital. And what was she talking about when she said she was not interested in the theater? There was no way in the world Jessica Fontaine would lose interest in the theater. It was her life.

I met a woman soon after I got to Arizona, a publisher of children's books, who asked me to illustrate a manuscript she was planning to publish. It was a sweet story and I could paint children—my new specialty—so I said yes and I had such a good time with it that I was sorry I finished so quickly. I'm sending you a copy; you should have it soon.

That was my first job and suddenly I was getting offers from all over, including France, England, Italy and Holland. By now I've illustrated books in just about every style from 19th-century Russian to folk-art American, and that was what kept me sane through twenty months of recuperation, four more surgeries, and mind-numbing therapy on alien-looking machines that fight back when one pulls, pushes, raises, lowers, rotates, straightens, stretches or curls them. You would not believe the number of ways there are to stress one's muscles and make them ache the next day. I was sure I'd end up as contorted as an octopus trying to scratch an elusive itch, but to my astonishment my strength came back and I felt whole again.

So now here I am on Lopez Island. I'm staying in a charming place called the Inn at Swifts Bay while I build a house on a lovely plot I bought: thirty acres with a private beach in a tiny cove bounded on one side by forests, and a cliff of reddish-gold rocks on the other. I worked with the architect in designing the house, including the fountain in the courtyard that reminds me of your fountains in Italy, and I used that for my stationery, as, of course, you've seen. Best of all, I'm beginning to be kind to people again. I think it's only when we're deeply unhappy about something that we're unrelentingly unkind. I have enough books to illustrate to keep me busy for at least a year, a woman to do cleaning and cooking when I move in (she irons, too, what a blessing!), and I've taken up horseback riding. I like it even better than walking, especially on this island, with forests, cliffs and beaches on the perimeter and farms and fields in the center. I hear roosters crowing in the morning (actually they keep it up all day; are they supposed to do that?) and the lowing of cows, and not another sound: no people, almost no cars . . . oh, an occasional seaplane coming from Seattle and circling before landing. I flew on it myself, to get here, and wondered, for just a moment, whether I was flying from, or flying to.

I'm so glad you feel better than you did last month. I think of you all the time, whatever I'm doing, and I think how interesting it is that both of us have settled into such good places.

Oh, yes, one more thing. I've met a man.

Take care of yourself. I love you. Jessica.

Luke felt a surge of dismay. *I've met a man.* And? Was she in love with him? Were they just good friends? Had they just started dating and she was thinking she might fall in love with him? Were they engaged?

Angrily he pulled the box to him to take out the next letter. But his hand stopped in midair. *What's wrong with me? I'm acting as if I'm jealous.*

As of course he was, he realized in the next moment. Because, somehow, against all reason, he had fallen in love with her.

# CHAPTER 7

"I think it's pretty conservative," Tracy Banks said, the point of her pencil resting on the number at the bottom of the budget for *The Magician*. "Salaries, renting the theater, Kent's advance and yours, and insurance, telephone, your production secretary . . . you know all that."

Luke nodded. He was having trouble concentrating, his thoughts skipping with every pause to Jessica's letters. He frowned to show that he was focusing on the numbers as Tracy went through each of them. Then he sat back. "Well, we'll try to shave it a little, but you're right: it's probably pretty conservative. Thanks, Tracy; just let me know when the numbers start to go through the roof."

"I'll let you know a long time before that. And Monte calls me every day, you know, checking up. Too bad he's not my lover; then I'd be thrilled with all the attention."

Luke was smiling as she left. He clipped the pages of the budget together and slipped them back into their folder. A million dollars to get to opening night. And that number would shoot up if they didn't have solid ticket sales in Philadelphia and in their week of previews in New York. After that, performance expenses would have to be met by performance revenues. He put the folder into his file drawer. A great play, he thought, with fine actors and talented people behind the scenes. And it all rests on money. One of those facts of theater life that don't occur to us when we direct our first play in college and revel in the romanticism of it. Then we start our apprenticeship in some little hole-in-the-wall company in Chicago or New York and we're plunged into the constant grinding battle to raise money and we think, Oh, but when I get to Broadway things will be different. And sometimes they are. But most of the time they aren't.

He stood at the window behind his desk, watching a building superintendent water the trees in a rooftop garden across the street. The water ran out of the bottom of each pot, glistening silver in the sun. Nearby, a mother settled her infant in a stroller, then lay back in her recliner and picked up a book. With one hand she pushed back her hair and it caught a slice of sunlight, glinting tawny gold. Jessica's hair, he remembered, had been tawny gold.

He looked at his watch. An hour before rehearsal. Just enough time. He left the office, merging with the languid crowds on 54th Street, making his way through them with gathering urgency to Fifth Avenue and then to the public library. Cool air curled around him as he crossed the marble lobby and turned into the periodicals room. At a long table he opened the volume of the *Reader's Guide* dated eight years earlier, the year his grandmother had moved to Italy, and found "Fontaine, Jessica," followed by a list of publications that had run stories about her that year. It was long, and he looked at his watch again. Time for a few. He paced impatiently until the librarian brought him the issues he had requested: *The New Yorker, Town & Country, Vogue, Redbook.*

*Town & Country* had run a five-page story, and

when Luke turned to the first page he found himself looking at Jessica, a full-length portrait,
standing alone on the empty stage of the Martin
Beck Theatre, looking pensively into the camera.
She wore a deep blue satin evening gown that left
her shoulders bare; her hair hung in long smooth
waves halfway down her back, and her hands were
clasped loosely before her. She seemed relaxed and
confident, perfectly at home. Beneath the photo
was a caption.

> Jessica Fontaine, winner of this year's Tony
> award for Best Actress in Clifford Odets' *The
> Country Girl.* "Not since the retirement of Con-
> stance Bernhardt have I seen anyone with this
> formidable talent," says producer Ed Courier.
> "Perhaps justifiably, since Ms. Fontaine was a
> protégée and close friend of Ms. Bernhardt's and
> credits her with much of her success."

Luke read the whole story, lingering over the
photographs, taken in Jessica's apartment in New
York, in her country home in Connecticut with an
attached studio for painting and wooded trails
along the river, where she walked in the early
mornings, and at the Martin Beck, in her dressing
room, on stage, and outside the stage door, where
crowds gathered every night for her autograph. He
had forgotten the haunting quality of her beauty.
It was not conventional and therefore was somehow elusive, as if in trying to picture exactly what
Jessica Fontaine looked like, one had to pursue

her. Her eyes were magnificent, large, heavy-lashed, a clear blue-green, but a little too close together for perfection; she had a brilliant smile but in stillness her mouth was a trifle too full, almost pouting; her chin was a smidgen too pointed, her forehead a bit too high, her eyebrows a fraction too heavy. Her skin was luminous and her hair the dark gold of a lioness, but on every other count she just missed the classic look of perfect harmony.

But none of that mattered because there had been vibrancy and radiance in Jessica's glance and smile, and in the moods that swept across her face that made her beauty unforgettable. And of course, Luke thought, there was her acting, which no one who had seen her ever forgot: her emotional intensity, her low musical voice that effortlessly reached the last row in the upper reaches of the top balcony, the gestures with her hands and long fingers that could rivet an audience's attention as they made a moment fraught with importance, the impact of her presence as she strode across the stage or hobbled or drifted or dashed, all eyes following her to see what she would do next. My grandmother was like that, Luke thought. And only a few others.

He turned the pages back and forth, skimming the text and pausing at photographs, and whenever she was quoted he recalled her voice and heard her say the words. He stopped at one line.

"I've thought about other ways of living, and I do have hobbies that give me great pleasure, especially painting, but nothing makes me feel fully alive and in touch with myself as the theater does. Without it, I could never feel whole."

So why had she told Constance she'd lost interest in the theater? It was as if she'd said she'd lost interest in breathing. Which is exactly how I feel, Luke thought, and Constance, too, who never got over it. Because it never goes away.

"Mr. Cameron," the librarian said at his shoulder, "you asked me to tell you when it's almost ten."

Luke looked at his watch. "Damn. I forgot. Thanks." Reluctantly he closed the magazine and left the library. He walked the few blocks to the rehearsal studio but, on the way, ignoring how late he was, he went into a bookstore and found the children's section. A clerk saw his frown and came to help. "These are by author," Luke said.

"Of course. How else would you find what you want?"

"I'm looking for an illustrator."

"Oh. Well, we have an index of illustrators; I can look it up. His name?"

"Her name. Jessica Fontaine."

"Oh, I know her books. She's very good, very unusual." The clerk squatted to take a book from the lowest shelf. "Children love her illustrations. Probably because they have so many secrets."

"Secrets?"

"Well, at least one in every painting." The clerk walked down the aisle, pulling books from different shelves. "And she does real paintings, not run-of-the-mill illustrations. Did you know she's won two Caldecott Medals?"

"No."

"She never went to the ceremonies to receive them in person; I understand she's quite reclusive."

"And the secrets?"

"All the paintings have something hidden in them: a face, a figure, an animal, a word, sometimes a sentence. As if she's saying that life is full of surprises and you never know what you're going to find. Of course children know that better than anyone, don't they?" She handed Luke twelve slim books. "I don't know which ones you want; as far as I know, these are all she's done."

"I'll take them all." He swung the plastic bag from one finger as he walked the long, hot blocks crosstown from Fifth to Eighth Avenue. I'll look at them tonight, he thought, and read some more of the letters. But even as he thought it, he knew that that was no longer enough. He had to see her. And so he would travel to the San Juan Islands, as soon as he could get away.

"*Leaving?*" Monte glared at him. "You've got to be kidding. Well, of course you're kidding; what am I getting excited about? You wouldn't leave a play in the fourth week of rehearsal."

"I said as soon as I can," Luke murmured. "What's with Rachel and Cort? They're behaving as if they hate each other."

"They do, at the moment. Just before you got here he criticized the way she read a line yesterday, she told him he didn't know the first thing about character development, he said she didn't know anything about character, period, or she wouldn't be hanging around with Kent Horne—"

"What?"

"They went to dinner last night."

Luke looked around. "Where is he?"

"She wanted a Diet Coke; he went to get her one."

Luke gazed at the actors sipping iced drinks. "Maybe he'll take up with Abby next."

Monte snorted. "She's three times his age."

"And the classiest woman here. I'll talk to him when he comes back. You'd think he'd be more careful, to make sure everything goes—"

Kent walked in, hugging a brown grocery bag patched with wet. "Afraid I'd lose it," he said, putting it down on the table. The wet spots had torn open and cans were jutting out. "God, I only walked a block, but, you know, cold cans, all that condensation . . ." He looked at Luke. "Something wrong? You were late," he added, as if whatever was wrong could be fended off with an accusation.

"Sit down," Luke said.

"Sure, but let me deliver this first." He took a can from the bag and carried it to Rachel, opening it as he went. They spoke a few words; then he came back and pulled out the chair beside Luke. "Shoot."

"We'll talk at lunch. Let's begin," he said to the cast. "Exactly where you left off. I have a few notes from yesterday, so let's stop at the end of act one and go through them."

Kent pulled out a small notebook. "I did my own last night. Cort's playing this whole act too sweet . . . I don't know how he does it, but he takes my lines and makes them jelly. You've got to sit on him, Luke. And Rachel should be dumber at first; she doesn't see what he's really like. I mean, she falls in love with him but it's more excitement than love, because he's really not a nice guy. Not yet."

Luke nodded. "I know. We're working on it."

They listened to the actors, who had known their lines since the second week but were still working on who they were, and how they would grow in relation to the others. There was too much moving around, Luke thought; their lines were lost in superficial activity. But that always happened in the growth of a play, and it did not bother him. And then, suddenly, the three actors on stage came together and for a few moments everything flowed and merged and was just right. It was as if the sun had broken through heavy clouds and everyone felt it. Monte was sitting straighter, Kent was grinning, and Luke was standing, driven from his chair by a surge of excitement.

Then it was over. In the middle of a line, Abby

suddenly wheeled and strode to the front of the imaginary stage, gesturing toward Rachel. "Luke, I will not tolerate this. She's like a toy some child wound up. Didn't anyone ever tell her to stand still?"

"Me?" Rachel said. "What was I doing?"

"*Moving,*" Abby declaimed, still looking at Luke. "Constantly, perpetually, *interminably.* It's like being in an amusement park with those cars that keep bumping each other. I won't have it."

"I thought I was getting out of your way," Rachel said. "You know, so I wouldn't upstage you."

Abby's eyes flashed and her neck lengthened. "You could never, ever upstage me."

"Rachel," Luke said mildly, "the idea of walking is to get somewhere. If you have a specific place to go to or away from, then do it. Otherwise, just stand still and react to the others. You should move in ways that feel natural, but you always should have a reason. Any problems with that?"

"No. I'll try. But . . . wasn't it *good* for a few minutes? You know, just perfect?"

Kent nodded dreamily. "It was."

"It will happen again," said Luke. "That's the wonder of it. Okay, let's go over my notes."

They sat around the table, pouring cold drinks, leaning forward in a small tight group with Monte at one end and Kent and Luke at the other. Luke glanced at his pad of paper. "I'd like to see everything happen a lot faster beginning about two-thirds into the first act, the lines coming on top of each other, the reactions split-second. This is the time when all of you first get an inkling that everything you've thought for a lifetime may not be true, and I'd like that to build, like a crescendo in a symphony. One way to get into that is to do the lines in slow motion. Abby, would you start? At the moment you come in from the sun porch. But don't lose the meaning of the lines; the trick is to hold on to the sense of what you're saying at all times."

He sat back and listened to them struggle with it. This was one of his favorite exercises, one that required intense concentration and made each phrase sound different not only to the actor speaking it, but to the rest of the cast as well. Speaking and moving in slow motion made everything seem larger and clearer as they had to focus on every syllable, and as they did so they often found new meaning in what they were saying and a new understanding of their emotions. It usually took about three minutes for them to feel what was happening, and when Luke saw their faces change he knew they had reached that sudden moment of feeling their characters expand. Cort and Rachel smiled at each other, their tiff forgotten. Abby put her arm around Rachel. The two supporting actors, who had only a few lines in the first act, watched enviously.

"Okay," Luke said at last. "We'll try that again this afternoon before we go back to act one. By then you should have a feeling for the tension that begins to build there, and I'm hoping your pace will reflect that. Now, this has been a long morning and I think we should go to lunch. Back in an hour, please."

He and Kent walked the short distance to Joe Allen and sat at a table along the red brick wall. Immediately the waiter was there. "You have just an hour, Mr. Cameron?"

"As usual; what's good today?"

The discussion was crisp and brief, and as soon as the waiter served their iced coffees, Luke looked at Kent and smiled. "You look like you're expecting a spanking."

"Isn't that what we're here for?"

"You're too old for one and I don't believe in them. What do you think you've done wrong?"

"Haven't a clue. I could just tell you were pissed."

"I was wondering how long it would take you to go through all the women involved in this play."

Kent stared at him. "That's what's eating you? What difference does it make who I date?"

"I'll tell you what difference it makes. I thought you'd have figured this out by yourself, but since you haven't, I'll try to make it clear. We created something new when we all got together for *The Magician*. We're almost a family. Not quite, but almost. We're almost a business, we're almost a club. Are you following this?" He looked up as the waiter brought their lunch, and shook his head as he saw the size of the meat loaf sandwich on Kent's plate.

"It takes a lot of energy to be a playwright," Kent said. "Oh, black-eyed peas, my favorite. Go on."

"This isn't some mystery I'm talking about: we've got a group of people depending on each other to bring a play to life, but also dealing with their own lives, and every day is a juggling act to keep them separate. Everybody knows—you sure as hell ought to know—that the minute you ask a group of people to work together in an atmosphere of make-believe and exaggerated passions, without letting their own passions interfere, you need to pay attention to what you're doing or it will get sloppy and destructive."

"Hey, all I did was date a couple of them," Kent said.

"You slept with at least one of them, but we won't go into that now." Luke ate some of his salad. "I don't want to sound pretentious about this, but there's more to it than just giving a few talented people a script and sending them up on stage to perform it. There are other things going on and we have to pay attention to all of them. There's almost no chance that this particular group will ever come together again, which is one of the reasons it's different from other groups, but that also means it's easy to get careless. I don't tolerate carelessness in my plays."

"Which means?"

"You know what it means. Put the same amount of effort into being a part of this theater company that you do into writing your play. Put the same kind of effort into getting this play to a brilliant opening night. It's yours, for God's sake; who has a greater stake in it? We have enough tensions that go with the territory; we don't need rivalries or sexual bravado. Especially we don't need a crude kid celebrating his entrance into the big time by screwing all the women who are part of his play."

Kent's face darkened. "You didn't have to say that."

"No." Luke shook his head slightly. "You're right, I didn't. I apologize."

*"You apologize?"*

"It was uncalled for. It doesn't help for both of us to be crude."

"Jesus, you don't quit, do you? Look, you never bothered to ask, but I'll tell you anyway. I didn't grab anybody. I mean, I let them know I thought they were dynamite, but they made the first move. Which I admire. But that's only part of it. Look." He put down his sandwich. "Look," he said again. "I've been all over the place—Europe, Africa, Japan—and I know a lot about the world, I know my way around, but you people make me nervous. This is your turf and you know what you're doing, you've earned the right to be here. I feel like a kid looking up at a bunch of grown-ups in a place where I don't know my way around, not yet anyway. So I grab—well, that's a bad word right now, isn't it?—I hold on to whatever I can. And Marilyn was—"

"We're not talking about specific people."

"Right, but I don't tell locker room stories, ever. It's just that I needed people to tell me how great the play is—"

"I do that. So does Monte."

"I need it all the time! If I don't hear it for a day or two I start to worry that it's no good, that pretty soon everybody'll realize it and you'll call the whole thing off. Or the critics will tear it apart. I've started a new play—I didn't tell you; I didn't tell anybody—and I wake up about two, three every morning scared to death because I'm sure the new one is no good, and neither is *The Magician,* and neither am I. So I grab—I latch on to people who tell me I'm great and then I feel okay for a while. You know, I used to smoke and I'd think I was about to curl up and die if I didn't have a cigarette? This is worse."

"I'll record it for you on a tape loop. You can play it anytime."

"Now, that is one terrific idea. What will you say?"

"Damn it, you know what I'll say."

"Tell me anyway."

"You've written an elegant play, a moving, personal, meaningful play. The actors love it and so do the rest of us and we're going to give it the best production it could have. Will that do?"

"Yeah. When will you do it?"

Luke contemplated him. "I wasn't serious."

"Well, I am. I mean, I know it's a joke and maybe it's stupid, but it'll be like my fix. Oh, what the hell, Luke, I'll behave whether you do it or not, but I'd really appreciate it. It would be my mantra."

Luke shrugged. It always astonished him how much writers needed to be stroked. But then, so did actors and painters and sculptors. Truly creative people were always reaching for more, and what woke them up in the middle of the night filled with fear was the knowledge that they'd never do it all, or even most of it, as well as they hoped to. "I'll make it this weekend," he replied. "Now, can you tell me anything about the new play?"

Kent leaned forward and lowered his voice conspiratorially. "You'll keep it to yourself, right?"

Luke knew it was a good idea as soon as he heard it, with powerful roles for a man and woman in their forties. "Perfect for Jessica," he murmured.

"Who? Jessica?"

"Fontaine."

"Oh. You know, I never think about her, but you're right; she'd be dynamite. I saw her a long time ago in London in *Medea;* she was awesome. But she's been gone forever, hasn't she?"

"Not quite that long."

"So what happened to her?"

"I don't know. I'm going to find out."

"And you think she might do it? God, Luke, if

we could get her . . . but I haven't got much to show her. I mean, I've got most of the first act, but that's all."

"Get me a copy. I'd want to read it, and if I find her, I might show it to her. I won't promise anything; we'll just see what happens." He reached for the check. "Let's go back; we have a lot to do this afternoon."

"Oh, let me. . . ." Kent moved in slow motion to extricate his wallet.

"No, I'll take it. If you learned something, it was worth every penny."

"Well, I did. You're good, you know. You're a terrific director and you're good with the cast, all of us, the crew, too. I'm not too good with people, I admit it, not all the time, anyway, so I admire people who are."

"You'll get better. Just pay attention to what you're doing. Let's go."

Rehearsals resumed with another slow motion exercise, and then went back to the beginning of the play. Kent sat beside Luke, making notes, muttering, fidgeting. Luke looked at him. "You feel it, too."

"Yeah, something's wrong. I don't know why."

"I think I do." He stood and walked to the taped border of the stage. "Abby, are you really angry with Daniel at this point? Why would you be?"

"Good Lord, Luke, he's not paying attention to me! He's thinking about this girl he's met instead of treating me with respect and love."

"So, he's distracted. How does that make you feel? Aside from angry, I mean."

She looked up at the ceiling, one hand rubbing the back of her neck. "I might be confused."

He nodded. "Because he's behaving in a way that you didn't expect. You thought you knew how the world functioned, but now your world seems to be turned upside down."

After a moment, Abby said, "You think I'd be bewildered."

"That makes sense to me."

"Well, now. Bewildered. Yes, I could see that. She's an old woman; she wants her world to be predictable. Well, we all do, don't we. But at her age it's harder to accept not understanding. Let me think about that. It changes everything, even the way I move. I'd move toward him, trying to understand, instead of away from him in anger." A slow smile spread across her face. "We'll try it. Right now. Cort, if we could go back to your entrance . . ."

Luke returned to his chair as the cast took their positions and began the scene again. "I love you," Kent whispered. "You're a genius. Will it cause consternation if I kiss you?" He leaned over and planted a kiss on Luke's cheek. "How did I get so lucky?"

"Shhhh." They watched Abby work through the scene. At first she was tentative, and Luke ached to have Constance up there. But in a few minutes she began to find her direction: she showed puzzlement, then uncertainty and bewilderment, and also, Luke saw with growing excitement, just a hint of fear. "She's got it," he murmured, and he saw the others change their behavior to mesh with hers. Luke and Kent looked at each other and grinned, and Monte said, "God damn, it's just right. What'd you do to Abby? Hypnotize her? She's usually such a terror."

"She loves the play," Luke said.

"And you know how to handle her. Good job."

"Tell her you like it when we break." Luke sat back, filled with the kind of deep satisfaction that came only with such a breakthrough. The feeling was powerful enough to stay with him all afternoon, and beyond, to the evening, when he drove Tricia to Amagansett for the weekend, a date they had made weeks before.

They were guests in Monte and Gladys Gerhart's starkly modern house and they had been given a wing with a sitting room and bedroom facing the beach, and two baths. "My, doesn't Gladys know how to do things," Tricia said, inspecting the rooms as she pulled off her clothes to dress for dinner. "And there's never been a breath of scandal about her. Him, either. Can you imagine a producer married to the same woman for thirty-four years? It violates all the laws of the universe. Luke? Do you agree?"

"About what?"

"The laws of the universe. Are you all right? You're mysteriously silent."

"I'm sorry." He pulled off his shirt. "You know how involved I am when we're this far along with the play."

"The play. Sometimes I think the play becomes a mighty handy excuse for everything. Have you found another lady?"

He shot her a glance. "You'd be the first to hear if I was seeing someone else. And write about it."

"True, but it has just occurred to me that something might be going on besides the play." There was a silence. "So you won't tell me."

"There's nothing to tell."

"Well, there is, but I'm damned if I know what it could be." There was another pause. "Claudia is still seeing Peruggia; did you know that?"

"No. It hasn't been in your column."

"Luke, do you really read it? I mean, more than now and then?"

"All the time."

She came up to him and kissed him. She was naked, her skin tanned and warm in the slanting rays of a setting sun. "And do you approve of it?"

*I can't imagine how someone can make a living putting rumors and outright lies into newspapers where readers will assume that it must be true. What an awful way to live.*

"I don't, and I tell you that every time you ask. But what difference does it make? You have hordes of devoted fans and almost no one in Hollywood makes a move without wondering what you'll say about it. That ought to be enough for you."

Distancing herself from him, she picked up a silk robe and slipped into it. "I like to think you admire me."

"I do. You've made your own way, with no help from anyone, and you do what you've chosen to do very well."

"And it's worth doing."

He chuckled. "No, but your tenacity is remarkable."

"Don't laugh at me. I do the same thing all those talk shows do on television that get millions of people watching. We give people information they want."

He nodded. "You're right. But from what I've seen, people watch those shows and read your column with a kind of malicious glee, and the only way I can figure it out is that watching or reading about a person having his guts scraped out makes them feel safe. It's as if they believe there's only so much agony floating around and if all those other people are suffering, there won't be any left to touch them. 'Serves him right,' they say, or, 'She asked for it,' or, 'Good looks didn't get *her* very far.' Passing judgement on pain that's usually quite real."

Tricia turned to gaze out the window at an occasional runner on the empty beach and the lazy waves of the sound, lapping the sand with little sucking sounds. In another part of the house, someone turned on a radio and a jazzy beat filtered into the room. "I could ruin you with my column."

"I doubt it. But why would you? Is that your goal?"

"Power is." She turned to him. "You know that."

He nodded, understanding again why he still was attracted to her. She was the most direct woman he knew, the most unsparing in her dissection not only of society, but also of herself. She often seemed naive, but in fact she was as tough and knowledgeable as an army general planning an assault on a fort he had studied for years.

"Anyway, I'm having fun," she said dismissively. "Let's stop, shall we? It's getting far too serious for me. Do you care if she's still seeing him?"

"You mean Claudia? *Care* if Claudia is seeing someone? Good Lord, I'd do cartwheels if she found a man she could marry. I'd give the wedding. I'd give the honeymoon. If I could find someone for her, I'd arrange it myself, but you'd put it in your column. 'What Broadway director is playing matchmaker for his ex-wife?'"

Tricia laughed. "I like that. I think I'll do it. I'll make up someone; it always adds spice. Not a director, though. I don't put you in my column."

"Yet."

She contemplated him. "Maybe never. As long as we're friends, anyway. I may have another item about Claudia, though. She and Peruggia are gambling a lot; she took him to the Phelans' and I'm told he's become truly rip-roaring, especially at roulette, more cautious with cards. If he keeps losing, I'll have to do an item on him. How could I ignore so much drama?"

"Why haven't you so far?"

"Well, you stopped that one item I was thinking of running. And he and I had a fling once and I did like him—well, no, not like: I was fascinated. Besotted, you might say, until I woke up. He's not a good guy, Luke. Some people say dangerous. Claudia should watch her step."

"I'll tell her that."

"I didn't know you still see her."

"Now and then. Trish, I'm going back to the city early Sunday morning. If you want to stay here for the day, I won't mind."

"No, I'm sure you won't. What's happening in the city?"

"I have work to do before rehearsal on Monday."

"You're two weeks from opening out of town. How much more can you have to do?"

"Sometimes most of the work is done in the last two weeks. I'm sorry, I know there's a brunch or something and you wanted me to go."

"Some people I thought you'd like to meet."

"Another time."

She untied her robe and let it fall to the floor, standing on her toes to put her arms around him, her breasts crushed against his bare chest. "This isn't to convince you to stay," she murmured, her lips close to his, "because I don't do that and anyway it wouldn't work. It's just because I want to."

"So do I," Luke said.

But by Sunday morning Tricia had orchestrated a chorus of guests and their hosts all urging him to stay for the full social schedule, including brunch for fifty and a cocktail party for two hundred just before they returned to New York. "Not this time," he said. "Another time. I'm sorry." Tricia stayed behind, to return that night with Monte and Gladys. Her eyes were cold and alert as she watched Luke leave.

He reached the city at noon and went first to the rehearsal studio. His footsteps echoed in the large bare space as he walked through parts of the second and third act on the makeshift stage, referring to a diagram as he shifted boxes and wooden chairs, working out new paths between them and a new pattern of movement. Better, he thought, studying it. Of course they'll have to like it, feel comfortable with it, but it adds to the tension and that should keep up the pace. He spent two hours drawing new diagrams, noting all the moves with crayons, one color for each actor. And then he became aware that he was famished.

Time to go home, he thought. Still some more work to do. The Sunday *Times.* Twelve children's books to read. And Jessica's letters.

Dear Constance, this island is no place for people who like to wander; it takes advance planning and some effort to get on and off it. One could own a private plane or boat (both terrific when the weather cooperates), but most people don't, and so their lives must harmonize with ferry schedules. This means lining up in one's car about an hour before departure, traveling for close to an hour to the mainland, then driving eighty miles south to Seattle or forty miles north to Bellingham. It makes grocery shopping quite a project! There is a very nice market in Lopez Village, but for the kind of selection we had in the city, the mainland beckons. However, it does not beckon to me because I have no desire to go anywhere. I'm completely satisfied to be solitary amid waters of a thousand colors—midnight blue, gray, silver, turquoise, blue-gray, dark green, jade—depending on the sky and the clouds.

Isolation is a big part of what makes Lopez beautiful: the pine forests wilder, the beaches more secluded, the cliffs more dramatic. And the island is very private, because most of the houses are tucked away in pine forests, invisible until you're practically at their front door.

My own house is finished. It's not large, but so bright and open it seems to merge with sky and water, serene and self-contained in its own world. I have an attached painting studio much like the one I had in Connecticut, and I've begun a garden. I've left most of my land wild, but a landscaper graded around the house and set down stones for walkways and helped me plant, so now I look from my windows upon overlapping circles of rhododendron, azaleas, blue blossom, fourteen kinds of iris, foxglove, roses . . . and a couple of dozen more I can't recall offhand. (By next year I'll have learned them all by heart.) My driveway and the road beyond it are lined with Scotch broom and when the bushes are in bloom they're a solid mass of yellow flowers that are so vivid it's as if they've absorbed the essence of yellow and left the rest of the world a little paler. I can almost watch everything grow here; the climate is mild and there's plenty of rain and sun. I never had a garden and I like the feeling of being connected to the earth when I work in it. I've planted a few vegetables, nothing very ambitious, though I may venture into more exotic varieties soon. The first time I ate a snowpea off the vine I had the most extraordinary sensation, as if I'd just discovered the absoluteness of food, instead of getting it third or fourth hand in plastic bags at the supermarket.

I hope you got the books I sent you: two novels I've enjoyed and my latest book for children, called *The Secret Room.* There's some talk of turning it into a movie or even a live musical, but none of that interests me. Anyway, it's such a long shot I'm not going to waste my time thinking about it.

Baffled, Luke shook his head. She wrote as if Constance were a casual friend, as if they had no history going back twenty-four years, as if they had not been as close as two women could be. And not a word, so far, to explain her exile—because that's what it sounded like—on Lopez Island.

And what about the man she'd met?

Dear Constance, I stayed awake last night, thinking about your letter. I'm sorry you think I sound remote and indifferent; you must know I never feel that way toward you. The truth is, I'm having a harder time adjusting to being here than I thought I would. Sometimes I sit in my garden, facing the beach and the blue-green water of this tiny cove, and it seems to me that I'm so far from everything and everyone that I hardly have any reality. (I know I said I liked the isolation, but my moods swing up and down with the wind or the hour or the angle of the sun.) All my connections to the people and places and things that once defined my life are gone. There was so much joy in my life that it's hard now to look around and find nothing to remind me of that other Jessica except my memories and occasional items about New York in the Lopez or Seattle papers.

So I feel disconnected. It's as if that train in Canada tore through the center of my life, ripping a huge chasm between then and now, and it changed everything so much that there's no way I can bridge the chasm and go back to what I was. When you ask how I feel, that's one of my answers: disconnected and truncated. Nothing lasts.

Am I sounding maudlin? I do love it here; I'm really fine. It's just that there's so much I have to get used to and learn to take for granted, now that it's my life. I know you felt you were going into exile when you went to Italy but I'm not saying that it's the same with me; I'd never call this exile. It's a new beginning and I'm making a new life.

And that's one reason, dearest Constance, that I can't come to Italy. You know I'd love to see you, but I don't want to leave the islands until I've made my life here and accepted it. I'm still too angry—at ghosts, at amorphous "maybes" and "what-ifs," like a boxer with only shadows to stand up against him—and I have to learn to deal with all of that.

I will deal with it, I will get used to this, I know I will, but, oh, Constance, I miss what I've lost. There's such an *emptiness* that wipes out the world when I stop being busy and suddenly find myself staring into space, longing for . . . everything. You're the one person in the world who can truly understand that, and understand my anger, because I know you had it, too (and probably you'll have it your whole life; I think I will), even though you've always tried to hide it.

Anyway, when I can be positive, I feel that I'm getting acquainted with myself again and I have to do that full time in the place I've decided to call home, so I can't leave it to go to Italy. I've already made friends—the island is so small I've gotten to know almost everyone—and I have my work. And I've got something else to think about. The Seattle Children's Theater is opening a new resident theater and they're commissioning plays for it now. After all the children's books I've illustrated I think I could write a play for children. I don't know, because I've never tried to write, but I may give it a whirl. It would be a way to touch the theater again.

So you see how much is going on in my life. In fact, I think I'll describe my day to you so you can share it. Every day is the same here, with minor variations, which is one of the charms of Lopez.

Luke skimmed the rest of the letter and the one that followed it. He was looking for a specific topic.

. . . usually ride very early, before breakfast, and then I garden, and as I work the sun climbs higher in the sky and slowly the plants turn pale green and then gold . . .

. . . paint in the afternoons when the light turns so clear it's as hard as a diamond with no soft edges or shadows . . .

. . . discovered Lopez Island Vineyards, a very good wine and they gave me a tour . . .

. . . ferry to San Juan, the largest island, and found myself being drafted by their theater committee to help direct . . .

. . . lunch with Rita Elliott, who designs jewelry and has her own . . .

Suddenly the earlier words registered and Luke went back to the line about San Juan Island.

. . . asked by their theater committee to help direct their production of *Pygmalion.* At first I refused, but they're quite impressive in their ambitions—it's a small company and none of them has seen *Pygmalion,* though they've all seen the movie *My Fair Lady*—and they were so excited about my being here that finally I said I'd do it, just this once. Do you remember that time in Chicago when you and I talked about how every actor dreams of directing? I've even thought that someday I'd combine acting and directing. But that's over and done with. I'm not part of the theater anymore. What I'll be doing at the San Juan Community Theater and Arts Center is a small diversion, a variation in my daily schedule. The play will run for three nights, and that will be plenty.

Luke shook his head. There was something odd about the way she wrote. It was too deliberate. Too careful. As if she didn't want to give anything away. The only time he found the liveliness of her earlier letters was when she wrote about riding or gardening. He skimmed a few more pages, until he found the topic he was looking for, and some of her old vitality as well.

His name is Richard; he's a sculptor living year-round on Lopez. I'd bought two of his pieces before I met him, a bronze horse's head which I've put in the garden, and a mother and two children in marble, an abstract of flowing lines and great tenderness that makes me think of my parents and of you. I met him one day digging clams in a tiny cove on the other side of the island. Picture this remarkably romantic meeting: two people at the edge of the water with large battered buckets beside them. They're using trowels to burrow beneath the wet sand, flinging water and sand in all directions, so that they have flecks of sand stuck in their eyelashes and pasted by seawater to cheeks and foreheads. Everything is shiny and dank with mist, and sand is under their fingernails and in the crevices of their shorts and T-shirts, as well. He's extremely handsome, medium height, blond, with dark brown eyes, a trim blond beard and an odd sort of lope when he walks. And we laugh together. I've missed that; I'd forgotten how much I need it.

Luke slammed the letter on the table. *Why am I wasting my time doing this? I should have been at work a long time ago, or at least reading the Sunday paper.* He took his tray to the kitchen, aware of the smothering silence of his apartment. It felt unlived in. Martin was away, no one was telephoning, and Luke had not spent much time there in the past few weeks, and when he was there he'd been mostly in the library. He stopped to pull up the roman shades in the living room, but at the first blast of sunlight, he lowered them again. Give the air conditioners a fighting chance, he thought; especially since no one is here to admire the view.

He cleaned up the kitchen, putting his dishes in the dishwasher and wiping the counters. Everything was spotless; Martin and the housekeeper took excellent care of everything and Luke was hardly a presence there. Invisible, he thought. Irrelevant. But it's a home, it's my home, and I ought to make it feel like one. He looked through the kitchen door at the dining room table that had been used only three times in the past year. I should make this place feel lived in. Entertain, host some benefits, invite friends and their kids to play billiards. Or I could put up the Ping-Pong table and plug in the pinball machine Monte gave me for Christmas a couple of years ago, as a joke. It would be nice to have kids around.

*Am I sounding maudlin? I do love it here; I'm really fine. It's just that there's so much that I have to get used to and learn to take for granted, now that it's my life.*

But I am used to it, Luke thought; I do take it for granted. This has been my life for a long time.

Except that Jessica wasn't in it, and now she is.

He went back to the library and was unfolding the next letter when the telephone rang. "Luke," Claudia said, "can you have dinner with me tomorrow night?"

There was something in her voice that told him he could not put her off. "Yes, but we'll be rehearsing late. Is nine o'clock all right?"

"Any time. Will you come here? I'd like you to."

"I don't think so. I'll meet you at Bernardin. If I'm a little late, ask Maguy to give you a wonderful appetizer and a bottle of the Guenoc Chardonnay."

"But you won't be late."

"Not if I can help it."

Hanging up, he thought wryly that he might never be off the hook with Claudia; she would never go away and he would never find a way to shut her out of his life. He went back to Jessica's letter. It was a description of her work on *Pygmalion,* oddly detached, he thought, as if she were writing not from pleasure or excitement, but from duty. But he did not linger over it; he was looking for a name. And then he found it.

Richard has his own high-speed launch, which is a great luxury now that I'm commuting for rehearsals. He delivers me to San Juan and then returns to Lopez to work in his studio rather than sitting about watching the cast stumble around the stage. Well, that's too cruel. But the truth is, they don't have much experience (some have none), so this is all going to take some time. Fortunately we have ten weeks. (Ten weeks, when we always thought anything more than four or five was a great luxury.)

That's all about the handsome sculptor? Luke thought. He riffled through letters and read more bits of paragraphs.

Well you were right, dear Constance, the play got better to a point and then got stuck there. We're working hard, but what we have now is probably the best we can do. I do like the people in the cast . . .

I flew to Seattle for the day and visited Elliott Bay Book Company to sign books and meet some schoolchildren who were visiting the store.

Two days to opening night and everyone is so wound up with excitement and nerves that I've become a kind of nanny . . .

. . . sold out for the three-night run and
we've extended it to a fourth night. Opening
night was wildly successful and I was the only
one who thought it was dreadful. But everyone
else was so *alive* with happiness . . . and isn't
that what the theater is all about? To make us
more alive?

. . . they asked me if I'd go back to New
York now, and I said of course not. I'm
perfectly happy here; I have everything I want.

Reading as he walked, Luke went to the kitchen.
He put water to boil and scooped coffee grounds
into the French press. Waiting for the water, he
leaned against the granite countertop and read on.
And found no mention of Richard.
*What happened to him?*
The teakettle whistled. He poured the hot water
into the coffeemaker and inserted the lid with its
plunger, then went to the library, took another letter from the box, and returned to the kitchen, once
more leaning against the counter, waiting for the
coffee to steep.

Dear, dear Constance, you sounded so
alarmed on the telephone. I wonder if you really believed me when I said I was fine. I'm
never sure whether you do or not, ever since
you pointed out, a long time ago, that two fine

actresses can fool anybody, even each other.
Well, I'm not trying to fool you; I really am
fine. I wasn't sure why you asked me, but the
answer is no: I've come to the conclusion that I
won't ever marry. It could be that I'm just not
ready—although, if I'm not ready at thirty-
seven I probably never will be—but more likely
it's that I just wouldn't be good at it.

But you mustn't worry about me. It's not
good for you and this is the truth: I love my
house and my garden, I'm truly happy when
I'm illustrating books and riding, and I've
made wonderful friends here, writers, innkeep-
ers, restaurant owners, shopkeepers, farmers,
and yes, Richard, too. And—my big news for
today—I'm getting a dog! My neighbor has a
litter of black Labs and he gave me my choice
and I chose the most beautiful and by far the
smartest. He's delivering her Saturday, and I'll
send pictures as soon as I have them. I've
named her Hope.

Luke took a mug of coffee back to the library
and ran his thumb over the letters behind the
marker he used to show where he left off each time
he stopped reading. There still were dozens he had
not read: the ones that had filled the three years
from *Pygmalion* to the time Constance died. He
remembered that he had wondered, when he was
in Italy, whether Jessica had known of Con-

stance's death. She must have known. Because the letters stopped.

He sipped his coffee and gazed at the jumble on the table. *Why did she name her dog Hope? What was she doing now? Did she change her mind and marry someone? Was she living with someone?*

And he knew that he could not wait any longer, spending time with Jessica only through her letters. He had to see her.

He reached for the telephone. His hand hovered above it. *The Magician* was opening in Philadelphia in eleven days. But there was no reason now that he could not take a weekend off. It had been one of the smoothest rehearsals on record and everyone knew it, even Cort, who had become an excellent Daniel as soon as Kent admitted that some of the changes Cort had demanded had made the play stronger. They would continue to rehearse; there still would be problems to deal with; but a weekend off would be good for all of them.

Besides, Luke thought, I have an obligation. I was supposed to deliver Constance's collection of plays. I should have done it long before this. She wanted Jessica to have it.

He felt a surge of anticipation as he picked up the telephone, the excitement of something new, something that had been building for a long time. He looked up the number for the airline. His travel agent would not be at work on Sunday, but airline desks would be open and it would not be difficult

for the agent on duty to get him tickets to Seattle
and Lopez Island on Friday evening, and back to
New York late Sunday night.

## CHAPTER 8

Claudia wore black, a lace blouse beneath a silk
suit that made her seem taller, her beauty more
formal, and people turned to watch as Maguy led
her to Luke's table. "Luke, dear, don't get up." She
bent and swiftly kissed him, then sat in the chair
Maguy held for her. "Were you waiting long?"

"A few minutes."

"I'm so sorry. But you know I hate sitting at a
table alone."

"So you made sure I'd be here first. Were you
watching for me?"

She smiled gaily. "Of course. From Palio. I saw
you walk across the plaza. Have you ordered
wine?"

"Yes." The sommelier arrived, and Luke waited
for the ritual of opening and pouring before turning back to Claudia. "You're looking very well.
That's a wonderful suit."

"Why, Luke, how sweet. And how lovely that
you noticed. I bought it just for tonight." She
raised her glass. "To us."

"You know I won't drink to that. I don't even

know what it means." He felt the familiar stirrings of impatience and frustration that always came to him when she behaved like a child, believing that if she repeated something often enough it would be an indisputable fact. "To you," he said, touching her glass. "Now tell me what's wrong."

"Nothing's wrong."

"Last night you sounded as if you needed help."

"Tell me about the play. Are you ready for previews in Philadelphia?"

"Claudia."

She studied the menu, then set it aside. "I heard your advance ticket sales are fabulous. You must be so pleased. Of course, it's because of your name. And I suppose Abby Deming's; but everyone knows it's mainly you."

"Is it about Ed Peruggia?"

"Luke, why can't we just have dinner and be happy together without all this probing?"

He contemplated her for a moment. "Did you ever call Gladys about volunteer work?"

Claudia sighed deeply. "She called me."

"And?"

"I said I'd try, one of these days when something interesting comes along."

"Interesting?"

"Luke, she does the worst kind of drudgery! Stuffing invitations into envelopes, for God's sake. Typing names and addresses into computers. Haven't they heard of secretaries?"

"Those organizations are raising money. They have to keep expenses down. That's what volunteers are all about."

"I know that; good heavens, do you think I'm a child? But they could afford at least one secretary if they were better organized. Anyway, I can't see myself sitting there all day stuffing envelopes. I said I'd help with flower arrangements, decorating the tables, things like that. Fun things."

"Maybe it's like any job: you have to serve an apprenticeship and work up to fun things."

"It's not a job; there's no salary."

"It's a job because it's work, and people with money and free time do it for the causes they care about. Why don't you let yourself try it? You spend more energy keeping yourself bored than you would giving some shape and purpose to your days. You wouldn't have to start out full time; offer Gladys two or three days a week. You might enjoy thinking about something besides yourself for a change."

"I'm going to order," she said defiantly, and beckoned to the waiter. "Salmon. Oh, wait a minute." The waiter refilled her wineglass, then watched attentively as she opened the menu she had examined earlier and once again studied each item carefully. "Salmon," she said at last. "I think." She scanned the menu again. "Yes, I think so. And bisque. Or do I want the salad? Luke, should I have the salad?"

"If that's what you want."

Claudia heard his voice tighten as it always did when she tried to force him to make decisions for her. She sighed. "Bisque." She waited until Luke had ordered and then said briskly, "Now tell me about the play."

"Tell me about Ed Peruggia," Luke said evenly.

"Luke, you know I like to save serious discussions for the end of dinner."

"So that if we're not finished we can go back to your place. I learned that a long time ago. But we're not going to do that, so if you want to talk you'll do it now."

She made a gesture of resignation. "He says he wants to marry me."

"Do you want to marry him?"

"I want to be married to you. I should never have agreed to a divorce; I should have—"

"I thought we were talking about Peruggia. Are you asking my permission to marry him?"

"I don't need your permission."

"My blessing, then."

"I don't need that, either. Damn it, why are you always *directing* me? Giving me permission, or blessings, telling me where to go and what to do, what would be a good experience for me, what would 'give shape to my days'—whatever the hell that means. You're always trying to manipulate me, as if I'm one of your actors who can't make a move until you say left or right."

"Keep your voice down."

"See? You're still directing me!"

Luke took a long breath. "Tell me what you want me to do."

"Take me back."

"I won't do that and you know it. What else?"

"Tell me what to do about Ed. I don't think he really intends to marry me. He plays with people— you know?—and sometimes he's mean. A mean person. He says things and then sits back to see how people react."

"And how did you react?"

"Where's the waiter? Would you pour me some more wine?"

"You're drinking too much, Claudia."

"Don't tell me—!"

"All right." He filled her glass.

"We need another bottle."

"No, we don't."

"Luke, please. We haven't even started eating yet. We have to have wine with food."

After a moment he shrugged and signaled for another bottle. "You were telling me how you reacted."

"I told him I'd think about it. I told him I didn't think he was in love with me."

"And he said?"

"That he adored me and wanted to spend the rest of his . . . you know, the usual stuff."

"The same things I once said."

"But you meant them. I don't think Ed means much of anything he says. He's not really very nice, you know—*do* you know him?"

"No. But I've heard that he's not a good man."

"Tricia probably told you that; she had an affair with him once and now she hates him. At least he told me she hates him and he hates her, too. I suppose I could end up hating him; sometimes I already do."

"Then why are you thinking of marrying him?"

"Because what else can I do? And don't tell me to call Gladys or I'll scream."

"I'm listening," he said.

"I can't stand being alone, Luke. I've got to have somebody fill the space around me. I've got to know whom I belong to and how I'm supposed to behave."

"No one can give that to you," Luke said quietly. "It has to come from within you."

"I don't know how to do that. Not everybody can, you know. Some people need help, because there's too much space around them and no boundaries. I need to know where the boundaries are, Luke, and how to make up a life. I just float. I don't belong anywhere." She put her hand on his. "I look at other people and they're busy organizing their lives as if they're organizing dinner parties or board meetings. They have all these *goals*. They have plans and lists and they're always *deciding* things. My God, it's like they cut notches in their belt to show how much they've done. Raised money, won prizes, bought a company, got elected to something . . . they're so damn busy! And they feel good about themselves. *I can't do that.* I never feel good about myself. I never know what I should be doing to feel happy or satisfied or just to get through the days without feeling lost and . . . loose. That's what I want you to do, Luke; help me be happy and settled. Not floating. I thought you cared about me enough to give me help when I need it."

He shook his head. "There's nothing I can—"

"There is. You know there is. Give me your name. Marry me. Then I'll really be Claudia Cameron. It's a fake now, it doesn't make sense to have your name but not be your wife. I know how to be your wife, Luke, I know what you expect of me. I know what everybody expects of me. I'll have goals and plans and I'll get things done."

"Because they're my goals and plans."

"Yes, of course; what do you think I'm talking about? You have enough for ten people; good heavens, you keep two assistants and a secretary busy full time. But you know I could help you in ways they can't. You told me I was a good hostess. How many dinner parties have you given in the past few years? I can take trips with you and talk to you about your plays and make love to you . . . whatever you want. Didn't I do whatever you wanted when we were married? All you had to do was tell me what you wanted and how you wanted it done, and I took care of it. Damn it, you do it for your actors, you could do it for me! Then I wouldn't be alone. And neither would you."

The waiter refilled her wineglass, then served their soup. Luke pushed his aside and turned his hand to clasp hers. "Listen to me. All of us are alone. We have to figure out by ourselves what we'll do with our lives, what name we want—which means what reputation—what we think people expect of us, and how we want to live and shape our days. You knew what I meant when I said that earlier. We fill our days and give them substance so that late at night we can look back and measure what we've done and how well we've done it, and think about what's waiting to be done tomorrow. I can't do that for anyone but myself. I can do it for actors on a stage because I'm working with a script and *I know how it ends.* But I don't have that luxury in life. All I have is each day, and my hopes for tomorrow and as far ahead as I dare plan, knowing that none of it may actually happen."

"You could help me do it."

"I can't. You wouldn't be happy and neither would I."

She put her chin up. "I'll marry him."

"From what I hear, I don't think he'll make you happy, either. But I can't stop you."

"You really don't mind imagining me in his bed. . . ."

"I'm sure you've already been there. And, no, I don't mind imagining it if I know you've chosen it freely."

"Oh, freedom." She made a dismissive gesture. "I've got too much of that."

"Do you want your soup?"

"No."

"You can take them both," Luke said to the waiter, and he and Claudia sat in silence while the soup was removed and their main courses were served.

Claudia sniffed several times, as if putting away tears, then gave Luke a trembling smile. "Well!" she said gaily. "The salmon looks wonderful, as usual. Did I tell you about the salmon at Ralph Lauren? He really is so on top of things, Ralphie. I mean there were these elegant packages of whole sides of smoked salmon from Scotland, and everybody was snapping them up . . ."

And Luke knew that she had decided that she had done as much as she could for this night and would wait for another one. He let it go. It was easier than forcing her to admit that she was living a fantasy—assuming he could force her to admit it—and he was in no mood to prolong the evening. In fact, dinner turned out to be more pleasant than he had expected. Claudia could do that when she wanted to and since, finally, he did answer her questions about the play, and smile at her anecdotes about people they both knew, they had enough conversation to see them through espresso and a shared caramel dessert.

But it was Jessica whom he thought about when he got home, and he thought about her the next morning when his airline tickets were delivered, because suddenly it had occurred to him that he was not sure she still lived on Lopez Island. Her letters about a new house, about gardening and riding and the production of *Pygmalion,* had all been written three years earlier. She could be anywhere by now.

At breakfast, he took Constance's box with him to the terrace and pulled out the last few letters, to look for clues. They were sparser than her earlier ones, warm and loving but almost completely barren of private thoughts or feelings. Whatever Jessica Fontaine was at this time in her life, she was not revealing it to Constance, even though she described in detail the books she was illustrating and others she had read, her gardens and a new greenhouse, and descriptions of people she knew.

Her garden. A greenhouse. Probably on Lopez, Luke thought. She was still using stationery with an embossed fountain in the upper left corner, but where once the words "The Fountain, Lopez Island, Washington State" had been below it, now there was nothing. Probably Lopez, he thought again, but it was a long way to go without being sure. And so, later that day, when rehearsal broke for lunch, he called her publishing house to get her address.

No one would give it to him. He was transferred from the publicity department to customer relations to the art department, the editorial department, even the sales department. They all said they did not know, and anyway, it was the policy of the publishing house not to reveal an author's whereabouts.

"She's not an author, she's an illustrator," he exploded to a secretary in the office of the president and publisher.

"We have the same rule for both," the secretary said. "And Miss Fontaine has been very specific, Mr. Cameron. She absolutely does not want her address given out. The people you talked to were telling the truth. They don't know where she lives. All her correspondence goes through this office."

"Let me talk to Warren," Luke said. He made it a rule not to use social contacts for private requests, and so he had not gone directly to the top when he made his first telephone call, or even his third or fifth, but he had to get back to rehearsal, and he was out of patience. And he had known Warren Bradley casually for years, at dinner parties and benefits, and even as a guest in his home for a few small dinners.

"Luke, it's always a pleasure to talk to you," Bradley said, "but I can't help you. Miss Fontaine has requested—well, in fact she's demanded—that we keep her address within this office. I wouldn't give it to anyone."

"Just tell me one thing," Luke said. "Does she still live on Lopez Island?"

"What?"

"In a house that she built. On a bay."

"God damn it, why have you been tearing through every department in this company if you already knew that?"

"Thanks, Warren. I knew she'd lived there in the past; I wasn't sure she still does."

"Luke, do you know her?"

"I met her years ago. Why?"

"Because as far as I can tell, no one's seen her and that's the way she wants it. We talk on the phone, we use faxes and FedEx for letters, contracts, memos, manuscripts . . . and that's it. Lopez is a small place and I'm sure you can find her if you want to, for whatever reason, but I'd think twice about it, if I were you. She must have powerful reasons for wanting to be left alone."

"I don't intend to batter her door down."

"But you are going to see her?"

"If I can. I want to take her something that Constance left her in her will."

"You could ship it to her."

"I'd rather not."

"Well, call me when you get back, and tell me what she's like now. I remember her so clearly . . . but of course that was a long time ago. She's become an important illustrator, but I can't imagine why she'd give up the theater for that. Let me know."

"I will. Thanks, Warren. I won't tell anyone we talked. Including Jessica."

For the rest of that week, he had no time to read Jessica's letters or her books. A hundred small details had come up, many of them issues that had been pushed aside in the early weeks of rehearsal, and now, with only ten days left, he and Monte and Fritz were together every night, smoothing them out.

"That entrance always was awkward," Fritz said as they looked at a diagram of the stage. "Martha complained about it a long time ago."

"Move the door," Luke said. They stared at him. "About a foot and a half downstage. Then when Martha comes in there's no way she'll miss seeing Lena; she'll practically stumble over her."

"I like it," Monte said. "Fritz?"

"Not a bad idea. Okay. What about the tea things in act two? The silver reflects the spotlights and there's these blinding glares shafting out to the audience."

"Use china," Luke said. "I know Kent wanted silver, but if we can't, we can't."

"China," Fritz muttered, and wrote it down.

"I was thinking," Monte said, "that we ought to hold a while longer before the final curtain."

"While they stand there like dummies?" Fritz asked.

"It's a very moving moment. Give the audience time to absorb it."

"Let's talk to the cast," Luke said. "I like it, but I want to make sure they're comfortable with it. Anything else?"

"Costumes," Fritz said. "Abby doesn't like her shoes."

"Get new ones. The greatest actress in the world can't act if her feet hurt."

"She doesn't like the way they *look.*"

"I'll say it again: get new ones. Fritz, we can't have her worrying about shoes, for whatever reason."

The lists went on and on and it was not until Luke was on the plane for Seattle that he finally settled down to read the twelve slender children's books he had brought with him.

The stories, for children two to six years old, were amusing and lively, some deserving close attention, but Luke was concentrating on the illustrations. And as he studied them, he knew that they would have captivated him no matter who the artist was.

Their styles varied, from Russian fairy-tale art to French folk art, from African tribal art to modern American realism, and they were done in watercolors, oils, charcoal, even crayon, depending on the style. But in spite of their differences, all the illustrations gave one overwhelming impression: that nothing was real.

Luke tried to put his finger on what made him feel that way. He found the hidden drawings, ingeniously flowing into and out of other parts of the pictures but clearly visible once discovered, and he knew how exciting it would be for children to discover them and show them to parents and friends. But they were not the reason that he felt this pervasive unreality. There was something else, something more elusive. It was not until he had finished dinner and put his head back, worn out from the long days and nights of the week just ended, that it came to him. "They're dreams," he murmured aloud. His eyes opened and he sat up and turned on his reading light again.

"May I bring you something?" the steward asked. "Another glass of wine?"

"Coffee," Luke said. "Thanks." He pulled his table from its niche in the arm of his seat and spread the books on it, opening them at random. The steward reached across to set a cup of coffee on the small ledge between the seats, but he barely noticed. He was absorbed in the drawings. And he saw that even the most mundane activities in them—a young girl raking leaves, a boy taking out the garbage after dinner, a dog hiding under a porch—were like dreams: a little bit distorted. Sometimes the pictures erased boundaries and ran into each other as dreams did. Sometimes they were multiple images that overlapped as dreams did. Sometimes they became blurred at the edges, then faded to nothing, as dreams did. Everything was recognizable, but nothing was exactly as it was in reality.

*Everything a little off center.* Marilyn Marks had said that about her first set for *The Magician* when she described it to Luke and Kent. *A woman who's always been different—and now she can't figure out what's gone wrong. That feeling of things askew, like a dream that she's trapped in.*

Luke put away the books and his table, once again turned out his light, and pushed back his seat. A movie flickered on the large screen at the front of the cabin, but he closed his eyes and saw Jessica, her photographs he had seen in the library, his memory of her on stage, the way he had pictured her with his grandmother in Italy from descriptions of her visits in her letters. *Trapped in a dream.* Was she? Nothing she had written hinted at that. Maybe he'd missed something; he'd read many of her letters so quickly, hungry for the next. *That feeling of things askew.* Well, it doesn't matter, he thought drowsily. Because I don't have to rely on letters anymore. I'll be able to talk to her about everything, find out everything I want to know.

He arrived in Seattle at ten o'clock—one o'clock in the morning, New York time—and took a taxi to Union Lake, where the seaplane he had reserved was waiting for him. They flew low over dozens of small islands, tiny islets and barren rocks thrusting out of the sea, and the pilot pointed out Lopez when it was still some distance away: a handful of lights in the darkness. Jessica's island, Luke thought, and suddenly realized how tense he was. She didn't want to see people from New York; she didn't want to see anyone except the cast of *Pygmalion* and her friends on the island. *I should have called. I should have pushed Warren to give me her phone number. But if she'd refused to see me . . .*

The plane banked and Luke saw the island at an angle, a dark sliver in darker water. He was struck by its compactness, and it seemed an act of desperation to him that she had chosen it, abandoning one of the most brilliant acting careers in history, and one of the world's greatest cities, to settle on this tiny piece of land floating in waters invisible and unknown to the rest of the country. Coming in low, they passed over the cluster of lights. "Lopez Village," the pilot said. "Downtown, if they had a downtown." Luke had a quick impression of other lights widely scattered about the island: isolated ones in open fields and single ones flickering like tiny stars amid the forests. Private homes, he thought. And one of them was Jessica's. His hands were clenched. Almost there.

They landed on an airstrip a few miles beyond the village. To the east a three-quarter moon was rising, its reflection a rippling pale ribbon that stretched across the black waters of Puget Sound to the dock where Luke stepped out of the plane. Angie's Cab Courier drove him along deserted roads winding narrowly through dark pine forests, then up a gravel drive to the Inn at Swifts Bay, where he had reserved a room. It was the inn where Jessica had told Constance she had stayed when she first came to the island, and Luke stood in the entryway trying to imagine her there.

The inn was vaguely Tudor on the outside, but the atmosphere inside was a riot of cluttered Victoriana. In the living room, the shelves of an antique hutch were crammed with fuzzy white rabbits dressed in Victorian costumes; a blue velvet wing-backed chair was adorned with lace antimacassars; a round skirted table was piled with books on flower gardens, architecture and art; shelves flanking the fireplace were stuffed with books, pictures, memorabilia and island artifacts, and on the top shelf straw dolls stood watch over the scene below.

Luke was smiling, thinking Jessica must have imagined she had walked onto a stage set, when his host came in, his hand outstretched.

"Robert," he said, "and of course you're Lucas Cameron. You must be totally out on your feet; it's halfway to dawn your time, isn't it? I'd show you around—hot tub, video library, all the rest—but I assume you'd rather see your room." He led the way down a narrow hall. "I think you'll find everything you want; would you like coffee, by the way? Or tea or port?"

"Nothing, thanks; they fed us all the way across the country." Luke took a swift glance around the room, appreciating the care that had gone into it, and smiled at more rabbits on the bed. Rabbits were not his style, but he admired anyone who was not afraid of excess.

"Will you be biking tomorrow?" Robert asked. "Carl Jones rents bikes and delivers to our door."

"No, I've come to see someone. If I can find her address. Maybe you can help me."

Robert's eyes narrowed. "You've come to see

someone and you don't know where she lives? We respect people's privacy here; I doubt that I could help you."

Luke nodded thoughtfully, and lied, which he knew, in a community this size, could come back to haunt him, but he was tired and it was all he could think of. "I had her address; I've lost it. I know she built a house on a bay about three years ago. Very private, she said, and the beach has a cliff on one side and a forest on the other. I'm a friend from New York. I haven't seen her for years, but my grandmother left her something in her will and I've brought it to her. I'd be grateful for your help. Her name is Jessica Fontaine."

Robert shook his head decisively. "Jessica doesn't see people, especially people who just walk in off the street."

"Of course she sees people; what are you talking about? Look, I'll say it again. I'm a friend. More important, my grandmother was probably her closest friend. She died a few months ago and I want to talk to Jessica about her. There isn't anything sinister in this; if she doesn't want to see me, I'll leave."

Robert contemplated him. "I'll think about it. Sleep well; breakfast is at eight."

Furious, Luke started to say something, but fatigue washed over him and he turned on his heel and closed the door of his room behind him. He paced three times from the fireplace to the sliding terrace doors and then he could not stay upright any longer and he went to bed. In spite of his anger, he slept soundly and woke with a start to the crowing of roosters, not knowing where he was. *I hear roosters crowing in the morning (actually, they keep it up all day; are they supposed to do that?).* And then he knew: he was on Jessica's island and soon he would be with her.

He dressed in chinos and an open-necked short-sleeved shirt and would have refused Robert's enormous breakfast to get started immediately, but he did not want to seem insulting. He ate as much as he could, then pushed the swinging door and went into the kitchen, where Robert was cooking while his partner, Chris, served.

"Not allowed," Robert said cheerfully. "No guests behind the scenes."

Luke nodded. "I want to thank you for breakfast; it was wonderful. But I can't wait any longer; I need to know how to get to Jessica's house. I have only today and tomorrow morning; I have to be back in New York Sunday night."

Robert flipped a pancake. "I called her, but she wasn't home. You did know her in New York?"

"I did."

"Socially?"

"Yes."

"And your grandmother was her closest friend? Big difference in ages."

"They had a lot in common. And they loved each other."

Robert used his spatula to lift the edge of a pancake and look at its underside. He stirred something in a pot at the back of the stove. "She's a very
nice person, very quiet, a good neighbor." He
glanced at Chris, who nodded, then he turned
back to Luke. "But she lives alone and she doesn't
have any social life and we think she ought to.
We've tried but she's turned us down. Very nicely,
of course, but very definitely. So we worry about
her. Well, she's on Watmough Bay on the south
shore of the island. You might miss the driveway
because it looks like a trail that doesn't go anywhere, but watch for her sign: it's the picture of a
fountain."

"Thank you. I'll call a taxi."

"Oh, take the truck. Nobody's using it; it just
sits there. Stop in the village, though, and get some
gas; I think it's pretty low."

"That's good of you." His anger was gone. He
had had an excellent breakfast, the sun was burning through early-morning clouds, he had trans-
portation. And he was on his way to see Jessica.
He felt wonderful.

The truck sat high off the ground and Luke saw
the panorama of the island as he drove on two-
lane roads between forests and open fields. He
caught glimpses of water through the pines until,
suddenly, the road curved and he was at the water's
edge, small waves lapping gently at narrow
beaches where driftwood bleached white in the sun

and dune grasses waved in the light breeze. A few minutes more and he was surrounded by forest again, dense pines and firs rising from a floor of ferns. At last he came to a broad open space of grassy fields beside the water, with a cluster of one-story buildings, all of blue-gray wood. Once again he thought of a movie set: a tiny village scattered over an almost treeless plain beneath an enormous sky. There was a food market, a real estate office in back of the barbershop, a bakery, an artist's cooperative, a bookstore, a post office up the road, a fire station, a library that looked as if it had once been a schoolhouse, a bank, a church, a thrift shop, and, oddly, an espresso stand. Two weathered buildings were the Lopez Historical Museum and nearby was an even more weathered performance pavilion.

At the gas station, he leaped from the truck and while he was filling the tank, several people greeted him, commenting that he must be staying at the Inn at Swifts Bay since Robert had loaned him his truck, and wishing him a good visit. Amused, Luke paid and drove on. A small community, he reflected, increasing his speed. A place that respects privacy. He laid Robert's map on the seat beside him and followed it, driving around the island to the south shore and Watmough Bay.

He was clenching the wheel as he slowed down, looking for a sign with a picture of a fountain. And he found it where the forest was most dense, hiding whatever might be within or beyond it: a beach, the water, a house. The sign was a wooden rectangle, darkened by rain and sun, with a deeply etched fountain that matched the one on Jessica's letters to Constance. There was no numbered address and no name.

Luke parked the truck off the road and walked down the trail of packed earth and forest grasses, barely wide enough for a car. The trail curved and he saw the gleam of water and then a low house of stone and wood. A woman was in the garden that stretched along one side of the house. She was cutting roses, moving in and out of sunlight and shadows, laying each rose in a basket that hung on her arm.

Luke's heart was pounding as he strode toward her. Then, abruptly, he stopped. He was hidden by flowering bushes and a large spruce tree, and he stood there in the dimness, puzzled and let down. This wasn't Jessica; he obviously had the wrong house. *Unless it's her housekeeper. Or maybe a friend.*

He stood still, less than twenty feet from her, frowning as his eyes grew accustomed to the sudden shifts in sunlight and shadow through which the woman moved. She was not tall, or perhaps she was, but her back was stooped and she limped, leaning heavily on a cane. Her face was thin and drawn, deeply lined and so pale it was almost colorless. What could be seen of her hair beneath her brimmed woven hat was pale silver-gray, cut short, leaving her frail neck exposed. She wore a simple white cotton dress that almost reached her ankles; it had a scoop neck and short sleeves, and when she reached out to cut another flower and Luke saw the curve of her arm, the strong, mobile wrist above her gardening glove, and then looked again for a long moment at her face, he knew that of course it was Jessica.

A shadow of Jessica. A faded image. A photograph, dulled and brittle with age. But she was not old. She was forty.

He stood there for a long time, his thoughts in turmoil. His expectations and certainties of what he would find had been so vivid that he felt as if he had been betrayed. He remembered how he had envisioned this moment when he was on the plane to Seattle. He had finished looking at Jessica's books and had lain back, half-asleep, imagining himself ringing her doorbell, being greeted by the woman whose pictures he had been poring over so recently, hearing again the vibrant musical voice that he had never forgotten. He had seen himself giving her the carton that was now in the back of Robert's truck, sitting in her house and talking about Constance and then about herself: about what had brought her to Lopez and when she might come back to New York. He had imagined hours of conversation filled with the intelligence and passion, the wit and sophistication, that had filled her letters.

Instead he had found a woman so plain she was almost homely, as insubstantial as a mirage, looking far older than her years, moving clumsily, without grace or vitality. He watched her limp around the corner of the house and out of his view, but he continued to look at her garden and the strip of beach and the bay beyond. Her roses were magnificent, tall and strong, their colors intense, and Luke thought their velvet richness had made her look paler still. He tried to remember what her eyes had looked like, but they had been hidden by the brim of her hat, even when she'd looked in his general direction. But he had seen enough of her face to know that there had been no passion in it, and, though she had been absorbed in her flowers, it was a quiet absorption, without fervor, that of a recluse who did not smile very much or string words together into conversations. She was a woman to whom he would never give a second glance if he passed her on the street. She was so unlike the woman of his imagination that he could not fathom now what had so captivated him in her letters. In fact, he could barely remember what she had written that he had found interesting or intriguing. What had led him to make this crazy trip?

He turned and almost ran back to the truck. Turning around in Jessica's driveway, he used Robert's map to find roads through the center of the island that would bring him to the inn in the shortest time. He saw Robert and Chris in the garden behind the house as he retrieved his suitcase, but he did not talk to them; he wrote a brief note, enclosing money for his one-night stay, and left the inn. Halfway down the driveway he remembered that he had no way back to the village. But anger and confusion kept him going along the road until he found himself beside a row of small houses facing a narrow beach cluttered with seaweed. He stopped at the first house and asked if he could use their telephone to call a taxi.

Within twenty minutes he was at the village and had called the seaplane. He had over an hour and so he walked the three miles to the airstrip. On the way, one of the men who had greeted him earlier stopped and asked him if he wanted a ride.

Luke shook his head. "Thanks, I'd rather walk. I'm catching the seaplane."

"Well, they take their time. You look pretty angry, friend. Robert's truck break down on you?"

"No. It was fine." He walked on; then, aware of his rudeness, he turned around. "I've got some problems to work out. Thanks for asking." Wallowing in my anger, he thought. Couldn't even return kindness with simple politeness.

But why was he so angry? He stood looking out over the water. Why so much anger?

Because he felt cheated. He'd come to this island to find Jessica Fontaine, whom he hadn't been able to get out of his mind since he'd begun reading her letters, whom he'd decided, in some kind of wild illusion, that he was in love with, and instead he'd found . . .

A different Jessica Fontaine, almost unrecognizable. Not the one he wanted. Nothing like the woman he wanted. Nothing like any woman he'd ever wanted or even looked at twice. *Damn it, I knew her. I knew how she sounded, how she felt about things, what she did with her days, the people she saw and worked with . . .*

*I saw her pictures. I knew how she looked.*

*Except that I was wrong.*

He pictured himself standing there, rigid with that sense of betrayal, watching the sky to see if the plane were coming, and he knew he was being petulant and shrill—*like a kid who didn't get the Christmas present he expected*—but he could not control it. Disappointment coursed through him; he felt he could not breathe with the pressure of it. He had to get away from here, from the images he had carried in his mind all these months and then had built to a full-blown fantasy. *As if I'd written a play and begun to direct it with one person missing . . . and when she showed up she was someone else.*

He gazed at a sailboat gliding through the harbor. Beyond it was the ferry from the mainland, and beyond that the tiny speck in the sky that was his plane, sunlight glinting off it so that it looked like a star and then a spotlight that grew larger as he watched. He kept his eyes on it, but what he was seeing in his mind, what, in spite of himself, he was reliving over and over, were those long moments when he had stood in the forest, watching Jessica cut roses and lay them gently in her basket.

# CHAPTER 9

The *Magician* opened to a sold-out house in Philadelphia on a rainy night in early September, nine days after Luke returned from Lopez Island. They had spent two days in dress rehearsals, for the first time with costumes, full sets and props; Luke had calmed Rachel's terrors at the idea of a real live audience, settled a tiff between Cort and Kent, and taken Abby to dinner because, she said, that was what her directors always did. And then it was opening night. The audience filled the theater and the lights came up on stage for act one.

Luke stood at the back of the theater beside Monte and Kent. He had focused on this night every moment since returning from his trip, except for the brief act, on his first day back, of stowing the box of Jessica's letters in a closed cabinet in his library. From then on, he had plunged into every aspect of the play, resolving the problems that still cropped up, soothing frayed nerves, refining the way his cast delivered their lines. Even so, at odd times, images kept intruding: the dark shape in a dark sea of Lopez Island from the air, forests and farms from the high front seat of Robert's truck, a weathered sign carved with an engraved fountain beside a faint path that led through dense trees to a house, a beach, a rose garden . . . But each time he would wrench his thoughts away, as he had wrenched the wheel of Robert's truck to turn from Jessica's house, and will himself to see nothing and think of nothing but his play.

Now, in Philadelphia, it seemed that Lopez and Jessica were as remote from him as were Tricia and Claudia and New York's hectic social life. In the darkened theater he leaned forward, tense and watchful as his actors moved past their initial hesitation and stiffness and settled into the rhythm and interlocking emotions of their lives on stage. Halfway through the act, Luke met Monte's eyes and they smiled.

At intermission the three of them mingled with the crowd in the lobby and those smoking outside until the bell rang to announce act two. "They love it," Monte said as the audience trickled back to their seats. "Good vibes all around. Nobody's bored and as far as I can tell nobody's leaving."

Kent came in with the audience, a beatific smile on his face. "They like it. *They like it.* Some of them were trying to guess how it would end. Can you imagine? They were talking about Lena and Daniel and Martha as if they were people they knew, trying to figure out what they'd do next. God, there's nothing like that in the world."

Luke watched the house fill up again. He felt the aura of anticipation as people took their seats, he saw the expectation in their faces, and he knew this was the true magic of the theater. The second act began and, as in the first act, he made mental notes of corrections and changes to be discussed with the cast and crew the next day. But then the energy of the audience and the actors swept him up and from then on he watched and listened uncritically, buoyed by the exhilaration that came only at such rare moments of accomplishment and fulfillment. From the corner of his eye he saw Kent smiling and crying at the same time, wiping his eyes with the back of his hand. "Can't believe it, too fantastic," he said softly to Luke. Luke put his arm around his shoulders and gave him a quick hug. "Great play," he murmured, and then they watched the final scene unfold before them.

"Bingo," Monte whispered as the sound of sniffling came from the audience. Luke saw men as well as women fumbling for tissues and he knew Monte was right. Bingo. The jackpot. To lead an audience into another world and to make them believe in it so completely that their emotions were those of the characters on stage.

*I can't imagine more power than that . . . as if nothing is closed to me, as if there is nothing I cannot do.*

The applause began the moment the stage went to black. The critics ducked out to write their reviews for newspapers and television, but the rest of

the audience stayed in place, their applause filling
the theater and washing over the stage as the cast
took their curtain calls. After that everyone went
to Roland's, where the air was charged with a
volatile combination of satisfaction, gaiety and
tension that was like mild hysteria; the noise level
rose as gaffes were relived and lighting, props and
costumes critiqued as if for the first time. Luke
had predicted that, and he knew that the next day,
when they came together for another rehearsal,
most of what was being intoned tonight would
have been forgotten.

What he had not predicted was that Abby would
propose a toast to him—"To Luke, a director fully
as good as his reputation, and a pleasure, a
*supreme* pleasure, to work with, putting all my
doubts, my *grave* doubts, to rest."—or that Cort
would tell him that now he, too, wanted to be a director and he was sure Luke would help him get
started, or that Kent would walk around all
evening in a kind of daze, uncharacteristically
quiet, even modest, as he accepted congratulations
and responded to the one question that everyone
was asking, saying that, yes, he'd started a new
play, and, yes, Luke had seen some of it and liked
it, but he couldn't say anything else; he couldn't
talk about it because things that got talked about
usually didn't get written.

And neither had Luke predicted their reviews—
everyone in the theater knew that was bad luck—
so he fell silent with the others as the early editions

of the newspapers arrived, and shared with them the rush of excitement when Abby read the reviews aloud, dramatizing their praise and dropping her voice to a sepulchral murmur when she came to anything negative.

The rest of that week in Philadelphia was much like the weeks before it: they rehearsed every day as audience reactions revealed weak spots or lines that did not get the reaction they had expected. Each afternoon, in the quiet time before the performance, Abby read novels, Rachel wrote in her journal, Cort napped, Monte and Fritz and the lighting director played poker, with Kent watching. And Luke walked.

He knew the streets of Philadelphia from other out-of-town openings, so he walked with barely a glance at his surroundings, lingering only among the faded red brick buildings where the United States had been born, but even there letting his thoughts float free. *After we open* came again and again, drifting through other images, lurking behind his actions so that when he stopped for a red light or glanced into a shop window, there it was. *After we open in New York.*

*Well, what? What happens after we open in New York?*

Something different, he mused. Something new.

The thought had been there since his grandmother's death, fueled by a recurrent restlessness and impatience. He wanted . . . something. And after they opened, he would find out what it was. And go after it.

He prided himself on that: knowing exactly what he wanted, moving straight toward it, ignoring obstacles or riding over them to get where he wanted to be.

*But sometimes I've been wrong about what I wanted.*

The streets of Philadelphia receded and he saw himself standing in that forest near Watmough Bay, taken by surprise, stunned, feeling betrayed as he watched Jessica in her garden.

*Very wrong.*

*Unless . . .*

He had reached his hotel. It was almost time to go to the theater for their closing night in Philadelphia, and his thoughts were shifting to the play. But one thought lodged itself before he pushed through the revolving doors into the lobby.

*Unless I wasn't wrong, and she's exactly what I thought she was in her letters.*

The next day everyone packed up and moved back to New York. They would rehearse once in the Vivian Beaumont before opening with previews leading to the formal opening night in the third week of September. This was so familiar to Luke that, no matter which cast and crew he was working with, he could almost plot their actions and emotions in the five nights of previews and then on opening night.

But still, standing with Monte and Luke at the back of the theater as the lights came up on stage, revealing Abby in her chair on her sun porch, and the audience broke into applause, his throat was dry, his hands clenched. Stage fright, he thought. Directors have it, too.

He began to relax in the second act, though he was alert to every sound in the audience and every small movement on stage. And that was why he saw Abby take three steps to reach Cort when she should have been leaning forward in her chair, her body reaching out to him. Now, as Cort stood looking out the window, she was beside him, her hand on his arm, and as she spoke he turned until he was facing her and could put his arms around her immediately instead of going to her in her chair, as he had always done.

"You've changed," Abby said softly, her face turned up to his. "For a while I thought I didn't recognize you; you were so different. Perhaps you didn't recognize yourself. Because nothing was planned. You didn't wake up one bright day determined to change your life; *it happened to you* and it was as if a chasm had opened between then and now. You were so surprised. I saw it in your face when you blurted out that you didn't want to spend Thanksgiving with me. No, you wanted to spend it with Martha, no doubt in her bed, and why shouldn't you? But I was surprised, too—I almost felt betrayed—until I looked for the Daniel I knew. And of course I found him: my fine loving grandson, different but still the same, changed but not transformed. And now you must embrace what you are. And I promise I will help you. If you will let me."

Luke looked into the distance. *A chasm. For a while I thought I didn't recognize you. Nothing was planned. Now you must embrace what you are.* It was as if he were hearing the lines for the first time. My God, he thought, she told us. In letter after letter, all the clues were there.

Monte nudged him. "I like it, the way she stands there and he turns while she's talking, the whole bit. Was it your idea?"

Luke shook his head. "I asked her to sit on the edge of her chair; I thought there should be some space between them. But you're right; it is good."

His tension built again as the third act began, and he concentrated fiercely on the actors and the audience reaction. But as the act built to its climax, and people in the audience sniffed and fumbled for tissues, he met Monte's eyes, and then Kent's, and spontaneously the three of them clasped hands. "You're on your way," Monte said to Kent beneath the applause that began a few minutes later, and Kent pulled away to wipe his eyes with the sleeve of his tuxedo.

Luke kept his eyes on the stage as the lights came up and the cast moved forward, holding hands, smiling into the smiling faces in the audience. Rachel took a step forward, then Cort, and then Abby moved ahead two steps, to stand by herself and make a deep curtsy, looking to left and right, acknowledging the applause that rose higher for her.

Then she raised her hand. Luke's eyes narrowed and he heard Monte murmur, "What's she up to?" as the audience quieted. Even those already moving up the aisle stopped and turned to look back. "Kent Horne," Abby said ringingly. "A brilliant young playwright. This is his first play and he should be here with us." She held out her arm.

The applause rose again. Kent looked wildly at Luke. "What should I do?"

"Get up there," Luke said. "It's true: that's where you should be. You deserve it."

"But so do you. I mean, where would I be if—"

"I'm exactly where I belong. Go on, now; they're waiting."

As they watched Kent lope up the aisle to the stage, Monte said, "I told you she was a smart lady. She just balanced the scales. When somebody says she's a terror, somebody else'll remember this."

Kent stood between Abby and Rachel, holding their hands. He bowed, Abby whispered to him, and he bowed again, more deeply. The lights went out, then came on again as the applause continued. Three curtain calls later, the stage remained dark and the houselights came up. The audience began moving toward the double doors that the ushers had flung wide. Opening night was over.

Later, when he wrote about it in his journal, as

he did with every play he directed, Luke described the party at Corelli's; the silence that fell, hours into it, when the newspapers were delivered, and then the rush of excitement as Abby, once again, read the reviews aloud. "All raves," he wrote. "They found more flaws than did the critics in Philadelphia—I'd have been surprised if they hadn't, and in fact a couple of points in the *Times* review are good enough for us to adopt them (and make me wonder how I missed them)—but everyone had high marks for Abby and Rachel, nice words for Cort, and praise for Kent. I got a line about my 'powerful, insightful direction with a constant thread of tension and self-discovery holding everything together.' More than enough to satisfy all of us."

He closed the journal and slid it into the top drawer of the desk in his library. He had used it as a log of each of his productions, ever since Constance suggested it when he was directing his first plays in college. "It will force you to think about why you choose some options over others," she had said. "It will make you more aware of yourself."

I should have kept a log of my trip to Lopez, he thought. Why I went. Why I left.

He stretched out on the couch. His tie and tuxedo cummerbund were off, his shirt open at the neck, and he propped his head on the arm of the couch and closed his eyes. It was after four in the morning and he was tired, but too energized to sleep. He knew that in the morning he would feel a letdown, with no rehearsal to attend, no schedule to follow, no play in formation, but for now he felt only exhilaration and triumph.

But as he lay there, he was not thinking about the play, or the reviews. He was thinking about letters. Writing them was like keeping a log, or a diary, he thought, organizing and trying to make sense of one's choices, even gaining some feeling of control over the events that crashed and tumbled through one's life. So that no matter what happened, one could turn to a piece of paper and a pen . . .

He opened his eyes. That was one of the reasons he could not get Jessica out of his mind: because so often her letters echoed his own life and thoughts. And so powerful were those echoes that every time he read a letter, especially late at night when he was tired and most open to suggestion, he opened a door to her and she walked through it. He had willingly, even eagerly, brought her close and made her a companion, a clear voice commenting on his days, and sharing them.

But the woman who walked through that door and became his companion was not the woman he had seen on Lopez Island.

*And I should have known she wouldn't be. She left clues in all her letters.*

He walked out onto the terrace. The air was cool and fresh from a brief rainstorm just ended;

by now the heat wave of August was barely a memory. As the clouds pulled apart into fragments beyond the dark steel of the George Washington Bridge, the sky turned pale opal shading to violet, with the city's skyscrapers outlined crisply against it, washed clean by the rain. Luke sat in a wicker chair in the corner where he liked to eat breakfast and, as the sky brightened and a brilliant daylight swept away the shadows and dim crevices of night, he thought about Jessica. Not the Jessica of the New York and London stage, but the Jessica of Lopez Island. A different person. And she had told them she was—if they had read carefully enough to see it.

*By the end of my stay in Arizona, I'd changed and I couldn't bridge the chasm and go back.*

*I won't—I can't—go back to what I was—too much has happened—so I have to get used to this.*

*All my connections to the people and places and things that once defined my life are gone, and I have nothing to remind me of that other Jessica except my memories.*

*I miss what I've lost, oh, Constance, I do miss it, and you're the one person in the world who can truly understand that, and understand my anger.*

*What's gone is . . . everything.*

Two women, Luke thought, exiling themselves to isolated places. But Constance had no choice but to leave the stage. And Jessica must have felt that she had none either.

He was asleep. He dreamt of his grandmother, and of Lena in *The Magician,* and when he woke to the smell of coffee and opened his eyes to see Martin arranging his breakfast on the brass chest beside his chair, he was remembering Lena's speech to Cort at the end of the play. *I looked for the Daniel I knew and of course I found him . . . changed but not transformed.*

He had not waited to find out whether she was transformed. He had stayed hidden in the forest, angry, dismayed, then turned and bolted. Why? What had made him so angry?

"Well, my dear Luke." He could almost hear his grandmother's husky voice. "You're used to everything going as you expect it to, without failures or major struggles. With Jessica, you'd been so sure of what you'd find that when something quite different appeared it was as if you'd been kicked in the rear. And you didn't like it."

"Mr. Cameron, congratulations," Martin said, pouring his coffee. "The reviews are quite glowing. I would call it a genuine triumph."

"Yes, we think it is," Luke said, sitting up. "Thank you, Martin."

"And I do thank you for my ticket. You know how exciting I find opening nights."

"I'm glad you were there."

When Martin left he reached for a plate of sliced melon and strawberries. Changed but not transformed, he thought. The woman he knew from letters, the woman he thought he had fallen in love with, might still be there. Or she might not. Her letters had become almost brittle after the accident, then sick with despair, then cool, chatty and remote, without the verve and optimism of the letters that had traced her brilliant career. So why would he think she was not transformed?

He had no way of knowing. Because he had run away.

He knew then that he would go back. He had to find out if the woman who haunted his thoughts was still there. He had caught only a glimpse of her; he could have been wrong about everything. It might have been a trick of the sunlight, of the shimmering reflections off the water, of the shadows and fickle light in the forest where he had stood. After all, she had written about a man she had met, about helping to direct a performance of *Pygmalion,* about friends she had made on the island. He had been too swift in his judgement; he should not have left.

So he would go back, and he would stay long enough to get to know her as she was now. But this time he would write first so there would be no surprises. The letter took shape in his mind as he drank his coffee. "Dear Jessica Fontaine. I'm sure you know that my grandmother died last spring in Italy, but I want to tell you about the time I spent there, closing her villa. . . ."

He would write about finding the box of her letters and about the collection of rare plays Constance had left to her. He would say he wanted to bring them to her personally. He would ask her to telephone at her convenience, to set a time for his visit. Right now would be best, he thought. No rehearsals, no schedules, no play in formation. Right now would be perfect. He only needed her reply, and he would be on his way.

# LOPEZ ISLAND

# CHAPTER 10

The familiar shape of Lopez Island rose from the turbulent waters of Puget Sound, dark beneath a pounding rain. The plane bucked and lurched as Luke tried to see the airstrip. "Shark Reef," the pilot said, tilting his head to indicate it. "And Rock Point Beach. Almost home." He banked the small plane, fighting the wind as he leveled off and roughly set down, braking hard to stop. He grinned at Luke. "Not my smoothest, but not too bad. Do you want to wait for a few minutes till it lets up?"

Through the streaming window Luke saw Angie's cab drive close to the plane. "No, I'll—" A crash of thunder directly overhead cut off his words. "How long do these usually last?"

The pilot shrugged. "Five minutes, an hour, hard to tell."

"I'll make a dash for it."

"Up to you." The pilot opened the door and pushed down the folding steps and Luke moved past him. Instantly he was soaked. He turned to the pilot. "If you'll hand me my suitcase and that cardboard carton . . ."

"Hold on." The pilot threw a large piece of plastic over the carton and handed it to Luke, who took three steps and put it on the backseat of the cab. His suitcase was next, and then he sat beside Angie in the front seat.

"Don't they have raincoats and umbrellas in New York?" Angie asked, inspecting his dripping suit.

"New York was seventy degrees and sunny. I'll dry off at the inn. You don't have to wait for me."

"I will if I don't get another call. Maybe Robert'll give you the truck again."

"Maybe." He cleared a spot on the foggy window as Angie turned onto Fisherman Bay Road. Lightning tore a gash through the sky over the water, followed almost immediately by a crack of thunder, and Luke thought of the cab as a small, vulnerable boat in a windswept sea as it splashed along the road, its windshield wipers whipping back and forth. He leaned forward, trying to see through the rain, and as he saw landmarks he remembered, and pictured in his mind the Inn at Swifts Bay and Jessica's house, he could no longer ignore the fact that he was on the island uninvited, as he had been the first time.

There had been no reply to his letter. After two weeks of waiting, he had telephoned, and telephoned again. Four telephone calls, with no answer, and no tape recording asking him to leave a message. With each failure, he had grown more stubborn until finally, almost angrily, he did what he had done the first time: he made reservations for the flights to Seattle and Lopez early the next morning, and then he called Robert, to book the same room he had had before. "And would you do me a favor?" he asked. "I've written to Jessica but

I haven't been able to reach her by phone, and I want to make sure she knows I'll be there tomorrow. If you could get a message to her that I hope to see her around noon or early afternoon, I'd be grateful."

"I can do that." Robert did not mention the peculiar getaway of his first visit, and Luke, grateful for his discretion, did not mention it either. But now, as the cab turned into the uphill driveway of the inn, he felt briefly paralyzed. It suddenly had occurred to him that if Robert had talked to Jessica, she might well have asked him to tell Luke to stay away. And if Robert did that, what choice would Luke have but to turn around and go back to New York?

"Let's go on," he said abruptly to Angie, who had turned to look at him. "I'll check in with Robert later. I'd like to go to Watmough Bay."

"You're pretty wet," Angie observed mildly.

"I'd just get wet again."

She nodded and as lightning flashed and thunder tore across the sky, she turned around in the empty parking area and drove down the driveway back to Port Stanley Road, continuing around the island toward Watmough Bay. The road followed the shore, then turned inland past a small rain-spattered lake, through broad farmlands edged with dense groves of cypress, and finally to the southern end of the island, where, once again, the shoreline came into view. Luke remembered it all as he had seen it from the high front seat of

Robert's truck, and as soon as he recognized the turnoff to Watmough Bay Road he said, "There's a driveway up ahead, almost hidden—"

"I know," Angie said. "Jessica gave me raspberries from her garden a couple of times. She's got a green thumb, that lady. And a generous heart."

Bemused, Luke said nothing. If Angie had known all along where he was going, how many others knew? How fiercely Jessica must have made her wishes known, he thought, if her privacy was guarded by everyone on an island that seemed to have no secrets.

The sign with the carved fountain was darkened by rain, and the driveway was like a path in a fairy tale, disappearing into a dark and moody forest. Angie drove to a curve in the drive that was about ten steps from the front door, and stopped. "You'll probably want me to come back for you."

"Yes, thanks. I'll call as soon as I know what time."

"Of course, Jessica has a car. She might drive you back."

"I'll let you know."

"I'd better wait now, though; she might not be home."

Luke looked at the closed garage door at the other end of the house. Her car was probably there; why would anyone go out in this rain? But there was no way to be sure. "Fine," he said. "But I'll pay you for this much. And would you mind taking my suitcase to the inn?" He did not want to look as if he were ready to move in when Jessica opened her door.

Finally he stepped out into the rain, just as lightning slashed and thunder broke above his head. Hurrying, he yanked open the back door of the car to lift out the cardboard carton, still draped in the plastic the pilot had flung over it. He tucked it under his arm and ran to the large over-hang that protected the flagstone entryway and the front door. There was no doorbell, so he used the fountain-shaped brass knocker. He heard a dog bark, but nothing else, and so he knocked again. He was about to knock a third time, when the door opened.

Her face froze in surprise as she looked up at him, and their eyes held for a long moment. She looked exactly as she had looked in her garden, though now, up close, he could see more clearly the faint outlines of the beauty that had been hers. Her eyes, blue-green as he recalled, were darker, still large and heavily lashed but deep-set and shadowed amid lines etched by pain. One could imagine the radiant smile that had drawn others to her, but deep lines of pain were there, too, flank-ing her mouth, stretching to her chin. Her face, once luminous and clear, was drab, pasty, almost colorless, sagging beneath its own weight. Her hair—those masses of tawny gold that Luke re-membered—was silver-gray, curling closely about her head, exposing her thin, corded neck. She wore narrow black pants with a pale pink silk shirt open at the neck, and her figure was still slim, but where she had been tall and stately, she stooped now, leaning on a cane, her body off center, almost twisted. Her dog stood beside her as she looked up at him with surprise turning to a stony anger.

"You had no right to come here."

It was the voice Luke remembered, the voice no one who had ever heard it could forget, flattened—perhaps deliberately—but still recognizable, and the shock of that voice emerging from her drab face and stooped body was so startling that for a moment he could not answer. But the rain was drumming above him and suddenly he felt very chilled. He heard Angie back up to turn around and saw Jessica look up sharply and raise her hand to stop the cab from leaving.

"I'm sorry," he said quickly. "I thought Robert would have told you I was coming here from New York. I asked him to call you."

"It doesn't matter. You had no right to come."

"I came as a friend. I brought you something that belongs to you. And now that I'm here, do you think I might come in?"

She hesitated, but just then lightning streaked horizontally across the sky and almost simultaneously thunder crashed like an avalanche above her roof. She stood to the side. "Come in."

Luke picked up the cardboard carton and walked past her into the house. Immediately the dog, black, sleek and curious, circled him, nosing his legs, his hands, his suitcase.

"Hope," Jessica said quietly, and the dog hesitated, then went to her side. She put her hand on its head and they stood there, a country portrait, Luke thought, in a very sophisticated room.

From descriptions in her letters he thought he knew what her home looked like, but he was struck by the dramatic beauty of the large living room: its white walls, white-cushioned furniture, pale gold hickory floors, and flashes of vibrant color in throw pillows, paintings, flowers massed in tall vases, and bold works of art displayed on table-tops and shelves, from Baccarat paperweights to Peruvian feather belts to a table covered with dozens of carved figures, arranged in a wedding scene, from Indonesia.

It was one of the most beautiful rooms he had ever seen. Its backdrop was a wall of windows looking out on shrubs and flowers bent almost flat by wind and rain, and, beyond them, a beach darkened by tumultuous waves. But no sounds of the storm invaded the house. Within its walls, everything was tranquil and hushed.

"Sanctuary," Luke murmured, setting down the suitcase and the carton in the small foyer.

"What does that mean?" Jessica had closed the front door and now she stood with her back against it, watching him.

"Your home is like my grandmother's in Italy, very beautiful, very quiet and serene. A retreat. A place to forget what you've left behind."

"You don't know anything about that." She

paused, as if realizing for the first time that this man was Constance's grandson. "I mean, you don't know about me. Of course you know about Constance." There was another pause, and Luke imagined her struggling between simple decency and her anger at him for intruding. Finally, decency won and she said, "You're very wet; please take off your jacket. I'm sorry I have nothing for you to change into."

Luke hung his jacket on a coat tree, then sat on a wooden bench and pulled off his shoes. "If you give me a towel to sit on, I'll try not to soak your furniture."

"Wait. I do have something." She walked through the living room and the dining space at its far end and disappeared through a doorway. In a moment she was back with a pair of faded khaki pants. "I wear them sometimes for gardening. They're oversize for me, so they might fit you. Go through that door and turn left."

"Thank you." He walked through the living room in the opposite direction from the one she had taken and opened the door at the end. He was in her bedroom, a high square room with an antique bureau and a white four-poster bed angled to have a panoramic view of Watmough Bay. The antique rug was pale rose and blue, and on the bed was an antique patchwork quilt of faded blue, mauve and ivory. Luke wanted to linger and study the photographs and paintings on the walls, but instead he turned left into the bathroom. He took a minute to admire the soft warmth of clear pine cabinets and countertops, and the freestanding tub on claw feet, angled, like the bed, for a full view of the bay and the horizon, and then he stripped off his wet pants and socks and pulled on the khakis.

They were cut large, with a drawstring waist, and once he turned down the cuffs they fit surprisingly well. He toweled his wet hair and face and it was then that he realized that the bathroom had no mirror. He looked into the bedroom. None. And there had been none in the living room. From what he had seen, Jessica's house had no mirrors.

He hung his wet pants over the edge of the bathtub and, barefoot, walked back through the bedroom, luxuriating in being warm and dry. He was also hungry, but he had invited himself into Jessica's house, and now was wearing her clothes, and he was not about to tell her he also needed to be fed. He opened the door to the living room and saw her standing at the window, looking at the storm. The dog was curled up nearby, watchful, its nose on its paws.

"Are they all right?" she asked without turning around.

"Yes. It's good to be dry. Thank you." There was a silence. "The carton is for you, from Constance." He went to the foyer and brought it to a glass table in front of the windows, near where Jessica was standing. Setting it down, he stared at an inlaid box in the center of the table, a twin to the one in

his library, filled with Jessica's letters. "This is extraordinary. Do you know that Constance had an
identical box?"

"We bought them together." She had turned
and was watching him pull off the tape that sealed
the carton. His face was in profile and the past
swept over her as she looked at his sharp features
and heavy brows. He was as assured and dominating as she remembered, even in a rumpled, open-
necked white shirt and drawstring pants, even in
bare feet. He was part of everything that once had
been her entire life, and she knew she should not
have let him into her house.

He pulled off the last strip of tape and opened
the box. "She left these to you in her will." Carefully he lifted out a layer of newspapers and then
several folds of tissue paper and laid them on the
table. He looked up. "You don't seem interested."

*I am, oh, I am, but I don't want you here. I want
to be alone with whatever Constance left me and
with my memories.* "Why didn't you send them to
me?"

"Because I wanted to meet you."

"We knew each other in New York."

"Barely. And a lot has changed since then."

She contemplated him and then, abruptly, her
glance went to the inlaid box. "Constance's was
empty," she said.

Luke shook his head. "Crammed full." He
raised the lid of Jessica's box and saw hundreds of
letters packed inside. "Why would you think she

could destroy yours any more than you could get rid of hers?"

*"You read them."* Her eyes blazed with anger, and Luke was startled to see how her face came to life.

He closed the lid. "I'll tell you why I read them if you want to hear it. But first I'd like you to see what Constance left you."

After a moment, Jessica came forward, leaning on her cane, her left leg swinging out with each step. When she reached him, Luke stood aside so she could look into the carton.

"Oh." It was a long sigh. She took out one of the slim books. Its cover was torn, the lettering worn and faded, but Luke had packed it and so he knew it was a first edition of Eugene O'Neill's *Strange Interlude,* and he knew that O'Neill himself had given it to Constance, and inscribed it. Jessica ran her fingers over the lettering and then opened the book. Her head was bent so that Luke could not see her face, but he heard her murmur the inscription. " 'To the incomparable Constance, with incomparable love.' " She looked up at Luke. "Constance laughed at that; she loved his extravagance. We talked about doing the play together, opening in Provincetown and then moving to New—" She cut off her words and stood still, her head bowed. A tear fell on the book and she hastily wiped it away. Then, with a small shake of her head, she looked into the carton, lifting books, reading titles. "The whole collection. It was so precious to her; she collected them all her life. I was sure she'd left them to a library." She looked up again. "Thank you. You packed them with great care."

"They were important to her. And so were you."

He had reminded her of her letters, and Jessica's face became stony. "Thank you for delivering these; I'm very glad to have them. Now that you've done it, I'll call Angie to pick you up."

"Wait a minute." Luke would have been amused at her stubbornness, but it was too desperate and sad to be amusing. "They weren't the reason I came; as you said, I could have sent them. I want very much to talk to you. It's a long trip from New York and I'd be grateful for a couple of hours before I go back."

"We have nothing to talk about."

"We have Constance."

She hesitated, then nodded. "Sit down."

He debated briefly among the two chairs and the couch that faced the windows. He chose one of the chairs and Jessica sat in the other, with the glass-and-beechwood coffee table between them. Rain lashed the windows; the room was as gray as the sky, but she made no move to turn on a light. "Were you with her when she died?"

"No. Her housekeeper called me in New York."

"Did anyone know whether she was in pain or . . . afraid? Whether she wanted someone near her?"

"It seems she died in her sleep. She was sitting in a large, deep chair in her library—"

"The blue one?"

"Yes. Next to a round table covered in white fringed silk." He was describing the room as if it were a stage set and Jessica closed her eyes, remembering it. "The lamp was still on; there was a volume of Shakespeare's sonnets with a book-mark in it; and the box of your letters, very close to her. It was probably around three or four in the morning and she probably was asleep—those were the few hours of sleep she got each night. I think she had no premonition, no time to wish that you and I were with her. I got there the next day and she looked peaceful and"—his voice caught briefly—"very beautiful."

Jessica heard the change in his voice and for a moment she forgot that she was angry at him and did not want him there. "She loved you very much."

"She loved both of us."

That was twice in one minute that he had linked the two of them. Jessica's resentment returned. Why was he forcing himself into her life? She looked away, at the rain whipping across her garden beneath dark, lowering clouds, but that only made her more aware of the snug enclosure of her house and the close presence of Luke, sitting with her, safe from the storm.

"You wanted to know why I read your letters," he said, and instinctively she tightened inside.

Luke stood and paced, as he did at home when he was organizing his thoughts. The wood floor was warm beneath his bare feet and he wondered briefly why he did not feel ridiculous, wearing borrowed clothes in a home where he was not welcome and wandering around without shoes or socks, but in fact he felt oddly at ease. Perhaps that was because many things reminded him of Constance, perhaps because he felt sheltered and safe while rain drummed on the roof and wind whistled around corners. "I was closing my grandmother's house, sorting and packing everything either for shipment to New York or giving away to the people she had named in her will. When I opened the box of your letters, I was curious—so many, and almost all in the same handwriting—so I read the first one. I liked the voice—an ingenue effusively thanking my grandmother for her praise after a performance in summer stock—so I looked at a few others and folded inside one of them was a newspaper clipping about a train accident in Canada." He paused, but Jessica said nothing. She was still looking out the windows, seemingly absorbed in watching the storm. "I could have stopped then, but I wanted to find out what had happened to you. I'd admired you for a very long time, I'd always regretted that we never worked together, and I was as baffled as everyone when you vanished. I once asked my grandmother, by the way, if she knew where you were. She said she did not. I assume you asked her to say that."

Still looking out the window, Jessica nodded.

"I didn't see that in a letter."

"It was in a telephone call."

Again Luke waited, but it seemed that was all she was going to say. When a silent minute had dragged by, he returned to his chair. "When did you buy the two boxes?"

"Seven years ago."

"Where? They look Italian."

"They are."

A low growl came from Luke's stomach. He tightened his muscles, trying to control it, but if Jessica had heard, she gave no sign. "Where in Italy?" he asked, and embarrassment and impatience were in his voice.

She turned to him then, her shoulders sagging. Every word he said, just the sound of his voice, brought everything she had ever cared about into her living room and she felt she hated him for forcing the past on her when she had worked so hard to erase it. But she could not push him out of her house as long as the storm continued, and she did want to talk about Constance. She had heard the growl from his stomach and knew that pretty soon she would have to give him something to eat—common decency, again—but she was not ready to do that yet. She felt lethargic and defeated and thought she would not feel good again until he was gone.

"Did you find them in that little town near her villa?" he prodded.

"No." She thought back, remembering. "It was the first time I visited her in Italy, and we drove to

Florence and spent the day at the Uffizi and the Pitti Palace. She was strong enough to do that, then, and we walked all day and talked—we always had so much to talk about; it seemed we would never have enough time—and then, on the way back to our hotel, we passed Signor Forlezzi's shop. The windows were dusty—well, they really were quite dirty—but we could see inlaid boxes piled every which way, and Signor Forlezzi sitting on a stool repairing something, a lamp, I think, and he looked up and said, 'Ah the sun has come out! Two such magnificent ladies to brighten my—' " She bit off the words.

"So you bought the boxes," Luke prompted after a moment.

She nodded. "There were two identical ones, the most beautiful, and we both said, 'For our letters.' When did you last see her?"

"A week before she died."

"Was she very sick?"

"Frail, but not sick. We walked through her gardens and talked about some of the directors and producers she'd worked with. . . ." He paused. "It just occurred to me. We covered a lot of territory, a lot of experiences, not exactly a review of her life, but as if she wanted to see it all in a kind of panorama before she died. I don't really believe in that, but . . ." His voice faded.

"What is it?" Jessica asked.

"I was remembering how her hand felt on my arm. We were walking through that damned maze she liked so much—I always felt claustrophobic in it, so I started walking faster—and she put her hand on my arm and told me to slow down. She said she kept the maze for the pleasure of solving its mystery and that I ought to give myself up to it, not fight it. 'You can't control it,' she said, 'the way you—' Well, that was the gist of it."

"Go on," Jessica said.

"It's not important."

"Please. I'd like to hear what she said."

He gave a small shrug. "'You can't control it the way you try to control everything else in your life; you must bend to its demands, as you do with poetry and fine wine.' "

Jessica smiled. "I can hear her say it. But didn't she include 'love' and its demands?"

Luke thought back. "You're right. Love, poetry and fine wine. I think you knew her better than I did."

"No, just differently. What else did she say?"

"We talked about my parents, and a nanny she'd hired when I first came to live with her, and about her work with directors and producers, including me. She had a criticism of something I'd done when I directed her in *Long Day's Journey into Night*. I couldn't believe it; it was almost ten years ago and she'd never mentioned it before, but it was there all the time waiting to be talked about."

"Was she right?"

Luke contemplated her. "I'm not sure."

"What did she say?"

"I'd asked her to think about the whole family as equally destructive because all of them kept saying unforgivable things to each other. So that was how she played Mary Tyrone: sharing the blame for the wreckage of the family. But that last week we were together, she told me I'd been wrong, that Mary was all victim."

Jessica shook her head. "You were right. Dependency is a curse and Mary used it as a weapon against all of them, James and their sons. I don't think she was aware of it all the time, but sometimes she knew exactly what she was doing." She stopped, stunned by the joy that welled up in her as she became an actress again, sharing with a director the analysis of a play. But she was frightened, too, to discover how close to the surface that other life still was, and she forced the conversation back to Constance. "What else did you talk about?"

Luke had seen the brightness in her eyes, and he saw it die. An ache of sadness filled him. He wanted to comfort her, but he had no idea what comfort he could give, nor did he think it would be welcome, and so he let Jessica guide their talk. "Mostly we reminisced. Or she did and I listened. As if she was trying to tell me, in a short time, all the things she thought were important." He gazed across the room, seeing Constance's library and her terrace overlooking the Umbrian hills. He turned back to Jessica. "There's one thing I'd like you to know. She wrote an extraordinary letter that week; I received it after she died. She used to sit on her terrace whenever the weather was good, and she wrote—this isn't exact, but it will be close because I read it so many times—'Sitting here, my whole being gathers in the wonders of this lush, serene landscape, and I feel I am its caretaker. But of course we all are, aren't we?—all of us who have been given a world filled with such richness and beauty and abundance. We are its—' "

" '—caretakers,' " Jessica said, her voice merging with Luke's. " 'And each other's caretakers, too, and there should be nothing but gratitude in our hearts.' "

Luke chuckled. "I should have known she'd use it more than once. She never wasted a good line, or a good paragraph. I found places in your letters where you quoted her saying something she'd said to me. I'll bet she ended that letter, 'I'm grateful for you, dear Jessica.' "

"And I suppose yours was, 'I'm grateful for you, dear Luke.' "

They laughed softly together. "You must be hungry," Jessica said suddenly.

"No. Thank you, but—" He saw her eyebrows go up, and he laughed. "Well, yes. I had breakfast on the plane, but that seems like three days ago."

She stood up, reaching for her cane. "We'll have a late lunch."

Luke stood with her. "May I use your phone? Robert expected me a long time ago. I suspect Angie's brought him up to date, but, still, I should call."

"It's on the counter between the kitchen and the dining room. If you want privacy—"

"No, this is fine. By the way, *did* Robert call to tell you I was coming?"

"Probably. He's very reliable. I didn't answer the phone for a few days."

Bemused, Luke gazed at her. "What if your publisher had called?"

"He knows I sometimes don't answer."

She reached out and turned on a lamp that curved over the coffee table. The room sprang to life and, startled by the sudden brightness, they looked at each other, across the circle of light. "I hadn't realized how dark it was," Jessica murmured. She turned and limped with her swinging, unbalanced gait to the kitchen. She turned back again as she opened the refrigerator and saw Luke watching her. Anger flared in her eyes. "You were going to call Robert."

"Yes." He found the number in the slim telephone directory that covered the San Juan Islands, and when Robert answered he told him where he was. "I don't know when I'll get to the inn, but I want to make sure you're holding the room for me."

"It's yours. I'd appreciate knowing if you're going to be very late."

"I won't be."

He hung up and walked around the counter into the kitchen. "What can I do?"

"Nothing; it's going to be very simple." Her

back to him, Jessica turned on the flame beneath a covered pot, then began to slice duck breasts on a wooden cutting board built into the dark green granite countertop. The kitchen was designed so that she had to move no more than a few steps to reach everything around the U-shaped counter.

"I'd like to help," Luke said quietly.

Her knife paused, then went on. "Can you make a salad?"

"I think I remember how, from the days before Martin."

"Martin?"

"Butler, chef, protector and moral center. He pronounces on whether or not things are proper and appropriate." He opened the refrigerator and found salad greens and endive and put them on the counter.

Jessica handed him a wooden board and a knife. "Tomatoes in the basket near you. Do you find him amusing?"

"Yes, but admirable, too. He believes in duty and concern for others and mutual responsibility, and I've never seen him bend his beliefs for convenience or his own desires. I find that so rarely that Martin seems quite special."

"You find it rarely in the theater?"

"Anywhere."

She was silent. She had almost asked him how strongly he believed in those things himself, but that would have made the conversation too personal. "Does he live near you?" she asked.

"He lives with me, in a sense. I built a separate suite in my apartment, with its own entrance. He's made my kitchen his own, so he says he has everything he needs."

"Except a place of his own and a family."

"Many people don't have families." He glanced at her, but just then she turned away to open a cabinet door and reach for a platter. "Let me do that."

"I'm fine," she said shortly, and took down the platter.

The room was very quiet. Luke watched Jessica overlap the thin slices of duck on the platter and scatter tiny Spanish olives around it. "Do you always have duck breasts ready for unexpected guests?" he asked.

"I keep them in the freezer. These are last night's leftovers."

Luke pictured her at dinner—not a casual fast-food meal to be gulped down while perched on the edge of the chair, but a thoughtfully chosen one, elegant, carefully prepared, artistically arranged— and eaten alone, with no conversation, no way of sharing the pleasure of good food and wine. It did not occur to him that he frequently ate alone; all he knew was that once again he felt an ache of sadness for her.

Jessica looked up and met his eyes. "The salad," she said coldly.

"Getting there," he said casually. He sliced the endive into thin strips and added them to the salad greens he had torn into pieces. He looked around for something in which to wash them. "In the cab-inet on your right," Jessica said, and he took out a salad spinner and spun the greens dry, then took a tomato from the basket. "Slices or wedges?"

"Slices."

Jessica adjusted the flame under the pot on the stove, ground beans in the coffee grinder, filled the coffeemaker with water and plugged it in. Her movements were brisk and economical but almost automatic; she was uncomfortable with Luke there, opening and closing her drawers, rummag-ing in her cabinets, using her utensils, running water in her sink. He was calm and quiet, for which she was grateful, but he was tall, with a powerful presence, and he took up a lot of space. It had been a long time since someone had taken up space in a room where she lived. We'll eat and then he'll go, she thought. The rain will stop soon, and I'll never see him again.

From beneath a covered towel she took a loaf of dark bread with a rough, floury crust and picked up a bread knife.

"I'll slice that," Luke offered. "Or would you rather I did something else?"

She took a breath. He insisted on being part of everything. "I just have to do this and set the table."

"Let me set the table, then. Would you mind? It was the one task Constance always trusted me with."

After a pause, she nodded, reluctantly, he

thought, and began to slice the bread. Luke walked around the counter to the dining space and opened cabinets. "Which settings would you like?"

"Anything you want," she said indifferently.

Annoyed because he wanted her to take some interest in their table, Luke shrugged and chose from the neatly stacked place mats two that were woven like tapestries in russet, blue and gold. He found blue napkins to match, and silver napkin rings. The round table was polished black granite with four white-cushioned chairs spaced around it, and Luke set the place mats before two chairs at right angles to each other, facing the windows. Then he changed his mind and set them on opposite sides of the table. In another cabinet he found six shelves of china stored in protective zippered cases, and below them two drawers crammed with silver, the kind of china and silver used for dinner parties in New York. Now they were here, as if she had not been able to decide what to give up. But how often were they used?

It came to him that Jessica's house and cabinets had the same look as his apartment on the day he had become aware of its emptiness and had thought he should entertain more. Her telephone had not rung once since he had arrived; no neighbors were close by. This small house on the edge of the water, its back turned to the people of Lopez Island, seemed as isolated and solitary as a castaway in the middle of a vast and indifferent ocean.

He unzipped the quilted cases and took out two

plates of white china bordered in an intricate floral pattern, two matching salad plates, and cups and saucers. From the drawers of silver he chose an openwork sterling pattern, then reached up to the open shelves above.

"What kind of glasses?" he asked.

"Red wine. And water, if you'd like."

He put them on the table, then took two sterling candlesticks from another shelf, and opened drawers until he found candles and matches. "Do you need help with the wine?"

Her silence said she did not need help with anything, but in a minute she appeared, holding a bottle and a corkscrew. "Would you like to open it?" She handed it to him, looking at the table. "How nice it looks. No wonder Constance trusted you."

He poured their wine. "I'll get the food." He brought in the platter of sliced duck, the salad bowl, and a basket of bread. "There's soup next to the stove," Jessica said, and he brought the tureen to the table while she set out soup bowls. Luke filled them and then he pulled out her chair and held it for her.

It was as if he had opened another door to the past. Somehow, without thinking about it, her back became straighter, her head came up, and when she put aside her cane and sat down she moved with grace and fluidity. But in an instant it was gone and Luke saw that she was in pain.

"I'm sorry," he said. "What can I do?"

She shook her head. "Please sit down."

The rain had lessened, but the wind still whipped it against the windows with a sound like a steady swishing of long skirts, and the sky was almost black. Luke lit the candles and their reflections danced in the windows. Jessica glanced at them and saw the faint glow of her face and Luke's. A moment of contentment came upon her unawares, overriding her annoyance at Luke's intrusion and the pain that had shot through her hip when she stood straight. It was good to have a companion with whom to share wine and food.

Of course, she knew that from a past filled with more than her share of companions. And Luke was pleasant and considerate. But he did not belong there and she knew that contentment was something that did not last. She would be glad when he was gone.

The soup was minestrone, thick with vegetables and pasta, steaming hot, and it was all Luke needed to confirm his feeling of having found sanctuary. If I needed a place to hide, he thought, this would be it. How distant it was from everything! How remote he felt from his apartment and office, from the Vivian Beaumont Theater, from New York, from everything and everyone in his life. "I haven't felt this relaxed in a long time," he said. "Thank you."

She nodded. They ate in silence. They finished their soup, then filled their plates with sliced duck and salad. Jessica held out the bread basket and

Luke took another slice. "A wonderful lunch. Do you do your shopping on Lopez?"

"Most of it. If I need anything special, Robert gets it for me when he shops in Friday Harbor."

"You must have been able to stock up, then, when you worked on *Pygmalion.*"

She gave him a startled look, and it suddenly struck him: If she was this isolated, not even answering her telephone, how could she help direct a musical? But it was not a question he could ask her, and he did not want to dwell on the fact that he had read her letters, so he moved smoothly on. "What about your house? It seems wonderfully well made. Did the architect come from Lopez? And the contractor?"

"They're from Seattle, but they both have homes here. It *is* well made; I watched every inch of it go up and Constance gave me advice about what to demand and what to watch out for. She told me she'd built a house once, but she didn't tell me where."

"She told you that? She never built a house. We talked about it when I thought I might build a weekend place on some land I own near Millbrook, but I never had time and neither did she. What kind of advice did she give you?"

"The hickory floor was her idea, and rounded corners instead of sharp ones, and the corner fireplace in the bedroom. I designed the kitchen because she didn't know I needed—she didn't have any thoughts about kitchens, but she had dozens of other ideas. Do you think she just made them up?"

"From old dreams that never came to pass." Their eyes met and they smiled together. "She probably thought of your house as the closest she'd get to one of her own. I'm sorry she never got to see it. She would have felt very much at home."

"I described it to her in my letters, but one night she called and said she was picturing me in my living room but I hadn't been at all specific about the pieces of art I'd put around the room and would I please correct that immediately."

They smiled again. It was easy and safe to talk about Constance, and so they did, loving her, missing her in almost the same ways, while the wind and rain lashed the windows, and the candles slowly burned down. The dog came for scraps and Luke and Jessica fed her until there were no more and she curled up and slept. They finished the bottle of wine and Luke, without asking, brought the coffeepot from the kitchen and filled their cups. "We always talked about the plays I directed," he said, sitting back and stretching out his legs. "Each time, she helped me get going when I hadn't yet found a way to focus everything. I missed her the most when I was working on *The Magician*. I missed her sitting beside me, reading a scene aloud, wearing those spindly reading glasses that sat at the very end of her nose; I missed her imperious finger tapping the table to make sure I got whatever point she was making; I missed her laughter when we shared a private joke—" He took a drink of coffee. "Sorry; I didn't mean to get emotional."

Jessica drew a long breath. He had brought Constance into the room and her sense of loss stabbed sharply. After a moment, she said, "What is *The Magician?* I never heard of it."

Luke looked up. "A new play by a young man named Kent Horne. He's a brilliant writer, which is amazing considering that he's unbelievably callow and usually not likable, but somehow he's written a magnificent play. So good, in fact, that it actually tamed Abby Deming."

"Abby was in it?"

"Is. We opened three weeks ago and it looks like we'll have a long run."

"Who else is in it?"

"Cort Hastings and Rachel Ilsberg. They've mostly done television, but they're fine, Rachel especially."

"What theater?"

"In Philadelphia at the Forrest Theater for one week. And then the Vivian Beaumont."

"And the reviews were good?"

"Raves. Even Marilyn Marks got high praise, in *The New York Times* and *The Wall Street Journal.*"

"Did she do sets or costumes?"

"Both. You worked with her, didn't you?"

"She did the set for *Virginia Woolf.* I liked her; she actually asked Constance and me where the doors would be best for our entrances and exits."

"We had to move a door in her set for *The Magician.*"

"Then she didn't check first with Abby or with you. She may have gotten burned on *Virginia Woolf;* everyone accused her of playing favorites by designing with Constance and me in mind."

"She did."

"Yes, but if you're the one she's playing favorites with, it seems quite reasonable." She smiled as Luke laughed, but then, suddenly, a warning clanged within her: *Getting too close, getting too comfortable, opening doors that shouldn't be opened. Change the subject, change the subject, change the—* But Luke's laughter filled her house with a sound it had not heard and she brushed aside the warning. *It's not important, because pretty soon he'll be gone.*

"Who was stage manager on *The Magician?*" she asked.

"Fritz Palfrey. And Monte Gerhart produced."

"Monte and his masks."

Luke chuckled. "He took them off for *The Magician;* I think I got to know him pretty well. And we worked well together. When did you work with him?"

"On *The Children's Hour.* I thought he was a bumbling fool."

"But, as you said, that's a mask." Luke leaned

forward and refilled their cups. "Monte was the one who wanted Abby Deming; I'd heard too much about her temper to want her. I'd never worked with her, but—"

"Oh, it was real. Awesome, in fact. I've seen her whip a cast into battle formation and turn a rehearsal into a civil war. Monte must have known that."

Luke heard the change in her voice: she was allowing its full resonance to come through instead of consciously keeping it flat. She sat forward, her hands curved around her cup, her arms resting on the table. In the candlelight the lines in her face seemed as deep as if they were carved, making her look even older than before, with not even a shadow of her former beauty. But Luke was not focusing on her face. Her head was tilted slightly, as if she were listening to the past, and in her pose he saw her hunger for news of the world she had left. It was as if he saw a door open. Now they no longer had to stay safely on the subject of Constance. Now they could talk about anything.

"Monte probably heard the same stories I heard," he said. "But he took Abby to dinner and she looked into his eyes and that seems to have done it."

"I've seen her do that. There's something quite biblical about Abby when she's with a man, as if she's giving him the choice of paradise or being turned into a pillar of salt."

Luke burst out laughing. "She was like that with Cort. And, from what I saw, with Kent, too."

"Did he rewrite scenes for her?"

"Only when we all agreed it was needed. She wasn't as demanding as I'd expected. Constance probably demanded more in her time than Abby, at least in *The Magician*."

"Constance understood character better than most playwrights. One time she made Hulbert Lovage rewrite the whole second act of *Madame Forestier*."

"That was a beautifully written play."

"Because he's a fine writer. He went through a bad time, writing dreadful plays and insisting they were fine and everyone else was wrong. His agent and his wife tried to get him to take a year off, even two or three, but he refused; he just kept writing, saying that his plays were perfect, that they didn't need one word changed. It was thoroughly depressing. Then, somehow, he pulled out of it; it was one of those mysteries that make us realize how unfathomable the universe of the mind really is."

"Even to Hulbert, I imagine, if he couldn't admit that what he'd written was bad."

"Oh, Hulbert never could tell the truth. He breaks out in a rash if he does."

Luke smiled, finding the same pleasure in her observations that he had found in her letters. "Hulbert reminds me of Kent Horne," he said, and he told her of the times he had forced Kent to bend to his demands as a director. "I could have been gentler, but I was impatient—"

"You were driving toward a single goal," Jessica said. "You couldn't see any side streets. Most people in the theater—" She stopped.

"—are like that," Luke finished, and their eyes met for a quiet moment of perfect understanding of the life they once had shared. Jessica broke the silence with another question, and then others, listening intently to everything he said, but all the while part of her was wondering at his candor. The Luke Cameron she had known and heard about in all her years in New York, even from Constance, had not been open about any of his failings; he had seemed cold and aloof except to those who had worked with him. She found his confession oddly attractive, not diminishing him but making him seem stronger: a man so caught in the tentacles of the theater that he sometimes lost sight of the gentle way of doing things. But the only reason I find that attractive is that I'm in the theater, she thought. And then, angrily, corrected herself. *Because I was in the theater, a long time ago.*

"And that was the time I called your agent about *Emily's Heirs,*" Luke was saying. "I wanted you as Emily. But you were in London."

"I was in *Lear* at Stratford, with Hugh Welfrith." She was staring into the distance. "That was the year Constance went to Italy. She stopped in London on her way, and stayed with me in my hotel suite, and we had such a good four days; she insisted on seeing *Lear* three times and on my night off we saw *Cats*. I loved knowing she was in the audience; I played to her, with little gestures and inflections we'd talked about over the years. It was like a code. We always had so much fun together; everything was so *right* between us." She clenched her hands, fighting back tears. She had no reason to keep her feelings from Luke, who also had loved Constance, but she was so used to keeping everything inside her that she could not now cry in front of him or even say that the world had a new bleakness since Constance had died. "Do you know what happened to Hugh?" she asked. "He was sick when he played Lear, though no one knew but his companion and me, and from his performance no one could have guessed."

"He died three years ago. We've lost a lot of good people in the last ten years."

Jessica nodded, her head down. "Hugh and I were good friends. And he was a great actor."

Into the silence, Luke said, "You probably don't know about Arcadia. It's a new acting school for children—I'm on its board—and it's very impressive." He talked about the directors of the school, and young actors who were coming from it, and from those stories he went on to others. The more he talked, the more questions Jessica asked, and he roamed widely through the world they both knew so well, spinning anecdotes about people and places, describing new actors and directors who came from television or from regional theaters, mentioning new restaurants and old nightclubs, and even vividly portraying the heat wave of the past summer and the view from his terrace of a wilting New York.

"But your rehearsal space was cool?" she asked, focusing directly on the only important thing to an actor in a heat wave.

"Noisily," Luke said, and they laughed, both having experienced plenty of old and laboring air conditioners in rented rehearsal spaces. Startled by her laughter, Luke stared at her, at the brief animation that gave a glimpse of the woman he remembered from the past. She would never look like that again, he thought, but if she laughed more often, if she took the world more lightly—

But even as he thought it her face sank back to its drawn, gray look. It was as if, for an instant, the sun had pierced through heavy clouds, and then was swallowed up again. Luke found himself wanting to make her laugh again and he cast about for some gossip or a humorous anecdote, but nothing came to him. To bridge the silence, he picked up the coffeepot, but it was empty. And that was when he became aware that the rain had stopped.

They turned to the window at the same time. They saw their faint reflections and those of the candles, now burned almost away, but they had not turned to see but to hear. And they heard nothing. No rain struck the windows and the wind had died. Luke felt a rising panic. He would have to leave. And all he wanted was to stay.

He had not found answers to any of his questions about Jessica; they had talked only on the surface and he was hardly any closer to knowing her than he had been when he arrived. He had done most of the talking, and whatever she had said about herself had never come close to revealing the person she had become. But that was not the only reason for his panic, or even the main reason. He wanted to stay because he was happy where he was.

But he could not invite himself, and so, in slow motion, giving Jessica time to stop him, he put his napkin on the table, pushed back his chair, and stood up. "I think by now my clothes and shoes should be dry." She turned from the window, and he was stunned by the sadness in her eyes. But she said nothing and so he walked past her into the living room and then to her bedroom, closing the door behind him.

Jessica did not move until she heard the door close. Then, automatically, she began to clear the table. She thought of calling Angie to take Luke to the inn, but instead she kept stacking dishes and carrying them to the kitchen, one or two at a time. *A quiet evening. Finally. I should have sent him away a long time ago.*

But the evening that she imagined was not quiet,

but empty, and, before she could stop them, the words *I don't want to be alone* sprang up and would not fade away. Alone in the dining room, with the cleared table and the candles flickering in melted wax, she looked about her at the perfection of the home she had created, and she imagined the silence of the hours ahead. She could fill her rooms with music and they still would be silent. She could move about the kitchen making dinner, with the sounds of a gas flame whooshing on, a refrigerator door opening and shutting, pots and pans clattering, and still she would be surrounded by silence. She could put on a videotape of a movie and still her house would be silent.

But this was what I wanted, she thought. Constance and I made the same kind of life.

No, that was not true. Constance had let the world into her life. Not in great numbers, but people came, mail and gifts arrived, the telephone was active.

*Dearest Jessica, I do not understand this life you have chosen, and none of your reasons make sense to me. What is this chasm you talk about that separates the past from the present? If you can help direct* Pygmalion, *what stops you from returning to Broadway and London, acting or directing, if that is what challenges you now? I read your letters again and again and I can only believe that you are still in some kind of shock from that dreadful accident. But my dearest child, if that is true you must seek help.*

*Do not cut yourself off from the world that you know. It is your nourishment, your life and your being.*

Constance had written that the year before, and Jessica had never answered it directly; she had only repeated that she was content and would not return to New York. After that, their letters fell into a pattern of news exchanged by old friends, without the intimacy they once had known. And then, just this past spring, a different kind of letter had come.

*Please come to see me. I miss you and I believe that you miss me. We need to be together. Please, my dear, dear Jessica, come to see me.*

The bedroom door opened and Luke stood in its square of light, still wearing her pants, still barefoot. "A damp day," he said ruefully. "Nothing dries. If you don't mind, I'll keep your pants and send them back with Angie after I get to the inn." He saw her glance at his bare feet. "I'll put on my shoes when she gets here." He walked toward her, through the living room. "Jessica, I apologize. I wanted so much to see you that I charged ahead without paying any attention to what you wanted. You made it very clear when you didn't answer my letter that you didn't want me here, but I ignored it. I shouldn't have come; I shouldn't have invaded your house, and taken up your whole afternoon, and forced you to feed me—"

"You didn't force me. I took pity on your audible stomach."

It stopped him short. She had so taken him by surprise that the rest of the apology he had spent time formulating in her bedroom flew out of his head and he could not think of anything else to say.

The dog stood, luxuriously shaking herself, and padded across the room. Jessica watched her, glad of the diversion. She wanted to ask Luke to stay; she wanted to tell him that he was her link to Constance and to the theater, but even more than that, she was happy to be with him. She knew he had enjoyed the afternoon, but she also knew he would not invite himself to stay. That had to come from her, and she felt rusty and halting. The words would not come.

Luke made the first move; he went to the telephone. "My stomach and I thank you, but it's far past the time for me to go." He picked up the receiver and turned, his other hand poised above the dial. "It's been a wonderful afternoon. I felt very much at home, and that had to do with far more than the fact that I've been wearing your clothes. I'm sorry we didn't get to know each other better, but perhaps someday—"

"I'd like you to stay."

Luke stood still, watching her. She had put her hand on Hope's head, as if for support. "We still have so much to talk about . . . we could have a late supper and then I could drive you to the inn. If you'd like that."

He hung up the telephone. "Very much." Hope

went to him and nudged his hand with her nose. He knelt and rubbed behind both her ears, and looked up at Jessica, smiling. "It's what I was hoping you'd say."

## CHAPTER 11

The Inn at Swifts Bay sparkled in the morning sun, washed clean by the deluge of the day before. The stuffed rabbits cramming the living room hutch eyed Luke with bright eyes as he walked through on his way to the kitchen, where Robert was making pancakes and muffins.

"Good heavens," Robert said, his whisk stopped in midair. "So early! After such a late night!"

Luke's eyebrows rose. "Eleven o'clock?"

"Well, later than I expected you'd be. I gather Jessica gave you a ride; I caught a glimpse of her car."

"Yes," Luke said, amused. "But I don't want to impose on her again and it seems there's no place to rent a car. Would it be possible for me to use your truck again? I'd pay you whatever a rental car would cost."

"How long would you want it?"

"I don't know."

Robert whisked thoughtfully. "You booked

your room for three nights; someone else is coming in after that."

"If I'm still here, I'll change to another one."

"We'll be full. A bike group from Vancouver."

"Well, I'm not going to worry about it now." Impatiently, he brushed it aside. He had awakened with a feeling of deep well-being and he was looking forward to the day that stretched ahead. He had no time for minor details. "I'd like the truck for three days, if you can spare it. I don't know what will happen after that."

Robert nodded. "We use it mostly in the winter, so it won't be a problem. I can't take money for it, though; just keep the gas tank full. Are you ready for breakfast?"

"No, I won't be eating here."

Robert looked alarmed at the idea of anyone leaving his inn with an empty stomach.

"We're going riding first," Luke said. "You're not ready to serve, anyway; it's far too early. No one else is awake."

"I make exceptions. Not even a piece of toast, or fruit?"

"Nothing except the keys to the truck."

Robert found them in a drawer and handed them over. He eyed Luke's blue jeans and cotton turtleneck shirt. "I could loan you some riding pants."

Luke shook his head, smiling. "I'll wear my own pants today; it will be a novelty. Thanks, Robert."

He turned to go, then turned back. "I don't know how late I'll be tonight. Is that a problem?"

"No, the front door will be open. Have a good time."

"I will." He walked back through the living room, stopping to pick up his leather jacket and Jessica's gardening pants, dry now from hanging over a chair in his room all night. Outside, he was surprised by the sharp chill in the air, and stopped beside the truck to pull on his jacket. Then, once again, he drove along the water, turning inland past the small lake, past Lopez Hill, to Watmough Bay Road, looking for the sign with the fountain. This time, unlike his first trip along these roads, there would be no surprise awaiting him; this time he anticipated what lay ahead.

He thought of the hundreds of women he had gone out with over the years. He could picture himself getting dressed to go out, and driving to pick them up . . . but he could not picture any of the women. Only Jessica was clear in his mind: leaning toward him as if memorizing everything he said, missing nothing as they talked about the theater and, always, about Constance. They always came back to her, as if she were their lodestar.

In fact, they never strayed from those two subjects, but there seemed to be no end to them, and so the afternoon had passed in anecdotes and memories and technical discussions of plays they both knew. Jessica made another pot of coffee and brought two mugs to the living room and they sat at each end of the white couch, facing each other, talking and talking with no break except when she returned to the kitchen to take a casserole from the freezer and put it in the oven. At nine o'clock Luke made a salad of sliced tomatoes, basil and *bufalo mozzarelle,* and Jessica set the table, choosing different place mats and china and silver, and placing them as Luke had, opposite each other. Following her directions, Luke found a bottle of fine burgundy in a small wine cooler near the kitchen, and then once again they sat down to eat, still talking, bringing the wide world of the New York and London theaters into that quiet house surrounded by darkness.

"Do you ride?" Jessica asked as they finished their coffee and cognac.

"Yes, as often as I can. I keep horses in New Jersey."

"I go out very early, before breakfast. I have a horse I think you'd like, if that appeals to you."

"Very much."

That was what he remembered as he drove to her house in the clean-washed early-morning air. And what he saw in his memory was her brief nod, almost somber, when he told her, stepping from her car in front of the inn the night before, that he had never known a more wonderful day.

She was waiting for him and they drove to her barn in his truck. Luke, occupied with following her directions, and then saddling the horse she chose for him, had only glanced at her, and so it was not until they were mounted and walking their horses from the paddock that he turned and contemplated her, and barely held in his surprise.

She was a different Jessica. An expensive riding habit softened her thin figure; a helmet covered her hair, and large dark glasses hid the shadows beneath her eyes. At ease in the saddle, holding the reins lightly, she had only a hint of the stoop she had when walking; in fact, her clumsiness had vanished. For the first time since he had been with her, Luke saw in her pose confidence and authority and a relaxation that allowed her to move with some of her former grace, and once again he realized how little he knew about her, and how little he could predict.

"Where would you like to ride?" she asked.

"Wherever is your favorite."

She led the way to a fork in the path and chose the left one that plunged into a dark forest, still dripping from the rain. The sun had not yet warmed the cold air, but the scent of wet pines and the leaves carpeting the path was so pure it gave Jessica the feeling of being at one with the earth. This was where she always began her ride. But this time her familiar solitude had been breached, and she felt tense and uncomfortable with the presence of another rider. But soon she became aware of how skilled Luke was, matching his horse's rhythm to hers as they trotted side by side on the wide path, and she began to enjoy herself. In a few minutes she turned at another fork in the path, and suddenly the rhythmic sound of matched steps was gone; she heard nothing but the soft trotting of her own horse and the piercing call of a bird. A feeling of aloneness descended on her and she almost stopped to turn around. But then Luke was beside her, once again in step, and she smiled, happy that he was there.

They rode in silence and soon the forest thinned until they were in the open, at the edge of a sheer cliff that plummeted to a narrow strip of rock-strewn sand far below, washed by frothy waves. The sky arched pale blue and cloudless over forests and farms, rolling pastures, grazing herds, and fenced yards where farmers raised a hand in greeting. And in a chorus all around them, the roosters crowed.

Luke drew in his breath. "Wonderful. It's more rural than I imagined. A perfect respite from—" He stopped.

"New York," Jessica said evenly, wondering when he would just come out and ask her what he wanted to know. "Though not many come here from the East Coast."

"How many people live here year-round?"

"I'm not sure. Two thousand, perhaps. Robert would know."

"And are they mostly farmers?"

"I don't know."

"I thought the solitude might attract writers and artists, sculptors, perhaps."

She gave him a brief look. "I don't think it's any kind of an art colony, if that's what you mean. I've heard of one writer, of mysteries, I think, and I've met one sculptor."

"Is there a school?"

"A very small one."

"Then most of the homes are vacation homes?"

"Many of them. Or weekend places for people from Seattle. I really don't know enough to answer your questions; you should talk to Robert. He knows everything about the island."

"But you've lived here for several years and you've worked with—"

"I have very little to do with the people on the island. Talk to Robert."

"He seems to be a good friend."

"He's been very good to me."

"And very protective of your privacy."

"He's protective of everyone. Most people are here for privacy." She saw in his face that he thought she went beyond privacy to isolation, but she would not be drawn into a discussion of the way she lived. "Robert can give you facts and figures, if that's what you want. He won't give you gossip."

"How did you find him?"

"Someone in Arizona had stayed at his inn and recommended it." She paused. "I assume you know I was in Arizona for two years."

"Yes."

She took a breath. "You read all my letters?"

"Not the last ones. I stopped reading when I knew I had to see you."

She paused at that, then decided to ignore it. "But all the others."

"Yes. You must understand—" Once again he stopped himself. "I'm not trying to avoid this; I do want to talk to you about it, but not here. It's complicated and I'd like us to be sitting still. Breakfast. Lunch. Dinner. Or in between. If any of that suits you."

Her eyebrows went up. He was planning their whole day and evening. But, then, why not? He had said he'd come here to get to know her, and how else would he do it? If she let him.

"Breakfast will be fine," she said, and urged her horse to a gallop. Again Luke matched her and they raced along the cliff, the sea wind in their faces, the sun burning off the last traces of the rainstorm and the early-morning dew. Dogs barked and children waved as they flew by; a woman hanging out her laundry picked up a young boy who shouted, "Hi, Jessica!" his words carried away by the wind. Horses came to their fences to watch them pass; a colt nursing at his mother's side turned toward them, briefly distracted; and two bicyclists on a nearby paved road held up their hands in the formal greeting of fellow riders.

Jessica took another trail, turning inland, and they slowed to a trot on a road between long fences guarding farmhouses fronted by vegetable and flower gardens. The fields stretching behind them were scored by perfectly straight rows of square hay bales turning golden brown beneath the blazing sun. A mechanic gave a small salute and said, "Nice day, isn't it, after all that rain," and a woman weeding her garden looked up to smile and ask, "Do you need fresh eggs, Jessica? I can drop some off this afternoon."

"Yes, thank you," Jessica said, and soon after turned at a trail that led back to the forest where they had started.

They had not spoken since the exchange about breakfast. Now, behind her, Luke said, "All those people know you."

"I ride this way almost every day and we say hello."

"But you don't know anything about them? When I asked about the people who live here—"

"I only see them when I ride past." Her words were brusque. Stop pushing me! she demanded silently. Leave me alone! She knew he was remembering her letters. She remembered them, too, word for word.

*I've already made so many friends—the island is so small I've gotten to know almost everyone—and I have my work.*

She felt her face flush, and a wave of anger swept over her. What right did he have to read her letters? What right did he have to come here and confront her with them? Damn him, she thought;

damn him for barging in where he has no right to be.

She rode ahead, her face taut with anger. When they reached the barn and had put the horses in their stalls, she walked to the truck in silence, not looking back. Luke came up to her. "I'm sorry. I should have known there's no way we can talk about anything outside the theater and Constance until we talk about your letters." She stopped beside the truck, not looking at him. "You knew yesterday that I'd read them," he said, and she heard an edge of impatience in his voice. "We spent a lot of hours together and you didn't make it an issue."

She looked down, absently drawing circles in the dirt with the tip of her cane. Finally, she nodded. "You're right. I didn't want to think about it and we had so many other things to talk about."

*And I was having a good time.*

But she could not say that aloud. "Shall we have breakfast?" she asked.

"I'd like that very much."

They drove to her house in silence. Hope's ecstatic greeting bridged the awkwardness of going in together, and Luke went back outside to throw a stick for her to retrieve, again and again, while Jessica went to the kitchen. She flicked the switch on the coffeemaker, took a pan from the refrigerator and put it in the oven, then went back to the front door. "I made something before we left, but it needs twenty minutes. Would you like fruit?"

"Yes, can I fix it?"

"It's all done." She took a bowl from the refrigerator and carried it to a planked table on the terrace, silvered from rain and sun and set with a pair of yellow place mats with small white flowers, and Provençal dishes in bright yellow, green and blue. Luke and Hope went around the house and met her there and she watched Luke pick up one of the mugs. "I bought them in Roussillon."

"The shop on the main square," he said. "On the corner. The place mats, too?"

"Yes."

"I bought a tablecloth for Constance there. And a length of Chantilly lace, very beautiful, and unusual because it was white and most Chantilly is black. I don't know what she did with it; I didn't find it when I closed up her villa."

"She gave it to me."

Surprised, he looked at her.

"She said I could use it for a mantilla, or something more mundane: a tablecloth or curtains. If I couldn't think of anything, she said, I should put it in my hope chest."

"Did you have one?"

"No."

"And the lace?"

"I had it made into curtains for my bedroom."

"I must have been too wet to notice. May I look?"

"Of course."

He went through the French doors into the liv-

ing room and across it to the bedroom. The delicate silk lace hung straight and softly billowing
across the three large windows. Its flowers and
leaves were woven of twisted silk and outlined by
strands of flat silk, and they twined and trailed on
a hexagonal mesh background that allowed light
and the colors of the beach and the bay to stream
through. The sun brushed the lace with pale gold.

"Constance would have been very happy," he
said, returning to the terrace. "It's very beautiful
here; the light brings it to life."

"I told her about it in a phone call and I sent her
a photograph."

"There were no photos," Luke said musingly. "I
wonder what she did with them."

"Probably destroyed them, as she should have
done with the letters."

Luke let it pass. "Would you show me the rest of
your house? We have time, don't we, before breakfast is ready?"

She smiled slightly. "It won't take long; you've
already seen most of it."

Leaning on her cane, with Hope at their heels,
she led him toward a door at the far end of the living room. Lagging back a little, Luke contemplated the finely shaped outline of her head and
her short, silvery-gray hair curling loosely just to
the top of her neck. From that angle, one could
almost believe that this was the Jessica Fontaine
of the past . . . until the eyes moved from her
lovely, long neck to her stooped shoulders and the

tilt of her frail body as she leaned on her cane. Then, even the expensive riding habit could not disguise the fact that this was a different Jessica.

She glanced back and saw his encompassing gaze, and her body tensed. Luke saw her visibly pull into herself as a frightened animal withdraws into a skin of protective coloration, and she flushed, deeply and painfully. "I'm sorry," he said automatically, because it had suddenly become obvious to him (and he cursed himself for being so slow) that a woman who had no mirrors in her house would surely resist being stared at, or even closely observed.

Without responding, she opened the door and stood aside for Luke to go past her. As he did, involuntarily he gasped. He was in a greenhouse that was an explosion of color, a maze of long, two-tiered redwood tables almost hidden beneath a profusion of orchids, amaryllis, begonias, geraniums, cyclamen, tea roses and chrysanthemums. One table was given over to herbs; Luke recognized thyme, rosemary, basil and chives, then saw a plant he could not identify. "They look like bay leaves."

"They are."

"I've never seen them growing. And this?"

"Tarragon."

"And this?"

"A Meyer lemon tree. It has a lot of growing to do."

*But I have a lot of time.*

As if she had spoken aloud, Luke thought he could hear her words. We'll talk about that, he thought, but not yet. He walked to the table covered with orchids: white *Phalaenopsis,* lavender *Cymbidium,* purple-and-gold *Brassavola, Oncidium* with arching stems covered with dozens of tiny yellow-orange flowers, and other varieties he had never seen. On the next table were tall, heavy-stalked amaryllis with massive flowers up to eight inches across, from pure white ones to the salmon-and-white double-petaled Lady Jane that dominated the table. "This takes an enormous amount of work," he said, moving to the table of cyclamen and roses. "And you have the garden outside, too."

Jessica said nothing, and he continued to move about the room, taking pleasure in the warm fresh scent of damp earth and leaves and flowers. A potting table stood near a door, its surface wiped clean, garden tools hung neatly on hooks mounted on the shelves above, where peat starter pots, plant food and bags of potting soil were carefully stacked. So this is her passion, Luke thought, though how it could replace the theater . . . But then he remembered her illustrations. They had not even mentioned those, yet.

"And this is my studio," Jessica said, as if she had heard his thought. She opened a double door that had draperies drawn across it on the other side and pulled open the draperies. "I control the

light with these, but usually I leave them open; I
like to look at the greenhouse when I work, especially in winter."

It was a large room with a skylight and tall windows on the far wall. Books covered the other
walls, surrounding a wide fireplace beneath a
carved wooden mantel. One of the shelves held
Constance's collection of plays, supported between two bookends in the shapes of theater
masks, one tragic, one comedic. The room was
crowded, with a deep couch and a matching armchair, two long worktables, several easels with
paintings propped on them, and a drafting table
tilted at an angle, with a high padded stool in front
of it. The floor was covered with a southwestern
rug, its earth tones repeated in dozens of glazed
and unglazed pots that Luke thought were probably Zuni or Navaho, filling tables and shelves
along the windows. "Totally different from the rest
of the house," he said. "Almost like traveling to another part of the country."

"Yes, that's just it." Her anger at his inspection
of her seemed to be gone. "That's exactly what I
wanted. Some people go to offices—"

"You go to the southwest." They smiled together. Luke wandered from easel to easel. "I have
all your books," he said casually, and from the corner of his eye saw the surprise on her face. "At
least, I have twelve of them. The bookstore clerk
thought that was the whole collection. I found
them extraordinary, quite satisfactorily haunting."

"Satisfactorily haunting?"

"It's always satisfying to be haunted by something, don't you think? There's so much that's ordinary all around us, and it blurs into other ordinary things and then it's gone, as it should be. Your paintings keep coming back to me; they appear at odd moments in the middle of whatever I'm doing. They're very fine."

"Thank you. That's the nicest thing anyone has ever said about them. I feel that way about Constance. She refuses to disappear."

"And she won't, for either of us, because we're holding on to her. I've always felt that one of our sharpest fears is that what is beautiful and special will slip away because we haven't tried hard enough, or haven't been able, to hold on to it."

Jessica gave him a quick look, wondering if he were trying to be clever. He had gazed at her often enough to make her uncomfortable and angry, but not once had he spoken about the way she looked. And when she had opened the door the day before, and they had seen each other for the first time, he had not even seemed surprised. It was as if he had known what to expect. But he could not have known. Robert had told her about Luke's first trip to the island, so short it made no sense: he had arrived after midnight, Robert had said, and he had left early the next morning, with no time to see anyone.

It was much more likely that when she opened her door to him he was the Luke Cameron she had heard about so often: a man who masked his emotions and kept his thoughts to himself.

Or when he rang her doorbell he was too wet and cold to think of anything but getting dry.

He was examining the paintings on her easels with an absorbed, concentrated look and it pleased her that a quick once-over was not enough for him. He studied the world he lived in; he did not take it for granted or skim with indifferent eyes.

Then why had he said nothing about her looks? Why didn't his face show surprise and revulsion, as she was sure everyone's would the minute she showed herself in places where she was known? For all of yesterday, that wonderful day, they had talked and talked, and not once had his face betrayed anything but interest in their conversation and pleasure at being there.

If it had, she would not have invited him to ride this morning.

"They're like dreams," Luke said, standing before the last easel. "That was what I thought when I first saw them. Nothing is quite what it seems." He glanced at her. "A lot of things are like that. And people, as well." Before she could respond, he looked at his watch. "Should we be checking the oven?"

"Oh, Lord, I forgot."

"It's been just twenty minutes."

She was hurrying, furious at her clumsiness as her leg swung out with each step, and she knew

Luke was just behind her. In the kitchen, she pulled down the oven door. "Oh, it's fine."

"I'll carry that if you can get the coffee," he said.

"You'll need a pot holder. In that drawer."

The large, irregular stones of the terrace, shading from buff to gray, shone almost white in the sunlight and long ripples in the bay glinted as they moved lazily toward the sliver of beach and Jessica's garden. Jessica had set the table in the speckled shade of a mimosa tree beside a small, slate-topped serving cart where Luke set the heavy black pan beside a serving knife and spoon. "I haven't had apple pancake for a long time," he said, sitting opposite Jessica. He watched her cut a wide wedge and put it on his plate, and the warm scent of apples and cinnamon rose in the sunlit air. "This is wonderful," he said, tasting it. "The cinnamon is different. Where is it from?"

"China. Most people wouldn't notice."

"It's spicier, somehow. More complex than the kind we usually get. Do you really find this on Lopez? Or Friday Harbor?"

"No, I send for it. A small spice house in Wisconsin called Penzey's, where they grind it every week. I have a long list of things I send for; it's the only way I can shop for everything, since I don't leave the island."

"Except to go to Seattle."

"No, I—" Her fork suspended, she met his eyes in a startled look.

Luke put down his fork and Jessica saw his eyes

change, as if he were taking a mental breath and plunging into a place he knew would be difficult. "You wrote Constance that you signed books for schoolchildren at Elliott Bay bookstore."

"You have an advantage over me," she said coldly. "You promised me an explanation."

"Yes, I owe you that." He looked out, at a small flat-topped island at the entrance to the bay and, beyond it, Mount Baker, snowcapped and serene, dominating the horizon. "The day I heard that Constance had died, I went to Italy. I arranged for her funeral, put her villa on the market, and then went through her rooms, following the directions in her will when there were any, otherwise making my own decisions on what to keep and what to give away. She seemed to be everywhere, you know; her fragrance followed me, her voice stayed with me . . . it was almost as if I were visiting and soon we'd have a quiet dinner—" His voice caught. As the silence stretched out, he deliberately took a bite of apple pancake, then another and another, and Jessica knew he was warding off ghosts. No, not ghosts, she thought; only the pain of knowing that a phantom is all we have left of someone so deeply loved.

She felt close to Luke now, relaxed and ready to listen. She ate some of her own pancake and, suddenly realizing how hungry she was, finished what was on her plate. Without asking, she served Luke another piece and took one for herself.

"Thank you," Luke said, and she knew he was

thanking her mostly for listening. "The box of your letters was in the library, beside her favorite chair. I'd seen it on other visits and thought it was simply decorative, but when I opened it . . . well, I've told you about seeing your letters and reading one or two from curiosity. I read a few more, I think, and then the telephone rang, and it was a woman in New York to whom I'd once been married."

Jessica saw her own surprise mirrored on Luke's face, and she knew he had not expected to say that. But then he gave a small nod, as if acknowledging that this was what he wanted to do, and he settled back in his chair and told her the story of that entire week in Italy and his return to New York. The hum of bees and the sweet trills of birds wove through his deep voice, and Jessica knew that he was responding, as she always did, to the isolation of this small space, seeming entire unto itself as it looked across the open water, leaving the islands and the continent behind.

"I haven't told you about Claudia." Briefly he told her about his marriage and the swath that Claudia still cut through his life. "What I found myself doing was comparing Claudia to you. Not fair to Claudia, of course, but it became so obvious that I couldn't avoid it. She's a woman who is incapable of shaping a life for herself, of finding meaning and purpose in her days. And you'd built a new life, almost from nothing. I didn't understand why you'd had to do it—nothing in your letters said exactly why the train crash forced you to abandon everything—but I knew you'd done it, and evidently without leaning on others. So while Claudia was demanding that I create a purpose and a direction for her, you'd had two careers, two ways of life, two purposes, two directions, and you'd done it by yourself. I didn't have to understand it to know how difficult that must have been, and I admired you enormously for it. I read a magazine interview you'd given, where you said you'd thought about other ways of living and you had hobbies, especially painting, that gave you great pleasure, but then you said, 'Nothing makes me feel fully alive and in touch with myself as the theater does. I think if I left it I would never feel whole again.' The reason I remember every word of that is because it's exactly the way I feel. So I think you must have gone through hell to get where you are." He paused, contemplating her. "And I think I'm beginning to understand it."

Jessica put her hands on the edge of the table as if to push back her chair and flee. "I don't want your admiration if it comes attached to a comparison with your wife—"

"Ex-wife."

"I don't want to be compared to her, or to anyone else. I don't want to be reminded, over and over, of what I was and what I said, as if you're rubbing my nose in the past."

"I would never—"

"I just want to be left alone! I don't want to

think about what's gone; I don't want to be dragged into places I've turned my back on. I don't want questions or advice. Or pity."

"I'm not pitying you. I'm not dragging you anywhere. I'm trying to tell you what your letters meant to me. And I haven't told you the most important reason I kept reading them." He was gazing outward again, watching a ship appear in the distance, hazily outlined, as if it were a mirage. "I found myself looking forward to coming home to you. To your letters, of course, but that meant to your voice and your descriptions of people and your comments on the theater. And you brought Constance closer, but that wasn't the main thing. The main attraction was you." He turned back to her. "Your companionship."

Jessica sat very still. He had caught her unawares again, and this time his words flowed into her, warming her. But when he paused, a sneer within her said, *Pretty dramatic stuff, but drama is easy, from a distance. Now that he's seen me . . .* And that sent her upright, no longer relaxed. "That was a fantasy," she said flatly. "You never had my companionship. And you don't know me, no matter how many letters you've read."

"I know that. It's the reason I'm here. I don't like open-ended mysteries; I need answers and conclusions."

"That's because you're used to two acts and a final curtain."

"It's because I don't wear blinders," he snapped.

"It's because I believe in understanding. Theater isn't all illusion; you of all people would know that the best of it tells the truth." He thought back. "A friend of mine, a director named Zelda Fichhandler, said something a long time ago; you know it because you quoted it in one of your letters. She said, 'Theater exposes our internal feelings so we can see them instead of having them just be fluttering around inside us.' You knew that it meant exposing feelings and *facing* them; you knew it and you believed it and I'll bet you still do."

"Constance told me you confuse theater and life," Jessica said angrily. "You thought your marriage should be like the one in a play you were directing and when it wasn't—" She caught herself. "I'm sorry; I shouldn't have said that."

"It seems my grandmother told you far more about me than she told me about you." His voice was light, but Jessica saw that he was surprised and hurt. "I'm sorry she told you that; it was very personal."

"So were my letters," she shot back.

"Yes, and I was prying and I apologize. But now that I've read them it doesn't make sense to keep arguing that point."

"It does as long as you keep quoting them. You have no right to throw my words at me, as if you're trying to force me to explain them or retract them. . . ."

"You're right, I apologize again. It seems I have

a lot to be sorry for. But you see, I don't understand you. How you could write one thing—"

"You don't have to understand me. Who asked you to?"

"I want to. *I want to.* That's reason enough."

"Not for me." She stood up and reached for her cane. "I think you'd better go; we don't have anything more to talk about."

"We have Jessica Fontaine to talk about."

"Then you'll talk to yourself. I have no intention of indulging you."

She was at the French doors, the dog padding beside her, when Luke said, "Jessica. Please," and she stopped, her back to him. "I'm not trying to force you to do anything. I doubt that I could, in any event. But I want to know you better and I'm willing to meet you halfway on that. In fact, I have already; I've been honest with you in everything."

She wheeled about. "Honest? You've lived a lie since the minute I opened my door to you."

"That's not true."

"Oh, yes, you're the expert on truth, aren't you? But you only use the parts of it that suit you. What are you really here for?"

"For Christ's sake." He was standing now and they faced each other across the terrace. "How many times do I have to say that I want to know you, who you are now—"

*"Then how can you ignore what you see?* Damn it, look at me! *This* is what I am now! Why do you

ignore it? You treat me like a child, or a fool, sitting here for hours and talking about the theater, about Constance, about New York, as if you were just passing by and stopped in to chat and found everything exactly as you expected it. Is that truth, to you? Or honesty? Do you expect me to believe that it is?"

The terrace was silent. The birds were still, the waves barely whispered as they rolled onto the beach, not even a breeze stirred the air. Hope sat motionless beside Jessica, waiting for whatever came next. "No," Luke said at last. "If you think I've been living a lie, you'd have trouble believing anything I say. The problem was, I didn't know how to begin. I did know what to expect, you see, when I rang your doorbell, because I'd seen you the last time I was here."

"Seen me? You never came to the house."

"Partway. You were in the garden, cutting roses. I watched for a few minutes and then left. I assume Robert told you I'd come to see you."

"Yes." Slowly, she repeated it. "You watched for a few minutes and then left. Of course you did; why wouldn't you? You were appalled by what you saw. What you saw sent you scurrying. So that's what happened; Robert and I were wondering. You read my letters and thought, for a kick, you'd track me down, but then, when you did, you were so revolted you couldn't even come up to the front—"

"Stop it! I wasn't revolted; I was surprised. I

have never been revolted by you. No one would be. Is that the certainty you've been living with all these years? It makes no sense."

"How do you know what makes sense? How can you have the faintest idea of what makes sense for me?"

"Well, exile doesn't."

"It does. For me."

"Because you're afraid of the look on people's faces when they see you."

She winced.

"That's it, isn't it?"

"Part of it."

"And the rest?"

She was silent.

"Let me guess. You imagined every director saying no when your name came up for a new play. You imagined every producer turning thumbs down. You imagined playwrights sending plays to all the top actors' agents except yours, and all your colleagues refusing to share a stage with you. And you didn't even trust Constance enough to share those terrors with her."

"It wasn't a question of trust," she cried, stung. "Her heart wasn't strong, and she already worried about me; why would I make her worry more? I'd written a couple of letters telling her how awful things were—" She saw Luke's face change. "But of course you know that. You read them."

"I couldn't get them out of my mind. Your despair was so devastating—"

"And that's what happened to Constance. She couldn't get those letters out of her mind. She lay awake at night worrying about me. She called me and wrote me—she thought I was about to kill myself—"

"She had reason to think that."

"I know, I know that. I should never have let myself go, but she was all I had and I loved her—"

"And you were sick and lonely and you needed her. You shouldn't be ashamed of being honest with her; if love is about anything, it's about that."

"Except that she was sick, too, and weak. And I couldn't bear the thought of her working herself into a panic over me. Even when I stopped writing about my injuries and therapy, she still worried. She worried about my being alone, and being unhappy, and leaving the stage, and coming here to live. I wanted to make her believe there was nothing to worry about."

"And so—" Luke walked toward her. "You made up a life."

"No. I wrote about the life I have: a home and a garden, a job, friends, a dog."

"And going to a bookstore in Seattle. But you never went there. You made it up."

She met his eyes with a fierce challenge. "Those letters were for Constance, no one else. I was talking only to her; it was *between us.*"

"How could it be between you when you were keeping the truth from her? You made up a life for yourself; you created your own fantasy. It was for yourself, not for her."

"That is not true!"

"Then tell me what is true. You didn't go to Seattle, to that bookstore."

Her eyes did not waver as she flung her answers at him. "No."

"You didn't make friends all over the island."

"No."

"And helping to direct *Pygmalion?*"

"A little. I made notes on the director's script and we talked on the phone almost every day."

"But you never went to the theater in Friday Harbor?"

"Twice. I sat in the audience and made notes. And I went to opening night."

"How did you know about everything that happened backstage?"

"The director told me, when it was all over."

"And the sculptor? The man you met digging clams?"

"My God, don't you forget anything?"

"Not much, when it's important."

She gave a small shrug. "Richard is a friend. We've visited each other's studios."

"How often do you see him?"

"Not often. But we're friends."

"Did he take you to rehearsals in Friday Harbor in his boat?"

"Yes, those two times I asked him, and he took

the time to do it. And we went to opening night to-gether. Some of his sculptures are in my studio; if you're interested, I'll show them to you. Have you had enough?"

"Not quite, but first I think we should sit down." He touched her arm. "Please."

She shrugged his hand away, but she turned and walked back to the table. Hope padded between them and lay at Jessica's feet, looking up now and then to make sure that the loud voices would re-main subdued.

"I'm trying to understand this," Luke said. "I'm not attacking you and I don't want to hurt you—my God, I would never hurt you—but I need to make sense of it."

"Why? What difference does it make? Why do you care?"

He started to say something, then stopped. "I'll answer that another time. I promise I will answer it, but right now I want to finish this. Why did you do it? Why go to all that trouble? You could have convinced Constance that there was nothing to worry about without those elaborate scenarios . . . by the way, *was* she convinced?"

"Not completely. She was very smart." Their eyes met in one of those moments when they were in perfect harmony, understanding Constance, loving her, longing for her to be with them again. Uncomfortable with that harmony, Jessica turned away to reach for her glass. The water was tepid and she thought of getting up to add ice to the pitcher, but she did not move. The air was electric with their intensity, charged with tension as they ricocheted from clashes to closeness and back again, and she felt pinned in place by it, and by the turmoil within her. Just as she and Luke swung wildly from one set of emotions to the other, so did her thoughts. On one side, it was very peculiar to be with someone who was almost a stranger yet knew so much about her; it was peculiar and distasteful, and whenever he quoted her or showed how much he knew and remembered, she wanted to tell him to take his prying eyes and get out.

But on the other side, she was beginning to feel at ease with him. At some point in the past twenty-four hours something within her had relaxed, like a knot abruptly coming apart so that all the taut cords sprang free, and she found herself settling into the comfort of talking about things that no one else knew, things she had thought were forever locked inside her, never to be shared.

"I had to write to her," she said slowly. "I loved her so and she was my connection with the world. I waited for her letters as if they were treasures—well, they were treasures—and I read each one over and over, until the next one came, and in between I wrote to her, and when I did that I was filling the silence of my house with our conversation. And then of course we had the telephone. She was always part of my life. The trouble with that was, that by keeping her with me, I kept my past alive. She *was* my past; we were so intertwined that sometimes I had trouble keeping us separate in my thoughts. So while I was trying to bury my past, every time I wrote a letter, or read one of hers, I resurrected it. So I tried to fill my letters with things that were different from anything we'd ever shared, and I thought that would help her, too, since she *was* ill and would be better off not worrying about me. So, after a while, I."

"Filled in the spaces," Luke said when her words trailed off. "Some shading, some coloring, a mosaic of small pieces."

Her eyes were wide with surprise. "Yes, exactly. The empty spaces." She gave a small smile. "There were a lot of them; I really had so little to talk about. So I filled them in and pretty soon it was as if I were in a play about Jessica Fontaine that would convince her I was doing all those things she kept urging me to do."

"And did that help fend off the past?"

Again he had surprised her by using the word she would have used. "Sometimes."

"But you said Constance wasn't convinced."

"I think she wasn't sure. About a year ago, she wrote that I shouldn't cut myself off from the world that I know. She said it was my nourishment, my life and my being." Again she gave that small, bitter smile. "I thought I was writing those fantasies for both of us, but neither of us completely bought them."

"You mean you weren't taken in by them."

"Of course not. Did you think I was? I liked writing them; it was fun to pretend a life, like Walter Mitty dreaming himself into a dozen heroic poses to deny the person he really was. But I never thought it was anything but a game."

"There was something in the way you wrote about that life . . . a kind of coolness. As if you were distancing yourself from it."

"Is that true?" She frowned. "I thought I was being so careful. Maybe that's why she never fully believed it. Maybe she always wondered if it were just a game."

"If so, she would have known it was a game you liked to play. It really was a fantasy for yourself as much as for her."

Her eyes hardened. "Do you always have to beat people into admitting their weaknesses? Can't you let them keep just a few illusions if that seems important to them?"

Luke's gaze turned inward, and there was a long silence. When he looked at her again, his face was bleak. "I think that's exactly what I do. I suppose I always have. No one has ever pointed it out so precisely. I'm very sorry, Jessica. I didn't mean to do that to you. I won't do it again."

"Why do you do it at all?"

"I don't know. I detest pretense, the masks people wear . . . No one can be a great actor without first understanding himself or herself—you and Constance knew that better than anyone—and I suppose I've been pushing my actors for so many years, I do it with everyone. Maybe. Or maybe I just like to control people and I do it by pounding them into submission."

"A little breast-beating there," Jessica said drily.

He laughed, and the tension was broken. "Actually I was paraphrasing my grandmother. She thought I overdid the need to be in control. I assume she told you that, too."

"Yes. But not maliciously. She worried about you."

"It seems she worried about both of us."

"Not all the time, but enough to talk about. She always wanted . . ."

"What?"

"I'll tell you another time." She saw the quick line that appeared between his eyes. "No, I'm not doing that to get back at you for keeping things from me. We each have our reasons."

Luke sat back and looked at her thoughtfully for a long time, and she did not turn away, though her hands were clenched tightly in her lap and she had to hold herself still to endure his scrutiny. She looked beyond him, at filaments of clouds trailing across the clear sky, and a sailboat tacking just beyond the bay, but all the time she was aware of his eyes on her.

"I'd like to take you to dinner tonight," he said at last. "Can you recommend a good place on the island?"

She met his quiet look. She knew the two of them were still springing back and forth, from tension to harmony, like bumper cars in a carnival, but she knew, too, that she did not want him to leave, at least not yet. She had been lonely for a long time and now the air was filled with a clamor of things to talk about, unresolved questions to settle, and the promise of companionship for dinner, and she was unwilling to let any of that slip through her fingers. "The Bay Cafe," she said, "if you don't mind something very casual. But I need to work this afternoon; is eight o'clock all right?"

"Fine. I'll pick you up."

"No, I'll meet you there. It's in the village, very small, you even have to look hard for the name. But it's easy to find."

After a moment, Luke nodded. "Eight o'clock. If you need me before then, I'll be at the inn." He stood up. "But I'll do the dishes before I go."

She was about to refuse that, too; she wanted to be alone, to think about everything that had happened, and to work at her drafting table through the afternoon hours, with music in the background and no one to intrude. But he was already stacking plates, and she remembered the easy way they had worked together the day before, and she did not tell him to stop. She watched him clear the table and carry everything on a tray into the kitchen, and when she joined him there he was rolling up his sleeves. He smiled at her. "I can do this myself; there's not very much. And you did the cooking."

She took a clean towel from the drawer. "We'll do it together," she said.

## CHAPTER 12

The Bay Cafe had no view of the bay, or indeed of anything but the wide, empty street that ran through the center of Lopez Village. The restaurant was small and spare, with a bare wood floor, simple wooden tables and chairs, white tied-back curtains in the windows, and a flowered curtain hanging in the kitchen doorway. It was not a place Luke would have chosen, had he glanced inside seeking dinner, but it was Jessica's choice, and he was waiting for her at a table in the back when she arrived.

"I'm sorry I'm late," she said. She wore a blue denim dress with long sleeves, a skirt that came almost to her ankles, and a narrow leather belt, and for the first time since Luke had been there she wore jewelry: a necklace of embossed silver beads and silver figured earrings. She sat in the chair he held for her, at right angles to his own. "I wasn't paying attention to the time."

"You shouldn't have to, when you're working."

"Usually I don't." But she smiled as she said it,

so that he would not think she was complaining about having nothing to do, night after night, but work as late as she wished.

A few hours earlier they had said good-bye casually, like old friends who knew they would be together again soon, and Jessica had gone to her studio while Luke let himself out the front door. He drove back to the inn, thinking about the fierceness with which she challenged him to be honest. She did not want his sympathy; she did not seem to care about his understanding. What she wanted was the truth between them. He remembered what she had said the day before, when they were talking about Mary Tyrone in O'Neill's *Long Day's Journey into Night.*

*Dependency is a curse and Mary used hers as a weapon.*

Was that what had driven her all these years? The fear of sinking into dependency and then finding what a devastating weapon it could be? She could not live with herself if she heard herself use those little tricks and stratagems that the dependent use. Yet another reason to withdraw from the temptation of others' sympathy and concern.

At the inn, he took from his suitcase the copy of Kent's new script, expanded now to two acts and an outline of the third. At some time during breakfast that morning the idea had come to him that Jessica, even looking as she did, might be able to figure out a way to play the lead—in fact, might possibly play it better than anyone he knew. He had almost said it aloud, but caught himself in time. He was sure that she was not ready to hear that, and he had to be convinced that this was not one of those wild ideas that bloom in the warmth of good companionship, excellent food, and the sunlight of a golden October day, later to spiral away to nothingness.

"You told Constance you miss the theater," he said in the restaurant when they had ordered dinner.

"That was a long time ago. This is a nice wine; I hadn't heard of it. Are you an expert in wine, in addition to all your other accomplishments?"

"I know enough to order what I'm familiar with and leave the rest to the sommelier. I gather that no matter how often I introduce the subject of your life in the theater, you'll immediately find something else quite fascinating to talk about."

A laugh escaped her. "Probably."

"Well, you choose. I'll be glad to talk about anything you like."

"Tell me more about *The Magician.* How you directed it."

It was an easy subject for Luke, and a pleasant one, and he talked about it while they ate their appetizer of mussels brought from the sea just an hour earlier, and the salad and main course, describing the decisions he had made and what came of them, the ones that worked and the ones that did not. "I think, on balance, it was a mistake to cast Cort as Daniel. He was fine, eventually, but it

took a long time to get there, through a lot of turmoil we could easily have avoided."

"Why was he the wrong person?" she asked.

Luke reflected for a moment. "He never liked
Daniel. He kept that to himself until he had the
part—or maybe he only began feeling that way
later—but once we were well into rehearsals it became almost an obsession and he kept insisting
that Kent make changes in Daniel's character. A
director should never cast an actor who doesn't
make it clear from the beginning that he or she
truly identifies or empathizes with a character,
or—if the character is evil—at least understands
him."

"That seems obvious," she said.

"It ought to. A lot of directors don't see it."

She sat back as the waitress removed their dinner plates. "And how is Cort doing now?"

"I haven't seen him since opening night, but I
haven't had any anguished calls from New York,
so I assume he's fine. You understand, he's not
bad, he's just not . . ."

"Daniel."

"Yes, that's it. He's a skilled actor pretending to
be Daniel."

"Like a parent humoring a teenage son but not
understanding a word he's saying."

Luke laughed. "Not that bad, but close. That's
very good; I'd like to use it when I need it. Would
you mind?"

"Of course not; it's hardly a line of immortal

prose. And anyway, I wouldn't know about it if you did."

"You would if you were there."

Very deliberately, Jessica set her wineglass down and folded her hands on the table. "I could just change the subject again, but I'll say this instead. I am not going back to the theater, or back to New York. I thought that was very clear in my letters to Constance, which you seem not only to have read but to have memorized. God knows I wrote it often enough for anyone to be convinced, but I'll say it again. I am not going back. I have a life here, a good life, and there is no reason for me to try to recapitulate the past."

"The reason is that that was your real life and your real identity and what you have now is Jessica Fontaine pretending to be whole on Lopez Island."

She shoved her chair back. The wooden legs squeaked on the wooden floor and struck her cane, propped against the wall beside her, knocking it over. The clatter seemed thunderous in the small room and Jessica's face flamed with embarrassment. Luke leaped to his feet. He came around the table and propped up the cane, then stood beside her, screening her from the other diners. "I'm sorry," he said, bending down so that he could speak softly. "I'd take that back if I could; it was rude and insensitive. Constance would say I'm still trying to control everything, events, people, conversation, the whole order of battle." He waited, but Jessica was looking at her clenched hands and did not look up or reply. "But this isn't a battle," he said. "I don't want one and I'm sure you don't; what we want is friendship. Jessica, I'm sorry. There are things I wanted to talk to you about, but they require a lead-in and if we can't do the lead-in, we won't talk about them at all. It will be enough for me just to be with you."

She looked at him then. "Why?"

"Because I like you. Because I'm having a very good time. Because I feel close to Constance when I'm with you."

A small smile played on Jessica's lips. When he isn't saying the absolutely wrong thing, she thought, he's saying the absolutely right thing.

"I'm sorry I made a spectacle of us," she murmured.

"It's already forgotten; the food is so good that that's what everyone is thinking about. I like your recommendation. May I . . . ?"

His hands were on her chair, and she stood slightly so that he could help her slide back to the table. "Thank you," she said.

He returned to his chair. "I hope the desserts are as good as everything else."

"I don't usually have any. You can give me a report."

"Then I'll have to try more than one. You know, one of the best restaurants in New York has a dessert that's an arrangement of five different caramel concoctions—"

"Bernardin," she said.

He nodded. "One of my favorites. But there are some wonderful new places, Nobu, for one. . . ." He talked about restaurants, then went on to concerts and operas of the past season, and then the fashion shows in Bryant Square, held in huge tents and attracting as much attention as the Paris and Milan shows.

"Did you go to all of them?" Jessica asked, amazed.

"I would have if they hadn't run simultaneously. They're a fascinating form of theater, and I went with a friend who gave a private commentary that almost made sense of the most absurd parts."

"Was she a designer?"

"No." Jessica could see that he was debating whether to tell her who it was. "Someone you don't approve of. Tricia Delacorte."

"The gossip columnist." She fell silent, suddenly seeing him as a whole person with an entire life. Until now, so much had been going on between them that she had thought of him only as a director whose work she had admired; as Constance's grandson who had read letters not meant for him; and as an unwelcome messenger bringing New York and the theater into her quiet life. Now she looked at him and saw a man who had been married and divorced . . . and perhaps had married again? She did not know. He wore no ring, but that was not definitive. His behavior with her did not seem to be that of a married man, but that was never definitive. In any case, she knew that, as a director and as a young, vigorous man, he would be deeply involved in the many-layered social life of New York, and, if he were single, of course he would have women to share his evenings, and his bed. A sharp stab of jealousy shot through her and she drew in her breath with dismay. Why would she care about that? She barely knew him and she had no intention of getting involved with him, or anyone else, ever again. Maybe it's New York, she thought. Maybe I'm jealous of his life there. Could that be? After all this time? Oh, when will that stop?

"I've known her for a few months," Luke said as the silence stretched out. "I know she's capable of writing drivel, but she's created a life for herself and she's very good at what she does, within its limits, and I admire that."

"Of course, you could say the same about a successful cat burglar."

Luke's eyebrows rose and Jessica drew in her breath again. "But I think she must have had a hard life at one time," she went on quickly. "I don't think she could unerringly spot people's vulnerabilities unless she'd spent a lot of time putting patches on her own."

*Not much better. It's time to change the subject.*

But Luke did it first, as if to save her from being obvious. "The other kind of theater at the fashion shows were the audiences. More casual and spontaneous than in Europe, I think."

"You mean they weren't stone-faced? When I went to the shows in Milan and Paris I always thought the audiences had practiced for months to perfect those masks. By the last day of the shows, they all looked like effigies that had been dug up from a Mayan tomb."

Luke burst out laughing. "They'd never go to another show if they heard you say that."

Their voices were low and they leaned closer as they talked. Luke ordered three desserts and Jessica took a bite of each while he ate all of one and parts of the others, and then they ranked them. "There are some we didn't get to," Luke said. "We'll have to come back."

They drank espresso and then ordered more, reluctant to leave, talking now about theaters in Europe, the Moscow circus, Finnish acrobats . . . until, finally, Jessica said, "We should go. It's very late."

Once again he helped her with her chair. At the door, she held out her hand. "Thank you for dinner. I enjoyed it."

Luke held her hand. "I'd like to see you tomorrow."

And then Jessica asked the question that had hovered over them all evening. "Are you here indefinitely?"

He smiled. "Not that long; I do have to get back. But I don't want to leave yet."

She nodded, as if she understood, though she had no idea what he was thinking or what he was waiting for. She slid her hand from his. "Would you like to ride again tomorrow morning?"

"Very much."

"The same time, then."

They said another brief good-night in the parking area, and then Luke drove off in the direction of the inn and Jessica turned toward Watmough Bay. The moon was almost full, so blazingly white that most of the stars were invisible. The sky belonged to the moon, as did the waters lapping the island, holding on their surface a rippling ribbon of light, and the pine trees along the road, every needle gleaming like a thin, pure white blade. Jessica was amazed at the clarity of everything, the beauty of her island enhanced so that it seemed newly created, the softly rolling fields as bright and welcoming as lighted rooms seen from afar. She breathed deeply of the cold, crisp air. The nights were chilly harbingers of winter now, while the days grew warm as the sun rose, and the gardens still bloomed. *And tomorrow we'll ride.*

The next day it seemed they had already fallen into a routine, riding very early through cool forests still wet with dew, along ocean cliffs and around the periphery of open fields, coming back to Jessica's house for breakfast on the terrace and a long, leisurely conversation, then parting for an afternoon of work, planning to meet again for dinner. They were more relaxed than the day before, as if they had broken through some barrier of strangeness to a place where they were familiar with each other and had begun already to use the kind of shorthand in their talk that longtime friends used without thinking.

"Where would you like to have dinner?" Luke asked as he put away the last clean dish from breakfast.

"There isn't much choice. The Bay Cafe is by far the best."

"Then I'll have a chance to try the other desserts. Do we need a reservation?"

"I'll take care of it. Eight o'clock?"

"Yes. I'd like to pick you up."

"Fine," she said easily, surprising them both.

He turned to go, then turned back. "By the way, I have to find a new place to stay; Robert has a bicycle group coming in. Can you recommend one?"

She was wiping the sink and her hand slowed. "There are several. I don't know anything about them; I've only stayed at Robert's. I'll think about it and we'll talk about it later. Is that all right?"

"Fine. I'm sure Robert will have suggestions, too."

"Of course," she said absently, thinking that Robert was a far better source of information than she was. But as she went into her studio and sat at her drafting table, she was trying to remember the inns she had heard of, especially one close to her house. She picked up her pencil and was bending over her sketch when suddenly she was struck by the extraordinary clarity of the light surrounding her. It was the same clarity as the moonlight the night before, and she put down her pencil and looked around the room at objects she barely noticed anymore. Now each was unique: seemingly polished to a brilliant sheen, the tiniest details standing out, perfect in their precision. The clear light washed over her, as well, and she saw her fingernails and the veins on the backs of her hands as sharply outlined as if she had drawn them with her finest pen.

Jessica looked with wondering eyes. As with the beauty of her island the night before, it was as if her studio were newly made, or as if she had just walked into it for the first time. I have never felt this before, she thought, and she knew that it had to do with Luke.

They had been together for most of the past three days, and in that whole time, they had been alone, seeing other people only at the cafe. No one had interrupted their nonstop conversation; the telephone had not rung, nor had the doorbell. No one had distracted them from each other since the moment he had appeared at her door.

And now she did not want him to leave.

She turned to her drafting table, concentrating on the pencil sketch she had begun the day before. Half an hour later, she took it to one of her easels. Hope lifted her head to make sure everything was in order, and Jessica smiled. "Nothing different, Hope; it's just an ordinary day." She clipped the sketch to the top of the large sheet of paper on which she would paint the enlarged watercolor version, pulled her cart of paints close to her, and picked up her brush. Then she paused, contemplating the sheet of paper. There was always this strange hesitation before she made the first stroke of her brush upon a blank surface, as if she were holding back before beginning a new adventure. Usually she imagined her first brush stroke, then her second and third, and then she would be ready to paint. But today she found herself thinking about Luke, and inns on the island. She reached to a nearby table and poured a mug of coffee from a thermos. I don't know anything about them, she thought, sipping the coffee; he's much better off asking Robert.

Five minutes later she put down her mug. It was not an ordinary day, she thought; it was, in fact, quite astonishingly different from other days. She took the portable telephone from its stand and called Luke at the Inn at Swifts Bay. "Has Robert given you any ideas about another place to stay?"

"I haven't asked him. I trust your judgement."

*After I told him I don't know anything about them? He's been putting it off, maybe hoping I'd call.*

"I do have an idea. You can—" Her voice caught on the words. It had been so long since another person had woven through the pattern of her days. But she knew this was what she wanted, and she rushed ahead before she could change her mind. "You can stay here. The couch in my studio opens into a bed and it's quite comfortable. The studio has its own bathroom and of course it's quite completely separate from the house. You're very welcome—" She stopped again as she heard her cool formality. "I'd be glad to have you here."

"Thank you," he said instantly. "You're very generous. May I come in a couple of hours? I don't want to interrupt your work."

She looked at her watch. "Three hours would be better."

"I'll see you about six, then. Thank you, Jessica. I'm very grateful."

How formal we are, she thought. And how comforting that is. Far better than the instant intimacy people seem to cultivate in New York.

But the idea of intimacy made her think she had made a terrible mistake. Why tantalize herself with other options when she had no intention of choosing anything but what she had? In other words, she told herself with a brutal directness she had practiced for years, why take the risk of falling in love?

She reached for the telephone, to call Luke again and tell him some lie to keep him from coming. But her hand hovered in the air until she gave up and let it fall to her lap. She wanted to see more of him. And she knew—though she had not told him this and perhaps never would—that that was what Constance had wanted, as well.

She turned to her painting, still not begun. This would not do, she thought. She had a schedule; she had a contract with her publisher. But then she thought of her front door. *If it's open, he can come in and I won't have to watch for him.* She walked back through the greenhouse and the living room to the foyer and opened the door a few inches. Hope followed her, puzzled by all the activity in what was usually five or six hours of perfect stillness, and Jessica rubbed her behind her ears. "Well, it isn't ordinary," she told her, "and I don't know how it's going to come out, but I'm sure I want to do this, and I'm not going to back out now."

After that she finally turned to her painting and when Luke arrived she was at her easel, completely absorbed. She would not have known he was there if Hope had not dashed into the greenhouse to greet him, tail wagging, nose nudging him for a caress. "Hello," he said softly, and knelt beside her. He looked up and met Jessica's eyes. "Hello," he said again.

She saw reflected in his face the brightness of her own, and she smoothed her features to a cool welcome. "I'm almost finished for today. Then I'll show you where everything is."

"May I see what you're doing?"

Automatically, she shrank back. No one ever saw her paintings until she sent them to New York.

"I'm sorry, of course you're not used to that," he said. "I'll wait in the living room."

"No, it's all right." She shook it off. Everything was different, so why not allow this difference, too? "I'd like you to see this."

With Hope at his side, he stood at her shoulder and Jessica looked at her painting through his eyes. The central figure was almost complete: a woman seated on a marble bench, looking into the distance, with a black dog at her feet. The rest of the painting was only a wash of background color, but the pencil sketch showed what it would be: on one side a forest, with a man building a log cabin in a sunlit clearing, and on the other an ocean with lightning slashing the dark clouds above. Almost hidden in the folds of the woman's long skirt were the words *The open door.*

The woman was Constance; the dog was Hope. The man was Luke.

After a silence, Luke said, "Why am I building the log cabin?"

"Because that's what you do. You create. You build."

He nodded. "I like that." After another moment of scrutiny, he said, "And Constance? And 'The open door'?"

"Constance was always opening doors for me, helping me make new discoveries about myself and other people and the whole world. She did that for you, too, didn't she?"

"Yes." He stepped back, looking at the painting and at Jessica together. "You've done a wonderful job with Constance," he said at last. "I don't remember seeing her in your other books."

"This is the first time a character reminds me of her. I've painted her portrait, though; I'll show it

to you later." She began to clean her brushes. "I'll
help you make your bed. The closet in the corner
has built-in shelves; the bathroom is through that
other door. We have a reservation at the cafe for
eight o'clock."

"I'll get my suitcase; it's in the truck."

Jessica watched him walk away from her. She
knew he was trying to accommodate himself to
the swings in her mood, and she was grateful for
that, because she had no intention of telling him
that they were caused by the small shocks she felt
each time she realized she already was getting used
to the idea of having him in her house.

Mostly that was because their hours quickly fell
into a pattern, and she was used to patterns. They
had dinner that night at the cafe and afterward sat
talking in the living room until they said good
night and Jessica went in one direction, to her
bedroom, and Luke went in the other, to the studio. The next morning they were riding by seven
o'clock and when they came back, at ten, they
made breakfast together and ate on the terrace.
By twelve-thirty, they had cleaned the kitchen and
Jessica was in her studio, and Luke was back on
the terrace, working on playscripts he had
brought. At seven they dressed and went to the
cafe or prepared dinner together, ending the day
in the living room with cognac and coffee and
more talk.

"It's very comforting," Luke said on his third
night at Jessica's house. He was laying a fire while

Jessica poured cognac and coffee. A Schubert piano sonata was playing and Hope was keeping a protective eye on everything. "There's a lot to be said for an unvarying routine. It's like a blanket I had as a child and brought with me to Constance after my parents were killed. It had a design of ships and boats and I knew every thread of every one of them. I could have closed my eyes and described the whole blanket, down to the bolts that held the oarlocks in place or the polka-dot curtains in one of the yachts. When I pulled that blanket around me, no matter what else happened I rooted myself. I was my parents' son."

Jessica looked at his back as he put crumpled newspaper beneath the kindling. "You miss knowing they're at home, talking about what you'll do when you come for a visit," she murmured, reaching back to a letter she had written to Constance, about her parents' deaths.

Luke turned quickly and quoted words from the same letter. "I miss having them miss me."

Their eyes met. "So long ago," she said, "but still so real. I wonder if we ever forget sorrow."

"I hope not," Luke said quietly. "I hope we recover from it, but never forget it." He turned back, took a long match from a holder and lit the fire. The flames leaped up and he sat on his heels, watching them.

"Do you still have the blanket?" Jessica asked.

"Yes."

"Do you ever look at it?"

"When Constance died, I hung it over an arm-chair in my bedroom."

"Is it still there?"

"It is, but most of the time I'm not really aware of it. It's become part of the background of my life. Like sorrow." He sat beside her and raised his snifter of cognac slightly toward her. "Thank you for another wonderful day. Three in a row with a rhythm and a pattern that are immensely comforting. I don't have a single day like it in New York, much less three."

Jessica sipped her cognac and contemplated the fire. The wood had caught and was burning steadily, with occasional crackles and small showers of sparks. Heat radiated through the room and she tucked her legs beneath her, feeling the rush of well-being that comes with warmth on a night that had turned very cold. There was a question she should be asking. Once before, she had asked it— "Are you staying indefinitely?"—and his answer had been vague, but now he had led them to it again. Three days of an unvarying rhythm were comforting. How many did he want?

*How many do I want?*

"Tell me about your parents," Luke said. "I read about them in your letters, but I'd like to know more."

And so the question was not asked. Instead, for the first time, Jessica talked about herself. "I think I had a truly magical childhood, the kind we don't appreciate until we're all grown up and wish for some of the security we rebelled against when we were young." She paused. "I'm sorry. You didn't have that security. You got it from a blanket."

"And from Constance, with abundant love, though the security was much different from yours."

They compared the ways they had grown up and Jessica did not need Luke's questions to urge her on as she reached back to find memories she had thought were lost forever. They alternated stories and anecdotes and had not run out when, finally, reluctantly, Jessica stood up. "It's been a long day. We can go on with this tomorrow." Luke banked the fire, their hands touched lightly, and with a murmured "Good night" they went in opposite directions to go to sleep.

The next day, on their morning ride, the conversation began where it had left off, with shared stories of families and schools, favorite teachers, friends, solitary times and daydreams, and so once again the question was not asked. And that night, Luke forestalled it by saying, "Robert once recommended a restaurant on Orcas called Christina's. If I can get a plane to fly us over and back tomorrow night, would you like to try it?"

"Oh, no, I—"

"Take a minute to think about it," he said quietly.

She did not have to think about it; she had told him she never left the island. This seemed like a step in some kind of deliberate campaign to get her away from home: first to Orcas . . . and then to New York?

"It's just one dinner," he said. "I'm not asking you to pack your bags for New York."

She felt a flash of anger, at herself for being transparent and at Luke for letting her know it. "We'll need a reservation," she said briefly.

"I'll take care of that." He went to the telephone and Jessica heard the murmur of his voice making one call and then another. In a few minutes he was back. "A small problem. We can get a plane over but not back. The pilot suggested a place called Turtleback Farm Inn; he thought we could get rooms this time of year. If that sounds all right to you, we could stay the night and come back early the next morning."

He looked at her steadily, challenging her to break out of the fixed pattern of her days, just for one evening, after which she could settle back into it, if she wished.

"I'll call the inn," he said. "There's no sense in thinking about it if they're full."

She watched him leaf through the telephone book and dial a number. "We have two rooms if we want them," he said, holding the telephone to the side. "Shall I reserve them?"

Instinctively, Jessica put her hand up and brushed back her hair. She saw Luke's face change and knew that he understood that for the first time in days he had made her conscious of herself as a woman, and the two of them as a couple.

"Jessica?"

"Yes," she said.

He finished his call and almost immediately they separated, Jessica to her bedroom, Luke to the studio. The next day there was a new kind of nervousness between them and breakfast was brief, leaving a longer afternoon for work. In fact, they barely spoke until they were sitting in the small plane, watching Lopez recede below them, and even then the pilot did most of the talking, giving a running commentary as they flew over the rugged contours of Shaw Island and then over the entire length of the inverted U that was Orcas, with Mount Constitution towering on their right and the smaller Turtleback Mountain rising from farmlands on their left. "That's where the inn is," the pilot said. "You look right across this narrow valley at Turtleback Mountain. Pretty place."

Jessica said nothing. She felt like a boat cut loose and swept away from shore, pulled this way and that by invisible currents. But at the same time she was excited by that very feeling of being un-moored, of gliding through a dusky sky with the evening star glimmering above and pale crescents of beaches encircling the dark islands below, of floating down and down as the Orcas landing strip came into view. It was as if this were a magic char-iot entering a kingdom where no one had been before. She shook her head, embarrassed by her own fantasy, and glanced at Luke, to see if he had noticed. Their eyes met, and she was so startled by the tenderness in his that she looked away, a little dizzy, denying what she had seen, because of course she must have been mistaken.

He had arranged for a car, and they drove in silence along winding roads through forests and farmland so much like Lopez that it seemed they had not left, until they came to Turtleback Farm Inn, its narrow yard neatly fenced, the last of the summer flowers drooping along the front of the large dark green farmhouse. Susan Fletcher greeted them and showed them their rooms, Jessica's off the living room, Luke's up the broad staircase of polished wood. "We didn't have two close together," she said matter-of-factly. Smiling pleasantly, she showed Jessica extra pillows and blankets and directed Luke upstairs, and not once did she betray the slightest degree of curiosity.

And yet, Jessica thought as Susan opened a window a crack and turned on another lamp, we must seem very strange to her: a tall man with a compelling face and a confident way of holding himself that shows he has mastered his world, and an ugly gray-haired cripple with a stooped back and a clumsy, lurching walk that requires a cane. Maybe she thinks I'm his mother.

The idea made her break into laughter, and she saw Susan's eyebrows go up at the change in her

face. Well, she can just guess, Jessica thought; I'm
not explaining anything and neither is Luke.
"Thank you; it's fine," she said to Susan, and
closed the door behind her. The room was so simple it seemed almost bare, but the bed was comfortable, the small dresser and night table held
magazines and dried flowers, and the bathroom
was an odd combination of paneled walls, a
pedestal sink, and a claw-footed tub with its
shower curtain gathered around it like a shawl
around an elderly man.

"Will it do?" Luke asked when they met in the
living room.

"Yes, it's very pleasant," Jessica said, thinking
that once again they were being very formal.

He opened the front door for her. "And are you
hungry?"

"Very. Breakfast seems a long way back."

"It was. And we didn't eat much. Nervous, I
suppose. Are you now?"

They stood beside the car and she looked up at
him. "No. Are you?"

"No. I'm very glad to be here with you."

She barely nodded, then sat in the car. *No more
formality. Maybe we won't need it again.*

Christina's was on the second floor, and Luke
cursed when he saw the staircase. "No one told
me."

"It's all right." She moved one step at a time,
self-conscious about her struggling pace. Luke

tried to take her arm, but she shook her head and went up alone. By the time she reached the restaurant, her breath was coming faster.

"I'm sorry," Luke said. "I should have asked."

"So should I. Let's forget it, shall we?"

The small room was almost as spare as their bedrooms at the inn, with a wooden floor and tables spaced far enough apart for privacy. An arrangement of copper molds covered part of one wall; a glassed-in porch and deck hung over the water of Eastsound. Jessica pretended to be intensely interested in the little there was to see, trying not to think of her cumbersome body, ready to cut off anything Luke said to try to make her feel better.

But he surprised her. "I may ask Christina if I can copy this room for a set," he said. "There's practically nothing here; a perfect way to save money on design and construction."

Jessica smiled. "Those copper molds are probably antiques. Very expensive."

"Oh, I'd eliminate them. They clutter things up, don't you think?"

They laughed, and Jessica began to relax. Her cane stood against the wall beside her chair, but she forgot it; she forced herself to sit straight, her hands in her lap, and saw the two of them as if they were on a stage: a lady and a gentleman dining quietly in a simple restaurant. But they were not on stage; they were part of the real world, two people sitting among groups of other people, and

when Luke ordered a Woodward Canyon Cabernet and they raised their glasses in a silent toast,
smiling at each other, she knew they had crossed
some imperceptible line and had become a couple.

"I never told you some of my favorite Kent stories," Luke said when they had ordered. His voice
was casual, backing away from the intimacy of
their silent toast, and he sat back, drinking his
wine and spinning stories about Kent Horne and
the weeks of rehearsal of *The Magician.* "One of
the most amazing things," he said as they finished
their appetizers, "was the way he began to feel the
presence of an audience even before there was one.
'We have to make them breathe with us,' he said—
it became his favorite line—'if we hear them
breathing with us, we'll know we have them.'"

"How did he know that," Jessica asked, "if he
hadn't ever seen his play performed?"

"He said he felt it. Something about the collective mind on stage—director, producer, actors,
stage manager—understanding better than anyone the collective mind responding in the audience. As if they breathe together."

"He knows a lot for a young man. Is he really as
young as you think?"

"Younger. You'd think so, too, if you'd seen him
in action. That's why his play is something of a
miracle. And his new one, too."

"He's written another?"

"It's not quite finished."

The waitress served their fish and refilled their

wineglasses, and Luke talked about rehearsals for other plays, and then Jessica said, "Do you know Orlando D'Alba?"

"No. Good name, though."

"It is good. I'm pretty sure he made it up, but why not, if it makes him happy? For eight years he sent my agent two plays a year, one in February and one in August, begging me to take them to Broadway and play the lead—always a woman who murdered various people and got away with it. I thought it was such an odd obsession; he never tried a different plot."

"And the plays weren't good?"

"They were quite dreadful, but he was so serious and determined that I wrote back every time with some suggestions, especially that he send the next one to someone else. But he didn't; they kept coming, always the same story set in different cities, with different names for the characters and different ways of murdering the victims. If you haven't heard of him, I guess he never made it to Broadway or anywhere else."

"He must have quite a stack of plays by now."

"Oh, I imagine he's sending them around; he didn't seem ready to sit on them. People usually don't cling to the past, you know; they let it go and find something new to hold on to."

Luke started to say something, but just then the desserts arrived, and with them Christina Orchid, asking if they had enjoyed their dinner. "We did," Luke said. "It was excellent."

Christina looked at Jessica more closely. "Aren't you Jessica Fontaine? I mean, of course you are. I saw you in *Anna Christie* a long time ago; you were wonderful. I heard you were living on Lopez; a vacation?"

"No."

"Oh. Well, I'm glad to see you. If you're living here, I hope you'll come back in spite of the stairs."

"I hope so."

"Enjoy your dessert." Experienced in the peculiarities of customers, Christina had learned long ago to recognize and end a dialogue that was not going anywhere, and with an amiable smile she moved to the next table.

Luke met Jessica's eyes. "Does that happen often?"

"Of course not. How could it?"

"You mean no one could possibly recognize you?"

She flushed. "I mean not many people up here have seen plays in New York and if they have they wouldn't remember who was in them after all these years."

The waitress brought their espresso and Luke changed the subject. They sat until late, the last diners to leave, and when they finally stood up and moved to the door, Luke stayed at the top of the stairs, letting Jessica maneuver down them by herself. In the car, she said, "It was a lovely evening," and he murmured, "As always," and then they were silent until they reached the inn.

The tiny living room was dark, with only a few embers glowing in the fireplace. "Shall we sit here for a while?" Luke asked, and without waiting for an answer put two logs on the embers and watched the flames catch and flare up. He went to a small table in the corner where a decanter and glasses had been set out and poured each of them a sherry. "I want to tell you something. It's the answer to a question you asked me many days ago. I don't know if you remember it—"

"I do." She sat on the love seat facing the fire and took the glass Luke brought her. "Thank you." A small table in front of the love seat was piled high with magazines and photography books of the islands, and she watched the reflection of the flames in their glossy covers as Luke sat beside her. They were closer together than they had been all week, but where once she would have pulled away, now she sat quietly, lulled by the flickering light, conscious of the solid feeling of Luke's body beside hers. She felt a little as if she had been running a race: tired but not ready to go to sleep, no longer running but not yet at the finish line, not even sure what she would find when she reached it but filled with an odd anticipation.

Luke set down his glass and turned to face her. "When I told you, the other day, that I was trying to understand you, you asked me what difference it made. You asked me why I cared."

"And you said you'd answer that another time."

"Because I wanted to be sure." Shadows danced

over them from the swaying flames and the walls
and ceiling seemed to dissolve, so that when Jessica saw Luke's hand move she thought it was a
trick of the light. But then she felt his palm against
hers, and saw him lean toward her, and she looked
down to see their hands locked together. "At some
point when I was reading your letters—I've told
you this, but I want to tell you again—I started
looking forward to coming home at the end of the
day and spending time with you. You became part
of my reality, one of the most important parts,
and that was when I knew that I was in love with
you."

"No." It was a whisper. She tried to pull her
hand away, but Luke was holding it too tightly. "I
told you: it was fantasy. It—"

"It was very real and I—"

"—doesn't make sense."

"—knew it when I'd been with you for a few
days."

They broke into brief laughter at the tangle of
their voices. "I knew it," Luke repeated. "I waited
to tell you until I was sure. What I loved in your
letters was very real. But it wasn't enough. That
was why I had to find you and why I kept trying to
understand what you wrote and what you are. Jessica, you're magnificent; what you've done with
your life—"

"No," she said again. She pulled away and
gripped her hands in her lap. "I'm not magnificent.
I was, once, but it's gone, all of it, and what's left is

a ruin—an ugly woman, a cripple, someone very ordinary who paints pictures and keeps a garden. Why do you romanticize that? You've talked yourself into loving me because it's different from anything you've done before, and very dramatic. As if it's a play. But if it were, it would be a comedy: a man talking of love with a woman who—"

"Stop it." He stood and began to prowl the small room. Jessica heard his footsteps as he crossed behind the love seat, saw his shadow stretch up the wall, bend across the ceiling, leap to the next wall as he turned to retrace his steps. "A terrible thing happened to you—no one would deny that—but you've pulled it around you like a shroud; you see everything through it; you're *smothering* in it." He stopped beside the fireplace and when Jessica looked up at him, his face was shadowed and his voice was hard. "You've defined yourself as ugly and a cripple and ordinary, you've locked away everything that was part of your greatness, you've shut yourself up in a house without a poster or photograph from the past, without a single mirror."

A log fell, sending up a plume of sparks. Luke sat on the edge of the love seat and took her clasped hands between his. "But my dearest Jessica, you live in a house of mirrors. You've surrounded yourself with mirages and illusions that keep reflecting back on themselves, and you've made them your reality. They're what you see from morning to night, and the rest of us, if you look at us at all, are without substance. You brush us away, like ghosts."

"That's not true. This whole week, we've talked about so many things, and I've been open with you, and honest. I haven't brushed you aside."

"But certain subjects were out of bounds. And you brushed me away just now, when I told you I love you. Why can't you accept that?"

"You know the answer to that," she said fiercely, keeping her voice low in the sleeping house. "You know everything about me; you knew most of it before you even got here. All those letters that were meant for Constance, that were the most open I've ever been . . . you read them, you should be able to understand them. And me. *I'm* the ghost! No one who ever knew me would look at me and see a whole person. They'd see a wreck, and they'd turn away. Oh, why did you have to bring this up? It's been a lovely week; why couldn't you leave it as it was? You would have gone back to New York and we would have been left with pleasant memories. Instead you keep pushing me to be someone I'm not: talking about going back to New York, talking about love . . . I told you this is the life I want—I told Constance, too, and you read it, more than once—why can't *you* accept *that?*"

"Because I don't want to."

"Is it so important, what you want?"

"It is to me. Look at you, doing what *you* want, refusing to try—"

"Doing what I can! This is all I can do!"

"I don't believe that. I don't believe—"

"Have you ever had anything happen to you that wrenched your life apart? That made you look at everything as if you were in a completely foreign place so that nothing looked the same, nothing felt the same? For two years I thought about this; I tried to see myself going back and putting together all the parts of my life that had once been familiar. But there was no way to do that."

"You were afraid."

"Is that so terrible? Of course I was afraid. I was terrified. I had no place anymore. There had always been a place for Jessica Fontaine; I knew it and so did everyone else. Doors opened, people welcomed me, everywhere I went *I belonged.* And then I didn't. I knew that the doors wouldn't open anymore, that no one would welcome me, and I'd be outside, where everything was foreign. Can't you try to understand that?"

"I am trying. I've been trying since I read your letters. You're a courageous woman; why didn't you even make an attempt? You could always run away; why did you do it before you were sure of what would happen?"

She shook her head. "You don't know anything about it."

"That's possible. But I know that any woman who cares about the stage as you do, any woman who wrote as you did to Constance, about the power you felt on stage, about the—"

"I don't want to hear myself quoted by you!"

"You're right; I shouldn't do that. I'm sorry. I was trying to make you see how big the stakes are."

"Good God, do you think I don't know that? My whole life is at stake! Years and years of building a life that protects me from—" She stopped.

"Memories and pain," he said quietly. "I understand that. But are they so devastating that you won't even try to get back what made you great? When I said you'd locked it away, I meant that: what made you great is still there—"

"That's another dream. You keep spinning fantasies, as if you could change me by talking long enough. What was in me is gone. Why won't you believe that when I say it over and over again? Once I knew exactly what my body would do, how to move across a stage, how to sit and open doors and pour a drink . . . It was an instrument that told an audience almost as much as my face and my voice. But that body is gone. And so is my face. Everything is gone; nothing is locked away. Now, I've said it all; you've forced me to say it all. Are you satisfied?"

He was silent for a moment. "I'm sorry. You're right; I shouldn't sit here and tell you what you want and what you don't want, or hold myself up as some kind of savior come to rescue you and return you to society." He stood up. "It was important to me to tell you that I love you, and that this has been a wonderful week for me. I don't think I've ever lied to you; I never pretended that you still have the beauty and perfect body you once had. But the more I got to know you the less important any of that seemed. I cared about the way we talked together, the way you saw the world and shared it with me, the way your spirit soars and your face is transformed when you smile, and even more when you laugh. To me, you *are* magnificent, and I'm sorry you can't trust me enough to believe I mean that."

He stood for a moment, a dark silhouette in the fading light of the fire. Then he bent down and kissed her, a light kiss, but not casual. "Good night, my dear," he said, and then he left, taking the stairs two at a time to his room.

Jessica stayed in the corner of the couch, trembling, her thoughts in turmoil. The fire burned down again to a bed of glowing embers and the room grew chilly, but still she sat, her hands clasped as they had been when Luke held them. The inn slept and no sound was heard, but her thoughts were clamorous.

How long had it been since a man had said he loved her? Oh, so long, so many years. . . . But that was not what had thrown her into confusion. Something else had done that.

She was in love with him.

No, she thought quickly. Not quite. But so close that she knew she would be, deeply and passionately, as she had never been before, if she allowed it.

But she could not risk it. She had a life to protect.

*You've pulled it around you like a shroud; you're smothering in it.*

A shroud, she thought. What a terrible word. As if I were dead. Well, the old Jessica Fontaine is dead—everyone knows that—but I'm not; I'm alive and busy and happy.

*You've surrounded yourself with mirages and illusions that keep reflecting back on themselves, and you've made them your reality.*

Anger welled up in her. If that was her reality, it was her choice. Who was he to say it wasn't right for her? He had his own reality, his life in New York, and when he returned to it, there would be no reason for them to meet, ever again.

She took her cane from its place against the arm of the couch and crossed the hall to her room, telling herself to stop thinking, to put the evening out of her mind and go to sleep.

"Did you sleep well?" Luke asked politely the next morning when they met in the dining room.

"No."

"Neither did I."

Susan Fletcher came through the kitchen door. "It's rather mild today, and there's a sheltered place on the porch. Would you like to have breakfast out there?"

Luke looked at Jessica.

"Fine," she said, thinking that breakfast would be uncomfortable anywhere, but since they had almost two hours before the plane would arrive, they might as well eat. "I'll get my sweater."

"I'll do it," Luke said. "Is it in your room?"

"On the bed."

While he was gone, Susan led Jessica through French doors to a small round table on the porch, set with a white cloth and two place settings, very close together. "I assumed you'd want to be here."

Jessica let out her breath in a long sigh. "How lovely it is." The long, wide porch looked over a deep valley, still lush with tall grasses shining beneath the early-October sun, with the gentle rise of Turtleback Mountain across the way. The trees had passed the peak of their color and many were already bare, but on others clusters of red, bronze and gold leaves clung stubbornly, and the same colors were on the valley floor, strewn among pink wild roses, white yarrow and bushes with shiny red berries. To the left of the porch, through dense trees, a pond glimmered, and a man pushing a wheelbarrow followed a path through a clearing, then disappeared into another grove of trees. "It's so different from Lopez," Jessica murmured. "We don't have valleys. Or mountains, for that matter."

"Orcas is by far the most beautiful of all the islands," Susan Fletcher said. "I hope you'll have time to see it."

Jessica smiled. The residents of each of the islands staked their claim to theirs being the most beautiful. We all need to think our own place is the true paradise, she thought. Even when it's an exile. The thought startled her, and she knew surprise was on her face when Luke came through the French doors.

"What a lovely setting," he said, and placed Jessica's sweater around her shoulders. She waited for him to ask what had surprised her, but he did not. "Another ideal retreat."

"I hope you'll see some of our island before you leave," Susan Fletcher said.

"I hope so. I think we'll have time. It depends on how soon breakfast is ready."

"It's ready now." She went through the French doors and by the time Luke and Jessica had seated themselves, moving their place settings slightly apart, she was back with juice and coffee. "Pancakes on the way."

Luke drank his juice and surveyed the view. He seemed content to let the silence go on. Susan Fletcher served their breakfasts, gave them a swift glance, then left, and once again the silence was complete. "There should be birds," Luke said, and at that they heard one, then two, and then a third.

"Perfect timing," Jessica said, and they laughed together, and she waited for him to say something about the night before, but he did not.

"We can take a drive around part of the island," he said after a few minutes. "I'd like to see as much as possible, if you would."

"Yes, I'd like that."

"I read the history of the islands last night. Did you know there was something called a Pig War on San Juan Island?"

"Yes, but wasn't it really just a quarrel over the shooting of someone's pig?"

"That was it. An American farmer shot a British farmer's pig and the British government of Canada, which claimed the San Juans then, issued a warrant for his arrest. American troops came in to prevent it; they camped on one end of the island and British troops camped on the other. But not a bullet was fired."

"Except at the pig."

He chuckled. "And the whole thing took thirteen years to resolve."

*"Thirteen years?"*

"Sometimes it takes people a long time to change their minds."

Jessica shot him a quick look, but he seemed absorbed in cutting a piece of pineapple. "Did anyone win?" she asked.

"Not in any traditional sense. They negotiated a boundary that gave the San Juan Islands to the U.S., but by then I'm not sure how much the British cared."

"Grown men acting like little boys," Jessica said. "Marching in with guns. Couldn't the boundary have been negotiated without armies?"

"Probably. If we could go back and act it out that way, then we'd know."

"That might make a good play. Maybe there were even three scenarios."

"Like points of view in *Rashomon*. You know, it does have possibilities. Maybe I'll try it sometime."

"To write it?"

"Yes."

"But . . . you're a playwright?"

"Mostly as a hobby. I've written two in the past six years. I don't have a lot of time. But I find it very satisfying."

"You haven't tried to produce them?"

"I wouldn't do it myself and I haven't shown them to anyone else. I'd like your opinion, though."

"I'm not an expert on what makes a good play."

"I think you are. No one could understand better what makes characters live, and whether they lend themselves to the interpretations of fine actors."

Once again Jessica felt herself being drawn into his life, away from Lopez. But he must know it won't work, she thought. After last night, there's no reason for him to stay another day.

"I brought them with me, as it happens. Those quiet afternoons on your terrace, I reread them. I think they're not bad. But of course I'm a little close to them."

She smiled absently. The truth was, she wanted to read them. It would give her a different way of knowing him. And she didn't care whether that made sense or not. "Could you leave them with me when you go back to New York? I'd return them quickly."

"Of course," he said without hesitation, and she felt a brief pang of disappointment. "But you could read them today and tonight, if you'd like. It seems I'll still be here; the airline is booked until the first flight tomorrow morning. I've overstayed my welcome in your studio, but I'm sure there will be plenty of rooms on Lopez; October is hardly high season."

"No, of course you won't do that. It would be absurd for you to move again."

"Thank you; that makes it much simpler," he said easily.

Jessica gazed across the valley at Turtleback Mountain. She and Luke both knew that there was regular ferry service from Lopez to the mainland, and rental cars available for the drive to Seattle. Why weren't they talking about that?

Susan Fletcher removed their plates, asking if they wanted anything else. "No, everything was wonderful," Luke said. "We'll be leaving in a few minutes. Can you recommend a good driving tour? We have about half an hour."

"I'll bring you a map."

The moment for talking about the ferry was gone. Luke and Susan Fletcher bent over the map, marking roads with a pen; and on their drive around the island there were shops and homes and restored public buildings to discuss. The plane was waiting when they arrived at the airport and on the flight back, Luke and the pilot talked while Jessica was silent. Her car was parked at the airstrip on Lopez and they drove to her house. Driving home together after a trip, Jessica thought. How domestic that sounds. How domestic it feels.

"I'd like one more ride together," Luke said. "Could we do that?"

"Yes, what a good idea."

They saddled the horses and rode for two hours, as fast as the trails would allow. The ride had a valedictory feel, and the sadness that went with it. As if in sympathy, the sky grew hazy and then darkened to a dense gray fog that swept in from the sea, obscuring everything beyond the nearest trees. They slowed the horses to a walk as Luke said, "Rain when I got here; fog when I leave. But what a glorious week of sunshine in between."

The house was muffled, like a cocoon, the windows gray with fog, the rooms dark. Hope ran ecstatic circles around them as Luke turned on lamps, moving with easy familiarity from one to the other, creating small circles of light that pushed away the gloom. He took Jessica's suitcase to her bedroom, then ran his hand over his hair, drenched from the fog. "I think we need to get dry."

Jessica was looking out the living room window. "Yes."

From across the room, he said, "What do you see?"

"Fog."

"And you find it interesting?"

She was silent. Luke went to her and put his hands on her shoulders. Her muscles tightened, but she did not move away. He ran his hand over her hair, as he had his own; it was soaking wet and plastered to her head, and she felt his fingers following the contours from her forehead to her neck. "Is it that you don't want me to look at you?"

They both knew the answer. He had been switching on lamps when she took off her riding cap and abruptly turned away. She knew how she looked: thin, gray, pinched. Like a wet mouse.

Luke turned her within his arms. "It doesn't matter. Don't you understand? I love you. What does the way you look have to do with that?"

Jessica met his eyes. She saw no revulsion in them, no pretense, no uncertainty. Just the tenderness she had seen earlier. And love. Within her, something let go. As if a dam had burst, warmth flowed through her and she put her arms around Luke, her body shaping itself to his. Pliant, suddenly free, she met him with a passion equal to his, one she had thought she would never know again.

But in fact she had never known this passion. What she felt for Luke was new to her, all-encompassing. She opened to him, and to the self she had tried to banish, with an intensity that made her draw back, her eyes wide.

"It's all right," Luke murmured. "I can handle it if you can."

She broke into laughter. "I'll try."

"It takes practice. Years and years—"

She kissed him. If they talked about the future, they would ruin everything.

"Jessica," Luke said, "if you don't want—"

"Yes," she said. "Yes. Yes. I do."

A quick breath escaped him and she knew he had feared that once again she would shut him out. Not now, she thought. Not today. Arms around each other, they went to her bedroom. Without her cane, her leg dragged, and for a brief moment, she tried to hold back. No man had seen her since the accident; no one had shared her bed. But Luke was helping her walk, and she wanted him—*Oh, I want him, I love him, whatever happens afterward, I want this now, please let it be all right, let him love me without second thoughts*—and so she stayed within his arm, letting him partially support her until they stood beside her bed.

Fog pressed against the windows, making the room seem like a cave as they undressed each other, letting their wet clothes fall to the floor. Jessica shivered; her skin was damp and cold. She pulled back the quilt as Luke turned on the lamp, and when they lay on the soft blanket he pulled the quilt over them. They lay quietly in each other's arms as Jessica's shivering subsided, and as they grew warm, their bodies began to shift, curve meeting curve, bone nestling within bone like the pieces of a puzzle coming perfectly into place. Everything happened so smoothly—Luke's mouth on her breast, her hand moving over his body in a long, searching caress, his body lying on hers, hers opening to receive him—that they flowed into each other as if they had become sound, weaving together into one pure note.

Jessica's body came to life. It had been both prison and prisoner for so long that the sudden rush of warmth and arousal burst the bonds she had forged and she felt her spirit soar. It was the exhilaration of freedom, of gathering in instead of pushing away, and for the first time in years she knew that what she was feeling was joy: something else, like love, that she had thought would never be hers again. And so she let everything go, the fears and angers of the past years, the tight control with which she had squelched her longings, the inward-turning, self-enclosed life of the recluse. She let it all go. For this moment, with this man, she was open to everything. And when she looked down, at her body beneath his, it was beautiful.

"My God, you are magnificent," Luke murmured, moving inside her, feeling her draw him deeper and make him more completely a part of her. At first he had been afraid to hold her too tightly; her bones seemed so fragile, her body so thin and pale. But he discovered how strong she was, and how intense her passion, and in the midst of his love and delight in her, his relief that she had let herself come to him, and his first stirrings of hope for the future, he felt a great pity at the depth of her need. She had gone through too many solitary months, and her fears had seemed to ensure that they always would be that way. But they won't, Luke vowed. She will never be lonely again. And then her arms came around his shoulders as her hips rose powerfully to meet him, and his thoughts scattered before her wondrous sensuality: a radiance that made every feeling so vivid, every response so intense, it was as if everything were new, as if they were discovering lovemaking, and all that it could be, for the first time.

They lay together through that long, gray afternoon, Hope curled guardian-like in the doorway, the lamplight encircling the bed in gold. They made love with their mouths and their hands, in frenzied bursts of passion that left them stunned and breathless, and in languid movements that brought them slowly to a pitch they prolonged until they could not wait another moment, and came together in a rush of joy and exultation that was reflected in the wonder in their eyes. Their bodies wrapped around each other like vines that curve and twine together in sunlight and showers until they merge into one. They lost track of time and space; they were so close they breathed together, and whatever each desired the other understood so instinctively that it seemed this had always been theirs.

"It doesn't seem possible," Luke said at some time in the afternoon. He was resting on one elbow, caressing Jessica's face. "I've been looking for you all my life and you were always there, so close to Constance, and because of that, close to me. Why didn't she tell me about you? About your letters?"

"You haven't asked that, all week," Jessica murmured dreamily. She was languorous and content; there was nothing more she wanted than this moment, this afternoon, this man.

"I wondered about it, but I suppose I thought it was one more of her minor eccentricities. But it doesn't really make sense. Does it to you?"

"She thought it made sense."

Luke's hand stopped moving. "You know why she didn't tell me?"

"We talked about it one time when I was in Italy." She looked up at him. "Don't frown, Luke. It makes you look like a medieval monk."

"You can think of me as a monk, after this afternoon?"

She laughed, a long, happy laugh. "No, how could I? Well, then, it makes you look like a Renaissance conspirator."

"Much better; it's nicely colorful. Why didn't Constance talk to me about you?"

"Because she wanted us to be together. Married."

Luke gazed at her. "If you wanted that for two people, you'd talk about them to each other."

"Not if you'd already tried to keep your grandson from marrying one woman and he'd told you that you weren't an expert in marriage and didn't know anything about the facts."

He frowned, then quickly smoothed it away. "You know too much about me."

"Look who's talking."

"Well. That's true. But, my God, Constance and I had that talk a long time ago."

"Yes, but it seems there were other times, and each time you told her, not too politely, that you'd find your own women. And do you remember the time, after your divorce, when Constance said you'd been angry at her for years for not marrying and giving you a father? That made you angry, too. After all that, she was sure that if she pushed me as a candidate for marriage you wouldn't even consider it. You'd tell her again that she wasn't the one to give advice, that you'd do your own searching."

Luke was silent. "She was probably right," he said at last. "I didn't shut her out as often as I did other people, but once in a while I did turn on her and tell her to leave me alone. Once, maybe more than once, she called me rigid. Others called me cold. You called me that, after we met at one of your opening night parties. And you were right."

"Have you changed?"

"I think so. I hope so."

"How?"

"Partly your letters. They made me see myself through your eyes. And Constance's illness, her move to Italy. I began to realize that she'd die someday—it's amazing how we ignore that fact until it hits us between the eyes—and I'd be alone. There was no one I loved besides her." He was silent. "But she should have talked to me about you, if she really wanted us to be together. You're sure she really wanted that?"

"Would you bring me the box of her letters?"

Luke went to the living room and brought back the inlaid box. Jessica sat up, reaching for a silk robe beside the bed and pulled it around her shoulders against the chill in the room. She took the box and walked her fingers across the tops of the folded letters crammed inside. The box, identical inside and out to the one in his library at home, gave Luke a sudden feeling of dislocation, as if he were in both places at once. And with that, he knew with brutal certainty how incompatible Lopez and New York were, and that Jessica would not easily consent to come back with him. "Jessica, I want to talk about—"

"Here," she said. She opened a letter and handed it to Luke.

Jessica, my dear, this will be short because I have so little energy. I've thought of dictating my letters to you, and that may come, but not

yet. I like to think I can fend off those
dramatic changes that all point to death. Luke
left a little while ago; we had a lovely visit. He's
lonely and, much of the time, angry as well,
but I can't guide him to happiness, or even pre-
sume that I know which path would lead him
there. I think he would be happy with you, and
you with him, but I will not propel him toward
you with one of those infuriating shoves mothers in Victorian novels always give their sons
and daughters. I'm leaving it to you, dear Jessica. Please find a way to him; give my dream a
chance. If it works, the two of you will drink a
toast to my memory and my foresight. If not,
you'll have lost no more than the time it takes
to dine together a few times. Oh, my dearest
Jessica, you've been my child and my dearest
friend for so long; I sit in my library at night
and picture you and Luke, hand in hand, and
it gives me great joy. I'm not at all ready to
die—damnation, I want to see the two of you
together!—but this is one role I cannot manipulate. I have not destroyed your letters as you
once asked me to do because I'm sure that
Luke—my wonderful inquisitive Luke—will
read them and then perhaps he will be the one
to find you. Dear, dear Jessica, take care of
yourself and ensnare my grandson. He needs
you. And I think you need him. And I will
send you, from very far away, my blessings. I
love you. Constance.

Jessica was crying. "That was the last letter I ever had from her." She touched the tears that were on Luke's cheeks. "I let her down, you know, and I can't forget that. She wrote to me, asking me to come to her. She said she missed me and thought I missed her—oh, and she was right!—and that we needed to be together. And she begged me to come. But I couldn't let her see what had happened to me, especially after all the letters I'd written . . . all those fantasies."

"She wouldn't have cared, any more than I do."

"She would have worried about me. Fretted over what I would do. She would have wanted to call people, write letters, *push* people to be kind to me. I couldn't stand that."

"But she was dying and wanted to be with you."

"I know." Her words were almost inaudible. "I should have gone. I kept thinking I might—someday. But then I read that she'd died and all I could think was that I should have been with her; I might even have been with her when she died. I can't stop thinking about that."

"And you didn't come to ensnare me, either."

She smiled faintly. "It was too late."

Luke slipped the robe off her shoulders and took her into his arms and kissed her. Their mouths opened together, their tongues met, and somehow all the unsaid words that had haunted them—between Luke and Constance, between Constance and Jessica—were put to rest as they held each other and drew each other in. "As if she's watching us," Luke murmured, "and finding a way to take credit for it."

Jessica smiled. "But she'd be right. She left my letters for you and you did exactly what she thought you would do. Inquisitive Luke."

"And a good thing." He drew her down so that they lay side by side, looking at each other, and then desire engulfed them and they came together with a new fervor and longing, as if now they believed that this was meant to be and that all the lost years could be made up.

Luke's mouth was on Jessica's breast, his hand searching out the places in her body that turned molten beneath his fingers, and as her breath came faster she slid down to take him into her mouth. She heard his gasp of pleasure and delighted in that, in what she could do for him, and looked up to smile at him. In a little while he moved as if to come on top of her, but she shook her head. "My turn." She lay on top of him, clasping him with her thighs and bringing him inside her, moving slowly, then faster, then very slowly, as their eyes met and held and they smiled together and she felt the sexual power that they gained from each other, and a new kind of exhilaration, that they had found this, too: the giving and exchanging of pleasure that came not from greed, but from love.

"I love you," Luke said when they lay side by side again. Night had come, and the black windows reflected their illuminated bed. "You're everything I fell in love with, and so much more. Beyond imagining."

Jessica shook her head. "You fell in love with a creature you imagined. You didn't know me from my letters."

"I knew a voice and an intelligence. I was only missing the rest of you."

She smiled. "Quite a bit. And even now . . ."

"I know. But we have years to fill in the gaps. A lifetime."

Jessica grew very still. "You're talking about New York."

"Not now," he said quickly. "We have to talk about it—you know that—but not tonight. We've torn tonight out of time. Out of the clock, out of the calendar. It exists by itself, and nothing can touch it."

"Oh, what a fairy tale," Jessica said softly, but she did not try to contradict him.

Sometime later, she once again pulled on her silk robe, and Luke took his from his suitcase, and they went to the kitchen where, quietly, with a harmony gained from their week together, they made a dinner of fresh fish they had brought from Orcas, and potatoes and snow peas from Jessica's garden. They talked about Orcas as they ate. "I'd like to go back to climb Mount Constitution," Luke said, to which Jessica made no reply, because she could never climb it and it was one more reminder of all the things they would never do together. Luke, cursing himself, changed the subject and they talked about Robert and Chris at the Inn at Swifts Bay, and Jessica recounted the few stories she knew about people on the island. They already had a store of shared experiences, the kind that could become the foundation of a life together, but Jessica knew that it was not a foundation they were building, but a collection of memories.

"I don't want to leave tomorrow," Luke said. "Could we have one more day here? We have so much to talk about."

"Yes." She wanted as many as she could have.

That night, they slept in Jessica's bed. Hope, waiting to lead Luke to the studio, was puzzled and walked through the house, looking into corners, as if to make sure that nothing else had changed.

"She likes things to be in order," Luke said, amused.

"Just like the rest of us. I'm not surprised she's confused; she's had more changes in one week than in the past two years."

Luke turned off the light and when Jessica moved into his arms he held her close, and kissed her. "Sometimes we thrive on change," he said.

The next morning, fog still enveloped the island, but they wanted to be outside and to hold on to the pattern of their days, so they rode anyway, a short ride in the fields and forest nearest the barn, two ghostly figures in a strange twilight that smudged the trees and erased the ocean, the cliffs, the sky. When they got back, there could be no breakfast on the terrace; they set the table inside and once again looked at blank gray windows that made the house seem wrapped in wool.

"We're like castaways," Jessica said, and her voice seemed hushed. "No horizon, no guideposts, nothing to tether us to the rest of the world." She smiled at Luke. "We could be floating in space, or drifting on a river, or sitting on the ocean floor; we have no clues, not even a hint. What a strange feeling."

Luke filled their coffee cups. "I like it. Cut off from everyone but each other, with the whole day stretching ahead of us, and no other plans but our own." Holding his cup, he sat back. "I'd like you to look at the plays I brought. Could you do that today, instead of my leaving them with you?"

"Yes, I'd like to."

"If you don't finish them, I could—"

"I'm a fast reader. I'll have plenty of time."

Luke took two bound folders from his suitcase. "I have some letters to write; will you be here or in your studio?"

"My studio."

So once again they spent the day apart, Jessica curled up on the couch in her studio, Luke writing at the glass table in the living room. He found it hard to concentrate, looking up every few minutes to wonder what she was thinking as she read. He had wanted to tell her they were rough drafts; that they needed polishing, more work on the details, more development of certain characters . . . but he had heard those excuses so many times from so many playwrights that he could not envision himself using them with Jessica. It wouldn't matter anyway, he thought; she'll say exactly what she thinks. She's not the type to coat her opinions so they slide down more easily.

Was that true? It was something he would have said about Constance, but did he know that about Jessica? The truth was, he did not, and it was only one of thousands of things he did not know about her.

But this much he knew: two things had not happened in the days they had spent together. Her telephone had not rung once, which indicated an isolation so cruel and complete that he could not contemplate it without aching with pity for her and vowing that he would do all he could to free her from it.

And she had not said she loved him.

Nor, of course, did she seem anxious to leave her island, her isolation, her very private life. But that was what they would talk about. Later, when she had read his plays. And when he had given her—though she did not yet know he planned to do this—the first two acts of Kent's new play, with a lead role that he hoped she would find irresistible.

At five o'clock, he turned on all the lamps, made a fire in the fireplace and put music on the compact disc player. Then, with that familiarity that he did not find at all strange, he went to the kitchen and found two kinds of pâté in the refrigerator and a loaf of French bread they had brought from Orcas. He arranged a tray and took it to the living room coffee table, added a bottle of Cabernet Franc and two glasses, remembered napkins and went to get them, and when he turned from the cabinet found himself face-to-face with Jessica. She looked beyond him, into the living room.

"How cozy it looks," she said. "Martin should watch out; you're about to take his job."

"I haven't time to do this in New York. Or the inclination. I'm surprised that you remembered him; I haven't mentioned him—have I?—since my first night here."

"No, but I remember everything. Sometimes I think that's a curse." She sat on the couch facing the fire. "Thank you for doing this. I feel as if I'm being waited on."

"You are. You deserve to be."

Jessica watched him open the wine and fill their glasses. "I enjoyed your plays. You're a very good writer."

"Thank you," he said. "Do I hear a 'but' dangling after that praise?"

"I think they need a lot of work. Polishing, more attention to details, more development of certain characters. What is it?" she asked as Luke began to chuckle.

"That was exactly what I was going to tell you they needed, but I didn't want to sound as if I were looking for excuses. Or asking you not to be too critical. Which characters?"

"Two in particular. Salk and Justine almost disappear just when they ought to be center stage. It's as if you were afraid to deal with the confrontation that's been brewing for two acts, so you let other people tell about it instead of showing it happening."

He nodded. "I didn't know how to write it without making them sound harsh."

"Because you think harshness is inevitable in confrontations?"

He scowled. "How would you know anything about that?"

"Oh, Luke, you had a reputation when I was in New York, for two things: you chose only beautiful women to spend your time with and you were a formidable foe, even a harsh one. Don't you know that's what people said about you? Constance knew."

There was a pause. "What else needs work?"

She leafed through one of the manuscripts while Luke watched her. He was unsettled by the change in their roles. For most of the week he had been the aggressive visitor from a hard-driving city; the successful Broadway director who led the way in so much that they had done. Now Jessica was the authoritative one, discussing his work and his character with a kind of cool distance that unnervingly put her in the role of director. But if it was unnerving, it also was intriguing, and he found himself drawn to her in yet another way: no pity now, just pure admiration.

"Here," she said. "Your dialogue gets stilted in a lot of places, but this is a good example." Luke leaned over to see the passage, but Jessica read it aloud, then said, "Did you hear the problem? A good cast would alter lines like those, loosening them up, but you should do as much as you can before it gets to that; it's your play and every word should sound the way you want it to."

"What else?"

"Something is wrong with the plot in the second play. There are some places that just don't make sense to me."

Luke moved closer and they bent over the manuscript, turning pages and discussing the twists and turns and coincidences that brought crises to almost everyone in the story. Now and then Jessica would read another passage aloud and Luke would hold his breath at the uncanny way she slipped into each character. She did it without thought or planning or an attempt to impress: she simply became another person as soon as she began to read. A great actress never stops being a great actress, Luke thought. Even if she thinks she has.

And how extraordinary to hear his lines come to life in Jessica Fontaine's voice!

"Thank you," he said when they turned the last page. "I showed Constance these, in an early version, but she was too gentle; probably she thought

I'd tell her she was no more an expert on plays than on marriage."

"But she was an expert on plays."

"I know. I hope she wasn't afraid of me."

"Never of you. Of your harshness, perhaps."

"Are you afraid of that?"

"I haven't seen it. I haven't seen anything in you to be afraid of."

"Oh, my love, thank you for that. For that most of all." He held her close, and as she put her arms around him and they kissed, the bound folders slipped off her lap and fell to the floor. Neither of them noticed. "I've wanted you all day," Luke murmured, "every minute of every hour. I almost went to the studio a dozen times to take you in my arms—"

"But you didn't want to interrupt my reading of your plays," she teased.

He laughed, his face close to hers. "Caught."

"But I wanted you, too," she said. "I thought of you in the living room, so close to me I imagined I could see you writing and frowning over a word, or daydreaming—but then I thought, oh, he'll worry that I'm bored with his plays if I come to him, and I wasn't bored, I loved reading them, but mostly I wanted to be with you, naked, with you on top of me, or whatever position we—" With her hand on the back of his head, she brought his mouth to hers.

And once again they found in each other the passion and exhilaration of unbounded arousal and fulfillment. They lay on the deep, yielding cushions, with the firelight playing on the walls and warming their skin as they undressed each other and maneuvered to touch everywhere, to kiss and stroke and suck every part of their bodies, to explore and discover everything about each other, to make every movement and every position completely theirs, so that they felt again and again, as they had the night before, that they had always been together yet still had endless discoveries to make.

They made love quickly, and then more leisurely, and later, wearing their robes, they made dinner and took their plates to the living room, back to the couch, where Luke opened another bottle of wine and they ate and drank slowly, lingeringly, sometimes in comfortable silence, listening to the music, sometimes talking in low, lazy tones. Until at last, with their coffee, Luke said, "I have one more play I'd like you to read. Not the whole play, just the first two acts. Would you do that?"

"Another one of yours?"

"No. A new one by Kent Horne."

"He wrote *The Magician.*"

"Yes."

"Why do you want me to read it?"

"I want your opinion. Especially of the lead."

She started to say she knew what he was doing, but she did not. Luke had told her so much about *The Magician* that she was curious about Kent Horne, and there could be no harm in reading part of his new play. She would give her opinion and hand it back to him, and then they would talk about his leaving. Because of course he had to leave, and she had heard him on the telephone earlier, booking the plane for the next day.

*But I don't want him to—*

She cut off the thought. "Yes, of course I'll read it," she said, her voice light. "Though there isn't a lot I can say about only two acts."

Luke went to the studio and brought back a folder identical to his, but much slimmer. He gave it to Jessica, then busied himself building up the fire and pouring the last of the coffee into their cups. With nothing left to do, he sat beside her, gazing into the flames, waiting.

He heard her close the folder, but she was still silent. He turned. Her eyes were closed, but tears ran from them and she was trying to brush them away.

"What is it?" he asked quietly, though he knew and his heart ached for what she was going through. But he steeled himself against it. She would go back to New York with him. He had decided that. And though he would rather she came because she wanted to be with him, he was willing to use Kent's play as additional ammunition. "What is it?" he asked again.

She opened her eyes. "He writes beautifully. It will be a wonderful play." She held out the folder.

Luke did not take it from her. "And the part? Felicia?"

"Powerful and exciting. But you knew that." She put the folder on the coffee table, and Luke felt a brief moment of shame for playing games with her, as if he could have forced her to hold on to it, and keep it. "You wouldn't have asked me to read it if it hadn't been the kind of part actors wait for all their lives. But I'm not acting anymore, Luke, and you knew that, too. I have no confidence in myself as an actress—good Lord, I could barely drag myself across the stage—I don't trust my body or my face to work for me anymore; audiences would feel revulsion when they see me instead of belief in my character. Is that enough? Do I have to say any more? This is the second time you've forced me to go through all my reasons, everything that's stopped me whenever I thought about going back. Did you think I hadn't thought about it? For months I thought of nothing else. But I can't. Whatever you may think, or want to think, I'm not the same person I was."

"You still love the stage, you still miss New York and the theater. If you could see past your fear, we could find a way to deal with everything else."

She met his somber gaze. "I am afraid. I've been honest with you about that. But you haven't been honest with me. You've been thinking about ways to get me back to New York for days now, but you haven't talked about it."

"You forbade it."

There was a pause. "You're right. I did tell you to

stop. But it wouldn't have mattered, Luke. I won't go back. This is my home and this is where I stay."

"After what we've found together."

"What have we found? How do you know if any of it is real? I'll tell you: none of it is real. Look at us. Two people absolutely alone, without city or society, with no other voices, no interruptions or schedules or clocks. 'We've torn tonight out of time.' That was what you said. 'Out of the clock, out of the calendar, and nothing can touch it.' And I told you it was a fairy tale. That's all it is. The most beautiful fairy tale imaginable and it has nothing to do with that world out there where you'll go tomorrow and fit right in, in your own niche, your own powerful place. You can't move a fairy tale to that world, Luke; it will crumble to dust."

"*You'll* crumble. The world will go on, right past you, but you'll stay here and dry up and your radiance will fade to—"

"There is no radiance! Good Lord, has a little sex made you so blind?"

"*A little sex?*"

"I'm sorry, I'm sorry. It was more than that. It was—"

"It was love, God damn it, and you can't pretend it was anything less. You've never said it, but you can't pretend now that it isn't true."

"I've never pretended. I just tried not to say it." She took his hand between hers and bent her head, resting her cheek on his palm. When she looked up, her eyes were shining with tears. "I love you, Luke. I love you with all my heart and with all that I am. I love you and I want you and this week has given me everything I could ever hope for with a man. But that's all it was, my darling, one week. You can't live your life here and I can't live mine in New York. We've both known that from the beginning. What we didn't know was how hard"— her voice caught—"how hard it would be to say good-bye."

"Then don't say it. We don't have to, don't you understand? Our lives have changed; you can come with me now. My God, Jessica, give us a chance! You don't have to decide anything about the theater for as long as you want, but come with me; marry me. This week was our beginning; I won't let you throw it away."

"I would never throw it away. It has all the memories I'm going to hold close. Luke, you cannot make this happen by willing it. What did you do, tell yourself you'd decided I was going with you to New York?" She saw his face change. "So you did. *You decided.* Oh, Luke, my dearest Luke, this time you're not the director. And you can't control what happens to us, though of course you'll try. But what do you think will happen if I go with you? What do you expect me to do? Go back to the stage? I can never do that. Live with you and watch you direct plays with other actresses in roles I'd love to play? Never, never, never."

She looked at his impassive face. "I'll tell you what I think would happen. One day I'd get a phone call from some director or producer with a too-hearty voice, offering me a part. He wouldn't tell me that you'd called him and asked him to do it, but I'd know it anyway. Or maybe you wouldn't have to ask any of them to do it; you're powerful enough that some of them would think of it on their own. And when I turn down the part, I'd go back to the life I'd made for myself on boards of directors and committees putting on benefits, and doing volunteer work in schools and hospitals— whatever I can find to feel useful and busy—while everything in me is aching to be where you are, in the place I . . ."

"In the place you love best in all the world," he finished.

Her head was bowed. "Luke, go back to New York. There's no happy ending to this fairy tale. I knew that, but I let it go on because I love you in a way I've never known before and that was so extraordinary that I thought it would be all right to . . . But it wasn't. I should have stopped it. Please, Luke, I don't want this to turn into an awful quarrel. I want to kiss you good-bye and remember that everything was perfect and very beautiful."

"Spoken like a true martyr."

She drew in her breath. " 'A formidable and harsh foe,' " she said.

"No, you can't get away with that. The truth

may sound harsh, but it's still the truth. You're wallowing in your suffering and you have no right to do that to us."

"Wait. Wait. There are so many things wrong with that. It's not the truth. Do you know what you've just done? Ignored almost everything I've tried to tell you. Accused me of wallowing, which I'm not doing; I'm making a life out of a wreckage that I have to deal with every day and every night, and no one can tell me how I should do that. No one! I have every right to live my own life the way I want, the way I feel comfortable. And if that affects us, I can't help that. I didn't ask you to come here or to stay or to love me; you came into my life on your own and if what I do offends you, that's just too bad. Oh, damn it, Luke, now I've said things we'll remember with pain, and I didn't want to do that. Luke, please, can't we have one more night and then say good-bye as friends? Please. I'm asking you for that."

Luke stood up and paced around the living room, through the dining area to the greenhouse and studio, then back, and once again made the same circuit, as if trying to see the house as a whole for the last time. He came back to the couch and stood behind Jessica. "Let's have a cognac, before we call it a day."

He left early the next morning. He had called Angie's Cab Courier at some time during the night and he was gone before Jessica woke. She had not slept until some time after dawn, when she dozed and woke and dozed again, and then reached out and found the other side of the bed empty. The fog had lifted and a weak sun filtered through the lace curtains. *So they'll be able to fly. He won't need a bed for another night.* But even if he did, it would not be hers. Not ever again.

Blankly, automatically, she did what she always did: she dressed for riding and drove to the barn and took down her saddle, debating which horse to ride. *No, not that one; that one is Luke's.*

She began to open the other stall door, then stopped.

*Yes. That one. Luke is gone.*

She heard the drone of a plane and limped outside to look up, just in time to see it climb through the pale sky and bank toward Seattle. The pilot had flown low over her house and then had turned east, leaving Lopez Island behind. Jessica felt faint and leaned against the barn. It was so quiet. No companion's voice cut through the cold morning air, and no birds sang.

*There should be birds.* And there had been. And they had laughed. *Perfect timing.* But it wasn't, she thought. We should have found each other years ago, when I was whole. Constance would have been with us then; she would have smiled upon us and the three of us would have been a family.

She was crying silent tears, leaning against the barn, shielding her eyes and trying to focus on the blurred plane as it grew smaller, becoming a fragile speck that vanished into tall clouds towering above Puget Sound. *It will be winter soon. I need more firewood.*

She rode all morning, and the next morning and the next, not thinking, going through all the motions she knew so well. Riding. Breakfast. Work. Dinner. A fire, a book, music. Bed. Again and again. *A rhythm and a pattern that are immensely comforting.* No, she thought. Not comforting. Numbing.

On the fourth day after Luke left, the telephone rang and Jessica almost fell, running to it. But it was Warren Bradley, her publisher, wanting to know how the new illustrations were coming. They had added a story; could she do a few more? Of course she could. That was her job.

"By the way," Bradley said, "I didn't know Luke Cameron was a fan of yours."

Her heart began to beat wildly. "What?"

"He owns all your books. Did you know that? Jessica? Are you still there?"

"Yes. Did he tell you . . . you saw him?"

"We were at a dinner party the other night and someone mentioned buying *The Greenhouse*—your first for us, wasn't it?—for her six-year-old, and Luke went on and on about how magical your illustrations were. Like dreams, he said, and of course I agreed. He also said—and you'll find this interesting—that he's thinking about adapting a couple of them for the stage. For adults, of course. He said he'd spoken to a children's writer, Sondra

Murphy, about the same thing and they agreed her books wouldn't work on the stage, but he thought yours might. Who knows? I'd never discourage him from exploring it." There was a pause. "But maybe you know all this. Did he ever get out there, to see you? He was all over our offices, trying to get your address a while back. Finally called me and of course I wouldn't tell him anything, but then he asked if you still lived on Lopez and I was so surprised I gave it away that you did."

"I don't see many people, Warren, you know that. Next time perhaps you'll be able to keep your surprise under control."

"Hey, what is this? He already knew it, Jessica."

"I'm sorry; I shouldn't have jumped on you. You've been wonderful, and I do appreciate it. I have to go now. Send me the new story; I assume you're extending the deadline."

"By a month. Are you all right, Jessica?"

"Of course. Would you send me a letter confirming the new date?"

"It's being written. I'll fax it tomorrow. Take care of yourself; you don't sound tiptop to me."

"I'm fine. Good-bye, Warren."

The next day her routine was back to normal and that day and the next passed in silence. But the next day, she found herself so hungry for another voice that when she rode she turned toward the Inn at Swifts Bay and found Robert in the kitchen. "Was it a good visit?" he asked casually.

"Yes. Tell me about your guests, Robert."

"Only one couple right now; slow time of year, you know." But he recognized her hunger for conversation and he talked entertainingly about the couple staying there, and went on with tales of other visitors in the past month. In between, he filled a plate with pancakes and fruit and put it in front of her on the kitchen table. "Eat. You're too thin."

"I'm always thin."

"You're thinner than always."

She smiled slightly. "Thank you, Robert. What a good friend you are."

When she left, she rode home slowly. The fields were turning brown, the trees were bare, and clouds scudded across the sky so that it seemed the world was speeding away from her. *The world will go on, right past you, but you'll stay here and dry up—*

Stop it! That was what she did lately: she clamped down on her thoughts, to keep them from swirling back to Luke.

But that day, riding silently through the stark forest on trails covered with soft, fallen leaves, she could not push him away. *You'll crumble. The world will go on and you'll dry up. . . .*

*The world will go on.*

And suddenly she knew that she did not want that to happen. The thought surprised her and she repeated it to herself. I don't want the world to go on without me. I don't want to miss it. I want to be part of it.

Why? Why now, all of a sudden?

But it really was not so sudden. For a week Luke had brought the world into her house, and they had talked about everything she had known and loved, almost as if she really were a part of it. And she knew that her feeling of loss as she watched his plane disappear was not only that he was gone, but that the outside world was gone, too.

Except that it wasn't. She could find her way back to it.

But what could she do?

The obvious thing. She was an illustrator of children's books; she could go where her publisher was, and be in the center of the publishing business. But that was New York.

*Then go to New York. Go to Luke. He's waiting.*

She shook her head wearily. She could not face those arguments again.

But what else was there?

The theater.

No, impossible. I told Luke . . .

Yes, but what about the theater without Luke? What about the theater without New York?

Doing what? Not acting, not ever again. But there were other jobs. She could help agents and producers evaluate and choose plays. Or she could be an assistant director, the kind of thing she had done with *Pygmalion*. Everyone had said she had been invaluable in getting that play to opening night.

I could do that, she thought. I could be an assistant director in a small town. It wouldn't be Broadway or London, but it would be the theater and I'd be part of it.

But . . . a small theater? In a small town? How long could I do that? It would be worse than here because it would be like nibbling at a feast I could never sit down to enjoy.

Well, then, a large theater. A city. And why should I be an assistant? I could be a director.

Why not? I know as much as most directors, probably more than most of them. Not more than Luke, but more than a lot of them. And I've thought of directing. Constance and I talked about it a lot.

A city. It can't be New York or San Francisco or Los Angeles. But maybe London.

No, London and New York are practically next door to each other. We all went back and forth all the time; we all knew everything that went on in their theaters and probably in their beds as well, and they knew what went on in ours.

So I can't do it.

The horse, left to itself, had taken her back to the barn. She dismounted and began to curry him with long, regular strokes. The rhythm soothed her and her thoughts slowed. I'm fine here; I know what I'm doing; I don't have any surprises. Why would I leave it? Well, it's settled. I won't.

But that night, restless in her bed, finally getting up and sitting in the living room before the cold fireplace, she knew it was not settled. And the more she thought about it through that long night, the more Luke's words hammered at her.

*—wallowing in your suffering.*
*You'll stay here and dry up.*
*The world will pass you by.*

They would not leave her alone; they stayed with her on her morning ride, and at the table where she had her breakfast. It isn't fair, she thought. I was all right until he made me want more. I was satisfied. Now I'm so hungry for everything he's gone back to, I can't stand it that others are part of it and I'm not, that it's passing me by, yes, he was right, that's exactly what it's doing, passing me by . . . oh, God, I want it again and I don't know how to get it.

*Go away from here.* It was as if Constance was standing beside her. *You must not turn your back on that world; it is your nourishment, your life, your being.*

I know that! she thought angrily. But I won't go to New York or London, so what good does it do to . . .

*There's Australia.*

She stood up sharply, as if listening. Australia. I never thought of that.

She cleared her breakfast dishes, her mind racing. She and Constance had both been to Sydney; audiences had loved them there. And what could be farther away from the places where she was known?

But . . . so far away. With nothing and no one to turn to if . . .

But wasn't that what she wanted? Nothing and no one familiar. A new place, to begin again. She remembered the nurse who had been so good to her when she was in the hospital, a young woman from Sydney who had written the letters she had dictated to Constance. A lovely young woman, warm and comforting, unpretentious, friendly. *Maybe they're all like that. Constance and I did think everyone was so kind, when we were there. Maybe they'll make me feel at home and give me a chance to make my way.*

Sydney. A vibrant city, English-speaking, with a famous opera house, a symphony, and lots of theaters. And Melbourne, with its theaters, close by. Mostly new theaters with good equipment; productions that were polished, if not as sophisticated as those in New York and London; enthusiastic audiences.

And so far away, she thought again. As far from New York as one could go without beginning to circle the globe back again.

*If I did go there . . . if I really did . . . I could work for the Sydney Theater Company. Or, if they don't want me, I could find a producer and we could rent a theater together. We could do two plays a season, or three, as many as we could han-*

dle. I'd be in the theater again, not on stage, but part of it; I'd be where I belong.

She went to her studio. Luke had restored the bed to a couch and had left everything exactly as he had found it. It was as if he had never been there. Jessica sat at one of the easels, gazing blankly at an unfinished painting. Without thinking, she reached for a brush and a tube of paint, and as she did so, she felt the rush of comfort that always came when she was working and settled in the closeness of her studio.

*If I left, I'd be risking all this. Why would I do that?*

Because, it seemed, she might not have that rush of comfort forever. Already it was diminished by the memory of the world Luke had brought her, and by the things he had said to her.

Sydney, she thought again as she painted. I could do it. I have the money to start again, and even back my own plays for a while, if I had to. I could do it.

Alone?

Yes, just as I've been for the past years. I know how to do that.

Her heart sank. *I don't want to be alone. I want to be with Luke.*

But she could not do that. Perhaps someday, after she'd become a successful director, with her own prestige and influence, she could go to him. . . .

*Nonsense. He won't wait that long, and why should he? He has his own life to make. I can't think about that.*

Think about making a new life instead. Think about making my own way, my own place, my own name. Not sitting on the sidelines letting the world get away from me, but part of it, part of the theater. Luke thought love was enough, but it isn't. I have to have my own value, my own self. That's what I have to create. With no connections to the past. And no connection with Luke.

And if it doesn't work out, I can always come back here.

*Of course it will work out. I haven't been gone that long; I remember everything. I can do this. I know I can. Luke is right: I can do anything if I really want to.*

At the end of the day she left her studio and went into the living room. She had forgotten to turn up the heat when she left and the rooms were chilly and forlorn, as if she had already gone away. She looked around, at the familiar rooms that had sheltered her for so long, and felt a moment of pure terror at the thought of leaving them. She waited for it to pass, but it did not. It settled within her, like a small knot at the base of her stomach. *What am I thinking of? I can't go out there, facing people, trying to . . .*

*Luke thought I could. Constance thought I could. If they really believe that I should, too.*

The terror was cold and heavy within her. *Well, I'll just have to live with it . . . for a while.*

She walked through her rooms and back to the greenhouse, and absently began picking yellowed leaves from a geranium plant. *Robert can find someone to rent the house, or at least to take care of it. And the horses, too.*

There were no more reasons not to go. After dinner, she made a fire and sat before it, as if warming herself before going out into the cold. The wind had come up and a branch scraped the window, causing the dog to bark. Jessica patted the couch and she jumped up, nestling beside her, her nose nudging for attention. Jessica stroked her sleek back and head. *I'm leaving everything else behind. But I'm taking Hope with me.*

# SYDNEY

# CHAPTER 13

Once again she looked out at water, but this time from far above, as if her white stucco cottage with orange-tile roof was floating through the pale blue sky above Sydney Harbor, its great glass windows framing the busy scene below. It was like a theater, Jessica thought, sitting in her living room and watching sailboats and ferries, catamarans and water taxis, yachts, freighters and ocean-going liners crisscross the harbor, miraculously avoiding collisions that seemed inevitable until the very last minute. And it was the closest to the theater she had come in the ten days she had been in Sydney.

She had arrived at the end of November. It had taken six weeks to finish her illustrations and arrange with Robert to have her horses and her house cared for. When she was almost ready to leave, she wrote to three producers whom she had met years before in Sydney, asking to see them. All three replied with flattering letters urging her to call as soon as she arrived. But from the moment she stepped off the plane, Sydney overwhelmed her.

It had been six years since she had been in a city. All those years, when she had been living so quietly in Arizona and then on Lopez, she had forgotten what a city sounded and felt like. Sydney, with its three million people and driving energy, seemed huge, deafening and frantic, as foreign as if she had landed on another planet.

The city sprawled outward from the harbor, old buildings and new piled together like blocks that children had tumbled out of a toy chest. The streets climbed up from the water on long hills lined with jacaranda and fig trees. Traffic was dense, fast and ruthless: a never-ending stream of cars and trucks that, to an American, seemed to careen toward disaster, since they drove on the left, as in England. The sidewalks were jammed with uniformed schoolchildren, tourists, business people and shoppers, all instinctively dodging each other, then clustering patiently at red lights even when no cars were coming from either direction. Often Jessica was jostled on street corners when she did not move with the crowd. Each time, she received a profuse apology, but she thought she was the one who should be apologizing, for being slow and stupid, for not fitting easily into city life—she who had fully mastered New York for so many years without giving its tumult a conscious thought.

But she had repressed all memories of New York, until now, when sights and sensations and the din of traffic brought it all back, and made her shrink from calling the producers to whom she had written. What am I doing here? she thought. I don't belong here. What did I think I could do here? I ought to go back where I belong, where I know what I can do.

But she did not go back. Instead, she began to look and listen, and soon found things that gave her pleasure. First was language, because language had been her whole life. She liked the Australian accent: a smooth version of Cockney, the words like notes sliding up and down the scale, as jaunty and cheerful as the people themselves. And she liked the names of places: sounds and syllables that rolled on her tongue like poetry or music. "Kirribilli," she would say. "Woollahra. Wooloomooloo. Taronga. Parramatta." They made her smile even when she did not feel like smiling.

Then she began to explore Sydney, at first tentatively, then more determinedly. She went again and again to the harbor, an enormous natural bay bisected by the great arc of the Harbor Bridge, with fingers of land jutting out all around its periphery to form coves, harbors, inlets and dozens of small beaches. From Circular Quay, she took a ferry crowded with tourists and a tour guide who gave a running commentary as they made a circuit of the harbor, complete with anecdotes about Sydney's history and the people, including American film stars, who owned the houses and apartments that climbed up the hills from the water's edge. She took other ferries to the suburbs close to the center of the city, thinking about a place to live. One day she took a ferry to the Taronga Zoo, built on a steep hill, where she navigated the paved roads in a small motorized cart for disabled visi-

tors and spent hours gazing at koalas and kanga-
roos, emus and wombats, and hundreds of other
animals and brilliantly colored birds never seen in
America.

In another motorized cart she drove along paths
in Sydney's vast Royal Botanic Garden, through
tropical forests, rose gardens, herb gardens and
stretches of lawn dotted with flowering bushes and
enormous eucalyptus, palms, and Moreton Bay
and Jackson Bay fig trees with trunks of thick
cords braided together and branches stretching
straight outward like welcoming arms.

To get around the rest of the city, she took
taxis, telling herself she was interested in everything. But she was lonely and it was difficult to
concentrate.

She was always alone. People looked at her with
sympathy and often made way for her as she
limped onto a ferry or across a crowded street, but
she spoke to no one except waiters in the restaurants where she ate. I'll meet people when I'm in
the theater, she thought. It will happen very
quickly. But until then she missed her house, and
her garden with its familiar view; she missed her
horses and the farmers waving as she rode past;
she missed her occasional conversations with
Robert, the sound of the waves as she sat on her
terrace, the moon through her bedroom windows.
She missed Luke.

She missed him in quick flashes that brought
back a sentence, a phrase, a smile, and then van-

ished, leaving her aching inside. She missed the sound of his footsteps in the house, the quiet way he worked beside her in the kitchen, the warmth of his body in her bed. She missed the feel of him. At any moment, when she relaxed her guard, she felt his arms around her and his lips on hers, she felt him inside her as she drew him deeper and heard his sigh of pleasure, she saw his smile and the long, absorbed look in his eyes when they sat by candlelight talking, talking, talking . . . oh, how much they had had to talk about!

He had written to her, brief lighthearted letters that arrived every few days while she was finishing her work on Lopez.

Martin has found a new cookbook and has decided to try every recipe, first page to last. My chances of getting into the kitchen have dwindled to nothing. But I'm not sure I want to. I prowled around it the day I got back and it struck me that it was unfinished: it desperately needed something to make it complete. And of course that was you, and the two of us, side by side, doing mundane tasks that seemed magical because we were together.

I saw your publisher at a dinner party the other night. I may have sung your praises too vociferously, because one of the guests asked me if I'd become an agent in my spare time. Only for extraordinary people, I said.

Tonight I sat in my bedroom, very late, holding the blanket I told you about, ships and sailboats and links to my parents. It occurred to me that I took nothing from Lopez that was a memento of my week there. I wish I had. That is a sentimental thought that would amaze many people who think they know me.

I've decided to cut out and frame the illustrations from your books that I like the best. There's a wall in my bedroom that's perfect for them, catching the sunlight.

New York is like a fabulous circus after the farms and forests of Lopez; I stayed home tonight to catch my breath. One has to get acclimatized to all the highjinks in order to survive. After dinner I pulled out my plays, thinking about your wonderfully perceptive criticism. I'm about to rewrite whole scenes. I can hear your voice reading the dialogue, with the fire sputtering and crackling in the background, and Hope watching over us, and I know that the magic we found was not just in the kitchen. I'll be working on the plays for some time, I think; I'm grateful for the time you gave to them.

Grateful, Jessica thought. Grateful. I did it because I love you.

She had answered him twice, her letters cooler than his, and then she had left Lopez without telling him where she was going. *It can't drag on; it's finished. It's the past and this is now, and I'm starting over again.*

And so she took ferries and taxis and kept moving, learning as much about her new city as quickly as she could. It was a hodgepodge, seemingly without rhyme or reason. There were frame buildings with lacy steel balconies that seemed transplanted from New Orleans; there was a stretch of George Street raucous with discount hawkers shouting their prices into microphones, Castlereagh with garish discount stores close to European designer boutiques, and William Street, where she saw her first Boomerang School. She thought there was no center to the city, but then her taxi came to a stretch of high rises near the harbor, where the crowds were more dense and parks and restaurants lined the streets, fountains played, the hospital stretched a full block—a sprawling pile of turreted and columned red stone straight out of the nineteenth century—and office buildings, shops and hotels clustered tightly, as if creating their own private city.

Just a few blocks farther were neighborhoods, called suburbs, crowded with mansions on private beaches clinging to the hills above, with apartment buildings scattered among them. Farther inland stretched street after street of smaller homes and cottages dwarfed by the trees around them, each with its own garden. Sydney in November was a city of flowers.

Three nights in a row, she went to the theater, applauding with the audiences while making a critical balance sheet in her mind of what she had found excellent and what was weak. As she did it, a ripple of anticipation ran through her and a small spurt of excitement, the first she had felt since arriving. *I'm ready for this. I've been away too long. If I'm in the theater, the city isn't important. I can feel at home anywhere, if I'm in the theater.* And then, on her fourth day in the city, impatient with taxi drivers who drove too fast when she wanted to dawdle, she rented a car and found, to her amazement, that it took only a short time to master driving on the left side of the street. That was a kind of triumph and once again she thought, Maybe I can do this after all. Maybe I really can feel as if I belong.

And so, on the sixth day, she rented a house, a pure white stucco cottage with an orange-tile roof that reminded her of Provence, fine furnishings much like those she might have chosen herself, and a deck cantilevered over the hill below. From there she looked down on the houses that seemed to be clambering up to her from the harbor's edge, and on the harbor itself, with its inlets and coves snaking in and out from distant headlands on her right to the great arch of the Harbor Bridge on her left. Beside the bridge, on a peninsula jutting into the harbor, was the opera house, its roof in the shape of huge white sails moving majestically out to sea. A theater and water, Jessica thought, and a quiet place of my own, above it all. She felt almost as she had on Lopez: alone and sheltered. Safe.

Hope sniffed, inspecting the rooms, always circling back to Jessica to be comforted amidst the strangeness. The rooms were overfurnished and no two pieces matched. After the clean, simple lines of her house on Lopez, Jessica thought she could not live amidst such a riot of color and patterns, but somehow the stripes and florals and solids and geometrics came together and were oddly harmonious.

She set the box of Constance's letters on the mosaic coffee table in the living room and arranged her collection of plays on a shelf in the bedroom. *I wish I had something of Luke's. Just one small thing to put somewhere and look at now and then. But I don't. Not a single thing. He said the same thing. We both parted empty-handed.* She flung a Scottish cashmere throw, brought from Lopez, over the back of one of the couches, and arranged fresh flowers in a Majolica vase she found in the dining room. The hotel sent over her luggage and she found places for her clothes in closets and built-in cupboards. The delivery boy brought groceries and she stocked cabinets and the refrigerator and freezer. The landlord came to make sure the hot water was hot, the cold cold, and the air-conditioning working, since it was November; almost summer in Sydney. A woman called and said she had been the housekeeper in that house for five years and did Miss Fontaine want her to continue? Emphatically, Jessica said yes. When she hung up she looked around and sighed. It was almost home.

So, at last, she made the first of her telephone calls and that afternoon met with Alfonse Murre, a producer whom she had met long ago in Sydney. She wore a summer dress of fine silk with a long skirt and long, almost transparent sleeves, and when the secretary announced her Murre came forward, hand outstretched, smiling broadly. He was fatter and balder than Jessica remembered, with a flimsy mustache that quivered anticipatorily before he spoke. He stopped when he saw her. "Jessica? My goodness." His face smoothed over and they shook hands. Jessica's was cold. "Come in; sit down." He pulled an armchair forward and watched as Jessica sat on the edge, propping her cane against the arm. He bypassed the armchair beside hers and sat behind his desk. "What brings you all the way to Sydney? I was surprised to get your letter."

He had not said he was surprised in his answering letter; he had said he could not wait to see her.

"I've been here before, as you know," she said.

"Of course. In *A Moon for the Misbegotten.* You were quite wonderful. I was new here and you made Sydney seem civilized, when I'd been thinking it felt like the end of the world."

Jessica smiled faintly. "I've been here three times and I like the theater here. So now that I've decided to direct plays, this is where I want to start."

"Direct. You want to direct."

"I've always been interested in it; I don't think that's unusual. You know how many musicians want to be conductors; it's the same thing with actors. They usually think they understand character better than—" *Don't explain so much; it sounds like pleading.* "Well, it's what I want to do now. I saw your production of *American Buffalo* the last time I was here and I thought it was excellent. I'm hoping you have some scripts under consideration and we can work together on one of them."

"Well. Interesting. I wouldn't have thought . . ." He drummed his fingers on the desk and frowned at the carpet. "Of course you stopped acting because—well, I mean, no one would . . . I mean you couldn't possibly . . . Dear me, Jessica, it doesn't seem likely, does it? I mean, to direct one of my plays, to be in the public eye, giving interviews, being written up in the papers, there's so much *public,* you know, about directing. I mean, you may think it's all behind the scenes, but even there, you know, where you have to instill confidence in actors and the crew, you have to be someone they look up to and— Oh, now, just a minute—" Jessica had stood up and he leaped to his feet as she walked away, leaning on her cane. "Jessica, dear me, you mustn't think *I* don't have full confidence in you, in your ability, that's not the issue, the issue is—"

"—your narrow-minded, frightened, ignorant prejudice," Jessica said icily. Standing in the doorway, knowing his secretary was listening, she turned back to him. "You think because I've changed physically, I've lost my brains, my competence, my ability to function as anything, much less a director. You—"

"Now wait a minute; you can't talk to—"

"You don't think, you react." Her voice soared, filled the office, swept over him as once it had swept over audiences. "You scurry away when something surprises you. Look at me! What do you see? Someone who isn't beautiful anymore. What does that have to do with my ability to direct a play?"

"I didn't say—"

"That's just what you said. No one would look up to me, no one would have confidence in me, no one would admire me. How do you know? Your pitiful little mind imagines it, but those are excuses to hide the fact that you don't like looking at me, you don't—"

"Goddamn it, I won't listen to this crap. What the hell is wrong with you? You were never a bitch before. You've gotten sour and mean, and if you think I'll forget this, I won't. I won't forget it, Jessica; you can't insult—"

"You fool," she said, her voice a despairing sigh. She turned and limped through the anteroom, trying to hurry, knowing she was even more awkward when she did, aware of the secretary watching her and seeing the image of Murre in her mind as he stood just inside his office, his lower lip thrust out, his eyes furious. She was trembling and her throat was choked with tears.

*Damn, damn, damn. I knew it, it's why I stayed on Lopez. I was right, I knew this would happen.*

She found a sidewalk cafe a block from Murre's office and sat at a table tucked in the shade of an awning. "Iced coffee," she said to the waiter, and clasped her hands to still their trembling. He's only one man, she thought, and not a smart one. There's no reason to think the others will react that way, have that look on their face. . . .

But it might be too late. Damn it, she thought, how could I let him get to me? How could I be so stupid? In every city, the theater is a small world; he'll tell everyone.

And he did. When Jessica telephoned the other two producers, their secretaries reported that they were out of town, and would be unavailable even when they returned; so busy, so backed up, right in the middle of one of Sydney's most crowded theater seasons; they were deeply sorry . . . perhaps when the season was over . . . they knew Miss Fontaine would understand.

From the aerie of her living room, she gazed at the harbor and the far-off headlands. She was halfway around the world from New York, but the nightmares that had haunted her for six years had followed her here. She felt bruised and lifeless; she barely had the energy to pet Hope, who sniffed

and licked her face and followed her in bewilderment as she walked indifferently through the
house. She paced aimlessly, seeing over and over
Murre's instinctive withdrawal, hearing the re-
proach in his voice, as if she ought to have known
how *public* a director was and spared him the entire interview. "The hell with him," she said aloud,
but he clung to her thoughts like a burr.

Once again, her house became her refuge. She
did not go out. With Hope at her feet, looking as
melancholy as she felt, she sat by the windows, filling her notebooks with sketches of the harbor and
scenes of Sydney from her memory. She listened to
music and read books and the morning paper that
was delivered daily; she ordered groceries by telephone and had them delivered. And at night she
lay in bed, her thoughts roaming where she could
not stop them.

*I never pretended that you still have the beauty
and perfect body you once had. But the more I got to
know you the less important any of that seemed. To
me, you are magnificent.*

Luke, dearest Luke, she thought, it's not
enough. The rest of the world doesn't agree.

*I love you. What does the way you look have to do
with that?*

Nothing, when it's just the two of us. I do believe that now. But to the rest of the world, the way
I look is all that counts.

*Come with me. Come home with me; marry me.*

Thank God I didn't. When this happened in

New York, you would have felt responsible; you would have argued with the Murres of New York, defended me . . . and for what? I could not work in the theater in that atmosphere and it would have poisoned our lovely fairy tale, and left us bereft.

But it seems I can't work in the theater in this atmosphere, either.

She moved through the days in a kind of trance, waiting . . . for what? For a way out. For the moment when she would stand up decisively and pack her bags and leave. But she did not. She sketched and read and listened to music and ate and slept. It seemed that this went on for a very long time, but one morning she noticed the date on the newspaper and saw that it had been only four days since her meeting with Murre. And at that moment, the telephone rang.

She jumped—good heavens, what a strange sound, and how loud!—and then thought, *Luke.* No, how could it be? He had no idea where she was. *One of the producers, then.* Not likely. *Well, probably the landlord. Nothing important.* She answered on the third ring.

"Jessica Fontaine?" The voice was strident and powerful, a woman's voice that was like a cross between a train engine and a trombone. She could knock down the walls of Jericho, one way or another, Jessica thought, and a giggle escaped her, her first laugh in days. "I'm calling Jessica Fontaine; have I found her?"

"Yes," she said. "What can I do for—"

"Hermione Montaldi here. You of course know who I am."

Jessica sat straighter. "You're the producer of *The Secret Garden.* I saw it a few nights ago. It was very fine. The best I've seen here."

"How many have you seen?"

"Three."

Laughter reverberated through the telephone, threatening to shatter it. "A small sample, but if you saw them all you'd still say it's the best. I hear from Al Murre that you came to see him, looking to work with him, but when he told you he didn't have anything right away you tore into him with all ten claws."

"No."

"No what?"

"I did tear into him, but it was for other reasons."

"Do you want to tell me what they were?"

"I'd rather you told me why you're calling."

"Right; that's fair. I'm intrigued by all this, I remember you with the greatest pleasure from the times I saw you here and in New York, I'd like to talk to you, I've got a play that might interest you, I'd like to find out if we could work together. Are those enough reasons?"

"Even after you talked to Murre?"

"Your mistake was, you took that little fart seriously. Nobody else does. Well, a few people do, but the savvy folk know better than to pay him any mind. How about dinner tonight? We're neighbors, you know, you could walk here in five minutes. I make an *ossobuco* you can't beat anywhere, and my house is much better than a restaurant for talking; nobody'll tell us somebody wants our table."

"How do you know where I live?"

"The telephone company is a fount of information. Come early, six o'clock, is that too provincial? It doesn't matter; I want to get started and so do you. Number forty-five, the pink stucco house two blocks down the hill from you. Palm trees in front; wrought-iron gates; high wall. I don't like gawking tourists. You'll be here?"

"Yes."

"See you then. Very casual, by the way; no silks or satins."

Jessica was smiling. She felt light, almost weightless; her heart lifted and excitement ran through her, buoying her up. The past four days were forgotten. It did not even give her pause when she reflected that nothing might come of this. She did not believe that. Hermione Montaldi—what a marvelous name!—would not have called if she thought nothing would come of it. From her voice, it was clear that this was a woman who made things happen.

She went shopping, escaping once again from a self-imposed prison. At David Jones, she mingled with the crowds as if she had not, only a few days ago, felt inundated by the city, and bought Armani slacks and shirts, Valentino cotton dresses, and

Yanono long silk skirts, flowered and striped. She ate lunch in the restaurant on the curved balcony of Dymocks Bookstore and, on her way out, bought histories of Australia and novels by Australian authors. *After all, I may be here for quite a while.* Driving home, she parked on one of the boutique-lined streets in Double Bay and bought bath salts, soaps, and sybaritic lotions and creams for herself, and an arrangement of orchids in a curved wicker basket for her hostess.

"Oh, spectacular," Hermione said as soon as she opened her door. "All four of my favorites. How did you know? Do you know their names?" She walked ahead of Jessica into the house, talking over her shoulder. "Red Beard, Flying Duck, Large Tongue, and Dotted Sun. Sounds straight out of a Chinese espionage novel, doesn't it?" She set the basket on a table before a broad window and turned, holding out her hand. "Welcome. I'm glad to meet you."

Their hands clasped. In the unsparing sunlight that flooded the room, Jessica gazed steadily at her, giving her a chance to show surprise or dismay. Instead, she saw a wide smile in a long, narrow face bare of makeup, with high cheekbones, black eyes close together beneath heavy brows, and a pointed chin, all surrounded by a flaring halo of frizzy black hair. She was taller than Jessica by six inches; she wore wide black pants and a long, loose, short-sleeved cotton sweater. Gold hoops swung from her ears. Her feet were bare.

"Well, you've had a rough time," she said, their hands still clasped. "Amazing, isn't it, how vulnerable our poor bodies are to change. What have you been doing with yourself since that train bust-up? Not acting, we all know that, but not directing, either, right?" She crossed the room to an open hutch with shelves of glasses and a built-in sink. She opened the cabinet below. "I have a terrific red wine, if that's all right with you. Then we can stick with it for the *ossobuco.*"

Jessica had not moved. She was stunned. No one yet had confronted her so casually with talk of the accident and what it had done to her.

"Red wine?" Hermione said again.

"Yes. Fine." She could not think of anything else to say, so she surveyed the room. The view through the huge windows was identical to hers, as was the strange collision of blazing sunlight and cooled air. The room was much less crowded than hers—most rooms in most houses would be, she thought—but almost as colorful, furnished with couches and chairs that were deep and inviting and covered in native fabrics from Bhutan and Nepal in earth tones spiked with startling deep blues. The rugs were woven in blues, reds and blacks; the lampshades, startlingly, were fringed. The walls were covered with paintings of old people, lined and craggy, sad, weary and wise, all looking past the viewer, at whatever lay ahead.

"They make me feel young," Hermione said, and laughed. She handed Jessica a glass of wine.

"That's not the main reason. Mainly they remind me that there's a lot of wisdom in the world and if I'm clever and pay attention, I may acquire at least a portion of it before I die."

"I like that," Jessica said, startled out of her self-absorption. "What a good thing to believe."

Hermione raised her glass. "To good beliefs and new friends."

"I like that, too." Their glasses touched and the faint chime made Jessica think of the bell that called them to their places on stage just before the play began.

Hermione settled herself in a corner of the long couch facing the windows. A rough-hewn coffee table held platters of *crostini,* mussels, and chicken *satay.* "I'm going to call you Jessie. Do you mind?"

"My parents called me that. No one else ever has. No, I don't mind."

"Good. Sit down, make a plate for yourself—dinner will be late; I forgot to turn on the oven—and tell me everything. If not everything, at least most of it."

"You know most of it from looking at me, and talking to Al Murre," Jessica said bluntly.

"Tell me anyway. If I get bored, I'll let you know."

Jessica laughed. She filled a plate and took a napkin, and sat in the other corner of the couch, facing Hermione. She felt herself curve into the curves of the cushions, relaxed and suddenly happy. "I like this room," she said. "I like you."

Hermione nodded. "Same here. We're going to do well together. But first we have a lot of talking to do. Eat something and then talk."

"If you will, too."

"I can talk your ear off if you have the patience to listen. But you go first. Take your time; we have all night."

They talked for most of it. Their closeness in the quiet room, with the sky darkening and Hermione lighting a dozen candles in ceramic holders on the coffee table, reminded Jessica of the evenings with Luke, hour after hour, enclosed in the safety of her house. But this time it was two women who were sheltered together and it took her back, beyond Luke, to her times with Constance; to a deep, fast friendship that had helped make her what she was today.

And so she began by talking about Constance, going all the way back to the beginning, when she was sixteen. Answering Hermione's questions, she told about those parts of her career Hermione did not know, and at last she came to the train wreck, and Arizona, and Lopez. "I was fine on the island; I was settled and busy, and I thought I was resigned to it. But it wasn't enough. I did like what I was doing and I guess I could have gone on doing it forever, but it never would be anything like the theater."

"Meaning passion." Hermione looked at her closely. "No passion in anything you've done since the accident. No theater . . . and no man? Good

God, six years with no man? Did you decide that a limp and gray hair made you sexless?" When Jessica did not answer, she said, "Not beautiful, no sexy bod, therefore, a sexless woman. Right? Oh, wait," she said after another silence, "somebody came along and changed all that. Am I close? Where is he now?"

There was a pause. "New York."

"And he wanted you to go with him and you said no. You said you weren't the clinging type and what would you do in New York? Of course you could have decided to be a director in New York, too. How come you didn't? Why Sydney? Jessie," she said gently, "you did promise to talk."

"He's a director," Jessica said briefly. "I'd rather not talk about him, at least not now. Maybe later, when I . . . Oh, I don't know. Probably not at all."

"Well, you poor darling, you're crazy about him and you sent him back to that zoo of single women and then came all the way out here to make your own name again. Are you writing to him? That's the last question; I won't ask any more."

"No."

"Does he even know you're here?"

"That's another question."

"It's part of the first. Are you writing to him and, if not, does he know you're here?"

They laughed together, and it was a good sound. "No. Now it's your turn. I want to know about you."

"I'll check the veal; we should be close to dinner. Have some more wine."

Jessica divided the last of the bottle between their glasses and sat back, nibbling on a *crostini.* Beyond the window, the clouds in the night sky glowed from the lights of Sydney. Lights glimmered on the water below, where ferries and water taxis plied their routes, and in houses and apartments in North Sydney, across the broad expanse of the harbor. Like a fairyland, Jessica thought, just as it is from my house.

It was the first time that she had used those words. My house. My city. My friend. And, maybe, soon, my work.

"Getting there, but it'll be another half hour," Hermione said, taking her place on the couch. "Therefore, salad in ten minutes. Can you wait that long?"

"Yes. I'm fine."

"Well, then. I'm sixty-two, divorced once, widowed once, two sons, one in the U.S. at Harvard, one in the U.K. at Cambridge; they're smart and fun and I miss them, but off they went with nary a backward glance, thank God, because I would have worried about them more if they hadn't. I was born in a dusty little town in southern Illinois; my father had a small grocery store with a hardware store in the back room—barrels of nails and screws and hinges that I'd play with by the hour; they don't have those wondrous things anymore—and he sort of made a living until a supermarket opened nearby with nails and screws in neat little plastic packages and that just about finished us. I'd hated the town even before we got to be dirt poor; I'd spent my childhood pretending I was somebody else living somewhere else—almost anywhere else. I was taller than the other kids and I read a lot and used long words and we were the only Jewish family in town, so they had lots of reasons to think I was odd, sort of foreign, and therefore untrustworthy, and they were always either ganging up on me or giving me the cold shoulder. So naturally I became a hellion at school and at home: some minor shoplifting, building booby traps, scaring my schoolmates—once I put a live frog in every desk in the classroom, including mine; you should have seen the action when thirty kids opened their desks to take out their books and pencils. Oh, my, what a happy memory. I've always wanted to use it in a play, but the frogs would get into the audience and some people might not be amused. Anyway, I was staging productions even then, hoping I'd drive my parents crazy and they'd send me to boarding school or the army or anywhere. They didn't, so I did the next best thing: I got married. Fifteen years old, to definitely the wrong man, but it got me out of Illinois, which was the whole idea. We split in New York a little before my sixteenth birthday and I got a job cleaning bathrooms in a couple of hotels, and that's where I met a terrific woman, the wardrobe mistress for a British repertory company in town for a month, who asked me if I'd like to be her assistant. I went to London with her, graduated college, got married again and had two sons, and when my husband died and left me with a modest pile of money I decided to be a producer. Got started in London, but Sydney was more fertile territory, so I settled here. It's getting tighter now, but I still do my best to shake it up. Is there anything else you'd like to know?"

"What do you like?"

"Good food, especially when I remember to turn on the oven, red wine, late Mozart and Beethoven, the Bach masses, all of Schubert, most of Poulenc. Biographies, novels, and history, adventure movies but no spurting blood—it gets so boring after a while—opera, ballet and everything in the theater."

"No sports?"

"Sailing. I like to race. And riding; I board horses with friends about an hour north of the city."

"No men?"

"Not at the moment. They come and go. The supply gets smaller and less interesting the older one gets. Anything else?"

"What don't you like?"

"Alfonse Murre, people who talk about money all the time, exhibitionists who are always yelling at the rest of us to notice them. People who don't feel a responsibility to their neighbors, anybody who makes a virtue of not thinking. A simple list:

stupidity, arrogance, pomposity and pretense. I'm sure there are more, but that gives you an idea." She stood up. "Let's eat."

They talked through dinner, through dessert and coffee and port in the living room, through the hours that bracketed midnight. "Oh, no," Jessica said when she finally looked at her watch. "I've stayed far too long." She reached for her cane. "I had no idea how late it was."

"It's not late for me, and I'm having a good time." Hermione was still lounging in her corner of the couch. "Unless you're too tired to stay. Are you?"

"No, but you must think I'm—"

"I'll tell you what I think. I think you're starved for friendship, especially with a woman. I think you've been a lonely little sparrow flitting around Sydney, trying to find something to make you feel at home but not having anybody to talk to. I think you miss your New York director and you haven't found anybody to make you feel good about yourself, or about the world, until tonight. And I think you ought to stay and have another glass of port and tell me why you want to direct plays."

Jessica leaned her cane against the arm of the couch. "Thank you for understanding all that."

Hermione leaned forward and filled their glasses. "And you want to direct because—"

"Because I can't go back to the stage."

"Why not?"

And for the first time, Jessica spelled it all out,

even more harshly than with Luke. "People are un-comfortable looking at me. When I'm on stage, when any actors are on stage, we create an intimate relationship among ourselves, but at the same time we're speaking to the audience, sweeping them with us into our story. We're characters and story-tellers at the same time. No audience would be able to identify with my character, or be swept up in my story, if all they can think about is how unpleasant it is to look at me." She gave a small laugh. "That sounded like a lecture on acting. I'm sorry. What I meant was—"

"I know what you meant. Have I seemed shifty and evasive, tonight? Generally uncomfortable? Was your New York director uncomfortable when you were together?"

"It's not the same thing. Neither of you paid money to be entertained, to be lifted out of your daily life to another place, some magical place that actors create for you."

"Well," Hermione said drily, "I'll wager your di-rector felt you'd created some magical place for him."

Jessica drew in her breath as the pain of loss stabbed her. It had been magical. And he had said so, so many times.

"Forgive me," Hermione said. "That wasn't kind. We all have demons to wrestle with and I shouldn't question yours. Let's go back. You've told me why you can't act anymore, but you haven't said why you want to direct."

"Because I know good theater. I know how to bring a script to life. I know how to work with actors. I know how to create mystery and reality at the same time so that audiences believe absolutely in what they're seeing. I've done all that on stage. I can do it from backstage, too."

"And besides, you're so hungry to get back to the theater it's driving you crazy."

Jessica gave a short laugh. "Put in its simplest terms. You're right. I don't know any other way to feel truly alive."

"You're sure you can do it, but you never have. Is that right?"

"I've never directed a play. I'm sure I can do it."

"Well, I'll tell you. I'm pretty sure you can, too. I have a few scripts I'm considering. Do you want to take a few days to read them, think about them, then call me?"

"Yes. Oh yes. Thank you."

"You should have started with me instead of that prick. Hold on." She left the room and returned with a stack of notebooks. "Six. Take your time. I want opinions. I think they all need work; some more than others. I'm sending you home; you look exhausted."

"I am. Thank you. Thank you for everything. I can't tell you how much I needed you."

"You didn't hide it." They stood and instinctively put their arms around each other. Hermione kissed Jessica on both cheeks. "I'm glad I found you, Jessie. I predict great triumphs for the two of us. Get a good night's sleep."

Jessica held her cheek against Hermione's for a thankful moment. Someone to trust. "I'll call you soon."

"Oh, one other thing," Hermione said casually as she opened the front door.

"Yes?"

"I'd write to him if I were you. It can't hurt, just to keep in touch."

Jessica stood in the doorway, leaning on her cane. "Good night," she said, and left.

But the words stayed with her and the next morning, very early, she took out a sheet of her new stationery and began to write.

Dear Luke, I've been in Sydney for a little over two weeks. I won't go into all the thinking I did to get here, but finally I just had to find out if I could be a part of the theater again. You brought it so crashingly into my life that I couldn't ignore it anymore, and so I looked for a place where I could begin again with a clean slate, not on stage but as a director, and that turned out to be Sydney.

I've rented a house and done the tourist things and finally I'm beginning to think I might like living here. It's odd how a place can seem strange, even faintly hostile, and then, be- cause of one special person, it begins to feel welcoming. That was what happened to me last night. I met a wonderful woman, a producer you may have heard of named Hermione Montaldi, and in a very long evening in her home we became friends and, maybe, partners. If that happens—she gave me scripts to read, to see if there's something I can direct—everything I hoped for by coming here will come true.

This is a lovely city, with its own peculiarities. All the glass-and-steel skyscrapers on the harbor are spanking new, built in the last twenty years, and behind them are buildings from the last century with all the decorative gewgaws that stonemasons used to make when time and money didn't dictate stark silhouettes.

The streets are crowded, and at first I thought the people were *so* friendly, waving to each other as they walked, but then I realized they were brushing away flies. It's quite fascinating: that constant fanlike motion of hands in front of faces, *plus* everyone seems to be carrying tiny cellular telephones cupped in their hands, almost invisible, so what you see are streams of pedestrians waving away flies while seemingly talking to themselves. Definitely living theater.

My house is in a section of the city called Point Piper, high above the harbor with lovely views of Double Bay (a fancy neighborhood called a suburb) and the city. Hope is with me and we've both settled in quite nicely. I hope *The Magician* is thriving, and that all is well with you. Jessica.

A cold letter, she thought, signing it. But she did not know how else to write. *I miss you and I wake up at night reaching for you.* There was no way she could write that. *I go through the city and find myself describing things to you.* She could not write that, either. *I love you.* No, of course not. All she could do was be friendly.

And why was she doing that?

Because she could not give him up. She desperately needed to feel close to him, even through letters, just as once she had used letters to feel close to Constance, and when Hermione said it was a good idea, it was as if she had been given permission. She had thought she could give him up completely, but it was too hard, at least for now. Maybe later, when she had a play to direct and was making other friends, maybe then she could cut him out of her life. But not now. Not yet.

The letter sat on the dining room table, which she was using as her desk, and she glanced at it as she read scripts that day and late into the evening, and the next day as well. Hermione called that afternoon. "I'm wondering if you've made friends with any of those scripts yet."

"There's one in particular that I like very much."

"But you're not about to tell me which one."

"Not until I've read them all."

"Good idea. Which means, that's how I'd do it. Are you all settled, or is there something you need? Can I do anything for you?"

"No, thank you. I like living here; it's beautiful and very private."

"Not the poshest of the posh suburbs, but definitely my favorite. Call me when you're ready to talk. I'm getting antsy to have a play in the works."

So there it was: she had a friend and a future. *I'm not dependent on Luke, so now we can be friends.* And she mailed the letter.

He replied by return mail.

Dear, dear Jessica, to go so far to find what you're looking for. I know you'll say it was necessary and I won't argue with that, but when I think of you (which is most of my waking moments) I have a disconcerting image of you teetering at the very edge of the world, clinging to Point Piper (I like the name) or to your new friend, Hermione Montaldi (I like that one, too).

I haven't heard of Ms. Montaldi; it's surprising how little we in New York know of the theater in Sydney, or they of us, I'm told. But of course you chose it for just that reason: because it was far away and not part of the two-way street between New York and London.

We're in the midst of an early cold spell and

I'm enjoying evenings at home, working on my plays, watching old movies and thinking about you. Martin is a happy man: I'm home for dinner so he can experiment in the kitchen, and both of us agree that he's on his way to becoming a master chef. He'd be happier if I had a companion, since it's much more fun cooking for two than for one, but I told him he has to be satisfied with me, at least for now.

You know how much good fortune I wish for you. I hope you write often, telling me all that you do; I can pretend you're close by, talking to me, when you do. With my love, Luke.

Almost as cold as mine, Jessica thought. Except for a few phrases. . . . She read the last one again. *I can pretend* . . . Well, that's the business we're in, both of us. Pretending.

And he had been anxious: her letter had taken four days to reach him, but he had sent his by overnight express mail. I could do that, too, she thought, sometime, if it seems important.

The next day she called Hermione and said that this time she would cook dinner. Hermione arrived at six o'clock and stood in the doorway, scanning the crowded room.

"Well, would you look at this. The lost and found for stray furniture. Stray patterns, too. But it's not unpleasant. Somehow it works. You don't get dizzy, living in this Arabian tent?"

"I like it. Three sides of protection and the

fourth is all sky and water." She flushed as Hermione gave her a quick look. "Protection is something I think about."

"So I see."

They sat as they had in Hermione's living room, at each end of the couch, with papers and manuscripts spread out between them. They went through Jessica's notes on each script, lingering over the ones that showed the most promise. After dinner they took their coffee back to the living room and worked on, coming at last to the play Jessica wanted to direct.

"So we agree, right from the beginning," Hermione said with satisfaction. "*Journeys End.* God, titles are so damnably hard to think up, but somewhere in Shakespeare there's always the perfect one. Now tell me why you want to direct it."

"I like the people; I like the story. Only four people in the cast, which makes everything easier, but mainly there's a kind of magic in the way they come together at the end, when they realize everything they've been searching for has been close by, but they hadn't recognized it, or even known how to look for it. There's a mystery in that—how people find each other in such a complicated and vast world—and I like that. The best theater is filled with mystery: all the wonders that make love and friendship and family and *belonging* possible." She paused. "I'm sorry. That sounded like another lecture. And a maudlin one at that."

Hermione gazed at Jessica for a long moment. "Did you write to him?"

"What? Oh. Yes."

"Did he write back?"

"Yes."

"Good. That didn't sound like a lecture, by the way, and you weren't being maudlin. The whole business of love and friendship and family is a mystery: how some people can stay married fifty years and others can't make it through the first six months, how some friendships go on and on, how some families thrive even though they're so stressful you'd think they'd explode, and others are always at each other's throats. Nobody understands it, and thank God. Where would we be without mystery? We'd be staging cookbooks. By the way, what's his name?"

Jessica began to gather up the scripts and notes. "Lucas Cameron."

"Well, you can't do any better than that. If he comes for a visit, I'd like to meet him. Okay, now, let's talk schedules. This is the second week of December. The Drama Theater at the Opera House is available for March and April; they told me I could have it if I let them know right away."

"More than enough time to be ready," Jessica said.

"It is if you know your way around, but you don't. You'll have to rely on me to recommend actors to read for the parts, and a stage manager and production secretary. You'll have the scene shop at the Wharf, and the Drama Theater lighting director and wardrobe and props crew, but it takes time to get to know them and be comfortable with them and have them be comfortable with you."

Jessica shrank back into the corner of the couch. *Have them be comfortable with you.* She had forgotten. Everything with Hermione was so easy and natural that she had let herself be lulled into forgetting. *Comfortable with you.* Of course they wouldn't be. Any more than Alfonse Murre had been.

"I'm talking about getting acquainted," Hermione said mildly. "It always takes a while, whomever we're talking about. But let's get this straight. You thought I meant they wouldn't work with you because you walk with a cane. Is that right?"

"Not just—"

"Oh, and also because you're not a glamour girl. That's it? That's why they'll refuse to work with you? They'll say, 'Great God, she has gray hair—' Why don't you color it, by the way?"

"Because it wouldn't change anything else. It would seem pathetic."

"Well, I don't know about that. But we'll let it go for now. Where was I? Oh, yes. You'll walk in and everyone will say, 'Great God, she limps. She has gray hair and a stoop. We make it a point never to work with anyone who limps or stoops.'"

There was a long silence. Then Jessica began to

smile. She had told Murre that it made no difference what she looked like, but it seemed that she
hadn't bought her own argument. But now
Hermione made her fears sound absurd. And
maybe—just maybe—they were.

"That's better," Hermione said briskly. "Now
we know where we are. I'm going to produce *Journeys End* and you're going to direct it, and we'll
work together every step of the way. I'd guess that
you're a fast learner, and you'll figure out our
whimsical Aussie ways in no time. By the way, one
other small problem: the playwright died a month
after finishing it. Young man, too, just dropped
dead. So we'll have to manage without the creator
explaining things or rewriting, if we want it, which
is sometimes a blessing, sometimes not. Okay, let's
look at dates. You're going to want to get your
ideas together and think about the kinds of actors
you want. How soon will you be be ready to start
casting?"

Hermione spread a calendar on the coffee table
and they bent over it, and began to make plans.

Dear Luke, we've started. Hermione and I
walked through the Drama Theater the other
day and it was as lovely as I remembered it
from the time I appeared there. It has only 544
seats (made with white Australian wood and
upholstered in blue Australian wool, which
everyone speaks of with great pride), but the
acoustics and sight lines are very fine. It's one

of two theaters on the lower level of the Opera House, with symphony and opera halls upstairs, so there are times when the whole building vibrates with rehearsals. Our sets will be made at the Wharf Theater, really and truly a wharf, converted to two theaters upstairs, and huge rooms below for set construction, props, costumes, and so on. We rehearse there, too, in a small rehearsal hall with a tiny balcony at the back where students come a few at a time to watch. Hermione asked me if I'd mind and I said I wouldn't . . . I don't think. How do I know what I'll mind? I've never done any of this before.

The play is *Journeys End,* written by an Australian who died, tragically young, soon after writing it. It's the story of a wealthy woman, one of Sydney's greatest benefactors, who, we discover, made her fortune by defrauding a couple she'd known most of her life. She's an influential, famous woman, but she has no feelings. She herself says she feels dead, without knowing why. The son of the people she defrauded buys the apartment next door (I hope to use turntables for the two apartments, if we can afford them) and the rest of the story is the way they discover each other (they haven't seen each other since they were children) and the way she comes to life, not only through him but through his parents, who are visiting him. It's the story of how an inhuman woman becomes human—a fairy tale, you'll say. Well, we need fairy tales, and every one that I've ever heard of is built around a kernel of truth, so maybe even inhuman people can learn and change. And this story has a strong dose of reality because at the end the parents understand her but never forgive her, so she doesn't get the clean slate she longs for. She's found love, she can *feel,* she'll be happy, but she can't erase the past.

We begin casting next week. Hermione has called several actors and also a management company; she thinks we'll find our cast very quickly. I hope so; I'm anxious to see this play come to life. I hope your writing is going well. Jessica.

She hesitated before sealing it. There were so many other things she could say. She could tell him how frightened she was, of failing, of disappointing Hermione, but mostly of working on a play without being in it. She did not know if she could bear that.

She shook her head. It was too personal. She'd told him enough. She sealed the envelope, stamped it and mailed it on the way to the Wharf for the first casting session.

Dearest Jessica, I'm wrapping this letter around a Christmas gift and I hope you accept it, since it comes not only from me, but also from Constance. The bracelet is from the collection that she left to me in her will, saying that she hoped I'd someday find a woman I wanted to give them to. She would have been very happy—and triumphant?—to know that you are that woman. With it I send my wishes for a very happy Christmas, and a joyous and fulfilling New Year.

Your letter about the Wharf and the Drama Theater just came. I know the excitement you're feeling; I still have it whenever a play begins to take shape. It's like working with a lump of clay for a while and suddenly seeing in it the shape of a head, the curve of a horse's mane, a leaf, a flower, a bird . . . still indistinct but waiting to be set free. That's what you'll be doing: setting free the hidden parts of the play—why people do what they do, the acts of love or hate they inflict or suffer, how they come to understand (or never understand) the life around them.

Nothing in the world brings the same good feeling as that. It almost makes up for the fact that we can't always shape our own lives the way we want. Almost. Nothing, after all, makes up for the absence of a loved one.

Hermione sounds terrific; I think you're going to have a wonderful time. As for the play, it sounds interesting, with a powerful lead, but it's hard to tell from a summary. Would you send me a copy? All my love, Luke.

The bracelet was of small square diamonds with a ruby clasp. Jessica put it on and held out her arm, the diamonds flashing in the sun. She had wanted something from Luke. Now she had something from Constance, too.

By now a letter from him arrived every day. Sometimes it was just a note scribbled in a taxi, more often it was a single page of news of the city and the theater, tales of people they knew and others whom Jessica had not met, recollections of Constance, suggestions for a movie to see or a book to read, the weather report, Martin's latest menu. He never wrote about a party or going on a date. One could assume, from his letters, that he had indeed become a monk.

Luke Cameron? Never. Of course he was seeing women, squiring them about the city, sharing their beds. There was no reason for him to write to her about them; the first she would know was when he wrote to tell her—for she was sure he would do this—that he was getting married.

But she would not think about that. She saved his letters, filling a drawer in the hutch in her living room. Then, one evening on her way home she stopped in Woollahra and saw in a shop window an Italian box covered in fine, dark green leather with a gold tooled border on the hinged lid. She brought it home and put Luke's letters inside—so many, already—then set the box on the coffee table beside the one holding Constance's letters. She stood back, gazing at them. *Not much personal contact, but there's a lot of paper in my life.*

"Handsome box," Hermione said later that evening. They were eating vichyssoise and cold chicken at the coffee table. "Good leather. Two Italian boxes. Both for letters?"

"Yes." Jessica filled their wineglasses and held hers up. "To the cast we'll find one of these days."

Hermione touched her glass to Jessica's. "Any day now. One box for Constance; you told me about that one. The other for Lucas Cameron?"

"Yes. He's asked to see a copy of *Journeys End.* Would you mind if I sent him one?"

"No, why would I? It'll be published in a month or two, anyway; he'd be able to buy it anywhere."

They ate in silence for a moment. "Well, what is it?" Jessica asked. "Something's bothering you. Is it that we're starting so late on the casting?"

"Hell, no. We don't start anything until you feel ready. That doesn't bother me at all."

"Well, something does. Come on, Hermione, you'll tell me eventually, so why not get it over with?"

"Why not, indeed. Well, the fact is, I'm not finding investors. I've got one, Donny Torville, a sweet guy, loaded, who doesn't care a fig about the theater, but he likes me. I was hoping for two or three more, but they don't seem to be out there."

"Because they don't think I can direct it."

"Right. I don't like to be brutal about this, but we have to face it. They ask me why I think you can come back after so many years, *and* come back as a director, which you've never been. And if you really could do it, they say, why not do it in New York?"

"What do they call me?"

"It doesn't matter. You know what it is, Jessie? They're mad at you for coming back. They remember you when you were the most gorgeous creature and the most brilliant actress, and they're mad because they don't want to know that looks can fade and bodies can be damaged; they don't want to know that bad things happen, because then they'd have to face the fact that bad things could happen to them. They want you to go away and let them believe that beauty and perfection last. What a bunch of assholes, turning their back on life."

"What do they call me?"

"I told you, it doesn't matter."

"It matters to me."

"Jessie, it has nothing to do with—"

*"What do they call me?"*

"God damn it, you're more stubborn than I am. Well, if you really want to know . . . Washed up and a cripple."

Jessica nodded, waiting for the sharp pain to fade. And it did, very quickly. She had felt it before, so many times, but now everything was different. "Well," she said quietly, "we'll have to prove them wrong."

Hermione's eyebrows rose. "Is this Jessica Fontaine speaking? A transformation. Maybe it's because we're two days from Christmas. But I didn't think you felt Christmasy, since it's ninety degrees outside and as humid as a sauna."

Jessica smiled. "It definitely does not feel like Christmas. Do you know how odd it is to see Christmas decorations next to silk trees in bloom, all those summery pink flowers like hundreds of birds perched on the branches? I can't get used to it."

"So Christmas didn't do it. What did?"

"You. And Luke. Knowing you both believe in me. And being back. Every time I walk into that rehearsal room, I feel alive and whole, because I'm where I belong. And none of your whining investors is going to take that away from me."

"Well, hallelujah. You're wonderful, I love you, I have absolute, total confidence in you. In us. This play is going to make money. Therefore, I've decided to back it. I would have told you earlier, but I wanted to know how you felt first."

"No. Hermione, you can't do that. You know you should spread the risk around; you can't assume it all yourself."

"Don't forget Donny."

"You need at least two more people."

"They aren't out there. For your second play

they will be, but not for this one. I'm okay with this, Jessie; I'm not worried."

"You should be. You've got an unknown playwright and a first-time director; that's hardly a sure thing."

"I'm okay with it."

"Well, then." Jessica went to the dining room table, strewn with papers and books, blocking charts, and scripts marked with colored pencils for each character, and rummaged until she found her checkbook. "How much did Donny put up?"

"Now hold on. This isn't your job. Your job is to direct this play."

"Let's not argue about money, Hermione; it's so boring. How much did he give you?"

"Two hundred thousand. Money is never boring."

"Arguing about it is. I'll match that and you can do the same. Can we produce this play for six hundred thousand?"

"Yes."

"With the turntables?"

"I don't know. I haven't priced them. Jessie, are you sure you want to do this?"

Jessica was writing a check. Without looking up, she said, "You and Luke aren't the only ones who believe in me. I'm beginning to believe in me, too."

She handed the check to Hermione. "This is on my money management account in the U.S., but I don't think you'll have trouble depositing it." She raised her glass. "I think we should drink a toast to our play. And to all the people who will be sorry they didn't back it."

Hermione grinned. "I haven't felt this excited for a long time. We'll knock their socks off."

Knock their socks off, Jessica thought two weeks later, after the Christmas holidays, when they were at the Wharf rehearsal room for their first casting session. She and Hermione had exchanged gifts on Christmas morning, then cooked dinner together for a few of Hermione's friends. On New Year's Eve they had visited a couple in Melbourne, spending the night and returning the next afternoon. "We don't want you getting gloomy about holidays," Hermione had said, and the week that Jessica had dreaded passed almost without pain.

Dear Luke, thank you for the wonderful bracelet. It means so much to me that it comes from both of you. I wore it to a quiet Christmas dinner, just ten people, and an even quieter New Year's Eve in Melbourne: four of us, Hermione and I and the couple we were visiting. He owns a construction company and she's a poet so the conversation roamed in all directions. You would have enjoyed it. I hope your holidays were good, and I wish you a wonderful new year. Thank you again. I love the bracelet. Jessica.

She had mailed it on the way to the Wharf and it came to her as she sat in the rehearsal hall that she had not meant to add that last phrase, but at the last minute she knew she could not send him a letter that was so cold, about something so special. *I love the bracelet. I love you.* He would not make that connection.

Sitting beside Hermione, she watched two actors come to the center of the room. She was nervous and it did not help that the room was very hot. The doors to the harbor were open, but the faint breeze off the water seemed to lose heart before it reached them, and no air stirred except from two floor fans that had long since conceded defeat. Thermoses of iced tea and water were on the table where they sat, and Jessica took a long drink of ice water. "Let's begin in act one where Helen discovers that Rex has moved in next door." She turned the pages of her script, so marked up in places she could barely make out her notes. She looked around as someone opened the door and walked in: a short balding man with bowed legs, long arms, and bright blue eyes in a deeply tanned face.

"Sorry, so sorry I'm late, it won't happen again." He held out his hand. "Dan Clanagh. Your stage manager. Hell of a way to make an entrance, but somebody rear-ended me at a stoplight and nobody but me was in a hurry to get all the paperwork done so we could resume our suicidal dash through rush hour. Anyway, how do you do. I'm looking forward to working with you. This is a truly fine play."

Jessica was smiling as they shook hands, re-membering what Hermione had said. "He's the best there is; you'll like him." And she did.

"Act one," she said again.

She had done this so many times that she felt disoriented when the actors began to read their lines. She was in the wrong place, on the wrong side of the table. Why was she silent while these people were speaking the lines of the play? She felt Hermione's hand on her arm. "Pay attention, Jessie. You're directing this play."

Of course. She was directing this play. She would not be on stage. She would be behind the scenes, invisible and anonymous.

*But I told Hermione I felt alive and whole and that is the truth. As long as I'm here, everything is all right.*

She began to listen critically. Actors walked in, read, and left, and now and then she felt a spark of interest, but it was not a big spark and it never lasted long. "It must be me," she told Hermione that night at dinner. "They're all competent; there must be something wrong with me that I don't think any of them are right for this play. Maybe"—she forced herself to say it—"maybe I'm jealous."

"Could be," Hermione said casually. "But I didn't think they were right, either, and I haven't got a thing in the world to be jealous about. Tomorrow may be better; Angela Crown's coming to read Helen and she's impressive. And the one for Rex, well, I'm not sure about him, but he might do. If nothing else, you'll like his name. Whitbread Castle."

"What?"

"You heard me. His mother probably got it out of a romance novel. If we use them both, we'll have a crown and a castle. How can we go wrong?"

"You can't take anyone seriously with a name like that," Jessica said, but when she heard him read the next day she sat up with sudden interest. He was extraordinarily handsome, with a deep voice and a powerful aura of sexuality, and when he and Angela Crown read together it seemed they already felt some of the tension that would build between Helen and Rex throughout the play. Jessica let them read without interruption. "He's too tight," she murmured to Hermione at one point. "Voice and body. But we can loosen him up, don't you think?"

"Worth working on," Hermione whispered. "He's okay."

"And Angela?"

"Better than him. I like them both. Don't you?"

Jessica nodded. "Angela," she said, "would you read the last two lines again, please? But first tell us whether you're annoyed or curious or maybe threatened, that he's now your neighbor."

Angela Crown was a large woman, a trifle over-weight, with masses of blond hair. A faint coarseness in her features kept her from being beautiful, but she was attractive, and audiences found her easy to remember, in part because of her size. She wore a red sundress with thin straps and a plunging neckline and Jessica found all that skin quite imposing in a woman almost six feet tall. "Annoyed, curious, threatened," Angela repeated in a well-modulated voice. "Well, maybe all three, but probably mostly curious. I mean, I don't know yet if he knew I lived here or if it's just an accident that he's moved in."

"But if you think he might have known you lived there, and deliberately chose that apartment, do you think you might feel invaded?"

"Invaded. Oh, you mean, what the hell is this guy from my childhood doing on my grown-up turf? I like that."

"Then would you think about that when you read those lines again? And go on from there, both of you."

"Oh, much more interesting," said Hermione as Angela began again. "She's quick, and that's all we need, besides talent."

. . . so we cast her,

Jessica wrote to Luke,

and Whitbread, too. I thought of asking him to change his name (telling him if it was shorter it would be easier for audiences to remember),

but I was pretty sure that would get me
nowhere and I'd rather ask only for things I
have a good chance of getting. He'll be very
good as Rex, once we loosen him up. One of his
problems could be that he's never had women
as both director and producer and, poor fellow,
he probably feels as if his mother is sitting here,
doubled, and he's torn between rebelling and
being a dutiful son. I've asked Dan Clanagh,
our stage manager, to pay attention to him so
he has at least one man to talk to. Once we cast
the other two parts, he'll have another man, and
that should help him feel he's not outnumbered;
the two of them can whisper together like boys
sneaking a cigarette behind the barn. We hope
to finish the casting tomorrow and have our
first run-through no later than Monday. Oh,
how familiar it is! But how strange, too. Do you
know how it feels when you look through an
airplane window at your neighborhood in New
York and you can't identify half the buildings
from that weird perspective? That's how I feel
now and sometimes it's so unnerving I begin to
feel disoriented, as if I'm not sure who I am.
But that will pass, I'll get used to all of it, and
most of the time I enjoy my view from the plane
a lot. I hope you got the play; did you like it?
Jessica.

Getting a little warm, she thought, reading it
over. What happened to that cool distance I was so

good at, no emotions, just facts? Maybe I should rewrite it; change a few sentences . . . it wouldn't take long.

Oh, but it's so good to be able to tell him these things.

And she mailed the letter.

Dearest Jessica, do you have a fax machine? Love, Luke.

"I have one," Hermione said when Jessica asked her the next morning. "But you ought to have your own. I'll have my secretary bring you one tonight. Is that okay?"

"Yes. Thank you." A man and woman walked into the rehearsal room and introduced themselves. "Let's begin in the second act," Jessica said, "where you first arrive to visit your son and you discover that Helen lives next door."

She was restless that morning and no one pleased her. They were in their third day of casting and she was increasingly impatient to get to rehearsals so that they could get to opening night. She wanted to discover how good she was, and she wanted to discover it right away. Now that she had let herself come back, all the years on Lopez seemed like marking time, and suddenly she wanted everything at once: challenge, achievement, success, acclaim. She wanted people to say she was wonderful, that in spite of all that had happened to her, in spite of what she looked like, she deserved admiration and praise and love.

*I love you. What does the way you look have to do with that?*

She brushed his voice away. It wasn't enough. She had to prove herself in other ways, stand on her own, become whatever person Jessica Fontaine would be from now on.

"Thank you," she said curtly to the two who had just read. "We'll let you know." Though of course they would not, because there would be nothing to say.

"Lunch," Hermione said, and they walked upstairs to the cafe. It was airy and open, with glass walls and open glass doors so that it seemed to flow into the terrace and then to the harbor and on to the farther shore, where a face painted on a Ferris wheel grinned at them from an abandoned amusement park. They ate quickly, saying little, both of them frustrated and anxious and worn down by the heat. "Well, I apologize," Hermione said as they walked back downstairs. "Can't seem to do a damn bit of good around here."

"You found Angela and Whitbread; that was wonderful. How many do we have this afternoon?"

"Four. One of the women might be okay. I haven't heard the men; they came from the management agency."

Jessica took her seat again, feeling hot and

sticky and vaguely annoyed. There ought to be a better way to do this, she thought. She looked idly around the rehearsal room, her gaze passing over Dan Clanagh's perspiring baldness, a technician's shirt stained with sweat, and then up, to a group of people crowding onto the tiny balcony. They were all students except for a gray-haired man, and she found herself staring at his sad face, long and gaunt, and deep-set, shadowed eyes. She touched Hermione's arm. "Who is that man?"

Hermione turned to look. "Director of the drama department at the University of New South Wales. Just got here a few months ago. God, he looks unhappy."

"He looks like Stan."

Hermione stared openly at him. "He does indeed. I wonder if he can act."

"He's head of the drama department."

"Not a guarantee. Dan," she said, leaning over, "could you run upstairs and ask that guy, the tragic one, to come talk to us?"

When Dan led him to them, Hermione thrust out her hand and introduced herself. "I'm bad at names and yours has slipped out of my head."

"Edward Smith."

"Not much excuse for forgetting that one. I apologize. This is Jessica Fontaine. We'd like to talk to you; can you leave your students alone for a few minutes?"

"They've taken over the cafe upstairs. What can I do for you?"

"We're staging a new play," Jessica said. "I'm directing it; Hermione is the producer. We'd like you to read for one of the parts."

"You've acted, of course," Hermione said.

"In Canada," he replied. "I never got very far. Why do you want me to read for this part?"

"Because you look like this guy," Hermione said. "His name is Stan, he's about your age, with a forty-two-year-old son, and he and his wife have had a rough time because twenty years earlier someone took them for everything they had and he's never found a way back."

"A loser."

"A victim. But he comes back, they both do, and in a way they're the ones who triumph in the end. It's more complicated than that and more interesting, but if you don't mind trying a scene with just that much and a quick read-through, we'd like to hear you."

He turned to Jessica. "Have you ever known anyone picked out of a crowd to be just what you're looking for?"

"No. It would be a first."

He gave her a long look. "Give me ten minutes."

He went outside, to the broad walkway that ran the length of the building, and stood in a shaded corner, reading the section Jessica had marked. When he returned, he said, "Who will read with me?"

"Nora Thomas," Hermione said. "Our last hope for Doris, at least for today. Nora? We're ready."

A stocky woman with steel-gray hair, a pug nose and full rosy cheeks closed her book and came to them from her chair in the corner. She took the script Jessica handed her, glanced at it and nodded.

She and Edward Smith shook hands, eyed each other, then sat on facing chairs some distance from Jessica and Hermione, and began to read a dialogue between Stan and Doris. Jessica clasped her hands in her lap, listening for what could be drawn out in the future, as well as for what was there now. When the voices stopped, she said, "Thank you. Would you please wait outside?" As they left, she turned to Hermione. "Well?"

"Neither one of them. Damn, this is taking forever. He's got a good voice and a couple of times I almost thought he had it, but he left me cold. No fire, no passion. He's so *down*. As for Nora, she's not bad, but I don't like her looks."

"What does that mean?" Jessica asked evenly.

"Nothing personal. She looks small-town. We want somebody who looks like she knows what it is to be rich even though she isn't anymore."

Jessica nodded thoughtfully. "I'd like to use both of them."

"You're joking."

"No, I like them. Give them a couple of weeks of rehearsal and you'll be agreeing with me."

"No way. You know how many times I've done this, Jessie? More than you can shake a—" She stopped. "Okay, I promised I'd never do that. I'm not holding it against you that you've never directed before; I'm just questioning your judgement in this one case."

"Two cases. They're better than you think, Hermione. I'm not guessing; I know it."

There was a silence. "Well," Hermione said. "A little conflict here. And everything's been so sweetness-and-light. What if I said absolutely not?"

"I don't answer hypothetical questions. You won't say it because you do trust my judgement. We wouldn't have gotten this far if you didn't."

"Well, God knows that's true." Hermione tapped her pencil on the table. "You know there's a lot of money at stake."

"A third of which is mine. I don't intend to lose it."

"Okay." She dropped the pencil and slammed the table with her palm. "Done. I hope to God you're right. I'll go get them."

When they returned and Jessica told them they had the parts of Doris and Stan, Edward Smith looked at Jessica. She was startled at his intensity. He was better looking than she had thought, and he was gazing at her with a kind of brooding interest she found attractive and intriguing.

"Can you take a leave of absence?"she asked him. "From now until at least the end of April. And if we continue the run at another theater, even beyond that."

"I'll find out." He went to the telephone on the wall. Nothing tentative about him, Jessica thought.

"I want to thank you," Nora was saying. "I'm so excited about this play, so incredibly excited, I've been praying for a week—"

"Have you ever been rich?" Hermione asked bluntly.

"What? Rich? Well, we had plenty of money when I was growing up. Why?"

Jessica let them talk, her thoughts wandering. When Edward hung up and turned and saw her looking at him, he smiled, the first smile Jessica had seen from him. "It's a little difficult, since I just took this position, but I think we can work it out. Summer vacation helps. I haven't thanked you for your trust. It means a great deal to me that you of all people think I have some ability on the stage."

Jessica's eyebrows rose. " 'Of all people'?"

"I went to New York from Toronto several times to see you on stage. I never dared hope we would meet. I'd like to ask you to dinner; is that improper, now that we're going to be working together?"

Jessica smiled. "I don't think so."

"Tonight, then?"

His eyes were gray; she had not noticed that. "I have a meeting with our stage manager at five; can we make it eight o'clock?"

"I'll come by for you. If you'll give me your address . . ."

Jessica wrote it down and handed him the slip of paper. "We have to know definitely about the leave of absence. If there's any doubt, we'll have to find someone else."

"There is no doubt," he said quietly. "I will play this part."

When he and Nora left, Hermione said, "He perked up. There might be something there after all. When are you going out with him?"

Jessica shook her head. "It always amazes me that you can be carrying on a conversation and listening to another one at the same time."

"I couldn't hear all of it; Nora talks nonstop, without commas, periods or paragraphs. We're going to have to slow down her metabolism. Which night?"

"Tonight."

"Fast work. Have you thought about it? It might not be a good idea. First of all there's something about him that bothers the hell out of me. Don't ask me what; I don't know yet. But I wouldn't trust him."

"Hermione, you don't know anything about him."

"Instinct, pure and simple. But my instinct and I don't usually let each other down. And there's something else. If you're his director, don't you think that's really all you ought to be? At least while you're directing. One thing at a time, one set of complications at a time."

"I don't see a problem."

"I do, Jessie. I don't think you should go out with him."

"One dinner. Then I'll rethink it."

After a moment, Hermione shrugged. "You're a big girl; I can't tell you what to do. You'll still be at the meeting with Dan at five?"

"Hermione."

"Well, yes, that was a stupid thing to say. I do know this play comes first with you. And second, third and fourth, too. What are you doing until then?"

"You and I are going to sit here and make plans. I'd like to have the read-through on Monday, if that's all right with you. Then we'll start rehearsals on Wednesday. I need to go back to the Drama Theater to make measurements, and I'd like to photograph the backstage: dressing rooms, prop room, everything. Could you arrange that? And you said you'd have scene and lighting designers for me to talk to this week."

"Monday afternoon for Augie Mack, the scene designer. I'm still talking to a couple of lighting guys; give me till next week on that. I'll let you know what time for the Drama Theater, probably this weekend, early in the A.M., before the tours of the Opera House begin. Do you have any idea how much you've changed since we first met?"

Jessica looked up from her list. "Changed? How?"

"How, she says. Listen to you. All of a sudden you're all put together; you know what you want and how to get it, or to get other people to get it for you. I'm very impressed. Particularly since I think I played a small but meaningful part in getting you out of those dumps you were in."

"You did." Jessica smiled. "And now I'm ordering you around. I apologize."

"Don't. I like decisive people. Now, here's my list of things to do. Oh, by the way, will you be home at seven-thirty?"

"Yes."

"Good. That's when the fax machine arrives."

Dear Luke, here is my fax number. I'm about to go out so I won't write now, but this weekend I'll tell you all about *Journeys End.* We have a cast and we're on our way. Jessica.

Dearest Jessica, here's *my* fax number. *The Magician* is sold out through March, which makes everyone very happy. Monte no longer worries about what he calls its "ultimate success"; as far as he's concerned, we've made it and he's looking around for another play. I've just given him Kent's new one, all three acts, though we agree the third still needs a lot of work. Would you like to read it now or when he's finished with the revisions?

I spent the weekend at Monte and Gladys's place on Kiawah Island (as big as their place in Amagansett). The beach is just outside, with joggers at all times of day and night, and, when everyone is asleep, only the sounds of the waves to break the silence. It was a lot of space and a lot of silence for one person and I thought about you all weekend. You would have enjoyed the conversations and the people. It was a weekend when all the vacation homes were filled with couples and I was more aware than ever of how the world prefers partners; how it subtly nudges to the side single people who, among many logistical problems, remind others that they, too, may be alone one of these days—and who wants to be reminded of that?

I hope I don't sound self-pitying. I enjoyed Monte and Gladys, but I did miss you. Congratulations on finishing your casting; do you have photos of your four people? Tell me about them. And about yourself. All my love, Luke.

P.S. I note from the time of your fax that you were getting ready to go out at about eight p.m. Are you having a busy social life?

Dear Luke, I went to dinner with one of our cast members, who is taking a leave of absence as assistant director of the university drama department. I plucked him from a group of students he was leading through the Wharf and it may be a gamble that fails, but what a triumph for him and us if it works!

It's late Monday afternoon now, very hot and humid, but in my living room it's blessedly cool and quiet. Today we had our first read-through, so I can tell you about that and the cast at the same time.

She wrote steadily for an hour, adding to her descriptions many of her ideas for staging the play. It was like thinking aloud; like talking to herself. It was like writing to Constance.

Thank you for listening to all this. Writing helps me make sense of all the parts that make up a play. I never realized how many thousands of details directors have to remember and make time for. I'm learning so much that sometimes it seems I'll burst from the sheer mass of it, but then I think of writing to you and putting it all in order and that's enough to make everything seem manageable again. Aren't faxes amazing? It's the closest thing to a conversation. Jessica.

Dearest Jessica, a telephone would be closer. All my love, Luke.

The telephone rang. "Jessica, it's Edward. Will you have dinner with me tonight?"
"No, I don't think . . . I'd rather stay home tonight, Edward. I'm sorry."

"Tomorrow night, then. One more dinner before rehearsals begin. I'm afraid of a lot of things changing after that."

There was a pause. "All right, then, tomorrow night."

"I'll come by for you as usual. Eight o'clock?"

"Yes."

*As usual.* After only one dinner together, he was trying to push her into a shared history. She liked him; she was drawn to him and enjoyed his company, but now she felt pressured and she reached for the telephone to tell him she could not go with him tomorrow night, either. But then she glanced at the one-sentence letter that had come that day from Luke. Everyone pushes, she thought. Everyone wants at least some degree of control. And dinner with Edward will be pleasant.

Dear Luke, I prefer the fax. Jessica

## CHAPTER 14

Edward drove, his face stern as he dealt with traffic, and they went to Bilson's, on the upper level of the International Passenger Terminal at Circular Quay. The restaurant, sleek in silver, black and gray, with a single flower on each table, made Jessica think of a stage set with the harbor as a dramatic background. Edward had reserved a table beside the wraparound windows that gave a panoramic view of the Opera House, the single steel span of the Harbor Bridge, and the bustle of boats trailing foamy white wakes across the choppy water. Below, lovers and families strolled on the Quay, stopping to watch slack rope walkers and mimes, a woodworker building models of sailing ships, and tourists lined up to board a paddlewheel showboat with a jazz band playing on the upper deck. Daylight faded as Edward and Jessica ate, and the lights of Sydney came on, outlining the bridge and the city's skyscrapers, illuminating the sail-like roof of the Opera House, and casting a pale glow on the water that was reflected in the restaurant's silvered ceiling.

Looking up at ripples that seemed to be moving above them, through the windows and out to sea, Jessica smiled. "I feel like a mermaid. Or at least my idea of one. What a good set this would make."

Edward waved the waiter away and refilled their wineglasses himself. "Maybe you'll use it in your next play."

"Maybe." She smiled again, familiar now with his attempts to get her to talk about herself. At their first dinner she had turned all their conversation back to him, always having a new question or comment ready when one of his answers began to wind down. She knew now about his family in Canada, his brothers and sisters, his father's career as a concert pianist and sudden death from a heart attack when Edward was sixteen. "My mother married again and we felt betrayed: a wedding less than a year after our father's death, and a stranger in the house. In fact, he was good to us and we had a good home, but we all left, one at a time, as soon as we graduated high school. Three of us went to college; the others found jobs in Toronto, Detroit and Los Angeles. We've never been together again."

"You must miss them."

"Not at all. Once in a while I miss knowing that people are somewhere close, but that's a weakness I try to conquer; a throwback to a time when I was young and wanted someone around to listen if I had a complaint or a problem. I suppose most people spend their lives searching for that, but I stopped long ago."

"Because you found it in the theater. Isn't that what you mean? That's as close to a family as you'll find. You haven't been married?"

"Once. We're still friends, but she's in Canada, and neither of us is any good at writing letters. Well, the theater. I'm not really in it, you know; at least I wasn't until now."

"But you said you'd acted in Canada."

"Not in major theaters."

"But still, that feeling of sharing, of creating something in harmony, don't you take pleasure in that when you have it?"

"I don't know. It seems that I'm a very poor

sharer. There's so much at stake when you open yourself to criticism—"

"It might be admiration."

"Possibly, but not likely. Most people find things in me to criticize. That's not a complaint; I understand what they see. I'm not smooth or sophisticated or witty; I hoard my emotions; I usually see the dark side of things. My mother said I was a nice kid who measured my life in empty rooms and roads I walk alone."

Jessica caught her breath. "*Is* that how you measure your life?"

"Mostly. I'm good with students, so I don't qualify as a hermit; it's just that I have no real intimacy. But that's not a complaint, either. We do the best we can with our lives and usually it's enough to make us moderately happy. I'm telling you more than I've ever told anyone; you're a good listener and you don't give the impression that you'll take advantage of any of this."

"*Advantage?* Good Lord, why would I?"

"People do, usually for power."

At that, she had changed the subject, not wanting to linger in his bleak landscape. But now, sitting across from him at Bilson's, she led him to talk about it again. "Where is your mother?" she asked.

"She and her husband bought a condo in San Diego. They like being warm."

"You don't see them at all?"

"Not for years. And we don't correspond; everything seems much too long and complicated to put down on paper. Some of us telephone now and then, but we've drifted so far apart that we find ourselves talking about the weather. I don't even think of them as part of my life anymore; they're something left behind, like people I've met and apartments I've lived in. And that's fine; I don't need them and they show no signs of needing me. The truth is, I've been satisfied to be alone all my life; I find it hard to give what people seem to need, so everything ends in unhappiness. I'm best at my work, where there's always a distance between people and there's no confusion about where we belong or how we're supposed to treat each other. I'm content with that."

Jessica contemplated him, thinking that he made her life of the past few years seem like a joyous social whirl. "I think in some ways you're very courageous, and I admire that, but I think you need people more than you admit. Why else would you ask me to dinner?"

"I asked you to dinner because your eyes are magnificent and I wanted to look at them for a long time. Why are *you* here?"

"To listen to extravagant praise."

"Why do you fend me off when I ask you questions about yourself?"

"Because I want to talk about you. How can you be an actor when you're so alone? Actors learn by being part of the world. You've been alone since high school."

"Except for the small blip of a marriage that lasted six months. Yes, but I do look at people, I analyze them in my mind, I think about them. The only thing I don't do is get close to them."

"Poor man," Jessica said softly.

He reached across the table and covered her hand with his. "You mustn't pity me. Especially now, when I have you to talk to. Thank you for being so understanding; I haven't felt this comfortable with anyone in years. You're an amazing woman, mysterious, fascinating, sensitive—" He stopped. "You'll call that extravagant praise."

"Yes," she said, but she did pity him, and admire his honesty, and the warmth of his hand on hers was enough to make her body stir and open to feelings she had tried to clamp off as soon as Luke left, and so her voice was soft, and she let her hand stay where it was.

"I want to see a lot of you," he said. "As much as possible. We've made such a fine beginning . . . I'm worried about what will happen when we begin rehearsals."

Jessica felt a flash of annoyance. She pulled her hand away. "We'd better talk about the play before we go any further. If we don't agree on that, we don't agree on anything."

His face folded into the long, melancholy lines it had had when she first saw him. He dragged his hand back to his lap. "You're going to tell me the play comes before everything."

"In just those words. I'd like you to feel that way, too."

"How can I, when I've just found you? No, don't frown, please, Jessica, please listen. It's true that I can be alone—that I *am* alone—but when I'm with you, even after such a short time, it's as if I've found an anchor. I'm usually afraid of getting close to people, but you make me feel at ease, with myself, with the world. I never meant to say the play isn't important, but I'd throw it away in a minute if I thought it would destroy what we have."

"We have very little," she said coolly. "Two dinners, which hardly adds up to a passionate love affair. Edward, this play means everything to me. If I fail . . . Well, I can't fail. This has to be my success, the kind of success I can build on, and nothing can distract me from that. I'm glad we're friends, but I won't go beyond that. Not yet."

He hesitated, then nodded brusquely. "Whatever you want." He signaled to the waiter. "Check, please."

"I'm not ready to go," Jessica said calmly. "I'd like another cup of coffee. And cognac." She struggled with pity and arousal and annoyance. She knew he saw this as a rejection—and there had obviously been many in his life or he would not so vehemently have made a virtue of solitude—and she wanted to bring back the smile that had briefly lightened his face. She wished for his hand on hers, again; the warmth, the weight of a man close to her, wanting her. The trouble was, when she contemplated going to bed with him, her thoughts skidded away, straight to Luke, to every moment they had spent together, in bed and out. But I wouldn't sleep with Edward anyway, she thought, not as long as he acts like a child who's pouting because he can't have what he wants at the exact moment he wants it. He'll be good in the play—he'll be terrific if he works at it—and that's all I want from him. At least for now.

Dearest Jessica, thank you for sending me *Journeys End.* It's a fine play; you're lucky to have it. I'll be interested in seeing how you develop Helen and Rex, and how you make their coming together at the end seem inevitable.

(Do you think it is inevitable that people who love each other will at some point come together? I'd like to think so.)

I'm in my library and I want to set the scene for you. Three feet of snow have paralyzed the city. Parked cars are smoothly mounded, like huge white truffles; cross-country skiers glide down Fifth and Park and Madison—though the plows, like dark fingers of Fate, are about to overtake them; and a strange and lovely silence has settled over Manhattan so that, suddenly, we are aware of how much noise we accept without thinking, day after day. (Of course I was aware of that on Lopez, but that was a different story.) Now that the snow has passed, the temperature has fallen to something below zero, and Martin keeps fires going in all three fireplaces in the apartment. It's a little after midnight here, early Tuesday, which means it's about three p.m. Wednesday your time—I've bought a clock which I've set to Sydney time so that I don't have to figure out hours and the International Date Line when I think of you—and your summer day is hot and humid (your letters and the television reports say), which puts us at opposite ends of the weather spectrum. I'll fax this in a few minutes so it will be waiting for you when you come home from rehearsal. Your first rehearsal. I hope it went so well that already you can see glimmers of the shape the play will take, and the intimacy your actors will create with each other and the audience. I could not wish anything more for you, now, than that.

Two new plays opened here this week. One probably won't last—it drifts and wanders and never gets to the point—but the other is causing quite a stir and I enjoyed it enormously. You would, too; I'm sorry you're not here to see it. Would you like me to send you the script? Which reminds me, you didn't tell me whether you want to read Kent's play now or after revisions. Or at all. Let me know. With my love, Luke.

*He can't be sitting home every night, not in New York where everything, and everyone, beckons. Where is he, in the evening hours before he writes to me? What is he doing? And with whom?*

The next night Edward had tickets for a play at the Footbridge Theater, and then took Jessica to the Regency for a late supper. They sat for a long time, talking about the play they had seen, and about other plays and books and music. It was the first time they had spent an entire evening without talking about Edward and, by the time they left, Jessica was having a very good time and was sorry it was almost over. "Do you like musicals?" Edward asked as they drove to her house. "I have tickets for the Theatre Royal for Friday. I tried to get them for tomorrow, but they were sold out. But I did make reservations for supper afterward. Would you like to go?"

"Yes," she said, smiling. "You're a thorough planner, Edward."

"That's usually a criticism—what a dull fellow, such a thorough, *rigid* planner. But there's nothing dull about making plans to be with you; it's the most exciting thing I do." He parked in front of her house and put his arms around her, and kissed her. "I love you, Jessica. You make me feel alive." He bent to her again and Jessica opened to him, absorbing his warmth, the enclosure of his arms, the pressure of his mouth on hers. He raised his head and she looked into his eyes, pale gray in the light cast by streetlamps. "I want to come in with you," he said. "I can't leave you now."

His hand was on her breast; he kissed her mouth, her cheek, her neck. Jessica, her eyes closed, arched toward him as his mouth moved to the hollow of her throat, followed the rounded neckline of her dress and moved down. Through the thin silk, his breath was warm on her breast; the warmth filled her and drew her into him. "Let me stay with you tonight," he murmured. "I want to be with you."

Yes, she thought. This is now, this is my life now. Luke is the past.

*He can't believe anyone would truly be attracted to him and he's terrified of being rejected.*

Her eyes flew open. She had written that to Constance, a long long time ago. Who was the man? She could not remember. Someone who had attracted her by needing to be stroked, encouraged, pumped up.

"I need you," Edward murmured. "My anchor. A place to belong and to feel alive."

*I seem to have a blind spot about men; it takes me a long time to figure them out. I have to work on that.*

Not about Luke, she thought. I didn't have a blind spot about Luke. But except for him, oh, Lord, I haven't learned anything at all.

Her body was cooling beneath Edward's long, sighing breath. "Edward," she said.

He lifted his head and when he saw her eyes his face changed. "What's wrong?"

"I can't do this. I'm sorry, but—" She felt him shrink from her; she could almost see his face shrivel. "I don't want this, not yet. It's not you, it's—"

"What else could it be?" He moved away from her and rested his hands and forehead on the steering wheel. "I went too fast. I must have seemed like some horny kid looking for—"

"Edward, stop." She was still trembling with arousal, but it was fading quickly. "Did it ever occur to you that I might be involved with someone else?"

He looked at her in shock. "No."

"Why not?"

"Well, because I thought you couldn't be."

*Because of my looks. You thought no one else would be interested, isn't that it?*

"I mean, you're new in town, you live alone, you're always working on the play . . . and you go out with me. Why would any woman look twice at me if she was interested in someone else?"

Jessica stared at him, then burst out laughing.

"What does that mean?" he demanded harshly.

"I'm sorry." She touched his face lightly. "I was thinking of something Hermione once told me was foolish, and she was probably right. Edward, there is a man I feel close to. That's all I'll say about him, except to tell you that I'm not with him and you and I are friends and that's enough for now. Besides, we're working together; why take a chance of complicating that? We have plenty of time to find out how much we like each other."

"I said love. And when you've waited for something all your life—"

"You can wait a while longer." She opened the car door. "Thank you for tonight. I'll see you in the morning." She leaned toward him, thinking of kissing his cheek, then decided against it. The slightest bit of encouragement and he'd be planning the next ten years. "May I have my cane?" He reached into the backseat and handed it to her. "Thank you. Good night, Edward."

She closed the car door and limped the short distance to her front door, knowing he was brooding as he watched her. I need someone who smiles a lot, she reflected, unlocking the door and going in without looking back. Do I think Edward will ever be that kind of person? Well, he might. What are the chances? Maybe one in a thousand.

But the next morning she awoke thinking about him, knowing that his loneliness and sadness were powerful attractions for her right now, because she needed to feel she could help someone who was even less self-confident than she.

"Are you thinking profound thoughts?" Hermione asked when she arrived at seven. "Much too early in the day for anything but breakfast."

"Croissants, brioche, muffins, fruit, coffee," said Jessica, leading the way to the dining room buffet. "Help yourself." A few minutes later the general manager for *Journeys End* arrived and the three of them sat at the cluttered dining table to go over the budget of the play. They worked for an hour, adding and subtracting to bring costs low enough so they would break even by opening night. "If we sell out in previews, we're all right," Hermione said at last. "Close but okay. The theater parties, bless them, will carry us through the first two weeks after we open, but we've got to get to them."

Jessica sighed. "We're going to have to give up the turntables and use the revolving circles that are built into the stage. I don't like it as much because they're one inside the other and the audience won't be able to see both apartments at once, but that's what we've got so we'll have to use it. Or just have a split stage, one apartment on each side."

"Dull and predictable," Hermione said. "Let's wait to see Augie's blueprints and costs. We'll decide then."

At eight, the general manager went to his next meeting and Jessica and Hermione left the coolness of her apartment to go to the Wharf, where Dan Clanagh was waiting for them. The heat was already building in the rehearsal room and they turned on the fans and opened their thermoses of iced tea. For the next hour, the three of them met with the lighting director, the managers of wardrobe and props, and the house manager. At nine-thirty everyone left, and Jessica was alone for half an hour, before the cast and the production secretary arrived.

She walked to the end of the rehearsal room, where bright blue tape formed the outline of a stage, and followed its perimeter, leaning on her cane, thinking about the first act of *Journeys End.* She went over the ways in which the four characters would come together, how they would look at each other and speak their first lines that would immediately create the tensions that would drive the whole play. But her thoughts kept skittering away, like drops of water in a hot skillet, and finally she stopped trying to concentrate, and stood still.

She closed her eyes. She was in the middle of the stage. She was looking at the audience. She saw the lights fill the set with brightness and focus on her. She heard the rustle of programs as everyone settled down. She saw the stage manager in the wings, and the other actors preparing to make their entrance. She felt the rush of energy and trepidation that swept through her each time she gathered herself together for her first line. She felt the pure happiness and exhilaration that buoyed her up after that first moment, and stayed with her through the play, through the night, through the weeks and months the play ran.

"God, it's hot," Hermione said, bursting in and whipping off her straw hat. "Too hot to do errands, too hot even to think; I drove back here by internal radar." She stopped short. "Shit, I'm a damn fool. Barging in, talking my head off. I'm sorry, Jessie. This is really terrible for you, isn't it?

One of the hardest things you've ever— Here."
She held out a handkerchief.

Jessica wiped her eyes. "Thank you. I won't let it
happen again; it's one of those indulgences that
lead nowhere. We ought to be able to edit our
memories so they fit the ways we've changed and
the times we live in."

"They wouldn't be memories, then. They'd be
lies."

"Well . . . fantasies."

"Which are okay as long as you don't organize
your life around them." She looked closely at Jessica. "Do you?"

"No. Hard, clear reality all the time." They
walked to their table as the cast came in and took
their places for act one. And Jessica knew that the
hard reality was that she wanted to be with them,
right there in that dusty rectangle marked with
blue tape, right there where Angela Crown stood,
and opened her mouth, and spoke the first lines of
the play.

*I'm jealous. Oh, God, I wish I wasn't, but I am. And
I have to get rid of it or I'll ruin the play and make
a fool of myself.*

"Angela, I'm sorry, but I'd like to start again.
These first few minutes, we have to believe that
you're angry, but also that you're sure you can control your anger. We have to get that feeling of control very early, because it spills over to your
greeting of Rex when he knocks on your door."

Angela nodded. She stood for a minute with her

head bowed, then took a few steps, began to pace, and once again spoke her opening lines.

Jessica did not interrupt again, but let them go through all three acts, while she and Hermione and Dan Clanagh wrote pages of notes. "Good," she said when the last line was spoken. "How did you feel about it?"

"Good," echoed Whitbread Castle. "I can already see the dynamics."

"It needs an incredible amount of work," Edward said.

Jessica smiled. If they ever were in danger of feeling happy, they could count on Edward to bring them up short. "Yes, it does, but I agree with Whit; this is a good start. We've got lots of notes here, but I want your ideas, too. This play belongs to all of us and we should talk out all our suggestions, problems, questions, whatever we think will make it better. I wish the playwright was here, but since he isn't, we'll have to make our own interpretations of the dialogue and the characters and I want you all to contribute to that."

Whitbread frowned. "But *you're* the director. I mean, you have the final say. The theater isn't a place for democracy, you know—*I* certainly don't want that kind of chaos—I want a director who *directs.*"

"If Jessica wants our ideas, I suggest that we provide them," Hermione said briskly. "Now let's take a short break—"

Whitbread put up his hand, as if he were directing traffic. "Because you're worried, is that it?"

*"Worried?"*

"People are talking, Hermione. You know. I mean, *I* get a little worried when I hear that my director doesn't have any experience or know-how, doesn't—"

"I'm going to fire him," Hermione muttered.

"No, you're not," Jessica said quietly.

"—doesn't have any, you know, *philosophy* of directing—except, I guess, asking all of us to pitch in with ideas and so on, which I must tell you I find alarming—"

"Have you heard of Lucas Cameron?" Hermione demanded.

"No."

"Oh, God, I wish Sydney would pay attention to New York. Well, for your information, Lucas Cameron is one of the world's top directors, and he asks every cast he works with to bring him their ideas, questions, problems, whatever, and *he pays attention to them.* He even gives out his private phone number so anyone can call him at home, anytime, to discuss the play. That doesn't sound like worry to me; it sounds like he's confident enough to listen to others. So is Jessica. She has powerful ideas of her own, but she wants to hear your ideas, too. Does anybody want to disagree with me on any of that?"

No one spoke.

"Where did you hear these rumors?" Jessica asked mildly, as if it were not really important, but as long as they were talking they might as well get it all out.

"Oh, well . . ." He was taken aback by her mildness. "Here and there, you know, nothing specific. . . ."

"Really? It sounded quite specific to me."

"No . . . more like fragments, you know, bits of conversations . . . I may even have been mistaken, you know how noisy some parties are. . . . Jessica, I want to work with you. I *do* see the dynamics of this play; I admire what you've done so far and your casting has been brilliant. I don't want—"

"Okay, we've covered everything," Hermione declared. She looked at Jessica. "Half an hour for lunch?"

"Yes. No more."

"Back here in thirty minutes," Hermione said to the cast. She watched them leave, then turned to Jessica. " 'Your casting has been brilliant,' " she mimicked, and they burst out laughing. "But it's not really funny; we have to talk about this. While we eat. I did tell you I was bringing lunch, didn't I?" She dug into her canvas bag and brought out two sandwiches and a container of vegetable salad, a thermos, plastic plates and glasses, and a wedge of chocolate cake. "Mostly leftovers from a small dinner party. Dig in."

"What is there to talk about?" Jessica asked.

"Closing the rehearsals. No visitors, nobody from the press, no more students. Just Dan, the production secretary when she starts next week, and the cast. That's it. I was thinking about this even before Whitbread made his little speech. It takes practice to be a director, you have to get your feet wet before you can swim and spread your wings before you can fly—good Lord, listen to me, I'm a stew of clichés today—anyway, you need time to make yourself the kind of director you want to be, and I'm not letting anybody butt in on that. You need space and privacy and you're going to get it."

"How often is that done?" Jessica asked.

"Now and then."

"But don't people always assume the worst when they're shut out of something?"

"They might."

"And that could hurt advance ticket sales."

"We've sold so many theater parties, I wouldn't worry about that."

"You said that theater parties fill the house for the first two weeks. But you still need individual ticket sales or you won't have any kind of a run. You've got your own money in this, Hermione."

"So do you. And you're right about ticket sales. But that's not what I want you to be thinking about right now. You just do the best job of directing that this town has ever seen; that's all I'm asking. Let me take care of everything else; you forget about it. Promise me you will."

"Just like that."

"Just like that. Think about the play. Think about dinner. Think about Edward. Who, by the way, was strangely silent, don't you think? Not exactly a knight in shining armor coming to your rescue in that whole conversation."

"Is that the conversation you've just asked me to forget?"

"Oh, my, tripped up. Okay, we won't talk about it. Or Edward. But I will say that he was good in rehearsal. He's studied the play and thought about it. Much to his credit."

"Yes. Thank you for lunch. Would you look at this list I have for Dan and add anything of your own? I want to give it to him when he gets back, and we'll talk about it after rehearsal. And I have a props list here, and some suggestions for wardrobe, and, I didn't mention it this morning, but I do have some alternative sketches for the set. What would you think of one turntable with an apartment on each side? Then we could show both apartments at once or only one. I thought we might talk to Augie about it after rehearsals. Can you stay?"

"You know I can. It looks like you've been working night and day. No time for sleep."

"I don't need a lot."

Hermione saw her look up as Angela Crown came into the room. "Bad dreams if you do?" she asked.

"No. Just . . . too much thinking."

"You know, Jessie, if I could make it easier for you, I would."

"I know and I love you for it. But I'm fine. You worry about theater parties and I'll take care of me. You forget about it. Promise me you will."

"Just like that."

"Just like that."

They laughed together. "Well, I won't promise, but I'll try not to harp on it. You'll work it out. You're good, you know: tough and smart. Can't beat that."

Not so tough, Jessica thought later that night. She had spent an hour with Hermione and Augie after rehearsals, then gone over wardrobe designs until almost eight. By the time she left, she was tired and feeling lonely, wanting companionship. Not even conversation, she thought, just the presence of someone else. She had not spoken to Edward all day and she missed his lugubrious commentaries and the sadness in his face that eased a little when they were together.

But as she maneuvered through the evening traffic and found herself going faster as she approached Point Piper, she remembered that a letter from Luke would be waiting for her. There was always a letter. He wrote every night, around midnight in New York, and his letter arrived instantly, in Sydney's hot summer afternoon, while Jessica was at rehearsal. And there it would be when she walked in at seven or eight o'clock, face up on her fax machine: crisp white pages filled with his handwriting. She would put off the moment of reading them by taking Hope outside and letting her run on her extra-long leash, then pouring a glass of wine and settling herself in a deep armchair beside the windows. And finally she would begin to read, and imagine that he was with her in the silence of her crowded rooms, with Hope curled up at her side and the sky fading to ocher and amber above the city's skyline and the ceaseless traffic in the harbor below.

Dearest Jessica, no letter from you for a few days, but I know what a busy time it is when you're just beginning rehearsals. You didn't say yes or no about Kent's play, so I've sent it to you without the revisions; I thought you might have suggestions that would help us with the third act. Not right away, of course; only when you want to take a breather from *Journeys End.* Kent, being Kent, wants to plunge right in, cast the play, and work on the third act while we're in rehearsals, a write-as-you-go method that causes me to break out in a cold sweat. Sometimes I wish I were as young as he is, filled with that absolute certainty that everything is possible, by brute force if not by intellectual savvy. But then I think it's better to be where I am, almost forty-six and perfectly willing to go slowly if I'm not sure what lies around the next bend or if I haven't got a fool-

proof answer for the problem at hand. I suppose that's what I'm doing with you, isn't it?
Kent probably would have been in Sydney long
ago, courting you and keeping alive the magic
of that week on your island. And maybe I
should have done that. In fact, whenever I see
an airline ticket office, I think how easy it
would be to fly to your new city and ring your
doorbell and, perhaps with Kent's cockiness,
invite you to dinner. Now and then I'm sure
you'd like that. But all the other times, I'm just
as sure that you'd tell me to get out of the way,
that you have a lot to prove and unless you
prove it alone you'll never be at peace with
yourself.

And maybe you'll never want me back in
your life, because I mean New York to you and
you're determined never to live here again.
Maybe you've met someone else who loves you
and has no connections with your past. Maybe
you don't know what you'll do next; maybe
you're waiting to see what's around the next
bend or what the foolproof answers are for the
problem at hand.

Whatever it is, I'll wait for you to find out. As
long as you write to me and keep me a part of
your life, I can wait. But perhaps you shouldn't
wait too long; you may find me, if you ever
come to look, grizzled, feeble and doddering.
Though no less in love with you. Always, Luke.

"Let's try it again," Jessica said the next day, "from Stan's entrance." She stood up, as if that might give them a feeling of urgency, perhaps even of tension, since tension was what she was after in this scene and had not found, though they had rehearsed it ten times already that day and it was only midafternoon. The trouble was, the heat was so oppressive they were all wilting and it made it more difficult to concentrate. "I have an idea. Edward, try stopping in the doorway instead of coming straight into the room. You thought this was your son's apartment and you're so shocked when you recognize Helen that you literally can't move."

"But how do I come in if he's blocking the door?" Nora asked.

"You don't have to, at least not right away. You start talking, right behind Stan; Helen hears your voice before she sees you. Then Stan comes in and you follow and the three of you look at each other for the first time in twenty years. Let's try it that way."

"I like it," Hermione said as Jessica sat down. "When did you think it up?"

"About two o'clock this morning."

"Still keeping your late hours."

"Yes." *But some of those hours were spent reading a wonderful letter over and over, because it was hard to think about anything else.*

Angela took her place on the couch and a moment later Edward simulated knocking on the door and opened it. "Rex, we're here—" He stopped, his breath coming out in an explosion, as if he had been socked in the stomach. His body seemed to draw into itself as he stared at Helen.

"Good, good," Hermione whispered.

"Rex? Where's my boy?" Doris was asking, behind Stan. Hearing her voice, Helen jumped to her feet. "Stan, you're in my way; I want to see my boy!" Doris cried.

Stan two took jerky steps into the room, with Doris right behind, almost pushing him. Helen took a step back as the three of them looked at each other.

"Much better," Jessica said. "How did that feel to the three of you?"

"Nice," Nora said. "It seems more natural."

"Angela?" Jessica asked.

"I don't see much difference from all the other ways we've been doing it, but it's okay."

"One difference is that now we know you've never forgotten Doris's voice; it helps explain a lot that follows. Now I want all of you—Whit, this includes you—to act out what you were doing before you came on stage."

They stared at her. "What?" Whitbread said at last.

"Make up lines, make up stage business, whatever works for you. I want to see where you were and what you were doing just before you came into the apartment. Angela, that means where you were and what you were doing *in* the apartment before the others arrived."

"Why?" Angela asked.

"Because your life doesn't begin the minute you step onto the stage. You're a whole person and the action on stage is *in between* other parts of your life. You're always coming from somewhere and when you exit you're going somewhere. If you can't feel that, nothing you do on stage will be truthful."

"I've heard that talked about," Angela said, "but *acting it* . . . I mean, why go through all that?"

"Because I'm asking you to. Whit, will you start?"

Slowly, agonizingly, each of them began to invent dialogue and action. "I don't know," Whitbread muttered. "I really have no idea what you're getting at."

Jessica sighed. "This is what I'm getting at." She took her cane and walked to the makeshift stage. "Angela, please." Angela moved away from the box that represented a couch and Jessica sat in her place, pretending to hold a pad of paper in one hand and a pencil in the other. "The zoo benefit next Friday," she said. Every word was audible, but it was clear that she was talking to herself. "The cancer benefit, the Botanical Gardens dinner, the Art Gallery dinner, and what's-his-name's costume ball . . . good Lord"—her voice rose, filled with pride and satisfaction—"I need a staff; one secretary isn't enough; this has gotten far too big for me to handle by myself."

She knocked on the coffee table, mimicking Stan's knock on her door, and looked up sharply, then spoke a few lines of the dialogue that followed, taking all three parts. "That's what I'm getting at," she said, standing up. "Of course, we don't know yet what Stan and Doris were doing before Stan knocked on the door, but we know that Helen was feeling very good about herself and therefore the shock of seeing her past suddenly appear in her doorway is even more devastating. Now you try it. Nora or Edward, one of you go first."

Nora was staring at her. "That was wonderful. You made Helen sound . . . I mean, if I could sound like that—"

"We're waiting," Jessica said flatly, sitting again at the table.

Hermione leaned toward her. "Did you see Angela's face? Total shock. I'll bet she's thinking you ought to be in her shoes right now."

"Angela? Believing someone is a better actress than she is? You don't really believe that."

"Well, put that way, probably not. And she really is pretty good."

"She's a good actresss; she'll be fine."

"I know she will. Well, would you listen to them now. They got the idea. Clumsy, but they're really trying."

Jessica nodded, and they were silent, listening. "Good," she said after a few minutes. "Now go back and do the scene again, but remember what went before, because it's part of you."

They went through the first five minutes of the scene. "Did it make any difference?" Angela asked. "It didn't seem any different to me."

Jessica took a long breath. "It was a little bit different. It will get better with time. If it doesn't, there's not much point in rehearsing. Let me tell you what I'm trying to do. I'm sure you've heard it all before, but I think you need to hear it from me. We're looking for truth. That means that when something surprising happens on stage, you are truly surprised. I know you'll think that's so elementary it doesn't need to be said, but actors forget it all the time. You're all so good you can act almost any emotion, but acting surprised or frightened or furious never convinces an audience as much as *being* surprised or frightened or furious. Once you've convinced them . . . well, you know this from all the times you've done it in the past: they believe in you and they'll follow you anywhere, into other emotions and other situations, until—at least this is what we hope—they discover something new about what it means to be human. For me, that's the true magic of the theater."

Edward shook his head. "That's too much to expect. How many actors can actually give audiences a new understanding of being human? A handful in the whole world. You're talking about a formidable talent, a very rare talent."

"Think of it as something to strive for," Jessica said coolly, finding Edward's lugubriousness less appealing by the moment. "Now please go back and begin act two again."

Dearest Jessica, I'm sending you two books that I've enjoyed; I hope you can find some time to read them. I know the feeling that you have too much to do before opening night (will you have previews?), but my homily for the day is this: small breaks for relaxation actually make everything more manageable, just as sips of wine make a meal go more smoothly, and brief separations between lovers intensify their feelings. Give yourself time for yourself. All my love, Luke.

Dear Luke, I'm having a problem with the opening of act two; I can't get the explosive tension it needs. It's better than it was, with Stan frozen with shock in the doorway and Doris behind him, heard (and remembered) by Helen before being seen, but it still isn't enough. Is there anything else I could do? Jessica.

Dearest Jessica, get Helen off that couch. The scene is too static in the moment before Stan comes in. Maybe she's been in the bedroom and comes in still brushing her hair or pulling on a jacket or tying a scarf—something like that—just as Stan opens the door. So they face each other standing, both of them

frozen in position for maybe three seconds before Doris says her lines behind Stan (a very
good touch, by the way). I hope this helps.
With my love, Luke.

"Yes!" Hermione exclaimed as she and Jessica
watched Angela and Edward face each other
across the makeshift stage. "Terrific! You finally
got it."

"A friend suggested it," Jessica said.

"Ah. The wonders of a fax machine."

"And of friendship."

"Speaking of which, how about dinner tonight?
Come over about seven; I'll rent a movie and we
won't talk shop at all."

"It sounds wonderful, but could we do it tomorrow night instead?"

"Sure. Shall I refrain from asking what's happening tonight?"

Jessica smiled. "It's hard to deal with such sub-
tlety. Edward is taking me to Manly for dinner and
a visit to something called Oceanworld."

"How romantic. *Is* this a romance?"

"No. We enjoy being together."

And that was what she said to Edward that
night as they sat on the terrace of the Headlands
Restaurant in Manly. They had taken the Jetcat
there, bouncing at high speeds across the choppy
water of the harbor, and then had gone to Oceanworld, a huge marine tank with a moving walkway
beneath the clear bottom, so that they looked up

at sharks, octopi, eels and dozens of other creatures from the ocean and the Great Barrier Reef.
"What fun," Jessica said. "It's the best way to pretend you're an eel or a shark. At least you see
things from their point of view."

"Not so long ago you felt like a mermaid," Edward said. They were walking slowly to the restaurant and he held her free arm, which annoyed her,
but she said nothing so that he would not feel rejected. "Are you tired of living on the land?"

"I'm not tired of anything," she said. "I like new
experiences and new feelings. New ways of looking at things."

He held her chair at the restaurant and propped
her cane against the wall. "Are you pleased with
our rehearsals?"

"I thought we'd agreed not to talk about work."

He picked up the menu and scanned it. "Everything here is very good. You might want to try the
Moreton Bay bug if you haven't had it."

"I haven't. The name definitely lacks appeal."

"It's just a local miniature crayfish, you know,
sadly misnamed. There's also the Victorian yabby,
a local lobster, quite fine. And the barramundi is
an excellent fish, found only here. Also the Tas-
manian scallops, grilled. I would recommend any
of those. Red wine or white?"

"Red. Edward, what is this sudden interest in
food? You've always seemed so indifferent, as if a
meal was just something that stood between you
and starvation."

"But I'm with you and that makes everything different. Jessica, I have to say this, how completely different my life is with you."

"We said we wouldn't talk about that."

"You said."

"Well, then, I said it. Isn't that enough?"

His mouth turned down. "I've disappointed you."

"A little, but not excessively. Come on, Edward; let's keep things light."

From then on, he let her lead the conversation, and she kept it firmly away from the two of them, until they had finished dessert and were drinking espresso. Then Edward took a deep breath, girding himself. "I asked you earlier if you were happy with rehearsals."

"And I told you—"

"I know, but we must talk about it." He took her hand, holding it tightly. "I have great confidence in you, Jessica, more than I have in anyone else at the moment. But right now I need to ask you how you think we're doing, because a lot of people in Sydney are saying that the play is a disaster, and I'm too close to it to know whether they're right or wrong, so I'm asking you to tell me."

Jessica's anger flared. "You're asking me to reassure you that the play isn't a disaster? What will you do if I say that it is?"

Shocked, he said, "I don't know. I don't expect you to say that."

"Then why ask it at all?"

"Because I need to hear you say that it's wonderful. I've put all my energies and hopes into this, more than anyone can imagine, and I need reassurance. Is that asking too much?"

She freed her hand. "I'd like to go home, Edward."

"No, no, we have to finish this. Why do you turn hostile when everything is so good between us? I asked a simple question: Are you happy with rehearsals?"

"We're going in the right direction. We still have two weeks and then previews. What else are people saying about the play? Or about me?"

"You don't want to know all that. I only mentioned it because the four of us are a little worried. Angela thinks the problem is closed rehearsals, but we can't be sure, so I said I'd ask you about it."

"You're the designated messenger? Does that mean none of you thinks rehearsals are going well?"

"We all did until we started hearing . . ."

"Until you started hearing what? I want to know, Edward."

"Jessica, this isn't easy for me. But we have to believe that what we're doing is good; we can't go for another two weeks wondering if it might be . . . might be . . ."

"A disaster. That's what you heard."

"Yes, among other— But none of it is true. . . ."

"If you really believed that, you wouldn't have brought it up. Go on. I want to know what they're saying."

"Well, it isn't true, we all know that, but some people are saying that you're floundering, that you don't know how to put a play together and build it, you know, develop tension, and you can't work with a crew or a cast. . . ."

"And you agree? With any or all of it? What about the last? That I don't know how to work with a cast."

"No, of course not. I told you, we know they're wrong about that. We all think you're the best director we've worked with. Even Angela said that and she's had the most experience of all of us."

"Then why are we having this discussion?"

"Because it's hard for us to be the subject of rumors."

"I thought I was the subject."

"We're involved. And they create an atmosphere, you know, of suspicion and mistrust, of *worry,* and we should be concentrating on the play instead of worrying about what people are saying."

"I agree."

"With what?"

"That you should be concentrating on the play. That you shouldn't be worrying about what people are saying. You've given yourself excellent advice."

"Jessica, you're being willful. You know what

I'm saying. We don't want to worry, but we can't help it. The atmosphere, you know—"

"Yes, I heard that. You all agree that I'm the best director you've ever worked with, but you begin to think you're wrong as soon as you hear ignorant people gossip."

"No, no, that's not what I said."

"Well, perhaps you'll tell me just what you did say."

"There's a feeling of insecurity, a *miasma* of insecurity. I should think you'd understand that; you're very sensitive to people's feelings. Angela asked if she could invite some friends—influential friends—to rehearsals, but Hermione wouldn't allow it. Why not? What harm could it do? It might help ticket sales, you know, and some people are wondering if we'll even get to opening night if this miasma lasts and hurts ticket sales. It shouldn't surprise you that we're worried about the future."

Jessica was silent. Everyone is worried about the future, she thought, but she could not share her own worries with Edward. "This is what we'll do," she said. "We'll begin publicity and advertising early and if Hermione can arrange it we'll start previews in Melbourne a few days early. That means we'll have early reviews from critics who haven't heard all your dire rumors. I'll have to push up all my schedules, which means I won't have time for anything else until opening night, but that should reassure all of you that I'm giving this play all my attention; that whatever needs to be done will be done. We're going to have a success, Edward. No one has to worry about the future."

He nodded gloomily. "You're saying you won't have dinner with me again."

"Oh, for God's sake," she said, her temper snapping. "Have you listened to me? I'm talking about the play, about the future. Didn't you just tell me that's what you're all worried about? Pay attention, Edward. I am telling you that there is nothing to worry about. Hermione and I have everything under control. Can you understand that? Can you remember it long enough to repeat it to the others in the cast? If not, I'll write you all a letter. Maybe I will, anyway." She paused. "That's a good idea," she mused, as if he were not there. "Review our progress, talk about the next few weeks . . . Something like a CEO reporting to a board of directors. Yes, that's what I'll do. And I'll do it tonight." She looked up. "I have to go home, Edward. I have work to do."

Dearest Jessica, what a good idea. What made you think of it? I can think of dozens of difficult situations that might have been avoided if I'd written that kind of letter once or twice during rehearsals. It's amazing how lax we get when we see people every day; after a while we assume they think the way we do. A very dangerous assumption. Anyway, I like

your idea and I hope you find it a form of flat-
tery that I'm going to imitate it in the future.
By the way, your letter, short as it was, sounded
unhappy. Would that have anything to do with
your letter to your cast and crew? Or to a social life I don't know about? Or to Moreton
Bay bugs? (I've been reading about Australia
and it occurred to me that you might have
eaten one of them in a moment of madness
and are suffering from its lingering effects.)
Good friends confide in each other; what else
are we here for? With all my love, Luke.

She wondered what she had written in her one-
paragraph letter that had given her away. It had
been very late when she wrote it, after she had finished the letter to her cast and crew, and she had
been exhausted and worried and feeling very much
alone. She longed for someone who had nothing
to do with this place or these fears. But as soon as
she began to write to Luke, she could not bring
herself to tell him what was happening. It was one
thing to ask for help in staging a scene; it was another to tell him her personal problems. Anyway,
there was nothing he could do about them, and
nothing she wanted him to do. She had come here
to fight her own battles and make her own way,
and nothing had changed that. She would handle
this alone.

Except for Hermione, she thought with a sudden lifting of the heart. Because of course she was

not alone; she had a friend. And a powerful one at that.

"So the bastard told you," Hermione said, holding a copy of Jessica's letter. They were on the couch in her living room, with appetizers and a bottle of wine on the coffee table. "Dinner can be anytime," she had said when Jessica arrived. "Cold soup, cold salad, warm bread. But you're not in a hurry, are you? Not rushing back home to do more work?"

"No. Small breaks for relaxation actually make everything more manageable."

"Is that so? When did you decide that?"

"Advice from a friend. I've been meaning to take it, but I've been too busy."

They burst out laughing, but when they were seated on the couch and Jessica showed her the letter to the cast, Hermione's eyes were furious. "Son of a bitch. There was no reason to tell you. You have a job to do and you're doing it fantastically—everybody is totally sold on you—"

"Everybody?"

"Almost. You should hear them talk about you. Oh, Whit still has doubts now and then, between rehearsals, but as soon as he's working with you he's yours forever. Your gallant swain Edward is another story. What a squeamish little bastard he is. What's he so scared of?"

"The world. And right now the world seems to be telling him that his director is a failure."

"And a director is like a mommy and he wants

his mommy to tell him that everything is peachy and she'll take care of him forever."

"Something like that."

"And you go out with this . . . person?"

"Not right now. I told him I'd be too busy with the play."

"And he sulked."

Jessica was silent.

"Well, okay, let's talk about those things you told him. You were bluffing, of course, but we can do just about all of it. Advertising and publicity actually began last week, but starting today we're doing a blitz. Ads in newspapers here and Melbourne and Canberra, posters everywhere, and a bunch of interviews set up for Edward. 'Drama Teacher Turns Actor,' that sort of thing. Also, I've made a deal with a friend running an AIDS benefit, very social, in two weeks. There's a program of musical numbers right after dinner and, if you approve, Angela and Whit will do a short scene from *Journeys End* as part of it. It's a very high-class affair and you ought to be there." She saw Jessica's face change. "Yep, you'll have to buy a formal dress. It's high time you did. It's important for successful directors and producers to mingle in society—you know that, Jessie—and that includes going to some of these very dull and very necessary affairs."

"I'll think about it. Have any theater parties canceled?"

"A few. Well, actually about half. But this is not

a devastation; I consider it a minor nuisance which someone of my forcefulness and incipient fury can resolve in a short time."

"What does that mean?"

"It means I have a considerable presence in this town. A lot of people who think they run things around here respect me, and they owe me for various favors over the years. I don't apply pressure indiscriminately; I wait for truly important occasions, and this is one. Well, I see you're still puzzled. Jessie, dear, you know all about theater parties: mogul types who own banks and run fat corporations buy out whole theaters for clients, friends, whatever. Some of them buy as many as thirty or forty thousand tickets a year for various plays and musicals, and every producer I know relies on them because they make a play look like a smash hit before it even opens. My friend Harry Miller says it makes plays critic-proof."

"And those are the people you're putting pressure on?"

"The ones who owe me favors. I guarantee you they didn't make the decision to cancel parties for our play; somebody down the ladder did. Once you go to the top, things change in a hurry. I'll take care of this, Jessie; it may take a while, but we'll pull out of it. Do you really think I'd let a bunch of sniggering bastards ruin my play? You know me better than that."

"Maybe we should open the rehearsals."

"Nope. We're doing fine. You're doing better

every day, and I'm not putting out a welcome mat for pricks who've been bad-mouthing you. It wouldn't help, you know; they'd have to find something to back up their lies, and then they'd spread *that* around town. Trust me, Jessie; we'll keep it the way it is. Now listen to me. I'll tell you what you told Edward. This play is going to be dynamite. We'll have other theaters on their knees—they would be if theaters had knees—begging us to bring *Journeys End* to them at the end of our two-month run. I'm telling you: do not worry. Just be the best damn director this town has ever seen. I ask nothing more."

Jessica gave a shaky laugh. She was so tired she could barely move. "Last night everything seemed so awful. . . ."

"Too many emotions, poor baby, you're worn out. Let's feed you some dinner and send you home to bed." She held out her hand and Jessica took it and felt herself being lifted to her feet. "You need food and sleep. What happens to our play if you collapse on me? There's nobody in town who could take your place. You and I and Donny Torville would be mighty distressed if you ended up in the hospital."

Jessica thought there was something odd about that sentence, but she was too tired to pursue it. She ate the food Hermione put before her, drank her coffee, and got up to leave. "I love you," she said at the door. "Thank you for being here."

Hermione held her close and for a moment Jessica felt like a child in her mother's embrace. "Thank you for coming to us," Hermione said. "I love you, too. Go home now. Sleep."

Dear Luke, I'm sorry it's been a week since I wrote last, but we compressed our schedule to allow a few more days of previews in Melbourne and I haven't had a minute to think of anything else. We're in the Drama Theater now, for three days of dress rehearsals. It's fun to be here, with a rehearsal next door in the small Playhouse, an opera rehearsing upstairs, and the symphony orchestra rehearsing next to the opera; it's like a vast hive with all of us little bees churning out words and music at fever pitch. What a good feeling to be part of it.

In our own little corner, we have full sets and real furniture, at last. I did get the turntables I've been dreaming of, so we have two apartments visible at the same time, and each turntable has three rooms. I know you can picture this: as each turntable revolves, the action can take place in a different room—living room, bedroom, kitchen—of each apartment. It's very exciting to watch. On Wednesday we'll go to Melbourne for ten days, then come back here for a week of previews. I'm very nervous, so jumpy I'm feeling a little lightheaded. It's a different kind of nervousness from the kind I had for all those years on the stage, but in a way it is stage fright—how astonishing after all this time to discover that directors have it, too—and it keeps me awake, worrying not about one part, but about all the parts, about all the people who are depending on me. And I keep thinking I've missed something—or many somethings—done things I shouldn't have done, not done things I should have done . . . and then I wonder how I could have had the arrogance to assume I could just jump in and direct a play, as if it didn't take years of training and thinking and study. . . . But right now I don't feel arrogant, just scared.

*I shouldn't tell him this, it's too intimate. But there's no one else I can talk to about it—everyone here, even Hermione, would think I'm afraid we're not ready, and I can't have that. Luke knows what it's like. He understands that I'm writing as one director to another. He understands everything.*

The play isn't really where I'd like it, but I think an audience will help. The cast seems to have reached a plateau . . . they're not getting any better (or worse, thank God), and they can't seem to do anything in new ways. Maybe we're overrehearsed; I know that can happen.

My main worry is Angela. She should go through so many moods—anger, guilt, fear of exposure, the discovery that she can be compassionate, the greater discovery that she can love—and she can't seem to handle all of them at once. It's as if she's sorted them into cubbyholes and takes out one at a time when she needs it. There's no flow in her emotions; she seems more calculating than passionate. Her understudy is younger and seems to have more passion, but we'll probably never know for sure because I can't imagine Angela allowing herself to get sick; she'd tell a virus or bacterium just where to get off . . . and it wouldn't be anywhere near her.

Nora is trying hard and I'm hoping an audience will energize her. The two men are excellent, especially our "find," Edward Smith. If you recall, he's the one we lifted straight out of his job at the university, and in the past few days he's gotten better and better. Sometimes he almost runs away with the play.

*Ever since I told him I'd be too busy to see him. Since then, he hasn't spoken a word to me except when absolutely necessary, but what difference does that make, since he's so wonderful on stage? If Angela was that good . . .*

If Angela was that good, I wouldn't feel this awful frustration and worry. I don't want just a good performance; I want a great one. And in my mind I know exactly what that would look like and sound like; I just haven't found a way to help Angela bring it to the light of day. You could. That may be the difference between a great natural director and one who's doing it as a substitute for something else.

I just read that last sentence over again. I hope it isn't true.

You haven't said anything about Kent's new play. Are you about to begin staging it? I did get the script, but I haven't had time to look at it. Maybe in Melbourne. How odd to be talking about a second strange city in such a short time. This must be called Australian immersion. Jessica.

Dearest Jessica, this won't make sense to you, but do it anyway. If mail comes to you from New York, ignore it. Burn it, throw it away, don't read it. Please trust me on this. Something has happened here, not dangerous, but difficult, and it might spill over to you, just at a time when you need to concentrate on your previews. I promise I'll tell you everything later, but please do as I ask now. Please. Trust me. I'll be thinking of you every minute in Melbourne. I love you. Luke.

She read the letter over and over that night, between packing and taking telephone calls from Nora and Whit, who had last-minute thoughts about everything from the set design to the timing of the final curtain.

*Trust me.*

For what? What could have happened that would spill over to her?

Now that she and Luke sent letters by fax, she received no mail. No one else knew where she was. So it would be someone he had told. Who? And why would he do that?

*Trust me.*

I do, she thought. In almost anything. But I should at least see if something is out there.

And so, sometime after midnight, she went to her front porch and opened her mailbox. The letter was there, gleaming white in the bottom of the black box. She took it out and looked at it in the light spilling from the foyer. Her name. Her address. Typewritten. No return address.

She carried it inside by one corner, as if it might be poison. *Luke wouldn't have told anyone but a friend. What could there be to worry about?*

*He's worried.*

The letter lay on her bureau while she finished packing. At one-thirty she got ready for bed. At one forty-five she began to open the envelope.

*Trust me.*

I'll think about it, she decided. She laid it on her night table, and went to bed. At three o'clock she turned on her reading lamp and tore open the envelope before she could debate it anymore. Her play was nowhere in her thoughts. She could think of nothing but this. Whatever was going on, it was happening to Luke and, somehow, to her, and she had to know what it was.

Inside the envelope was a clipping from a newspaper, raggedly torn out.

### Behind Closed Doors
### by Tricia Delacorte

What oh-so-successful Broadway director has become a virtual recluse because he's smitten with an Australian wallaby? Or is it *wannabe,* as in aiming to make a comeback on the coattails of a Broadway hot shot who can smooth the way for anybody . . . even a washed-out has-been?

## CHAPTER 15

The Melbourne Centre Stage Theater was sold out for opening night. Edward paced, propelled by anxiety. "They should have left one seat unsold. No one should tempt the gods. The American Indians wove blankets with one mistake to keep them from being perfect. The gods think perfection means we're trying to rival them, and they knock us down."

"Gods never come to out-of-town openings," Hermione said. "They'll be waiting for us in Sydney." She grinned at Edward's startled look, but a little later, when she found Jessica coming out of the makeup room, she said, "Of all the things I'm worrying about, the gods knocking us down is very low on the list."

Jessica smiled faintly. "They'll barely notice us, we're so far from perfection."

"Not *that* far. We're in good shape, and you know it. What's wrong, Jessie? Something's been bothering you since we left Sydney and I can't believe you're that worried about the play."

She made an effort to smile and to make her voice confident. "There's just so much to think about; I never knew there were so many loose ends before an opening. But we'll do fine. A lot of problems disappear with an audience."

"Jessica, the lighting in the third act . . . ," said the lighting director, and they had a brief conference, deciding to lower the lights gradually through the final five minutes, leaving one turntable in darkness and the other with a single lamp holding Helen and Rex within the circle of its light.

"Why didn't we think of that in Sydney?" Hermione asked. "It's wonderful . . . and so obvious."

"It's only obvious after you've thought of it," Jessica said, and then Dan Clanagh came through, saying, "Places, please, everyone," and, automatically, she started forward, to take her place on stage.

"Jessie." Hermione's hand was on her arm and

Jessica stopped, almost holding her breath, because this was the moment when it truly came to
her that others would answer that call and move
onto the set and share the play with each other and
the audience, while she would only watch. "It
doesn't get easier, does it?" Hermione asked.

"No. But it will. Someday." She kissed
Hermione's cheek. "I'd rather be here, doing this,
than anywhere else doing anything else. It's mostly
wonderful, you know, just being back."

"Good. I'm counting on that. Now come on;
we're going to be part of the audience and watch a
terrific play."

In the back of the theater, Jessica leaned against
the wall, too nervous to take the seat on the aisle,
beside Hermione, that had been reserved for her.
As soon as the lights came up on the stage, she was
leaning forward, urging the actors on, silently saying their lines just before they did, her eyes moving
to the places they would move, always half a beat
ahead of them. Her hands were clenched, her
body rigid with tension, as if she were pushing and
pulling her cast to remember everything they had
learned in rehearsal and then to go beyond that, to
be better than that, because she knew that often
happened in the exhilaration of performing.

The audience was friendly. They had applauded
the set when the lights came up; they applauded
Angela Crown, who was well-known to them; and
they laughed and were quiet in all the right places.
By the third act, Jessica was beginning to feel ex-

cited. Her hands were still clenched, her body still pushing forward from the wall, but she was no longer terrified that she and Hermione had been wrong. There were trouble spots, but they had time to smooth them out. Angela was still too mechanical, but they could work on that. Nora was responding to the audience and giving a better performance than in rehearsals. Whit had a few clumsy moments, but mostly he was a strong and sympathetic lover. And then there was Edward.

"He was incredible," Hermione said as she and Jessica left the theater while the audience was still applauding. "You were right—thank God you didn't let me talk you out of him—he was absolutely incredible."

"Yes." Jessica felt closer to him than at any other time. It seemed possible that she could love him. He had made the audience weep and he had touched something deep within her, a longing for powerful emotions that had been closed off in her years alone. They had flared brilliantly with Luke, but then had been damped down again. Until tonight, when Edward had made them stir.

"Champagne?" Hermione asked. They were the first to arrive at her hotel suite, where the cast and the crew heads would wait for reviews. She poured two glasses. "The food should be here in a minute."

When the others came in, superstitiously afraid to say it had gone well, Hermione oversaw the buffet. "Scampi and Chinese stir-fry. My own private tradition: the same supper after every opening. It goes back too many years for me to remember how it started, but it makes me feel good, so I impose it on everyone."

"Tastes terrific," said Whitbread through a mouthful of stir-fry.

"It tastes like straw," Edward retorted. "How can any of you eat, with this terrible waiting?"

"Damned if I know," Hermione said cheerfully. "I just know I'm hungry."

Hours later, several copies of the early edition of Melbourne's major newspaper were brought in and there was silence while everyone read.

*Journeys End,* which opened last night at Centre Stage prior to its run at the Drama Theater in Sydney, is a powerful, finely crafted play that almost realizes its potential. Jessica Fontaine, the American actress, in her debut as a director, has focused emotion and tension in just the right places—I thought the audience was holding its collective breath at more than one point, not sure what would happen next—and the stage set is a triumph: two turntables representing two apartments whose inhabitants are at odds and always just missing each other, as the metaphor of the revolving turntables perfectly illustrates.

The weakness is in the interaction of the cast. Angela Crown is almost powerful enough for Helen and Nora Thomas has found her breakthrough role in Doris, but the two women never clash with the ferocity the script begs for. Whitbread Castle is a strong Rex, but he and Angela

Crown, even in their extraordinarily beautiful love scene at the end, did not convince me that their coming together was inevitable. I thought to myself, "What luck that this worked out," and I would guess that that was not the intent of the playwright, or of Ms. Fontaine. The true star of the evening was Edward Smith, a drama professor plucked from obscurity with marvelous insight on Ms. Fontaine's part. In a breathtaking performance as Stan, he is totally convincing, pathetic and admirable at the same time—no mean feat for the most experienced actor, much less one in his first major role.

Jessica skimmed the rest, knowing that most readers never finished reading a review: they only wanted the overall thumbs-up or thumbs-down. And this was definitely thumbs-up. It was not a great review, but it had good quotes for advertisements in Melbourne and Sydney, and it was positive and tantalizing enough to sell tickets for the remainder of the week. They would rehearse each day, smoothing rough edges, dropping lines that had not worked with the audience, adding movement where the stage had seemed static. They would do the same for a week of previews in Sydney. And then they would be ready for opening night.

"Jessica!" Angela stood on a chair, holding her champagne glass high. "A toast! A round of applause!"

The others began to clap. "You're wonderful, Jessica," Whitbread said loudly. "We love you."

"You're all wonderful," Jessica said. "I told you earlier, you're the best cast I could have found, and the best crew. I don't need reviews to tell me that. It was a wonderful opening night." She had told them that before, too. Everything they were saying now, and would say for the next few days in the exhilaration and relief of good reviews, would be a repeat of things they had said before. "Thank you, all of you," she said, repeating something else she had said a dozen times that night. "And don't forget rehearsal tomorrow, ten o'clock."

There were groans and laughter and as they began talking among themselves again, Jessica folded the newspaper and slipped it into the large tote she carried. Now she could think about other things.

"I'm going to bed," she murmured to Hermione beneath the chatter of the others. "Will you make notes before rehearsal?"

"Already thinking about it. Are you all right?"

"I just need to be alone for a while."

"A good thought. As soon as I can, I'm kicking everybody out of here. Good night, Jessie. At the risk of repeating myself, I want to tell you that you've done a tremendous job and we're all pretty damned proud of you. And grateful."

They held each other for a moment, and then Jessica left.

522 — J U D I T H   M I C H A E L

In the living room of her suite, she kicked off
her shoes, took off her suit jacket, and sat on a soft
couch that shaped itself to her body and made her
immediately want to go to sleep. But she could not
do that. Because she had to call Luke.

She struggled to sit upright in the clutches of
the cushions. What time was it in New York? She
tried to calculate it, then gave up and reached for
a pencil. Four A.M. Friday in Melbourne. One P.M.
Saturday in New York.

*He'll be home. Unless he's out of town, in which
case I guess I'll talk to Martin.*

Her hand was trembling as she picked up the
telephone and placed the call. "Luke Cameron,"
he said, answering it on the second ring, and at the
sound of his voice Jessica's eyes filled with tears.

"Hello?" he said.

"Luke, it's Jessica."

She heard him draw in his breath. There was
a brief pause, and then he said, "You read the
article."

"I had to. It involved both of us."

"I didn't want you to be distracted from— Wait,
this is opening night. How did it go? Was it a triumph?"

She laughed with the sheer pleasure of hearing
his voice. "Almost. We have some work to do."

"And Angela?"

"Pretty good. One critic said the love affair
didn't seem inevitable. I seem to have failed there."

"It must have been hell, directing someone in

that role. I wanted to write to you about it, but I thought I'd let you say it first."

"There was nothing to say."

"Not even to me?"

She was crying and said nothing. She should not have called him. She was all right as long as she did not hear his voice.

"I'm sorry. Jessica, my darling, I don't ever want to make things worse for you. But we're so damn far apart and I keep trying to reach you in one way or another—"

"Luke, tell me about that column."

"Do you know how incredibly wonderful it is to hear your voice? I will tell you about it, but this comes first. I miss you. I love you. I love your letters. I look for them every day; I can't wait to get home to find one."

She forced back her tears. "Luke, please tell me."

"Well, then. First of all, it's my fault. I should have known better, and it's been driving me crazy that I let you in for this. Claudia sent it. I haven't mentioned her in my letters because I thought it didn't concern you, but she's gotten worse lately, always a little drunk and on one drug of choice or another, always antagonistic, as if she's daring people to slap her down. Peruggia dropped her and even the Phelans don't want her gambling there anymore. I may be the only one who tolerates her, and I give her money because I assume some of it goes for food, even though most of it probably goes for drugs and alcohol. She comes here at odd hours, early morning, late at night, wanting money, but mostly wanting company, someone to tell her that everything will be fine tomorrow or next week or next month. I think about you, and what you've done with your life, and I look at Claudia, and I suppose I'm not very sympathetic, which makes her even angrier. Anyway, she showed up a couple of weeks ago when I was at breakfast and she wandered around the apartment and found your letters on my desk. I'd bought a box for them and she opened it and started reading. Your early letters were in envelopes with return addresses and she came storming in, carrying one of them, demanding to know all about you. I would never talk to her about you so I changed the subject, which I should have known was just the wrong thing to do."

"So she called that gossip columnist. Your friend."

"Tricia. I haven't seen her since I got back from Lopez. She isn't any happier with me than Claudia is. So there they were: two angry women concocting a vicious piece of garbage that doesn't hurt me but does hurt someone they don't even know. But it isn't important, Jessica, no one pays attention to those things."

"They did when I lived there. Mostly for titillation, but also because they got clues about how to behave with certain people. Have things changed so much since I left?" When he was silent, she said,

"It may be a piece of garbage, but it says what everyone would say if I came back to New York. I told you that when I said I wouldn't go with you."

"Look, these are two women who want to hurt someone because they think they've been hurt. Why do you assume the rest of New York would be anything like that? They'd remember you and welcome you. And if some people are cruel, we'll deal with it together. Jessica, my love, we're stronger than they are."

"Luke, please stop." She had drawn herself more tightly into the corner of the couch as if to defend herself against his arguments, and she knew that this time he could hear the tears in her voice, but she was too tired to care. "I can't argue with you; I'm so tired"—*and I miss you, I love you, I want your arms around me, I want to be in bed with you, I want to be riding beside you and seeing how beautiful the world is when we're together*—"and I've got to get some sleep. We're rehearsing tomorrow morning and I have meetings after that . . . you know all this; you know what I have to do. I'm sorry you have to deal with Claudia, I know it's hard for you, but I can't help you . . . I can't do anything at all. I couldn't even if I was in New York; all I could do is watch people snicker. . . . I'm sorry, I think I'm talking in my sleep. I'm sorry, Luke, about so many things. . . ."

There was a pause. "I'll write to you. Goodnight, my darling. Sleep well."

She heard the click of the telephone and then

there was only cold emptiness where his voice had been. She put down the telephone and in another minute, still curled up on the couch, she was asleep.

"Our last night of previews," Hermione said. "I'm going to miss Melbourne: such fine audiences, such sensitive, discerning critics. And," she added casually, "advance sales in Sydney are roaring along; I even got two new theater parties for later in the run."

Jessica looked up from her packing. "I'd forgotten the theater parties."

"That was your job: forgetting them. I told you I'd take care of everything. Right now the previews are sold out; ditto the first three weeks. We broke even up to tonight; we'll make a profit in Sydney. You and I will not be sleeping in doorways for the foreseeable future."

They smiled together.

"I do like this business of women hooking up together," Hermione said. "I'm having fun, I'm making money, and I don't have to play any sexual games or build up any egos."

"You built up mine," Jessica said.

"And a good thing I did. I meant male egos; yours was worth building up. Have you heard from your New York director lately?"

"Speaking of male egos?"

"Speaking of males."

"I forgot to tell him the name of my hotel here. I imagine I'll have something waiting for me in Sydney."

Ten letters waited for her in Sydney, lying neatly on her fax machine, and she rushed, almost tripping, to get them. The maid was cleaning the spare room where she had stayed while Jessica was in Melbourne, and Hope was making joyful dashes about the living room, as if rediscovering it now that everything was normal again. Jessica had the whole day to herself. Dan Clanagh and Augie Mack were overseeing the installation of the turntables and sets at the Drama Theater; Hermione was in meetings; there would be no rehearsal until the next morning, with the first preview that night. Jessica took coffee and a basket of apples to the living room and sat down to read.

My love, I'm sitting at my desk watching spirals of snow swirl past my window. Every few minutes a bunch of flakes cluster together like politicians plotting a campaign and then a gust of wind shoots them straight up and out of sight. The prediction is for a foot of snow by morning, which is absurd for March, but New Yorkers, of course, will deal with it quite handily, as they did the last dump that shut us down for a few blessed hours. Martin has gone out to buy groceries and cross-country skis before there's a run on either one; I think he's quite pleased with the sense of impending crisis that the howling wind and swirling blizzard have created.

Puzzled, Jessica read to the end, then went on to the next.

Well, my love, I've just been cross-country skiing down Fifth Avenue, an exhilarating experience. I didn't do it in the last storm, but this time I couldn't resist. I wish you could see the transformation here: nothing moves but people who have taken over the streets as if time has turned backward a couple of centuries. No, even farther back, since there are no horses, no carriages—nothing but the whisper of skis on snow, the slap of snowshoes, and the exuberant shouts of children (and quite a few adults) as the city becomes a village—*their* village. It is bitter cold, but the sun gives the snow a silvery sheen and the shadows of buildings lie across it like long blue-gray spikes. I skied as far as—

They were all the same: casual, warm, friendly, almost impersonal, talking about the opera, an auction at Sotheby's, a ballet at Lincoln Center. No mention of Claudia or Tricia, no mention of her coming to New York, not even a question about her play during the rest of the week in Melbourne. He's given up, she thought. He finally believes that I won't be part of his life, that what we had on Lopez is over, that what we have left is friendship. Perhaps he's already found someone else, so he won't write anything about his personal life. Ever again.

A sense of loss swept over her. She pushed the letters into a pile and left them on the couch. There seemed to be no reason to put them in the box with all his others.

When the telephone rang, she answered it dully. "Jessica, are we still on hold?" Edward asked. "Tell me we aren't. I want to take you to dinner tonight. We can celebrate Melbourne or talk about the previews starting tomorrow or not talk about work at all. Or not talk about anything; we could just eat and drink and be happy together."

This was a new Edward. His jubilant voice made her sit straighter. "You're not worried about tomorrow night?"

"Not much. A little, of course, and it might get worse tonight—one is never sure whether anxiety will go up, down or sideways—but Melbourne, you know, those reviews . . . They were like wine, don't you think? I feel quite intoxicated by them."

"It was just tryouts in Melbourne," Jessica said, alarmed by his jauntiness. "Sydney will be tougher because this is where we'll have our run. And we still have work to do; we're rehearsing tomorrow at nine."

"Then dinner should be early. Shall I pick you up at seven?"

She glanced at the pile of letters on the cushion beside her. Why not? she thought. He cares for me and it will help the evening pass. "Yes. I'll be ready."

She looked through her window at the hazy late-summer sky and the trees just beginning to turn color across the harbor. I'll have to talk to Hermione about another play, she thought. I have to keep busy.

Maybe one of Luke's plays.

The idea seemed to come from nowhere. But then she knew she had been thinking about it for a long time. They were fine plays; she knew they would be better when he finished rewriting them. And if she directed one, he would know there were no hard feelings.

But she could not do that. Because of course he would come to Sydney to take part in the rehearsals.

What a ridiculous idea.

She heard a click: the fax machine switching on. She looked at her watch. Three o'clock. Midnight in New York. Turning, she watched the sheet of paper inch into view. She imagined Luke standing in his library, watching his letter disappear into his fax machine. *Giving it to me to read.*

She gazed across the room at the white sheet of paper with lines of handwriting that she recognized as Luke's. *I don't want another friendly hello. I already know what that looks like.*

In a little while, she took the bowl of apples

back to the kitchen, skirting the fax machine. She went to her bedroom and found a book to read. She changed the disc she had been listening to, putting on the Mozart clarinet quintet, one of her favorites. And then she could not stand it any more and she picked up the letter and began to read.

My dearest love, by now you must be back in Sydney. I've seen some of the Melbourne papers at a newsstand that seems to carry every major paper in the world, so I know how well you've done. I'm not surprised, but I'm enormously impressed, because I know that a brilliant acting career doesn't guarantee a smooth transition to directing, where you have to deal with everyone, not just your own character. I'm very proud of you. I hope you're as proud of yourself.

I must confess, my love, that I don't know how to write to you anymore. The letters waiting for you when you returned from Melbourne were written while I was trying to figure out what to do next. I love you, I want to marry you, I want us to be together, to achieve as much as we can, together and separately. But I don't think you want to hear me say that. I don't know what you want to hear me say. All I know for certain is that, if you don't tell me to stop, I'll go on writing, indefinitely, I suppose, because I cannot break my connection with you. Any bond between us is better than none.

If you aren't yet ready to tell me what you want, I can wait. I have no more cross-country skiing to write about (curses on a city that clears its streets all too soon), but there is always my work, and yours, and, as a last resort, opera and ballet and Sotheby's. I love you. Luke.

The sun shone brilliantly; the clarinet soared in a joyous melody. Jessica went back to the couch, picked up the earlier letters, and tucked them in with the collection in her box. *But not this one, not yet. I want to read it a few times—a few dozen times—before I put it away.*

And then she thought of Edward. She had no desire to go to dinner with him—what could she have been thinking of? I'll call him, she decided, and tell him I just don't feel like going out tonight. But before she could pick up the telephone, it rang beneath her hand.

"Yes," she said, thinking of Edward.

"Jessica Fontaine?" A woman's voice. Jessica sat on the couch, frowning, trying to place it. Too loud, aggressive, almost antagonistic, a little slurred, as if she were— She clenched her hand around the telephone. As if she were drunk.

"Yes, who is this?" she asked, though she already knew.

"Claudia Cameron. You don't know me; we

never met, but you seem to know my husband. Luke Cameron."

"Your husband?"

"He was. But we're still close. *Very close.* We care about each other— we're very close!—and I want to know why the hell you're writing letters to him."

*I don't have to talk to her. I should just hang up.*

*What would Luke want me to do?*

*He tries to protect her; he'd want me to do the same.*

There was the sound of ice clinking in a glass. "Damn it, answer me! Are you afraid of me? You ought to be, you know, I can ruin you, I can smear you—"

Stung, Jessica snapped, "By planting lies with gossip columnists."

"Oh, so you did get it. Then you know I can smear you all over New York if I want to. And I may want to. Answer my question! *Why do you write letters to my husband?"*

"I write letters to your ex-husband because we're friends."

"'Friends' is what people say when they're sleeping together. I read some of those letters, all about the theater and Australia . . . who do you think you're fooling? I could tell you're sleeping with him."

"That would be hard to do, since he's in New York and I'm in Sydney."

"Oh, clever, clever. You actresses, you're all the same; there isn't an actress in the world I'd trust.

You're trying to take Luke away from me, get him to go to Sydney so I won't have him close anymore. I asked him, and he said you were."

"What?"

"He said you were sleeping together."

"He never told you that."

"He did. He said—"

"He said we were friends. He said I'm directing a play for the first time, and he helps me with problems I'm having."

"You don't know what he said!"

"I know him. I know what he would say."

"If you think you know him that well, you're sleeping with him."

It was so illogical that Jessica burst out laughing.

"Don't you dare laugh at me!" Ice clinked in her glass. "You're finished! Do you understand? You won't have Luke—ever!—and you won't get any work in this town. Ever! I have powerful friends who'll stop you, and when Luke hears how you laughed at me he'll never look at you again. He'll throw away your letters, and if you call and beg and beg he'll hang up on you. I know how he is when he's pushed. So stay away from him! If you do, my friend won't print those other things she has."

"She has nothing. You don't know what you're talking about." The hell with her, Jessica thought furiously. They've been divorced for over eleven years; who does she think she is to tell me whether

I can be with Luke or not? And does she really think she and her gossip friend could keep me away if I really wanted to come back? "This is crazy—"

"Don't tell me I'm crazy!"

"You're being ridiculous. I'm not after Luke and I'm not coming to New York, but, believe me, if I wanted to you couldn't stop me."

"Oh, can't I. The minute you get off that plane—"

"There is no plane. What is wrong with you? I told you I'm not—"

"You're lying! Listen, I'm telling you, if you take Luke away from me, I'll kill myself. I mean it! He's all I've got."

"You said you had powerful friends."

"I do. Or I did. I don't know exactly what happened to them; I haven't seen them lately. Maybe they're out of town. But it's not important because I've got Luke, he cares about me, and if you take him away, I'll kill myself. I've decided, you know; I'm serious. You should know that before you get on that plane."

"Claudia, listen to me." Jessica's anger was gone; she felt only a deep sadness. "I'm not coming to New York. These are terrible things you're saying and there's no reason for them. You have so many things to live for—"

"Like what?" Jessica heard her crunch ice in her teeth. "You don't know anything about it! You've always been in the spotlight, you've never suffered or failed at anything, you're clever and beautiful and people applaud and say how fantastic you are. What do you know about failing? What do you know about waking up every day and not having *any idea* what you'll do that day *because you're not good at anything!* I lost Luke, you know, and now I don't see my friends anymore, I've lost people all over the place, but what would you know about that? You haven't lost anything, you *find* things, like other women's husbands, and then you take them away. You take and take and take, and people clap for you, but nothing works for me; everything's a failure. *I'm* a failure. Luke doesn't care; he loves me anyway. He doesn't love you! And if he does . . . If he does I'll kill myself."

"Don't say that. You're young, you can get help—"

"You mean a shrink?"

"Someone to help you find things to fill your days and give shape to your life. You have years to meet new people and find new ways of living. I know what it is to feel despair and loneliness—"

"Bullshit."

"I've had some terrible times; I had to—"

"Bullshit, bullshit, bullshit. God, you actors, you lie through your teeth. I hate all of you. I hate the theater. I hate New York. I hate Luke. No, that's not true, Luke is all I've got. I love Luke. He'll miss me when I'm dead. He'll cry and say it's his fault. No, he'll say it's your fault. Then he'll hate you. And kaput, that's the end of you and Luke. I wish I could hear him curse you for what you did, but I won't be here, will I?"

"Claudia, stop it. You're not going to kill yourself; you don't *want* to kill yourself. You need help."

"Don't give me any fucking advice, lady, I don't need it! Just stay away from my husband. *STAY AWAY!*" The phone slammed into its cradle.

Jessica sat for a long moment still holding the telephone, as if Claudia's voice might miraculously reappear. But at last she hung up. She was shaking from the violence of Claudia's rage and desperation, and from her own helplessness. There must have been things she could have said that would have been more helpful, more encouraging, less confrontational . . . And if Claudia really did kill herself . . .

But she wouldn't, Jessica thought. People who talked about suicide seldom actually did it; talking seemed to diminish the urgency. Was that right? Hadn't she read that somewhere?

The truth was, she knew almost nothing about suicide and almost nothing about Claudia.

*I should call Luke. He should know she's talking this way.*

She looked at her watch. Damn it, she thought, why can't we be in the same time zone? Almost one A.M. in New York. He would be asleep. I'll call later, she thought.

The telephone rang. "Jessica," said Edward, "how about Catalina for dinner? I don't want to make a reservation if you don't want to go there."

"Edward, I'd rather not go anywhere. I'd rather not go out tonight. I have some work to do, a telephone call to make, and I'm nervous about tomorrow night. I wouldn't be good company."

"You're the only company I want, however you're feeling. Jessica, you can't let me down; you're all I've thought about since we talked this morning." His lightheartedness was gone; now his voice was deeply melancholy, with that strain of neediness that always in the past had made Jessica want to stroke his brow and comfort him. "We've been apart so long—we have so much to talk about—my God, it feels like years. Jessica, Jessica, don't shut the door on me, please don't shut me out."

She frowned. It was not just that his lightheartedness was gone; now there was something calculating in his voice and his words, as if he had done this dozens of times before. *Whenever he meets someone like me, who responds to a needy man.*

"Just a few hours," he said. "Whatever you have to do can wait that long, can't it? You can give me a few hours of happiness . . . I've waited so long, been patient so long . . ."

He's a taker, she thought. This isn't love; it's appropriation. He doesn't care about me at all; he cares only about what he wants, what he can take. Just like Claudia. Maybe Luke and I attract them.

Except when we're attracting each other. But I can't keep propping up Edward the way Luke props up Claudia. I have too much to do, and that's not what I'm looking for.

Oh, Edward, she told him silently, what a shame that you're a fake. We could have had a good time, being friends and working together. And who knows where we might have gone, if we'd had a chance?

But she could not say any of that. A week of previews, and opening night a week later, meant that she had to have a cooperative Edward, not a hostile one.

"I don't want to shut you out; you know I enjoy being with you. But I can't take any chances with this play, Edward; everything I want to do in the future depends on it. That goes for you, too, doesn't it? We both need a success. Please try to understand: I need to be alone right now. There isn't anyone I want to be with; I just want to be quiet and alone."

"There's no one you want to be with?"

"That's what I said. Did you think I'd singled you out?"

"No, I don't think you'd do that. But this is foolish, Jessica. We could be anxious together, about the play and about each other."

*My goodness, he is very good. Why didn't I see before how skilled he is?*

She eased the conversation to an end and stood up. *I've got to get out of here. This is too much for one day.* Tucking her notebook and pencils into her tote, she drove to Circular Quay and took the first ferry leaving the dock for Manly. It was a slow one, not the Jetcat she and Edward had taken, and sitting in a sheltered spot on the deck, she took out her notebook and settled back to work.

But she did no work. She was nervous and suddenly feeling depressed, and she forgot Claudia, and forgot about calling Luke, as she let her thoughts roam. She gazed at the shoreline: huge stucco houses in various shades of pastel, densely wooded slopes with leaves so dark green they were almost black, small crescent-shaped beaches with private docks and boats rocking gently against them. The sun shone fuzzily through a haze that turned the sky almost white, and the water was gray and choppy. Jessica felt a stab of nostalgia for Lopez Island and her house on its small beach between the cliffs that had always symbolized protection and safety. No protection here, she thought. Nothing stands between me and previews and next Tuesday's opening, not even Hermione, though she would if she could.

But it was Hermione to whom she turned when things began to go wrong at the first preview. The theater was almost full, but the audience was restless, and when the stage went to black at the end of the first act and the houselights came up, Jessica and Hermione quickly ducked out. In the lobby, they stood beside the podium where an usher was selling programs, and watched the audience come out. A few of them kept going, and left the theater.

"What's happened to Angela?" Jessica asked. "She's so distracted, as if she's worried or angry or frustrated . . . something's bothering her. She was fine at rehearsal this afternoon; has she said anything to you?"

"No, but when I got here she was hanging on the phone like a lovesick teenager. Maybe a lover's spat?"

"I don't know. She's married, but her husband isn't here; he's in Los Angeles, in a touring company of *Phantom of the Opera.* I hadn't heard anything about an affair."

"Neither had I. Do you think the audience notices it?"

"Yes. Oh, maybe not; I don't know. They seemed awfully restless to me and some were leaving just now."

"Most likely they're out there smoking. Shall I talk to Angela? Or do you want to do it?"

"My stomach is in such knots, would you mind doing it? I think the others are reacting to her; they're not as good as they were in Melbourne. . . ." Her voice trailed away. She felt sick, and she waited in line with some members of the audience to get a seltzer at the bar at the end of the lobby. She took it outside, to the plaza lapped by the harbor's waves and lit by large bright globes. Clusters of theatergoers from both theaters were drinking champagne and coffee, talking and smoking. *Of course they didn't go home; they just came out here because it's a pleasant night and they can smoke.* She hovered beside groups of people, eavesdropping, but before she could hear any comments about the play someone called her.

"Jessica!" She turned and saw Alfonse Murre sliding sideways through the crowd. His thin mustache was quivering, his bald head sparkled beneath the globe lights. He shook her hand, averting his eyes from her cane. "My dear, dear Jessica, it's been far too long. You absolutely vanished after that day in my office. But you've been busy, haven't you? And to such good purpose! This is quite fine, you know. Of course, the prudent man does not make judgements on the basis of just one act, but so far, so far, dear Jessica, I am having a very pleasant evening."

And that was how Jessica knew that *Journeys End* would be a hit.

And that Alfonse Murre would be delighted to talk to her about working together in the future.

And that she and Hermione, so close to the play, had exaggerated any troubles Angela Crown might be—

"There *is* a problem with Angela, isn't there?" Murre asked. "I mean, she's definitely not on top of every line, and that's not like her. I've worked with her, you know; a very competent actress. Perhaps she's not well?"

"I don't know." There was no point in lying; the audience might or might not know something was wrong, but people who knew the theater would not miss it. "Hermione's trying to find out."

He gave a little nod, acknowledging her honesty. "Let's hope it's a small matter, and brief."

"Thank you," Jessica said, and their eyes met, for the first time with interest and the beginnings of respect.

Backstage, she found Hermione in the makeup room, at the end of a row of small cubicles partitioned off for each actor. At the other end, Angela was redoing her makeup.

"What happened?"

"Her husband's got lung cancer and it doesn't look good. Surgery next week. She says she has to be with him, and I can't blame her." Their eyes met. "Jessie—"

"We have an understudy," Jessica said. "She's not as good as Angela, but she's young and quick and we can work with her. She'll be all right."

"In one week?"

"In one week, night and day if necessary. She'll be fine. She's never missed a rehearsal, she knows her lines, the blocking, everything. She'll never be Angela, but she's all we've got. I'll start working with her tomorrow morning. You'll have to take the cast rehearsals."

"I can do that if you'll give me your notes after each performance."

"Of course."

Dan Clanagh walked past. "Places, everybody, for act two."

"What were they saying outside?" Hermione asked.

"I didn't hear much, but they seem happy. Alfonse Murre wants to know where I've been keeping myself."

"Son of a bitch. But that means he knows we've got something good. And he probably talked to some critic who also thinks it's good. I could strangle newspaper editors; they aren't supposed to send critics to previews, but one or two always show up and run an early review, and if it's a killer the play might never get to opening night. Who came tonight?"

"I asked Dan; he told me it's Gregory Varden. I don't know him; do you?"

"Sharp, savvy, brutal when he wants to be. Probably the smartest, most feared critic around. Reviews for the *Sydney Herald* and has a weekly column. Likes new playwrights, to keep the blood supply fresh. His words, not mine."

"Do you suppose Alfonse talked to him?"

"I'll bet my house and car he did; Alfonse likes to know he's not alone in his opinions. So I predict a rave in tomorrow's paper. And that gets us home free, you know. I wouldn't pop the champagne yet, but, based on experience, a rave at this point means lines at the box office."

"Alfonse knows Angela is having trouble."

"Shit. Well, of course he'd see that. If he told Varden, it could be a problem. We'll have to get out a release on Lucinda stepping in, before it gets written in stone that our leading lady is less than wonderful. In fact, Varden's probably noticed something himself. Do I talk to him about it at the second intermission? No, no, and no; what a blunder that would be. We'll have to let him do his own thing. And she might be terrific from now on. Keep your fingers crossed."

She was not terrific, Jessica thought, standing in the back of the theater for the second act, but she was better than in the first act. If she could keep it up, the preview week would be all right. Not great, but all right. If she couldn't . . . *Well, Lucinda Tabor is about to get the chance of a lifetime, and she and I are going to work twenty hours a day if necessary so she'll be ready to step in at any time.*

At the next intermission she went backstage and found Lucinda in a corner, reading a newspaper. "Lucy, something's happened. Angela has to leave the cast, and you're going to be playing Helen when we open next week."

Lucinda grew deathly pale. "Why?"

"Her husband is ill; she's going to Los Angeles to be with him. She'll stay for this week. At least that's what she says now. You and I are going to spend the next few days working harder than we've ever worked before, so you'll be ready to step in whenever she takes off."

"But this doesn't happen!" Lucinda's voice rose.

"Keep your voice down. We're not telling the others until they finish the third act."

"Telling the others. Oh, God, then it's true. But it can't be. Jessica, talk her into staying. You can do that, can't you? Tell her she has to do it; her husband will be fine; I mean, she doesn't have to be there every minute; she has to stay here!"

"I said keep your voice down," Jessica snapped. "What in God's name is wrong with you? This is what every actor dreams of; this is a phenomenal chance, Lucy."

"But I'm not ready for it! Oh, God, oh, God, Jessica, I can't do it."

"You took the job of understudy."

"Because I knew it was safe. Angela never gets sick, nothing *ever* happens to Angela. I never *ever* thought . . ."

"Well, you have all tonight to think about it before we get to work in the morning. You do know the part."

"Yes, but that doesn't mean—"

"And you took notes? You wrote down all the suggestions I gave Angela, all the things we discussed?"

"Yes, you told me to. But, Jessica—"

"This isn't a debate, Lucy, this is the way it's going to be. Now I want you to go home and read the play a few times tonight."

"Read it?"

"Get a stronger feel for all the characters, and

the way the story flows. Think about it as a whole, not just about Helen. We'll start early tomorrow. Can you be at my house at seven-thirty?"

Lucinda looked at her helplessly. Jessica held her eyes. Finally she gave a little nod. "I guess."

"You know where I live? The top of Point Piper. I'll see you then. And Lucy . . ."

"Yes?"

"You'll be all right. We're going to work very hard and you'll be fine. You must believe that."

"I don't know why *you* believe it. I don't know why you chose me in the first place. I shouldn't have tried out. I should have said no. But I thought, you know, I'd learn a lot, watching you and Angela, and then someday I'd work up to a part like this. All the other parts I've played were smaller; you knew that."

"They were good parts and you played them well. Your videotapes were good."

"But they weren't leads. And I didn't have to follow somebody like Angela."

"Don't think about that. You'll be your own Helen, quite different from Angela's."

"And I'm too young. Helen is forty. I'm twenty-eight."

Jessica gazed at her. "You look older. You told us you were older. Thirty-two, I think."

"Because I thought I wanted to do this. Everybody was pushing me, my parents and my boyfriend and my acting coach in Melbourne . . .

they said I had to take chances or I wouldn't get anywhere. But Jessica, Helen *scares* me."

"Why?"

"Well, she reminds me of my mother, she's—" Jessica burst out laughing, and Lucinda said, "Please don't. Don't laugh or be impatient; just listen, please. I never told you this because I was so sure—I mean, I *knew*—there was no way in the world I'd ever have to play Helen, but she does remind me of her . . . I mean, she's so sure of herself, so *sweeping* the way she goes through life with everybody admiring her, and my mother's like that and she's always expected me to be like her, but I'm not! People keep telling me to do this and do that and behave this way or that way, but it's like they're asking me to run up a mountain: *I can't do it.* Maybe someday I'll be ready for Helen. I'd love to have you direct me when I am—if I am—but until then, I'm sorry, but I just don't think I can handle it."

"*You're sorry?* You're an actor, a professional; we gave you this position in good faith; you've sat here through weeks of rehearsals and tryouts, and now you say you're sorry? You don't do that in this business. You have a job to do and you're damn well going to do it." She stopped. "I shouldn't have said that. Let's start again. All actors worry that they might not be able to handle some role at one time or another. When that happens, they study the play to understand it so well that it becomes a part of them, and they ask others to help them.

I'm here to help you. You're going to play Helen and I predict you'll make a name for yourself—"

"I'll make a fool of myself, and ruin your play."

"You won't do either. I'll make sure of that. I'll tell you what. I'll come to your house tonight after the party and we'll read through the play together. I don't want you stewing over this all night; we'll get a jump on it and you'll feel much better tomorrow. You've got to get some confidence in yourself, Lucy, or you really won't be able to play this part. It's just a question of confidence. Believe me."

Lucinda looked at her with the eyes of a frightened child and Jessica's heart sank. *Is it too late to call a management company and find someone else? Of course it is. And word would get out that things are worse than the worst of the rumors.*

"I think you're a little bit in shock, Lucy; give yourself time to get used to this. What time shall I come over tonight?"

"Oh, don't do that. It makes me feel like you're afraid to let me out of your sight. I do want to please you, Jessica, I mean, I don't want to disappoint you because I think you're wonderful—I've loved watching you direct all the others, and I kept wishing we could work together—"

"We will. Starting tomorrow. You won't disappoint me, Lucy; you'll make me proud of you."

"You really think so? You really believe that?"

"Absolutely. You wait and see how well we work together."

"Oh, God, I hope so. It's just that, you know, I'm so scared. And ashamed. Because it's awful, isn't it, to be so scared?"

"Scared is okay. Terrified would be a problem." She kissed Lucinda's pale cheek. "Read the play again tonight. And keep telling yourself you're going to do just fine."

*But she is terrified. And she won't even be adequate if she doesn't get some confidence. So that's my job: building up her confidence while rehearsing the whole play with her. Do I think she can do it? We don't ask that question. She has to do it. She will do it. With luck and an incredible amount of work, she'll be all right. No better than that, but at least we'll still have a play. Oh, damn, why did this have to happen, when everything was going so well?*

"Will you drive with me to the party?" Edward asked later, after the second curtain call, when Jessica went backstage to congratulate everyone. Hermione was talking to the wardrobe director about duplicating Angela's wardrobe in a smaller size; Angela was on the telephone. "I've stayed away, just as you asked me to," he said, "but now we could have some time together."

"I'm not going to the party, Edward. I have a lot to think about and I'm going straight home."

"Then I insist on driving you."

"No, you're going to the party to celebrate with everyone else. Hermione will have an announcement to make, and you must be there to hear it.

You were wonderful tonight, Edward. I hope you know how impressive you are."

"If you say so."

"Oh—" She cut off an exclamation of annoyance and impatience. "I do say so. I'll see you tomorrow."

At home, she thought of writing to Luke, to ask his advice about working with a terrified understudy, but as soon as she thought of him she remembered Claudia. She had to call him. Even if Claudia had not been serious, even if it had been nothing more than dramatics, she had to tell him. And if she waited, she would have no time; the next week would be for Lucinda, and no one else.

She did not bother checking times; she was tired of it. I have to talk to him, she thought; if I wake him up, that's too bad.

"Luke Cameron," he said, answering on the first ring, and Jessica felt again the jolt of pleasure at the sound of his voice, and a longing to be next to him, close to him, in his arms.

"Luke, it's Jessica. I hope I didn't wake you; I couldn't bother figuring out the time."

"Seven-thirty Monday morning. Are you calling because of Claudia? No, you couldn't be; you have no way of knowing."

She caught her breath. "Knowing what?"

"That she's dead. Sometime last night, we don't know exactly when."

"Oh, no. Oh, Luke, how terrible. I really didn't

think she would . . . I meant to call you . . . Oh,
dear God. How did she do it?"

"We don't know if it was deliberate or not.
What did you mean, you didn't think she would . . .
what?"

"It may not have been suicide?"

"It isn't clear. She had enough drugs and alcohol in her to kill two or three people, but she
was consumed by drugs and alcohol; they were
her life. And her death. She'd never talked about
suicide—"

"Yes, she did, Luke; she called me. We talked
for—"

"*She called you?* When? Why?"

"Yesterday afternoon. To tell me to stay away
from you."

"Good God. As if she could have the slightest—
Is that all she wanted, or did she want to talk?"

"She wanted to talk, so I did, because I didn't
know what you would want me to do—I thought
you'd want me to try to protect her, but I didn't do
a very good job, did I? Oh, Luke, I'm so sorry. It's
so terrible, so unbelievably awful to feel that life
has *nothing*—how can anyone feel that way? And I
wasn't kind to her; she made me angry and I
showed it."

"She was good at that; she forced people to be
cruel to her. And we were." His voice was shaking.
"It is awful; you're right. To be so desolate . . .
Would you tell me what you told her?"

"That I wasn't coming to New York. For some reason she was convinced that I was. I told her that you and I aren't together; that we're friends. She kept calling you her husband and said you were the only one who cared about her. I said she needed help, that she had a lot to live for but she needed help to find a way to give shape to her days and meaning to her life."

He gave a short, bitter laugh. "You and I gave her the same speech. No wonder she didn't believe you."

"About what?"

"Our not being together. I used those same words—giving shape to her days—every time I lectured her. Oh, Christ, I did lecture her when I should have been helping her; there was so much more I could have done . . . there's always more that we can do."

"Not always. Luke, you took care of her for years. And she knew it. She told me you did. She told me you were very close."

"Oh, for Christ's sake, she knew damn well we weren't. She was my welfare project, the one I made time for, the one I threw money at because that was easier than taking her hand and walking her through some solutions that might have worked out. I let her down a hundred ways."

"So did I. I even laughed . . . oh, Luke, what a terrible thing I did. I laughed."

"At what?"

"She said something that was so absurd that I . . . well, I shouldn't have. I wish I hadn't."

"Jessica, you are not responsible for Claudia's death."

"But neither are you. Luke, from what she said, a lot of people let her down. I think that must be a big club: people who have disappointed Claudia. And I did let her down."

"Maybe. But if you did it was only once. And you owed her nothing."

"She was a human being. I owed her attention and sympathy."

They were silent. "You know," Luke said at last, "she kept accusing me of treating her like a character in a play, and in a way she was right. But she was always asking me to do it, to direct her life. Until finally she found a way to direct it herself. To direct her death."

"If it was deliberate."

"If it was."

"Are you mourning her?" Jessica asked.

"I'm mourning a failed life. She never really gave herself a chance; that's the real tragedy of Claudia. You know, Constance and I talked a lot about the way we lived our lives: as if each of us was in a play with openings and closings, dramatic peaks, brief intimacies, a new plot every few months or years. Not particularly admirable, but that's how we lived and it was enough for us. No, not for Constance. She had more; she had your friendship. And then I found you and knew I wanted more, too: a real life, as messy and unpredictable as it is. Claudia—my God, I can't believe she's gone—Claudia never could face life with all its messiness and unpredictability, and I did nothing to help her learn how. I suppose that's what I'm really mourning: her refusal to grab life and make it hers, her insistence on living her fantasies when so much richness and beauty were all around her. That's a lesson, isn't it? For all of us."

Jessica was silent. She knew he was waiting for her to say that she wanted a real life, too, one that was more substantial, deeper and more permanent than the one she had now. That she wanted him. But too much was happening; too many emotions were churning inside her. In a strange way, Claudia had brought them closer than ever, but she could not focus on that now.

"Luke, Angela is leaving the play; her husband is having surgery next week and she wants to be with him. I really have to concentrate on our understudy right now."

"Is she ready?"

"No. And she seems to be in total terror. Can we talk about it for a while?"

"As long as you like. But isn't it getting late there? We can talk tomorrow if you'd rather."

"I'm not tired. Could you wait a minute while I get some coffee?"

"I'm refilling my cup now. We can pretend we're

sitting at the breakfast table. I know, for you it's close to midnight. But since we're pretending anyway . . ."

"Yes," she said softly. "I can picture a breakfast table."

When she came back and settled into the couch again, they talked for two hours. "Well, you've got a problem," Luke said at last. "You can pump her up for a week and she still may be convinced she's not ready. Maybe you ought to try to change the focus a little bit from her to the other three, especially the man . . . what's his name?"

"Whitbread."

"Good God, how did he handle that when he was a kid? Well, you might think about accommodating Lucinda's weakness—"

"Helen can't be weak."

"No, but maybe you can mask it. Try to think about what the others have internalized. If you take it scene by scene . . ."

Jessica listened, absorbing and memorizing everything he said. She pictured his face and his smile, the way his eyebrows rose in amusement, the gestures he made with his large hands. She brought his deep voice into her, making it part of her. When she offered her own thoughts, he listened in silence, never breaking in, commenting only when she had finished, often praising her, always making her feel that he thought of them on the same plane: two directors, two professionals.

"It has a chance, if you build her up enough,

and put more focus on the other parts," he said at last. "The trouble is, you don't have much time. Maybe you ought to think about hypnotizing her; make her think this is the best thing that's ever happened to her."

"They didn't teach hypnosis at the Actors' Studio. I'll have to work on her without it."

"But that's the goal. If she gets intrigued, she'll work like hell and cope with her fear. So you have to do a selling job with her, rehearse with her, and work with the others to help them carry at least some of the scenes. It's going to be a rough week."

"To put it mildly. Thank you, Luke. I needed the help and the pep talk."

"They're both available, whenever you want."

"I'm sorry about Claudia. I know it's hard for you in so many ways. I wish I could have been more helpful."

"We always wish that when something goes badly. I feel sadness about Claudia, but not much more. Maybe that's the true tragedy of her life: her impact was so shallow that no one feels a sense of real loss. Now *there's* something to mourn."

"A terrible thing," Jessica murmured. She shivered, as if feeling the loneliness of it.

"My love, you should go to sleep."

"Yes. Thank you, for everything. Good night, Luke."

"Good night, dear heart. Sleep well. Let me know how Lucinda does."

"I will. Luke—"

"Yes?"

*Come to Sydney; come for my opening night. Could you come just as my friend?*

"Jessica?"

"Nothing. Good night. I'll write to you." She hung up before she could say anything else. She could not ask him to come to her.

He had not asked her about her plans after the run of *Journeys End,* and in fact she was not sure what she would answer if he did. She had known for weeks that she would not return to her reclusive life on Lopez. Whether her play was a success or a failure, she would find a way to stay in the theater, probably in Sydney, almost certainly alone. Someday she might feel ready to join her life to someone else's, but for now she still had too much to learn about herself, as a director, perhaps as a teacher at a university or an acting studio, perhaps as a writer about the theater. She had to forget the memories that haunted her—forget them, not simply keep pushing them away—and make more friends and do more work, much more work, until at last she could say to herself that she had made yet another new life on her own and was self-sufficient in it.

"Oh, bullshit," said Hermione the next day at lunch in the wharf cafe when Jessica told her about her call to Luke. "Since when are you so dumb that you think you or anyone else can go very long without needing other people? Riding

through the world on a white horse, mowing people down, doing whatever you damn please and
get out of my way because I'm just fine and I don't
want any help, not even that traffic cop over there
keeping other horses from smashing into me, *no
help at all.*"

Jessica laughed. "You have the most amazing
way of making what I say sound absurd."

"Only when it is absurd. How did Lucinda do
this morning?"

"Not good." Absently, she tore her paper napkin into small pieces. "This is my fault, you know.
I shouldn't have approved her. I knew her background was weak, but I was so anxious to finish
casting and begin rehearsals—"

"Hold on, you didn't do this alone. Her reading
was good; did you forget that? And her videos
were good. So were the letters from Melbourne;
they liked her there. We had plenty of reasons to
approve her."

Jessica shook her head. "I should have seen that
she wasn't ready for a major part. I should have
seen her fear."

"Right, if you were a sorcerer. None of us saw
it."

"It's my job to spot those things."

"Well, we'll take you to the woodshed some
other day. Right now, what do you think about
her?"

"I don't know. I'm trying to convince her that

she's good and that Helen is a great part for her. If I can do that, I'm pretty sure she's got the talent to pull it off."

"Hypnotize her."

Jessica laughed. "You and Luke would get along. He thought of that, too."

"Well, great minds. I wish I could help with Lucy. *Is* there anything I can do?"

"You're doing it. A sympathetic ear and a friendly face; the most important things I need right now."

"Then let's do more of it. Come for drinks tonight, seven or seven-thirty, whenever you're finished with Lucinda. I might even cook dinner."

"Don't forget to turn on the oven."

"I'll keep it in mind." Hermione watched Jessica limp down the corridor from the cafe to the small rehearsal room where she and Lucinda were working. *That damn cane; that would be a problem.*

*But not insurmountable.*

She finished her cappuccino, scowling fiercely, so that a friend coming to talk to her veered off, thinking another day would be better. Hermione never saw her; she was too deep in thought. The night before, she had lain in bed, consumed by an idea that was absolutely crazy, that even a gambler such as she would be wise to avoid, but that became absolutely irresistible the more she thought about it.

*Go over it again. Why do I want to do this?*

*Because I love her. She's the daughter I always*

*wanted, and my dearest friend, and even though she won't admit it, she's being eaten up inside by directing other women in that part instead of playing it herself. Who wouldn't risk a lot for a daughter and a best friend?*

*And one more reason. I do not want Lucinda Tabor to play Helen.*

*That does it. A list of reasons no one could quarrel with.*

She fished in the clutter in her vast and sagging purse, brought out her cellular phone and walked to a corner of the empty cafe, peering in all directions like a secret agent watching for spies. Leaning against the wall, she got the number from an operator and made the call.

When she was finished, she switched the telephone off and paced around the silent room. *Dear God, if this doesn't work I will have screwed a lot of people who'll think a lynching party is much too good for me.*

She folded the telephone into its slim rectangle and put it away, staring unseeing at the harbor, the water dancing with raindrops, the trees swaying in the wind. Finally she gave a decisive nod. *Let's do this right. Either I'll be a pariah for the rest of my life, or the heroine of the Pacific Rim.*

She drove home and sat at her computer, composing a letter. She typed the single paragraph and printed it out. Then she called the long-distance operator. *Please, please let him be one of those farsighted people who list their fax number in the phone book.* "Both numbers," she said. "Office and fax." The operator read two numbers and Hermione let out a long sigh. *It was meant to be.* She took the letter to her fax machine, skimmed it once more, and then sent it.

Dear Lucas Cameron, there is a ticket for you at the box office for opening night of *Journeys End,* next Tuesday: the seat next to mine. I hope you'll consent to have dinner at my house first; it's time we got acquainted. With my very best regards, Hermione Montaldi.

## CHAPTER 16

"You've gone mad." Jessica flung the words from the other end of the room. She had walked into Hermione's house carrying a bottle of wine, a loaf of bread and a book she knew Hermione wanted to read, but within a few minutes, her gifts, and dinner, too, were forgotten. "You let Lucy go? Why? How could you? My God, Hermione, what have you done?"

"Can we sit down and discuss this? Maybe open that excellent wine you brought and talk in leisurely, dulcet tones?"

"In one week we've lost the star and her understudy, and you want a leisurely conversation? I want to know what happened. What did you tell her? Where is she? We have to get her back. Hermione, damn it, where is she?"

"Melbourne, but—"

"Oh, thank God. So close. I'll call her—"

"Don't do it, Jessie. And don't glare at me." Hermione let out a long breath, trying to control the tremors of fear that suddenly were racing through her. *I shouldn't have done it. What got into me? Jessie's right; I was mad. And what do we do now?* She felt unsteady on her feet. "Listen, I'm sitting down, even if you're not." She took her place at the end of the couch and reached to the coffee table to open the bottle Jessica had brought and fill two glasses. "Very nice," she murmured, swirling her glass and tasting the wine. "Penfold's Grange Syrah." Each word was clipped in her effort to keep her voice steady. "You've learned a lot about Australian wines."

"Why shouldn't I call her?"

"Because she's a hell of a lot better off where she is than she was with you browbeating her into playing Helen."

"*Browbeating?* Who said I was—"

"She did. She said you reminded her of her mother. You and Helen both. She said the more you told her how good she was, the worse she thought she was and she couldn't stand the idea of letting you down. She couldn't face you, either, to tell you herself. She hopes someday you'll forgive her."

"I can't believe— When did she tell you all this?"

"Jessie, sit down; we can't talk this way."

"When did she tell you?"

Hermione sighed. "About five o'clock this afternoon when you finally quit for the day."

"She went running to you because she was unhappy with me?"

"I went looking for her. A friend of mine has the perfect part for her in a new play in Melbourne, and I thought she ought to know about it."

Jessica's eyes narrowed. "How did your friend happen to think of Lucy for that part?" Hermione did not answer. *"You* thought of it. *And you called him.* Why? *Why?* I know you've never been crazy about Lucy, but why would you do this? How could you do it?" Hermione still said nothing. "How could *she* do it? How could she just walk out like that, knowing she'd leave us with no one?"

"Well, she didn't know that. I told her we had someone else to play Helen. That made her feel—"

"You what? But it was a lie! Hermione, what's gotten into you? I could have gotten her ready, I know I could. She would have been ready by opening night."

Hermione's tension exploded. "I don't give a damn whether she would or not! I didn't want her to play Helen."

"You had no authority to make that decision."

"Right. You're absolutely right. I'll never do it again."

"This is not a joke!"

"I know it isn't. I'm sorry, Jessie." *I'm sorry, I'm sorry, I shouldn't have done it, it was crazy, but I can't tell you that, because I have to convince you—*

"Why did you do it? What in God's name were you thinking of?"

"You know damn well what I was thinking. Jessie, please sit here with me. We have a lot to talk about, and standing there glaring at me isn't going to get us anywhere."

Jessica did not move. "You are mad. You think I'm going to play Helen. I won't do it. I can't. *You knew that.* You've destroyed our play because of a ridiculous idea that you can force me onto the stage, as if—"

"Cut it out, Jessie." She took a long breath and plunged ahead. "It's not a whim and I'm not forcing you; I'm clearing the way. I was awake all last night thinking about this. You're so hungry to be up there you can taste it; it's eating you up inside. Well, now's your chance. You know every word of that play, you know *Helen*—everything about her, probably back to the time she was in kindergarten. You'll play her the way she ought to be played; you'll *be* her. Angela couldn't do that, and God knows neither could Lucy. You'll be the Helen the author, may he rest in peace, dreamed of."

"In my imagination. *Not on stage.* Can't you understand that? I've told you over and over why I can't."

"Well, I forgot. Tell me again. Come on, sit here, have some wine, and tell me your reasons."

Jessica stood where she was, taut with anger and frustration and a growing panic. "What's wrong with you?" she cried. "You know my reasons; you can see them! Look at me!" She limped across the room, leaning on her cane. "How clever do you have to be to figure this out? How can I walk across a stage? This is what they'll look at"—she had reached the couch and she threw her cane onto the cushions—"they'll see this, and the way I walk, *and the way I look,* and then everything stops. Don't you see that? Every time I take a few steps everybody watches this cripple pretending to be like everyone else. We're trying to pull an audience into our story so they believe it. What do they believe when they see me?" There was a silence. She sat on the edge of the couch. "That was a question!"

Hermione was eating appetizers nonstop, trying to calm her churning stomach. "How about—" she began, but her voice came out in a croak.

Jessica looked at her closely. "You haven't got an answer. You're as worried as I am. My God, Hermione, what are we going to do?"

"No choice anymore." Hermione cleared her throat. "I haven't given us much choice. Wait. Give me a minute." She took a long drink of wine, then put her glass down and pushed it away. This was no time to feel mellow. "If your only problem is walking across the stage, you don't have to do it.

Why can't we reblock the scenes so that Helen stays pretty much in one place? She can stand, sit, take a couple of steps to a desk or chair, whatever, but basically she stays in one place and lets others come to her. That shouldn't be too hard for a bunch of intelligent people to figure out in an hour or two."

"No."

"No, we're not intelligent? No, we couldn't figure it out? No, it couldn't be done in an hour or two? Try some of your wine; it's excellent."

"Hermione, don't turn this into a farce. When I gave up the stage it was like dying, but I've come to terms with it, I'm content, and if you think—"

"You're as content as an eagle with its wings cut off, or a koala that can't climb trees. What are your other reasons?"

"You know them."

"Tell me."

"Helen is forty and beautiful; she has a powerful presence and great pride in herself. She's not ugly, she doesn't stoop, *and she's not lame.*"

"Are you telling me why you can't be in this play, or in any play?"

"Right now we're talking about this one."

"So if the play was about a gray-haired hag with a cane, you'd do it?"

Jessica broke into laughter.

"Oh, I'm so sorry." Hermione turned down the corners of her mouth. "Have I made you seem foolish again?"

"Don't do that, Hermione. This isn't funny."

"Well, God knows I'm aware of that. Okay, you win, Jessie; you've got all those reasons, so I won't fight with you. We'll cancel opening night. We'll find another Helen and open by April first. We'd lose March, but that's not as bad as losing everything. I'll call the management companies tomorrow so we can have readings by the end of the week." She stood up. "How about some dinner? I did remember to turn on the oven, so for a change everything is ready."

*Cancel opening night.* To anyone in the theater, those words were like a bell tolling death. Jessica looked past Hermione, through the windows. The rain had diminished to a drizzle that misted the glass, making the view of the harbor and the opposite shore soft and dreamlike. Unconsciously, she put her hand on the cane lying on the cushion beside her, and ran her palm up and down its length. Hermione was right: they would find another Helen. A skilled actress could fit herself into the cast in two intense weeks of rehearsal and they would have a run of one month, enough to establish her name as a director. And then—

Then it would all begin again.

But that's my life now, she thought. One actress or another, what difference does it make?

Hermione leaned forward and refilled Jessica's glass, and picked up her own. She was beginning to feel better. "I always wondered why you never colored your hair," she said casually. "Didn't we talk about this once before? I mean, I have mine done, and so does just about everybody else, so why didn't you? Not drastically; just enough to make you look blond, ash blond, something like that, instead of gray."

Jessica turned to her, frowning, as if trying to make sense of what she was saying.

"Your hair," Hermione said. "Blond instead of gray. You know, one of those sexy silvery-blonds, maybe even streaked a little as if you'd been out in the sun. How come you never did it?"

"Because it wouldn't have changed anything else. My stoop, my leg, my face . . . We did talk about it and I told you I'd look pathetic: trying to be something I wasn't, pretending to be young and pretty. I wouldn't look any different just because my hair was another color."

"Well, we have a difference of opinion on that. We should do a test to find out. It is a great look, you know, especially when you're forty. Like you. And Helen."

Jessica's face hardened. "I will never look like Helen."

"Then God damn it, *make her look like you!*"

A startled look flickered across Jessica's face. Of course. That was what she always did. How could she have forgotten it? You're an actress, she told herself. Make her look like you. You're an actress; make the audience believe she looks like you.

Make them believe Helen *is* you. You can do that. You haven't forgotten how. Because you're an actress.

A wild excitement began to build inside her. *I'm going back. I'm going back.* Tears slid down her face. She was afraid, she was exuberant, she was joyful, she was hollow with fear. *I'll try. Dear God, I will try.*

*Oh, Constance, I wish you were here now.*

*I wish Luke was here.*

Hermione, her heart pounding, took a long breath and slowly let the muscles in her neck and stomach relax. She had a terrific headache—but who cared about that? Nothing was important now but the look of vivid excitement on Jessie's face . . . and how much work they had to do in the next few days. But that didn't matter either. They'd get it done. They'd get everything done, she thought jubilantly. Because the hardest part was over.

She handed Jessica a tissue and took her in her arms. "Okay," she said softly. "Not to worry. We're together in this. We're a hell of a team, remember?"

Jessica nodded. She was wiping her eyes, but the tears still came. "Please talk to me until I can stop crying."

"Well, let's see. I've already talked to Wardrobe about altering Angela's clothes for Lucy, so they can deal with making everything a couple sizes smaller; they're wizards over there; they'll take care of it. You'll have a fitting tomorrow. What else? Your hair. That'll be tomorrow, too; I know Sistie will fit us in; she's the best hair colorist in the world. Makeup . . . well, that's easy. I'm sure you're an expert at it, but you haven't done it for a while so we'll ask one of our local experts for help, just to make sure, and to see that it works with the lighting. We may want to change the lighting, too, to do the absolute best by you; better talk about that tomorrow morning. How about seven o'clock with Dan, at the theater, to begin reblocking the show? I'll bring breakfast. Angela told me she's definitely staying through the week, so we won't dump this on the cast until Saturday; that gives us the weekend plus Monday to put everything to-gether—lights, blocking, three rehearsals with the cast, wardrobe, makeup, props—you may want to change a few things when you start using them. How does all that sound?"

"Six rehearsals. Probably more."

"What?"

Jessica kissed Hermione's cheek and sat straight, freeing herself from her embrace. "Two rehearsals a day, maybe three. We have a lot to learn and we'll go through the play as many times as it takes to learn it all. Also, you'll have to call the publicity people for new posters for the lobby; we need to have them for approval in two days so they'll be ready for the weekend, when people come to the box office to buy tickets. Be sure to tell the house manager what's going on. And call the printing company; we need an insert in the program for Monday: a loose sheet we can slip in, announcing the change, with a short paragraph about me. I'll write that tonight when I get home. And publicity has to get out a press release for Sunday. Not before; I don't want Angela, or anyone else, thinking we're trying to upstage the preview week. Also the newspaper ads have to be changed; you ought to be able to do that with a phone call, but somebody should proofread the new ad. Can you think of anything else?"

"I'm having trouble thinking of anything but you." Hermione gave a small salute. "To a courageous lady. I love you."

"No, wait, there is something else. Hermione, what are we talking about? You know I can't act in Australia; I'm not a member of MEAA. I didn't need to be, as a director, but every actor does. And they're always Australian; you know how protective they are here. How could we even think I could do this?"

"If they're famous enough, they can work here. Glenn Close could do it. Bernadette Peters could do it. Jessica Fontaine could do it. But you're right; it's a lot easier if you're a member of the actors union." Hermione raised her wineglass. "I propose a toast. Come on, it's about time you tried this wine." When Jessica picked up her glass, she went on, "To my dearest friend, Jessica Fontaine, who has been a member of Media and Entertainers Arts Alliance for over a month, ever since I took it upon myself to sign her up." She beamed again. "Are you going to join me in this toast or not?"

"You made me a member—?"

"Well, how could I predict what was going to happen down the road? It was like taking out an insurance policy. And now it's paying off. Jessie? Are we drinking to this?"

Jessica touched her wineglass to Hermione's. "Thank you. I know you meant well. Even though you were—"

"Butting in. You're absolutely right. But I knew damn well you wouldn't do it yourself, so I had to. And it's a good thing I did, because look where we are. About to launch your newest career."

There was a pause. "Do you know how terrified I am?" Jessica asked.

"That's okay, at least for a while."

"I told Lucinda that scared was okay but terrified wasn't."

"She's not in your shoes. Anyway, you'll get over it as soon as we get to work."

"I never got over having stage fright."

"Then my guess is you'll have it again. It is not on my list of things to worry about."

"What is?"

"I have no intention of telling you. It might disturb your concentration. Now I have a suggestion. Let's have a quick dinner so we can get to the theater, and afterwards come back here and talk about everything in the world but work. It'll be our one small break before the next few days, when we are going to eat and sleep and breathe this play. What do you think?"

"If we can do it."

"Of course we can."

But they could not. They went to the theater, where Angela gave one of her best performances before an enthusiastic audience, and came back to Hermione's house talking about the weather and assorted uninteresting topics until they stepped into the living room and at once began talking about the play. They talked for hours, until Jessica said she had to go home. "I don't know if I'll sleep, but I ought to try."

"Pretend. It's almost as good as the real thing."

Hope dashed rapturously around her when she came in, and because the rain had stopped Jessica took her outside on her leash instead of letting her into the small yard. They did not walk far, but it felt good to be out and moving, even slowly, even limping. The sky was still overcast, the strange yellow-orange sky of cities at night, and she thought of the velvety blackness of Lopez, with the stars clustered thickly and brilliantly above her house, and the Milky Way a scattered path from horizon to horizon. My safe haven, she thought. And now everything I do takes me farther away from it.

For years she had been sure she was doing the best thing, choosing solitude, staying away from the stage. How could she be sure that what she was about to do now was the best thing?

She sat at the dining room table with Hope curled up at her feet and began to write the insert for Monday night's program.

> The role of Helen has been assumed by the American actress Jessica Fontaine, who is also the play's director.
> Jessica Fontaine has appeared previously with the Sydney Theater Company in *All's Well That Ends Well* and *The Crucible.* In America, England and Canada, she has starred in *Anna Christie, The Country Girl, How Green Was My Valley, The Importance of Being Earnest, Mrs. Warren's Profes*

She stopped writing, and read over the list of plays. So many triumphs. These plus another two dozen. All of them triumphs, for her or for her and Constance. The two of them had dominated the American stage until Constance retired, and then Jessica dominated it herself, with one great success after another. How could she think of presenting herself to an audience as that actress? "Fraud!" they would cry. "She's not Jessica Fontaine. She's a fake. Who's she trying to fool?"

She put her head in her hands and sat for a long time. Finally she went to the kitchen to make tea. Constance, I need you, she thought as she waited for the water to boil. I need wise words from someone who knows as much about the theater as I do, and who knows me. I need someone who knows what I once did, what I might do again.

Constance had written about working through fear, she recalled. It had been in a letter written close to the time she died. It shouldn't be too hard to find.

The water boiled and she poured it into the teapot, then went to get the box of Constance's letters. On the way, she passed the fax machine. A letter was waiting for her.

My love, this will be short, but I'll write again soon. It's after three in the morning; I've been sitting in a bar talking and drinking Scotch—I never drink Scotch except when I'm excited about something—with an actor who may be the male lead for Kent's play. I saw him in a play at the Westside Theater and in five minutes I was pretty sure he was what Monte and I are looking for. I'd seen him before, but Kent's script made me think of him in a new way. You'd like him: he's got a deceptively easygoing style that barely masks a terrific amount of tension. Audiences love him (I've seen the play three times).

We buried Claudia yesterday. Monte, Gladys and I were the only people there, other than a minister we found, who, of course, did not know her and talked about her as if she were an anonymous woman who died in a vacuum.

It was one of the saddest days of my life. I remember there was a short time, years ago, when she talked about bouncing back—she liked the image, as if she were buoyant, airy, untethered—and finding herself, or maybe a new self. I wish I could have helped her do that. I wish she could have found her own way to do it.

The snow is gone, the tulips are up, I miss you. All my love, Luke.

She went back to the dining room table. It was not Constance she wanted, or letters. It was Luke.

Luke, I'm going to play Helen in *Journeys End.* I'll explain it all later, but right now I need someone with me besides Hermione; I need you. Could you come to Sydney? Could you come right away? Jessica.

At seven o'clock the next morning she was at the theater with Dan Clanagh and Hermione, sitting at the desk in Helen's living room on the turntable closest to the audience. Barely paying attention to their breakfast of coffee and croissants, they began to reblock the play, diagramming everyone's movements so that Helen's were reduced to a minimum and the others' were changed to bring them into her orbit. Jessica was tight and nervous as they began to read lines that led to specific actions. Dan and Hermione read from scripts;

Jessica spoke her lines as if she were already Helen. "This would have been a good idea, even with Angela," Hermione said, watching Dan, taking Edward's part, move around Jessica. "It makes Helen much more central; it enhances her own attitude of self-importance. We should have thought of it earlier."

"Angela would have loved it," Jessica said with a smile.

"It would have scared Lucinda," Dan said. "Too heavy of a burden."

Hermione and Jessica gazed at him in bemusement. "Do you have us all analyzed and categorized?" Hermione asked.

He gave a small, wicked smile. "You can't stage-manage people if you're being taken by surprise all the time. You need to be ahead of everybody."

"But you never make suggestions," Jessica said.

"You never asked."

She nodded. "Okay, what do you think about my playing Helen?"

"Terrific. You don't feel superior to her—which Angela did—and you're not afraid of her—which Lucinda was. You'll be great."

Hermione and Jessica exchanged a look and burst out laughing. "How simple everything is," Jessica said. "Thank you, Dan. That means more to me than almost anything." They went back to work and by ten o'clock they had finished the first two acts, and were putting their diagrams away as the cast and crew arrived for rehearsal.

Edward went to Hermione and stood close to her, crowding her. "Angela is leaving and no one can find Lucinda." He looked slightly rumpled, and the folds in his face seemed to have deepened into permanent depression. "Everything is falling apart."

"Give me some space," Hermione said tartly. More gently, she said, "I'll be delighted to answer all your questions, but first I have an announcement. Angela will be with us through Friday, the last night of previews. Lucinda has been asked to read for a major part in a new production in Melbourne, and that is where she really wants to be right now and I would not stand in her way."

"She's gone?" Edward cried.

"What the hell," Whitbread exclaimed. "I mean, *what the hell!*"

"She told me," Angela said. "Does that mean you're canceling opening night?"

"We can't," Nora moaned. "We have to open. We can't let it die, not after all this work."

Hermione waited patiently. "We open Tuesday night; that hasn't changed. What has changed is the person playing Helen. That will be Jessica, who has graciously consented to—"

*"Jessica!"* Edward turned a frenzied look on her. His eyes slid to the cane propped against the desk. "How?" he asked bluntly.

"We always appreciate expressions of support," Hermione said drily. Ignoring Edward, she spoke to the others. "This is what we're doing—"

"Hermione, this should come from me," Jessica said. She stood beside the desk. "Six years ago I left the stage. I'd been in an accident and afterward I looked so different, and felt so different, that I thought I'd never act again. But it's not easy to leave the theater when it's been your whole life for most of your life, so I came back, to direct *Journeys End.*"

"And did it brilliantly," Hermione said. "But Jessica Fontaine belongs on the stage. I knew that only a great actress could replace Angela, and that's why I begged Jessica to do it. And thank God she said she would. Does anyone have any problem with that?"

"I think it's absolutely wonderful," said Angela. She engulfed Jessica in a hug. "I was worried about Lucinda . . . not terribly strong, you know . . . no real sense of self . . . but now . . . well, Hermione, you do understand how much alike Jessica and I are. It's a very wise choice."

Hermione nodded modestly.

"What about the cane?" Edward asked.

Nora sucked in her breath; none of them had dared mention it.

Hermione began to answer, but Jessica put out her hand. "We're reblocking the play. Helen will stay in this small area and you'll be moving in and out of her orbit. In other words, you can't assume anymore that she'll come to you with a lead-in to a line or to open the way for some stage business. You'll have to do that yourselves. We're figuring it out now and by the weekend we'll be rehearsing it."

"Tomorrow," Edward said. "We need all the time we can get."

"We're all professionals," Hermione said. "We'll have the weekend, plus Monday, Monday night and Tuesday morning if we need it. That's a lot of rehearsing for three people who by then will have performed this play for more than two weeks."

"You're all so good," Jessica said, and thought briefly that she and Hermione were like a vaudeville team, tossing their routine back and forth. "You've all gotten better and better—I've never seen so much progress in two weeks—and I'm sure we'll be ready for Tuesday night. I hope I come up to your level; you're all very fine."

"Well, my goodness," Nora said. *"You're* the one . . . I remember that day you took all our parts . . . Jessica, this is *very* exciting. It will be an honor to work with you."

"We'll give you our best," Whitbread murmured, raising Jessica's hand to his lips. "Good actors are always prepared to surmount the unexpected."

They all looked at Edward.

"Edward, are you prepared to surmount the unexpected?" Hermione asked.

"I don't like risks—this is incredibly foolhardy—but I don't see that we have any options. I can only hope that those of us who have so much to lose will—"

"Not lose it," Jessica said evenly, wondering what she had ever seen in him. "I think we all have a great deal at stake here. Thank you all for your support. Now the schedule. We'll still rehearse every day during previews, at ten o'clock. On the weekend and Monday we'll start at eight. The new blocking will be ready tomorrow; you'll get diagrams to take home to study before Saturday. If you have questions or problems with my work, or anything that involves direction, and you're uncomfortable coming to me, talk to Hermione. We all want to succeed."

After that, the cast rehearsed until one o'clock, then scattered for the afternoon. Hermione and Jessica ate a quick lunch at the outdoor cafe on the lower terrace of the Opera House, not talking much, gazing across the water. The day was cool and they did not linger. "Time for your hair," Hermione said, and led her to Sistie's Salon.

"Nice hair, good texture, good body," Sistie said as she lifted and let fall strands of Jessica's hair. "Hermione said you wanted blond. Very light, with streaks?"

"Yes," Jessica said.

With a broad paintbrush, Sistie painted Jessica's hair in small sections that stood up like rays of the sun until she combed them all down, tight to her head. Jessica looked in the mirror at her thin, drawn face, its deep lines even deeper without a frame of softly curling hair. In the bright, unsparing light, she looked stark and ugly. "Wait," she said, tensing to stand up. "Hermione, I can't—"

"How about a manicure?" Hermione said loudly.

"We could do that," said Sistie. "You'll be sitting here for twenty minutes anyway, and Amy is free right now." She picked up Jessica's hands and inspected them. "Definitely a good idea."

Two hours later, when they left, Hermione was jubilant. "I knew it, I knew it. What do you think? You were very polite to Sistie, but do you really like it? It's very good, Jessie."

"There isn't much difference, is there?" They reached her car and she looked at herself in the rearview mirror. Far better than in that awful moment when her hair had been plastered to her head, but still . . . "It's a nice color, but I don't really look any different."

"You look younger. Believe me. Now wait until we get to makeup."

"I'll look so young I'll be sent back to kindergarten."

Hermione hesitated as Jessica pulled out of their parking space. "You're not happy about this?"

"I'm okay. It's just going to take some getting used to."

"You will. I'd guess it will take about fifteen minutes. Do you want to go somewhere for coffee?"

Jessica shook her head. "I'm going home to study until curtain time. I thought I knew this play, but I'm finding all sorts of little things I'd never thought of."

That night, after the performance, she rushed home and almost tripped over Hope as she hurried to read the letter that would be on the fax machine. But there was no letter; the tray was empty. And it was empty the next two nights as well. He never got my letter, Jessica thought, gazing at the silent machine as if she could will it to life. The housekeeper misplaced it when she was cleaning the library. Or it fell on the floor behind a chair. Or his fax isn't working. Maybe he's out of town.

Or maybe he hasn't written because he doesn't want to. He's decided that he isn't about to come running when I finally get around to asking him. Why should he, after all the times I told him I intended to make my way alone, without clinging to him?

No, she thought. I don't believe that. Not after his last letter. And she picked up the telephone and called him.

There was no answer. Not even a tape recorder on which she could leave a message. *They've all disappeared. Luke and Martin and the housekeeper.*

She slammed the telephone down. It served her right, she thought. She'd do it alone after all.

She took Hope outside and limped behind her as she sniffed her way up and down the block.

When they went back, the house felt hollow, like a shell. It was as if she had populated it with Luke when she wrote her letter and now that he was not coming it seemed emptier and quieter than ever. But I do have Constance's letters, she thought as she changed into a robe and went to the kitchen for tea. And Hermione. Manipulative, domineering, crafty, scheming, and absolutely wonderful. And she loves me. That's more than most people have; it's all I need.

On Saturday morning, the cast of *Journeys End* began rehearsals for opening night. There had been a party the night before, to say good-bye to Angela and to celebrate a sold-out week of previews, with one powerfully good review by Gregory Varden that had brought lines at the box office. But they could not celebrate success, because no one had seen the play that would open on Tuesday night. With Jessica in the lead, everything would be different and the critics would forget everything they had said and start from scratch, prepared to sneer, not only because she was famous, but also because she was American.

By Saturday afternoon, fear had settled over them like a cloud. Because Jessica was not doing well. She stumbled over lines she knew perfectly well and had been practicing at home all week. She forgot cues; she forgot the new blocking and found herself lurching around the set because she thought she was holding up the others. They could not get through more than two or three lines of dialogue before they had to go back and try them again.

"A disaster," Edward growled backstage after the first rehearsal. "My whole life is riding on this play; I put my future in her hands and she's destroying it. I can feel it crumble; there won't be anything left."

Jessica heard him through the thin wall of the women's dressing room, where she was being fitted for alterations to her wardrobe. She looked down and met the eyes of the wardrobe designer, who was pinning her skirt.

"Fuck 'im," the designer said, making no attempt to lower his voice. "I saw you in *The Crucible* and you were fantastic. There ain't nothin' you can't do. You'll make him look like a horse's ass. Which of course everybody knows he is." Jessica laughed. "Now that's better," he said. "You hear him sounding off again, you come to me. There's always the other side, you know. Mustn't lose sight of it."

"Thank you," Jessica said gravely. "I think you're very wise. I'm glad you're here."

The trouble was, she could not get used to standing still on the stage and letting others come to her. All morning, she had instinctively sprung to her feet, or taken a step forward, propelled by the emotions of the dialogue, only to be brought up short, remembering. She felt like a stick of wood, propped like her cane against the desk, or stuck on the couch, or standing between two pieces of furniture.

And she thought the others were always aware of the differences between her and Angela, too polite to say anything, pretending not to notice that she was thin and stooped where Angela was tall and assertive, that she looked older than her years where Angela had looked exactly the right age, that she could not use the blocking she herself had worked out, while Angela had been able to do anything.

Instead, they were being very kind. Nora had said, "Oh, I do like your hair. What a good idea." Whitbread Castle had said, "Very nice. You look younger, if I may be so bold as to say so." Edward had been surprised. "I liked the way you looked before."

*Because, in Edward's melancholy world, no one should be good-looking.*

"You look grim," Hermione said. "Relax. It will come."

"It should still be there. Like bicycle riding: once you know how to do it, you never forget."

"You're rusty, that's all. Out of practice. Loosen up, Jessie; you're making everybody as nervous as troops going off to war."

"That's what it's beginning to feel like."

But when they returned to rehearsal that afternoon, she masked her fear and frustration and concentrated on her lines. She stumbled less over words and phrases, but she had no vitality and the others reacted by walking through their parts as if they were automatons.

"Not great," Hermione said when they had struggled through all three acts. "But it's only Saturday. We have plenty of time. Are we coming back tonight?"

Jessica shook her head. "Everybody needs a break. Tomorrow at eight."

"I'll tell them. How about dinner tonight? Do you want to come over and laugh or cry or just talk?"

"No. Thank you, Hermione, I just want to be quiet." She drove home slowly, no longer hurrying to find a letter waiting for her. She unlocked her door and barely glanced at the empty fax machine. She took Hope's leash and walked outside with her, then came back, automatically looking that way again, though she had told herself not to. Finally, with Hope curled up beside her, she sat on the couch, nibbling leftovers from the refrigerator, drinking coffee, going over every line of the play.

What was wrong with her? It was more than being forced to stay in one place; more than self-consciousness about her looks. She knew her lines, her emotions, her expressions; she knew her moves, the few that she had. But the exhilaration she remembered so clearly—that moment, like a wrinkle in time, when suddenly she would break through a barrier and become her character—was not there. I've lost it, she thought. I'm like a dancer whose body can no longer do the stretches and swooping bends it once did. I had a talent, but I didn't nurture it, and it shriveled and died.

The telephone rang. *Luke. Finally.*

"Jessica?" It was Nora. "I hope you don't mind my calling, but I just wanted to tell you that I know how it feels to be doing badly, I mean, you know, not doing as well as you can, and you mustn't worry, because it will get better, really it will, and we're all sure you're going to be absolutely great."

"Thank you," Jessica said. "You're very kind."

When she hung up, she was smiling. The wonderful irony cut through her self-pity and frustration. Nora, she thought, who has done almost nothing in the theater, consoling Jessica Fontaine, encouraging her, telling her she'll be absolutely great.

Well, then, I will be.

She remembered something Constance had written when they were beginning rehearsals for *Mrs. Warren's Profession.* Bringing the box of letters to her lap, she scanned them until she found it, a quote from a director named Alan Schneider.

"There are no secret shortcuts, there are no formulas, there are no rules. There's only yourself and your talent and your taste and your choices."

The next morning—*Sunday; only two more days*—she arrived at the theater before everyone else. She walked across the dimly lit turntables, coming at last to the place at the desk where she would stay for most of the first act. She stood there for close to an hour, her thoughts floating free: she was part of the stage, part of the set, part of the theater. When the others arrived and Dan turned up the lights she blinked, as if awakening. "We'll go straight through," she said as they took their places, "but we'll stop whenever anyone has a question or a comment."

There were no questions or comments. It went more smoothly; everyone felt it and a few times they seemed to relax. Jessica had laid the new blocking diagrams in key spots on both turntables, and simply knowing they were there helped them remember their moves. And, as their movements became more natural, they could concentrate on their lines and on the way Jessica spoke hers. She still stumbled over words, and missed cues, but fewer than before, and they were all so absorbed they barely noticed it. What they did notice was that they responded to Jessica differently from the ways they had responded to Angela, and because of that they heard new meanings in their lines and discovered new ways of relating to each other. By the end of the second run-through, though they still were having problems, they all knew that the play was becoming richer and more intriguing than at any time before.

"I'd like to go through it again this afternoon and after dinner," Jessica said. "Does anyone mind?"

"No," Edward said, surprising them all. "It's getting quite interesting."

On Monday—*the day before we open*—the morning rehearsal went almost without a hitch. "We're getting there," Whitbread said outside the dressing room. "I think we're definitely on top of it."

"Jessica is not good," Edward said, his voice despairing. "She's not *alive.* She seems distracted and—oh, God, I don't want to believe this—afraid."

Once again, Jessica met the eyes of the wardrobe designer, who was making a final alteration on the sleeves of the evening gown she would wear in the third act. "Assholes never learn," said the designer sadly. "Greatness works slowly. If I had to design a dress in half an hour, what would it look like? A lunch bag with a buttonhole. Don't they know you need time?"

*We have today, tonight and tomorrow morning.*

"Forget that you're the director," Hermione said as they finished lunch. "I'll be the director. I'm sitting in the fourth row counting the times you blink."

"I'm blinking a lot?"

"Not more than usual. If you do I'll let you know. Now listen carefully. I want you to forget everything but Helen. That's what you always did before, isn't it, thought of nothing but your part? Well, how did you do it? You and Constance: how did you do this transformation you're always telling me about?"

"I don't know. At some point it just happened."

"Then do that now."

"Do what?"

"Let it happen."

"But—"

"You're blocking something. Maybe you're still hung up on how you look. Maybe you're afraid you'll be wonderful because then you'd agonize over why you wasted all those years. But those years are gone, Jessie, this is now, and you are going to *be* Helen. Let it happen; let the past go."

"But we never completely get rid of the past. That's the theme of this play."

"Then use it. Use your past to make us believe in Helen. Damn it, you ought to be able to do that. That's your job. That's what you're good at."

They began again, a little before two in the afternoon. This was a full dress rehearsal, with makeup, lights and props. In the third act, Jessica wore an evening gown of deep red satin, closely fitting, flared at the hem, the long sleeves ending in lace that lay lightly over the backs of her hands. When she took her place, Whitbread rushed up to her. "My God, Jessica, I am *stunned.* I mean, the makeup, the dress, your hair . . . I am stunned. No wonder Helen impresses everyone. Such an impressive woman!"

"Not bad," said Hermione complacently. Before she took her seat in the audience, she whispered to Jessica, "If you're as free of your fears as you look, we haven't got a thing to worry about."

Jessica watched the others take their places. *Free.* That was what the theater was all about. The freedom to explore new worlds, to learn more about human nature, to discover and rediscover the wondrous variety of life.

The freedom to grow from the past to the present.

And she knew that, for the first time, that was how she felt. Free.

The opening lines of the third act were spoken by Edward and Nora, in their apartment. Then Jessica spoke, standing beside the couch in her apartment, talking to Whitbread. And that was when, in an instant, she caught fire, and became the Jessica she had been. And became Helen.

It happened so easily that it was a few seconds before the others reacted. But then Nora said, "Oh!" in a short gasp and Edward dashed from his set to Jessica's, to see her face.

"Places!" Hermione said sternly from her seat in the fourth row.

Edward half turned to her. "I just wanted—"

"We're rehearsing," Hermione snapped. "Jessica, as soon as Edward is ready, would you repeat your last line?"

With frustrated backward glances, Edward returned to the other set. Jessica had not moved; she still faced Whitbread, her body holding the sense of urgency it had had when she had begun. And, as Hermione was the first to see, her stoop seemed almost gone. Somehow she had moved her shoulders just enough to give the illusion of standing straight, her head high.

Thank you, God, Hermione breathed. She wanted to do a dance, she wanted to shout, but she sat still, her clipboard in her lap, and scrawled HALLELUJAH across the top sheet of paper. Backstage, Dan Clanagh and the wardrobe designer grinned at each other. The lighting director, in his booth high up in the back wall of the theater, nodded, as if he had known all along that everything would work out down there. And from that moment on, it did not occur to anyone in the theater that the woman standing by the desk had a stoop and a limp, that her face was thin and lined and her body frail. As the play moved to its conclusion, all they saw was Helen. And they believed in her.

Tuesday morning the final dress rehearsal did not go well and Jessica called it off at the end of the first run-through. "We've overdone the rehearsing; we need to get away from here. Go home and relax. Take a ferry ride. Do yoga in the park. Meditate in the Chinese Gardens. Think about anything but the play. I'll see you back here at six. I think you're all wonderful and we're going to give a splendid performance tonight."

"We think you're wonderful," Nora said. "You're so exciting to watch, Jessica: the way your voice changes, and how you stand and sit, even the

way you put your hand up—you know, like this—
and brush back your hair . . . I mean, I've never
seen you do that."

"Because that's something Helen does," Edward
said. He touched Jessica's arm. "Dear Jessica, we
have so much catching up to do. I'll call you early
tomorrow and we'll take the whole day, go somewhere private, get to know each other again. We've
been apart much too long."

She looked at him blankly. What was he talking
about? But as the silence stretched out and she saw
the folds in his face deepen, his lips tightening and
pulling down, she knew she could not risk tonight.
Tomorrow he would be on his own, but for
tonight, she could not risk anything. Tonight they
needed Edward at his best.

"We'll talk in the morning," she said softly.
"After Sydney discovers its newest actor, tonight."

"We could have dinner first." He took her hand.
"We've waited a long time."

"I never eat before a performance. I suggest you
don't either. Unless you don't get nervous before
going on."

"I do."

"Then it's better to have an empty stomach."
She smiled at him and went to join Hermione, who
was waiting in the wings. "I hope you don't mind
that I sent them all home. We were—"

"Stretched too thin. I know. You did exactly
right. What are you going to do this afternoon?"

"I think I'll go to a movie."

"What a good idea. Would you mind if I tagged along?"

"I'd like that."

"By the way, I won't be back here at six. Do you mind?"

"No, it's not necessary."

"You haven't asked, but the fact is, I have a date."

"On opening night?"

"I got him a ticket."

"That's nice," Jessica said absently. "We're sold out, aren't we?"

"We are sold out for four weeks. Between Varden's review and the theater parties, we're into April. Which makes all us investors very happy. What movie are we going to see?"

"Let's get a newspaper and throw darts. Whichever one we hit."

It turned out to be an American film, a deafening jumble of machine guns and bloody cries of pain, bodies smashing through plate-glass windows and an occasional lull for the lead actor and actress to tumble into bed. "Good sex, lousy story," Hermione said as they drove home. "Reminds me of an affair I had once. Why do filmmakers think people like all that mayhem?"

"Because a lot of people do like it."

"Probably reminds them of their home life. Are you nervous?"

"Yes."

"You're terrific, you know. Have I told you that? There's something magical about the way you turn into Helen; you'll have them on their feet: standing ovation, cheers, applause, the whole thing."

"It's bad luck to say that before a performance."

"They won't move, they won't applaud, they won't even clap politely."

Jessica laughed. "I love you, Hermione. I couldn't have done anything in these past months without you. Go home to your date; I hope you have a very sexy dinner."

Hermione pulled up in front of Jessica's house. "You know you're a lovely lady. I've never had as good a friend or anyone as fine to work with. This is going to be your night, not mine—"

"Our night."

"—and you deserve it. You deserve all the good things in the world. You're the best person I know, and a great actress." She kissed Jessica on both cheeks. "I'll wish you luck now. Or is that bad luck, too?"

"Not coming from you." She watched Hermione drive away, then went into her house. She glanced at the empty fax machine and felt a sharp pang of loss. She wanted Luke to be there. The excitement of yesterday had not been perfect, because he was not there to share it. *Oh, damn, damn, damn, Luke. Why couldn't you be here?*

A cup of tea, she thought. A hot bath. Then a book or a magazine, or just staring out the window, gathering strength. And then the theater.

I've done it so many times. It's just a routine by now.

But by the time she arrived at the Opera House, very early, and parked in the underground garage, she was trembling so that she could barely walk. The next two hours were a blur. She did her makeup, with help from the expert Hermione had hired; she dressed and organized her other clothes to make sure they would be ready when she needed them; she checked props to see that they were all laid out; she spoke to the cast, encouraging them, helping them with a line or phrase they suddenly could not, for the life of them, recall because they were gripped by fear. But she was barely aware of any of it, until Dan went through, calling, "Places for act one, everybody."

She stood in the wings, waiting for the house-lights to go down so that they could move onto the set, in the dark, and be in their places when the stage lights came up. Her breathing was quick and shallow, her stomach was a knot of fear. To distract herself, she looked through the small opening in the wall, invisible from the other side, to see if the house was indeed sold out, and if the audience was settling down.

And she saw Luke.

He was sitting in the sixth row, on the aisle, in animated discussion with Hermione. His profile was to Jessica, so familiar but so strange: his sharp features and heavy eyebrows, his deep-set eyes and wonderful smile. In one hand he held the program, in the other the insert that announced Jessica's starring role.

She stared at him. She could not believe he was there. Why had he come, without telling her? I have known him for one week, she thought, and I love him with all of my being. But maybe I don't know him at all. Why is he here? Why didn't he answer my letter?

Hermione knows.

*You haven't asked, but the fact is, I have a date.*

Oh, Hermione, Jessica thought. Another scheme. You wrote to Luke, or called him, saying you had a ticket for him. But I wrote to him, too. And he never answered.

"Ready?" Dan asked her. "Houselights down?"

"Yes." Her mouth was dry, and she leaned against the wall for support. The excitement of Monday night's rehearsal was gone. One day's success never guaranteed the next; every actor and painter and writer knew that. Each new day, each new project, was like starting from the beginning. And tonight, Jessica thought, there is an audience, there are critics . . . and Luke. And I can't remember my first line.

But that always happened. She could not worry about that. She moved onto the dark stage and stepped up to the turntable, setting her cane down softly, silently with each step as she followed tiny reflectors in the floor that led to the desk. She sat down, laid the cane on the floor behind the desk and picked up the telephone. Whitbread was on the other turntable, seated at his dining room table with Edward and Nora. The stage lights came on, illuminating the double set and the four actors.

Applause greeted the set. Then the audience fell silent, and Jessica spoke the opening line into the telephone, remembering it perfectly, as she had known she would.

Luke leaned forward, gripping the arms of his seat. It was Jessica . . . but not Jessica. She was not the woman he had known on Lopez, nor was she the world-renowned actress of another time. She was Helen—proud, arrogant, self-satisfied—and Luke knew that if others noticed that her face was thin and drawn, they would have thought that that was exactly what Helen looked like. Her hair was pale blond, Luke saw, wondering briefly why she had not done that before—and longer than he remembered it; her makeup was skillful. She moved hardly at all, staying in one place or taking only a few steps while holding onto the back of a chair or the edge of the desk, but the blocking had been done so skillfully that the way the others moved made her stillness seem natural. Her body seemed frail and stooped . . . no, she wasn't stooped . . . yes, of course she was, but the way she held her shoulders created the illusion that she was standing straight. Few people would notice—directors would, dancers and athletes would—but most of the audience, Luke thought, would never realize the effort that went into that controlled posture. They would see only a woman who was not beautiful but who held them with the force of her will, the art of creating a complex character with great simplicity of motion and gesture, and her voice.

It was her voice most of all that made Luke catch his breath: that vibrant, musical voice that he had heard on Lopez Island, but not for many years in a theater: passionate, intense, reaching the farthest rows without effort, conveying in every word, every phrase, love or scorn, fear, longing, elation, anger or the wistfulness of a dream.

He sat without moving through the first act, waiting for Jessica to look his way so that their eyes could meet. But of course she would not do that. She was sharing the play with the audience, but at the same time she was Helen, sharing the story with the other members of the cast, and Helen did not know Luke Cameron or care that he was there.

The minute the houselights came up, he lunged from his seat, driven by the need to go backstage. Hermione grabbed his hand and held it tightly. "You know better than that," she said firmly. "What do you do to people who come backstage at intermission in one of your plays?"

He chuckled. "Kick them out. You're right."

"Well," Hermione said as they moved up the aisle. "Was I right about Jessie?"

"You know you were." They stood at one end of the lobby, far from the crowded cafe at the other end. A few people braved the light drizzle to go outside and smoke, but most stayed inside, talking

about Jessica. Luke caught snatches of their conversation and felt an enormous pride, as if he had
had a part in the evening. "She's extraordinary,"
he said to Hermione. "It's been so many years
since I saw her on stage that I'd forgotten how
compelling she is. It's as if she gathers the stage
around her and carries it with her . . . and she isn't
even moving! My God, all these years, she could
have been in New York, London, anywhere."

"Don't tell her that."

"No, of course not. And maybe I'm wrong.
Maybe she needed those years to get ready for
tonight."

"Incubation?" Hermione asked.

"Something like that. I think, when really terrible things happen to people, the ones who come
out strongest in the end are the ones who accept
the fact that when they put themselves back together they can't be exactly the same as before,
that they might even have to make a new self, a
new life. So I suppose it really is like being reborn,
or re-created."

"You helped her do that."

"By the time I found her, she'd done most of it
herself. You probably helped more than I did."

"It's not a contest," Hermione said drily. "We
both love her and admire her. She really did figure
out what to do with her life, and how to do it."

"You haven't figured that out yourself."

"Sure I have. This is my life; it won't change. I

told you all about it at dinner. You're a good listener, so I talked a lot."

"But you might marry again."

"Nope. It won't happen. There aren't a lot of good men out there, Luke, especially when you get to my age, and the man I had was as special as they come. What are the chances of finding two like that in one lifetime? Zilch. I've had some nice affairs, but they weren't great passions and as long as I can support myself why should I settle for anything less? Are you thinking of taking Jessie back to New York?"

"If she'll come."

Hermione nodded.

"I'm sorry," Luke said. "I know how much she means to you."

"We mean a lot to each other. And she's got a terrific future here, you know. Not only with me; there are plenty of other producers . . . well, you can guess all that, from tonight. She'll be able to write her own ticket. Without any of the crap she'll get in New York."

"You told me she had her share of it here. Rumors and such."

"She got past them. They're gone. She doesn't have a gossip columnist here who hates her guts."

"Let me tell you something about gossip columnists. They think they have the power to make or break careers, but in fact their only real power is to hurt relationships. They create nothing, they only try to damage or destroy, and it's not a pretty way to make a living, but neither is it important if you're talking about careers. No one is going to refuse to see a play because of anything they write."

"No one?"

"No one. You know why people go to the theater: because they've heard something is terrific or because they want to see the star, or both. Gossip can't change any of that. If Jessica comes to New York, people will say she looks different—older, no longer beautiful—but as soon as they see her on stage they'll forget it. Her acting will take her back to the top, almost as if she hadn't been gone. I'd think that's what you'd want for her."

"I want the best for her. But New York isn't the center of the world, you know; she could be at the top in Australia, and travel to London and America now and then and have the best of everything."

"New York is the center of the world to Jessica. It is to anyone who's been in the theater there."

"Well, nobody can decide that but Jessie, can they?"

Luke held out his hand. "Peace. I don't want to quarrel."

"Oh, were we?"

"Come on."

"Well, okay, we were." She shook hands with him, then kissed his cheek. "Silly to fight over Jessie, isn't it, when we know she's going to make up her own mind. Sorry, Luke. I do like you; I'm just feeling sad that we won't all live happily ever after in the same town."

He gave her a long look. "You can't be sure of that."

"An educated guess. I know how much she loves you."

The second and third acts seemed to fly past; Luke recognized the strong hand of a director who was making the action seem to go by even faster than it was. The cast picked up on each other's lines, almost overlapping; their actions were sharply defined; the lighting subtly changed, leaving the periphery in shadow, making the center brighter and more urgent. By the time the final love scene between Helen and Rex was played, there was not a sound in the house: tension held everyone still. And then the action slowed and the lights began to dim, so gradually that it took a minute for Luke to identify what was happening: slowly, slowly, the stage lights faded until at last, with the final few minutes of the play, only one lamp threw its soft circle of light around the lovers. And then it, too, went out.

There was a faint sound, almost a collective sigh, and then applause rose like a huge flock of birds taking wing. It thundered through the house and in a moment everyone was standing. "Quite right," Hermione said, standing up and applauding loudly. There were tears in her eyes. "A wise audience, don't you think? Very wise, very discerning. Oh, God, Luke, wasn't it *wonderful?*"

"Wonderful," he echoed. He was standing beside her, straining to see through the darkness on the stage. *Look at me. Tell me you know I'm here. Let me share this with you.* The stage lights came up, revealing Jessica and Whitbread still in the same pose, on the couch in Helen's apartment. It did not seem possible that the applause could grow louder, but it did, and it continued for a long moment, as Nora and Edward came from the wings to stand at the front of the stage, bowing. They stepped apart and turned, and Jessica and Whitbread came to stand between them. Jessica used her cane to take the ten paces and when she reached them, the other three stepped back and stood there, applauding with the audience. And then there came a chorus of "Bravo's," a sustained, deep bass note rising through the applause, almost drowning it out. Jessica's eyes glistened; her face was radiant. A stagehand brought flowers—two dozen roses from Luke, bouquets from Hermione, Edward, Nora and Whitbread, Dan Clanagh, Alfonse Murre—too many for her to hold, and they piled up so that she seemed to stand in a field of flowers. She bowed her head as the applause and cheers continued. And when she raised it, she looked straight at Luke.

The applause went on; even the critics sitting in the fifth row had not left. But then Jessica stretched out her hand, palm up, to Luke and Hermione and the audience, uncertain of what was happening, slowed their applause. "Please,"

Jessica mouthed; there was still too much noise for her to be heard.

"She means us," Hermione said. "I don't know what she's up to, but what the hell; right now I'd follow her anywhere. Let's go." Holding Luke's hand, she led him to an unobtrusive door beside the stage. It led to a narrow corridor, and when the door swung shut behind them the applause was cut to a faint hiss. They followed the corridor to a stairway with a closed door at the top. Luke went first, opening the door and waiting for Hermione. They were in the wings, looking at the stage and the actors in profile, Jessica alone in front, acknowledging the applause that had risen again.

She turned and saw them and held out both hands. Hermione turned to Luke. "What do you think?"

"She wants us with her." He and Jessica were looking at each other, and their look held as he led Hermione onto the stage to stand beside Jessica. Edward had begun to scowl, but remembering the audience, he smoothed it away, allowing only his eyes to show first bewilderment and then a growing anger as they settled on Luke.

Still looking at Luke, Jessica raised her hand to quiet the audience. "I love you," Luke said beneath the applause. "You were magnificent. As always."

The applause stopped and Jessica turned to the audience. "I want to introduce two people to you. This is Hermione Montaldi, the producer of *Journeys End,* who has been my good angel since I

came to Sydney, who took a chance on me when
no one else would, who gave me help and advice,
and scolded me when I began to lose confidence in
myself, and finally—when Angela Crown had to
leave the cast—forced me to take a chance on myself and play the role of Helen."

The applause began again, sweeping over them.
Luke had never stood on the stage for curtain
calls, never felt the force of that surging wave, and
he drew a sharp breath of wonder at what it carried with it: adulation, gratitude, love . . . and
power. No wonder giving it up is like dying, he
thought.

Jessica's hand was up and once again the theater
grew hushed. "But most of all, what Hermione
Montaldi gave me was loving friendship. Without
that, I could not have directed *Journeys End* or
taken a role in it. Without that, I probably would
have given up a lot of hopes and dreams a long
time ago. She knows she has my love and my
thanks; I hope she has yours."

Once again the applause stormed over them.
Right on cue, Luke thought, admiring Jessica's
perfect timing. He saw Hermione make a gesture,
as if to say she had no idea what to say and so
would say nothing. She bowed her head in thanks,
then put her arms around Jessica and kissed her
on both cheeks. With her mouth at Jessica's ear she
said, "You neglected to tell them you put your own
money into this play."

"Not important." Her hand went up, once more

quieting the audience. "And I want you to meet Lucas Cameron, a director from America, a good friend who first made it possible for me to come back to this life. Some years ago, I was in a terrible accident, and I thought that it had ended my life in the theater. Luke insisted on believing in me when I had stopped believing in myself. He had faith in what I was inside, when I had lost the courage even to look. He loved me when I thought I wasn't worth loving." Her eyes met Luke's and she took his hand and looked at the rapt faces turned up to her. "He knows he has my love and my gratitude. I hope he has yours."

The applause rose, the audience stood, clapping, smiling, and Jessica beckoned to Nora, Whitbread and Edward to come forward. Hermione and Luke stepped back—like a minuet, Luke thought; in a minute we'll be twirling each other—letting the cast stand in the spotlight, bowing again and again. The critics left, a few people were walking up the aisle, and Jessica turned then and limped to the wings at stage left. Nora and Whitbread followed, Luke and Hermione just behind them. Edward, still stunned by Luke's appearance, hung back, and so had his own curtain call before the applause died away and the audience began to break up, pulling on coats and jackets, moving sideways to get to the aisles, talking among themselves. Opening night was over.

Except for the party at Bennelong, the restaurant just above them, off the foyer of the Opera

House. "You go ahead," Jessica said to Hermione backstage when they all had changed into their evening clothes. Nora and Whitbread had gone to the restaurant after stopping to talk briefly, euphorically, to Jessica; Edward was wandering around, trying to decide whether to let his anger at Jessica and Luke spoil the triumph of his performance.

"But you will come," Hermione said. She looked at Luke, then back to Jessica. "You can't stay away. I have to find a quiet minute to thank you, I mean, my God, Jessie, I was almost crying up there. Don't do that again."

Jessica laughed and held her cheek against Hermione's. "I think this was a one-time event."

"And you'll come to the party."

"Yes."

"Not too late."

"Hermione."

"Sorry. I know you two have a lot to talk about. I'll see you upstairs. Luke, I'm glad you're here. I'm glad we're friends."

"So am I. Thank you for dinner. And especially the ticket."

The crew was cleaning the stage, adjusting furniture that had been shifted out of place, returning props to backstage. One by one, they finished and drifted off. Backstage was lit by the bare bulbs of safety lights, stark shadows crisscrossing, stretching to climb the walls and disappear into the blackness above. The stage was dark except for a safety light high above the couch. "I don't have a private dressing room," Jessica said. Luke took her hand and they walked to the stage and sat on the couch. He put his arms around her and they held each other, their bodies instinctively fitting together, remembering. "I wrote to you," she said, pulling back. "You didn't answer."

"Wrote to me? When?"

"Last Tuesday. A week ago. I asked you to come to Sydney. I said I needed you."

"My God, I never got it. Jessica, my love, you know I would have been on the first plane if I had. I was out of town and I gave Martin a couple of weeks off because Hermione had written and I knew I'd be here."

"I wondered whether she wrote or called. What did she say?"

"That there was a ticket for me for opening night and she wanted me to have dinner with her first. No reasons, no explanations. But I didn't need any. I went to Monte's place on the Island for a few days; he and Gladys weren't there, I just wanted to get out of the city for a while and finish one of my rewrites. Then I left for Sydney. I'd planned to stop at home and see if you'd written, but the time got very tight and I knew I'd be seeing you so I didn't go into the city at all. Damn it, you must have thought . . . My love, I'm sorry, forgive me. Damn it, I should have been with you all this week."

"No, it was all right. It really was all right. In

fact, I suppose that's why Hermione kept your coming a secret. She didn't know I'd written to you and she probably thought I had to get to opening night on my own so I'd never think I'd clung to you or anyone . . . good Lord, I certainly made a point of that with everyone, didn't I? And I really wasn't alone; I had Constance, in her letters, and Hermione. Two incredible women. Didn't someone say that that was all you needed to lift the world?"

"Three incredible women. And here's the third. Do you know that you were more brilliant tonight than in any of my memories of you? You've become a different actress; completely mesmerizing. My love, we have to—"

"How am I different?"

He grinned. To actors, discussing their performance came before anything else. "You have more depth, I think; an underlying sadness, maybe even sorrow. I don't know if it will be right for other roles; it was perfect for Helen." He kissed her lightly. "Do you mind if we put off that discussion to another night?"

She laughed, a low, happy laugh, and kissed him. "I like the way your mouth feels on mine. I like having you close to me. I like the way our hands are clasped so tightly that neither of us can get away."

"If we wanted to, which we don't. Jessica, my darling, I love you. I've missed you in ways that were unbearable, because everything I did was incomplete without you. I kept turning around to tell you something, or to ask what you thought about something, or to share a smile at something amusing. I told myself it was impossible to feel that way after only one week together, but that was the way I felt. I think you've felt the same way. Your letters were very careful, but I thought that came through, maybe because I wanted so desperately to believe it. And if you could write that you need me, you must feel the same way."

"Yes." She kissed him, softly at first, then with the passion she had held back for all the months in Sydney. "I love you, I need you, I want you. I stop thinking about you and then, all of a sudden—"

"You stop thinking about me? How can that be?"

They smiled, so filled with happiness it did not seem possible. "When I'm working," she said. "And I'll bet you do the same. I hope you do."

"Then and only then." He leaned back, studying her face. "My love, have you done everything you needed to do? After tonight, the most incredible triumph, a double triumph, you must feel you've proved almost anything you would need to prove."

"To do what?"

"To marry me. To be my partner, my friend, my wife. To become part of my life and let me be part of yours. To depend on me and let me depend on you. To build a life . . . my God, to be everything Constance hoped we'd be."

Jessica laughed. "The ultimate reason."

He grinned again. "Shall we do it for her? Or because we finally got as smart as she was and found each other and love each other. And because we know, as she did, that we'll be greater together than apart. For all those reasons, and probably a few hundred more. Enough to last a lifetime."

"In New York?"

"Yes. And Sydney, if you want. And London or Cape Town or Papua New Guinea, if that strikes your fancy. And Lopez for restorative holidays. My love, we can do anything we want. I can't give up New York entirely, and I think you should come back and conquer it again. But we aren't tied to it. You and Hermione will want to work together again; maybe the three of us will work together. Why not? I want you to star in Kent's play; we can do that in New York and then think about doing something here with Hermione."

"One of your plays," Jessica said.

His eyebrows rose. "Thank you. We'll talk about it. Does that mean yes? That you'll come back with me? That you truly believe we can do all that, and much more?"

There was a long silence. The theater seemed alive with echoes of all that had happened that night: the shuffling of feet and rustling of programs, the breathing of hundreds of people, the words spoken on stage, the work behind the scenes, the applause. My life, Jessica thought. My place.

But it was not enough. She laid her hand along Luke's face, his dearly loved face, and her fingertips recognized the warmth and texture of his skin, the prominent bones that sculpted his features, the heavy brows above eyes so intent on hers. *I need this, too. Luke is my life and my place, as much as the theater. I would never be whole without him.*

She smiled, and Luke said, "What?"

"Once I said I'd never be complete without the theater. Just now, I thought I would never be complete without you."

He took her in his arms. "Thank you for that. I think I've been waiting all my life to hear those words, and a very long time to hear them from you." Their arms were around each other, their lips barely touching. "I love you, my darling," he said, and their lips met and all the passion they had known on Lopez swept them up as the applause had earlier; desire clamored within them, denied for so many months, overwhelming them now.

"This is not the place," murmured Luke.

Jessica laughed softly. "It was all right for Helen and Rex."

"Helen and Rex only make love in the audience's imagination. We're going to make love in real life, in a real bed, if we can find one."

She kissed him. "I have a house. You're always coming to my house, have you noticed that? Luke, my darling, we have to go to the party upstairs. But later—"

"Later we'll go to your house and make love and let nothing interfere, all night, all day and evening . . . well, you do have to get to the theater. We'll make an exception for that." They stood up, close together, their bodies reluctant to separate. "And as soon as we can, we'll go to New York and make love in my house. This is an equal opportunity marriage. Which reminds me." He bent down and retrieved her cane and handed it to her. "I'd like to get married right away. In Sydney. We'll have a small, very private ceremony and eventually take a trip to some small, very private place. Would that be all right with you? Or did you have ladies-in-waiting and a cast of thousands in mind?"

"I hadn't thought about it." She smiled mischievously. "But you're the famous director; are you sure you don't want a milling crowd scalping tickets to your wedding? All of New York's reporters and producers and actors and theater critics and—" She stopped.

"—and gossip columnists. No. None of the above. I want you. And, very briefly, friends to stand up with us. Definitely Hermione. Perhaps Whitbread. I gather from glowering looks that Edward would not be agreeable. And then, my darling, you. Only you. For now, for always. When can we do this?"

"There's no performance on Monday."

He laughed, and the joy in his laughter rang

through the empty theater. "Monday. Our wedding day."

They turned away from the rows of empty seats stretching into the shadows and Luke paced his steps to hers as she limped backstage, past the dressing room and long row of makeup cubicles, past the tables of props and Dan Clanagh's small desk, past the cables snaking across the floor, past the storerooms, and so to the outside door. Luke held it open for her, but she stopped for a moment in the doorway. Behind her was the stage, in readiness for tomorrow. Ahead of her was the world with all its diversity and challenge, its troubles and triumphs, waiting for her to come back. Because together she and Luke could do anything. She believed that now.

Luke put his arm around her shoulders and she looked up, meeting his eyes. They were still in the doorway; they were still backstage. Everything at once, everything together. Dearest Constance, Jessica said silently, thank you for helping me find my way home.